OPEN SEASON ON MEN

"So who's it going to be?" Diane ran down the list of Fleur's most recent victims. There was that Wall Street broker.

Fleur shook her head. "Huh-uh! Guys like him come six in a box."

The Lufthansa pilot.

"The sex was lousy. He was always coming in for a landing even before I got off the ground."

The model from last month's cover of *M*.

"We were three in a bed," Fleur replied. "Me. Him. And his ego. Nope. The man I have in mind is someone very special. Everything you'd want in a husband."

"My my!" Diane said. "Sounds terrific. Where'd you find him?"

"Around," Fleur said. "Problem is, he already *is* a husband. Someone else's. But one of these days, that man is going to be mine."

Her face sad, Diane slowly stood up. "Don't do it, Fleur. Don't even think about it. It's emotional suicide. Besides, they never leave their wives. I should know."

Fleur shook her head. "I remember you mishandled it, start to finish. The fact remains, you let him get away. Well, I don't share your scruples. As far as I'm concerned, it's open season...."

SINGULAR WOMEN

FREDA BRIGHT

BANTAM BOOKS

TORONTO • NEW YORK • LONDON • SYDNEY • AUCKLAND

SINGULAR WOMEN

A Bantam Book / November 1988

ISBN 0-553-27330-2

Published simultaneously in the United States and Canada

Bantam Books are published by Bantam Books, a division of Bantam Doubleday Dell
Publishing Group, Inc. Its trademark, consisting of the words "Bantam Books" and the
portrayal of a rooster, is Registered in U.S. Patent and Trademark Office and in other
countries. Marca Registrada. Bantam Books, 666 Fifth Avenue, New York, New York 10103.

PRINTED IN THE UNITED STATES OF AMERICA

O   0 9 8 7 6 5 4 3 2 1

To Susan Ginsburg,
but for whom etc.

... when they had been running half-an-hour or so, and were quite dry again, the Dodo suddenly called out, "The race is over!" and they all crowded round it, panting and asking, "But who has won?"

... the Dodo said *"Everybody* has won, and *all* must have prizes."

Lewis Carroll,
Alice's Adventures in Wonderland

How come a nice girl like you isn't married?

Anon.

ONE

$P_{ing.}$

Rosemary Marshall tapped the edge of her knife against the water glass.

"The meeting of the Wednesday Club will now come to order." This said, she buttered a roll and regarded her two friends with satisfaction.

She was a large, comfortable woman, yellow-haired, blue-eyed, endowed with a china-doll complexion, a soft southern accent, and a passion for organizing all unincorporated items that fell within her grasp. Give Rosemary sweater drawers, pantry shelves, children's parties, dinner menus, or the entangled lives of her dearest friends, and she would set about bringing order out of chaos.

The Wednesday Club was a case in point. Technically speaking, it wasn't a club at all, simply an irregular series of get-togethers at one or another midtown restaurant. On Wednesdays, usually, so Rosemary could combine lunch with a raid on Bloomingdale's, a Broadway matinee, or the occasional lecture series.

"Membership" was confined to four old friends who had once shared earrings, English lit notes, dates, and dorm space at Smith. Now, ten years later in their busy lives, lunch was their way of keeping in touch.

But if there had been a "club"—a proper club with a charter and bylaws and duly-elected officers, then Rosemary would certainly have been president. Not every high-powered executive, she believed, worked in an office. Ability

1

was ability, no matter the outlet. Some people spent their energies building careers, others preferred to channel theirs in private pursuits. Rosemary was one of the latter persuasion.

Take her house for instance. It was a showcase, a model of taste and efficiency, proof positive that had she but chosen, Rosemary could have operated a decorating service or run a restaurant of formidable distinction. Instead, she reserved those talents for her family's pleasure, setting one of the finest tables in one of the loveliest houses in all Fairfield County. According to her husband, there weren't half a dozen places in all New York where the cuisine was as good. And given his expense account, Alex should know.

She hoped today's lunch would meet her own exacting standards of food and elegance. It looked promising.

The Café Karnak was a handsome place, decorated in soft peach tones and shades of gray, with biting jet accents. Art deco blended with Ancient Egypt in the high pale columns, the plaster-of-Paris acanthus leaves, and the smoked-glass torchieres that shed a golden desert light. Tiger lilies bloomed in alabaster vases. Everything looked smart, stylish so very New-York-Today! Rosemary felt the lilt of anticipation.

"I hope the food is a match for the decor," she said, looking first left, then right, at her two nearest, dearest friends.

On her left sat Fleur Chamberlain, slim and vibrant in a sexy slither of Italian silk jersey. Every man in the room was sneaking glances—and didn't she know it! Ten years on Madison Avenue had polished Fleur's dark beauty to a glossy peak. Time, care, and above all money had gone into the effort, and she had come to resemble one of her own high-fashion ads. Chic. Sleek. Perfect. Every detail was state-of-the-art, from her shiny cap of dark hair to her jewel-toned eyelids to the lacquered stiletto nails to the tip of her Maud Frizon shoes. Beautiful Fleur. Simply to be in her company could make you feel tacky by contrast.

And on Rosemary's right, Diane Summerfield. Dear Diane! "The Brain Trust," Rosemary used to call her with a mixture of awe, envy, and affection. Smart but nice, was the verdict, once one pierced the upper-crust shell and scooped out the very warm human being underneath. In the old days, Di could always be counted on for a quickie loan or help with term papers. She gave ungrudgingly, never asked favors in return. Why should she? What reimbursement could one offer the girl who had everything: smarts, class, and money?

Law school had changed her though. Toughened her. Sometimes Rosemary wondered if Diane was still such a soft touch. Today, for instance, Diane was looking every immaculate inch the corporate lawyer. "Don't mess with me," the dark suit proclaimed. "I mean business." Power resided in those padded shoulders, in the knife-sharp cut of the lapels. Only a head of rebellious red hair broke the steely monochrome and suggested something less than absolute control.

Two very impressive women, Fleur and Diane, in their different ways. Rosemary felt a vicarious pride in their accomplishments.

Still, she thought, what a pain in the ass it must be, dressing for success every morning. The coiffed hair, the clothes-that-made-a-statement, the three-inch heels, the weighty briefcase. And all for some job, some boss. Rosemary wriggled her toes in her black leather flats and felt good.

Next her glance fell on the empty chair opposite. Not a sign of the woman, and here it was nearly one. Time, Rosemary reckoned, to get organized.

"We're a quorum," she announced. "So what do you think? Should we go ahead and order or wait until Bernie gets here?"

"Wait another few minutes," Diane said, pushing back her chair. "It's so rare that we all get together."

"Order now," said Fleur. "A. I'm thirsty. B. I'm starved. And C. Waiting for Bernie . . . well, it's like waiting for Godot. Entire generations have grown old and toothless waiting for Bernadette Hong. Lord knows I love her, but she's incapable of keeping appointments. Unless, of course, they're job-related. She'd be late for her own funeral, as the cliché goes."

"Or wedding." Rosemary nodded. "She was late for mine, as you know. Almost twenty minutes late. The organist kept on pumping away, some boring piece by César Franck. We wound up having to pay him overtime. Alex was furious."

"You actually remember?" Fleur asked. "My God, what a head for trivia! That was a zillion years ago."

"Ten years last June, to be precise. And of course I remember—almost as though it were yesterday. Your own wedding," she added, "is not an event you're likely to forget."

"We poor singles will have to take that on trust," Diane murmured.

"Like it was yesterday," Rosemary repeated. "That wonderful smoked salmon. Diane tripping on my train. Mother weeping like it was the end of the world, although truth to tell, she was very relieved. And of course we have most of the high spots in our album. Plus the movies. Sort of an *aide mémoire*. Although"—she frowned faintly—"darned if I can recall who caught the bouquet. One of you two, was it—or was it Bernie, do you think?"

But no one else could remember either.

"Somehow I recollect it being Bernie," she mused. "Not that it matters. After all—knock wood—who's superstitious?"

Diane glanced impatiently at her watch. "Perhaps we ought to order. I've a two-thirty meeting, and if memory serves, Godot never did turn up. I'm sure Bernie will forgive us if we eat. Waiter—"

The next five minutes were spent in serious menu consultation.

"Decisions, decisions." Rosemary rolled her eyes. In a city where fashionable restaurants vied for creativity, the Café Karnak determined not to be outdone. The loot of the earth's larders seemed to have been rounded up and trotted out in new and astonishing combinations.

"Poached cojo salmon with shitakes and baby vegetables, gingered mako shark on a bed of radicchio—"

The waiter reeled off the daily specials with the gusto of a budding Dustin Hoffman. He was a husky blond with blinding white teeth and a Fire Island tan.

"—breast of Muscovy duck with green peppercorns—"

Fleur tuned out. Tuned in on the waiter instead.

"I'm impressed"—she leaned toward him, her voice suddenly seductive—"the way you manage to keep all that in your head. And your delivery's superb. I bet you're an actor."

He gave an acquiescent nod.

"I knew it!" she breathed. "A young man just dripping with talent. What did you say your name was?"

"Rusty." He leaned forward and inhaled her perfume. "Rusty Barnes."

"You don't look rusty to me." She gave him a wicked

grin. "I happen to employ a lot of actors in my work. Tell me, you ever do any modeling? Perhaps I could fix you up with a little something."

Dishes were discussed, decisions made while Fleur, who subsisted on grilled fish and meager salads, continued her flirtation.

"Mousseline of trout garnished with white grapes and pimento," Rosemary mused. "Would that be delicious or revolting? What the hell—I'll try it."

"Go ahead," said Diane. "Live dangerously."

"And what would you ladies like to drink?"

"White wine," said Rosemary.

"Pellegrino," said Diane.

"Bloody Mary." Fleur smiled up at him with a lavish of dimples. "Long on the vodka. Short on the tomato juice. I don't want to fall awake back at the office."

Rusty grinned and moved off.

Fleur watched him go. "Yum, yum, yum." Then she contemplated the contents of the bread basket with naked lust.

"The sesame buns?" Rosemary was almost afraid to ask.

Fleur laughed. "No, darling. I was referring to our chewy little waiter. Did you see those teeth! All fifty-eight of them. The better to eat you with, my dear. Although now that you mention it, his buns weren't too bad either."

"Fleur!" Rosemary clucked. "Have you no sense of decorum? This is a public place. And the way you came on to him, telling him you could fix him up with modeling jobs—"

"And so I can."

"—as a centerfold for *Dentistry Today*. Poor kid. He was so embarrassed he didn't know where to look."

"It seems to me"—Fleur reached for a breadstick. Thirty-six calories. How fat can you get on thirty-six calories?—"he knew exactly where to look. Right down my cleavage."

Rosemary reddened. "That dress doesn't leave much to the imagination, does it?"

"Enough," Fleur said. "Don't you like it? It was featured in last month's *Vogue*."

"Gorgeous." A covetous note crept into Rosemary's voice. "Wonderful color. I wish I had the nerve to wear clothes like that. But Alex would kill me. He has very conservative notions as to what's suitable."

"Does he now?" Fleur smoothed the silky fabric over her thighs and smiled. Rosemary's envy, the waiter's hot eyes—all combined to give her a sudden rush, like a cocaine high.

Appearances count. That was one thing she had learned in advertising. "You are what you look like" was as close as anyone at the agency came to formulating a philosophy. And right now she knew she looked like a million—even if she had to starve herself to do it.

"Maybe I'll give him my card," she mused.

"Who?"

"That waiter. He looks like a pleasant afternoon's diversion."

"Oh, come on," said Diane. "He's a kid. Besides which, he's probably gay."

"Only one way to tell."

The breadstick was delicious. Fleur nibbled it slowly, trying to make it last. Each bite seemed to go direct to her waistline. Someday, when she was old and rich and beloved, she would pig out in a giant carbohydrate orgy, eat herself to blissful death. Crusty ryes, Russian pumpernickels, seeded rolls, baking powder biscuits, English muffins lathered in butter. Cheezits. Oh God, yes! "A box of Cheezits, a jug of wine, and thou . . . Talk about paradise enow."

"The trouble with you, Fleur"—Rosemary watched her performance with the breadstick and found it vaguely obscene—"is that you think about sex too much."

"I do?" Fleur's tongue darted out to rescue an errant sesame seed. "Why, I haven't thought about it in fifteen seconds."

"Way too much," Rosemary reproved. "You always did, even in college. You ought to settle down and get married."

"Do you mean"—Fleur licked her lips, already regretting the breadstick—"that marriage is the cure for sex? What a novel idea! Though I can't say that's much of a testimonial to Alex's prowess."

Rosemary turned crimson, but she'd be damned if Fleur would have the last word. At least she *had* a husband, which was more than Fleur could say. "Alex, it just so happens—" she began, but Diane cut her off.

"Okay, you guys. Let's break it up and play grown-ups for a while. We're not back in the dorms. Besides which"

—she raised her voice and waved—"there's herself. Miss Bernadette Hong!"

"Star of stage, screen, and television."

Bernie swept across the length of the restaurant, jet propelled. There were quick brushes of the lips to cheeks, murmurs, and greetings. Then pulling out the vacant chair, she began unloading her burden: briefcase, jeans jacket, Liz Claiborne scarf, straw hat, and, atop the pile, a bulging leather satchel that had seen hard service. After which she grabbed a vacant chair from a neighboring table and plopped down.

"What a day!" she pronounced with the gusto of someone saying, "What a life!"

Her small, well-muscled body exuded energy. Her high cheekbones and straight black hair told of Chinese ancestry. She had the kind of smile that wore well both on TV and off. She flashed it now.

"Waiter"—she clapped her hands—"on the double!"

Rusty appeared, ready to repeat the specials, but Bernie cut him short. "Give me a cheeseburger, if you've got one. If not, a steak and french fries. Well, any kind of meat as long as it's red and doesn't take more than five minutes to cook. And, oh yeah, a big Diet Pepsi."

She looked around. The layout was faintly familiar; the peach-and-silver color scheme was not. "Sorry I'm late. I had a helluva time finding this place. Pretty, though, with the columns. What do you call this stuff? Art deco? Art nouveau? Loews Orpheum?"

"Deco," said Rosemary, who took courses at Cooper-Hewitt.

"Very attractive. But it used to have another name, didn't it? Swamplands—something like that? They did blackened redfish. I remember getting heartburn—"

"That was last year," Diane said, "when it was the Maison Bayou. Creole cooking."

"Bayou it was Creole, by me it was Cajun," Fleur said.

"Ouch!" Rosemary simultaneously winced at the pun and wished she'd made it.

"And before that it was the Belgian omelet place."

"Good old New York," Bernie said, "where nothing stays the same ten minutes running. No wonder I couldn't find it. That would be a cute human interest story, though. Long-lost lovers promise to meet after a twenty-year separation beneath the clock at the Astor. Eternal love, all that crap. Only when they get there the Astor is no more."

"Wasn't it turned into a welfare hotel?"

"No," Diane corrected. "That was the Martinique."

"You're so literal," Bernie chided. "Anyhow, it would make a terrific segment for *Five on Ten*. The TV Show That Captures the Heartbeat of New York," she mocked. "But enough of my shoptalk. How about yours? Fleur, you're looking terrific. So what else is new? How are things at Marsden-Baker?"

"Total jungle," was the answer, "with a little chaos thrown in. Jesus, six months in an ad agency is all the proof you need that Darwin was right."

"Well, I hope you're one of the fittest. And, Di, what's with your lawsuit—anything in it for my show? Or is it one of those cases only a lawyer could love?"

"Of course I can't talk about it freely, but. . . ." Diane launched into the latest installment of professional woes: a complex litigation between two behemoth companies that had occupied her attention for the last two years. Rosemary yawned. Fleur studied her nails. Only Bernie listened with a show of absorption until the food arrived, at which point she called a halt. Attention was something she could turn on and off with a switch. It was one of her best professional assets.

"Enough of this New York career crap. Now let's hear from the civilian population. Rosemary! How's life treating you? How's that cute little Chris of yours?"

"Wonderful!" Rosemary visibly expanded. Job talk bored her, left her feeling voiceless and numb. She considered herself an emissary from the real world: the world of mortgages and motherhood. "He began kindergarten last week."

"Good school?"

"Marvelous."

"And how's Alex?"

"Terrific! You know, they promoted him to exec VP."

"And how's the house shaping up?"

"Sensational! We're putting a pool in next month."

"How about the dog?" Fleur interjected. "We don't want to forget beloved Sandy. Arf, arf. I presume he's superlative too."

"Actually," Rosemary said, glowing, "it's Shelby, not Sandy, and we plan to show her at Westminster next year."

"Fabulous," Fleur said darkly.

"And how about you, Bernie? What big story are you up to? I watch the program practically every day at five, and so would Alex if he were ever home that early, which he never is, but still! We always hope we're going to catch you on it live! If you ask our opinion, they don't give us enough of you."

"Thanks, pal. My opinion too. Seems to me I get all the grunt work—like standing knee-deep in snow on the Long Island Expressway or cruising through Battery Park in a heat wave asking people if it's warm enough for them. I've got to get myself something meatier. After all, I'm just a reporter, not an anchorwoman, so whether I get on the box or not depends on what I've got to say. As a matter of fact, right now I'm on the track of a hot one." She reached over and patted the worn satchel. "You're lookin' at a load of Dyn-a-mite!"

"You got a bomb in there?" Diane teased her.

"You said it." Everyone at the table turned to her. Bernie paused, then assured that her audience was rapt, lowered her voice. "Yep. There's enough explosive in this old Coach bag to start a riot or"—she grinned—"to get me a neat bit of exposure on the show. I just did interviews with a team of academics, and it could be a helluva story. My friends, what you're looking at is nothing less than the future. Our assorted fates, believe it or not."

"Do tell."

And Bernie did.

A team of social scientists had recently completed a statistical study of marriage patterns. Their subjects were career women: white, college-educated, successful ("That's us," Fleur gasped)—and single.

Their conclusion: "Dear hearts," Bernie said. "It looks like we're single for life. Except of course for Rosemary."

The women at the table fell silent. The statement was too shocking to be absorbed.

At last Diane spoke up. "Says who?"

"Says this Harvard-Yale team, and they've got heavy credentials. I spent the morning going over the data. What it comes down to is this: If you're not married by the time you're thirty, your chances are approximately one in five of finding a husband."

Fleur sucked in her breath. "I'll be thirty-three next month."

"Plus," Bernie barreled on, "if you're not married by thirty-five, the percentages drop to about one chance in twenty."

"And if you're still single at forty, God forbid?"

"At forty," Bernie declared, "according to statistics, you stand a better chance of being killed by a terrorist than you do of meeting Prince Charming. After that, your chances deteriorate rapidly."

"Very funny," Diane said. Her face was grim.

"Does that mean," Rosemary asked, "because I'm the only one of us who *did* get married, I've statistically doomed the rest of you to staying single?" It was a question no sooner asked than regretted.

"Only kidding, ha ha," she added hastily, but no one laughed.

"Statistics suck!" Fleur finally burst out. "Research is rubbish. And all the experts are assholes. Categorically. Listen, Bernie. If I wrote my ads according to the dictates of what the surveys said, I'd be collecting unemployment by now. Christ, I spend my life fighting off the market researchers, with their little charts and graphs and computer printouts. It's all hype! As if you can measure what makes people buy perfume or eat Gorgonzola or fall in love. Well, according to research, the Edsel was destined to be the car of the century while McDonald's was just another hamburger joint. What research is really about is a bunch of social scientists hanging on to their jobs. And I'll be damned if I'll let them tell *me* whether Fleur Chamberlain gets married or not. No way! That's a decision I plan to make for myself, thank you very much. With a little help from Mr. Right."

"Whoa!" Bernie signaled for a truce. "I don't invent the news, I only report it. And maybe you're the one who'll beat the percentages. But if you ask me, I think the research hit it right on the button. Look around you. No, not just here but all around. On the job, in bars, at parties, when you go to the beach. Do you see this huge fund of available men? Wonderful guys who can't wait to tie the knot? Listen, the only place you'll find bachelors these days is under *B* in the dictionary. Any argument?"

Diane nodded. "Too true. There are very few men out there for women like us."

"There are scads of men," Fleur retorted. "Whole fucking armies. You want to throw in the sponge, that's your privilege. But speaking for myself, I could have married a dozen times over, going all the way back to high school." She began an inventory of scalps collected, of hearts left broken in her perfume-scented wake, but Bernie would hear none of it.

"That was then, this is now," she said crisply. "You probably blew it by waiting. It looks like we all did, except for Rosemary. Anyhow, you can't argue with facts, and the fact is: Here we are, three terrific women—attractive, smart, successful. And single. Yes, there are men, Fleur, and some of them are even—quote—available. But consider the quality! Prince Charming is extinct. And who's taken his place? Let's take a look at your so-called army of available men. For openers, the forty-year-old bachelors. Never married, never made a commitment."

"Ouch!" said Diane.

"Then the fags."

"Double ouch."

"Plus the usual nerds"—Bernie was building up steam, finding a rhythm, just as she did on TV—"the turds, the walking wounded, the geriatric ward, the losers, the boozers, and all guys named Dwayne. Dare I mention the Peter Pans? We're too old for those jokers. God forbid they date a woman over twenty-five. And lest we forget, the card-carrying narcissists complete with gold chains and Nautilus biceps. The only romantic relationship those guys are capable of is with the mirror. So step right up, ladies, and take your pick. Not me, pal. And even if we stooped to marrying men like that, who says they want to marry us? It's a buyer's market, after all, and these guys aren't buying."

"In other words, the options are no longer ours," Fleur said.

"Afraid so, given the acute shortage of eligible men. We're not talking quick lays, mind you. We're talking husband material. Well, all those men who would make good husbands probably *are* good husbands." Suddenly Bernie switched targets. "Tell me, Diane, are you beating them off in droves? How many terrific guys do you meet these days?"

"I don't have time," Diane protested, "I work eighty hours a week." But her passion for accuracy got the better of her. The entire conversation was painful, close to the bone, and there was no comfort to be gleaned in the knowledge that her plight was shared by a multitude. "Correction, that's not strictly true. I do meet people in the course of business, only they're not, well, they're either not suitable, or else they're not very interested in me, to put it bluntly. My mother says"—she sighed—"that when you're ready, you'll find somebody."

Fleur laughed. "Everybody's mother says that. It comes with the territory."

"What do mothers know? They grew up in a different world. But for us, the likelihood is," Bernie concluded, "that we three are single for life. Which is not necessarily a tragedy," she added.

"You can say that," Diane observed, "because you have a long-term relationship with Steve, so loneliness isn't a problem."

There was a hum of agreement around the table. For the past five years, Bernie had shared her life and her loft with a TV production manager, Steve Godwin. It was a nonmarriage made in heaven.

"Granted," she admitted. "Steve's terrific. But even without live-ins, we have plenty of compensations. Exciting jobs, good friends, no real money problems. I for one never thought that marriage was the be-all and end-all."

Diane contemplated the infant vegetables on her plate: baby carrots, newborn zucchini, tiny peas, tender and vulnerable. "I refuse,"—she said softly, then raised her voice. "I refuse to accept as a given that I will never have a family. Because that's what those so-called facts of yours come down to, Bernie. You're saying that it's already too late, and I'm condemned to be childless forever, unless I decide to go it alone. That's horrible—horrible!" Her blue eyes misted over. "I'm thirty-two years old, and I don't have forever."

"All I'm saying is, there's no point hanging around the waiting room when the train's already left. I'm talking generationwise, Diane. You shouldn't take it personally."

"Well, of course I take it personally! My God, what could be more personal than getting married, having kids. I take it very personally when some research report tries to rob me of my future. Maybe you don't want to get married,

Bernie—that's your decision. But I can't write it off so easily."

Bernie observed Diane with heightened interest. She had never seen her so emotional, so vulnerable. Mentally, a set of tumblers began clicking into place. This story might be even bigger than she thought.

Rosemary, who had remained quiet since her unintended gaffe, now moved to smooth things over. "All that research is stuff and nonsense," she said. "You can't predict human behavior. Remember, you're talking statistics, not prophecy. If you really want to, you'll get married."

"Hear hear."

"As I said," Fleur added, "research is bullshit."

"Yes indeed," Rosemary replied. "But you know what else is even bigger bull, if you'll excuse the expression? That myth about waiting for the right man to come along and sweep you off your feet. Let me tell you, there is no fairy godmother. Happiness is hard work, and you mustn't expect it to come to you without effort. I wish"—she leaned across the table, warm and intimate, encompassing her three friends in a maternal glow—"I wish you could all share the joy that I've had out of marriage and motherhood. I wish you this happiness because I love you all dearly."

"That's sweet." Diane began to feel teary, but Rosemary had not finished her say.

"When I got married right after graduation, you all thought I was copping out. Now don't deny it." She raised her hand to quell a protest that never materialized. "You were all so much more ambitious than I was, more career-oriented. I guess everybody was back in the seventies. But I did the right thing—right for me, anyhow. Okay, maybe my life didn't turn out to be as glamorous as if I were a TV personality or an advertising hotshot or—" She looked at Diane and groped for words, lawyering always having struck her as boring and abstruse. "Well, you know what I mean. I'm proud of all three of you for being so successful, but I wouldn't trade places for the world."

"It's not either/or," Fleur put in.

"Of course not. Have your careers. Enjoy them. But get yourself husbands too. You're all attractive women, and there are plenty of men, if you go looking. Nice men. Sometimes I wish," she added, smiling, "that I could clone my Alex and give each one of you a copy. Of course to me he's very special, very unique, but there must be other men out there almost as nice. You simply have to put in the work. After all," she added, "you may recall, I didn't land Alex by sitting on my duff."

Bernie giggled, for they all remembered the discovery, stalking, pursuit, and capture of Alex Marshall that had absorbed Rosemary's entire senior year. It was a campaign worthy of a Clausewitz. In the dorms they had dubbed it the "Winter War."

"Stowe," Rosemary reminisced. "I caught my sweetie on the slopes at Stowe, Vermont. Chasing up there every damn weekend, including two awful blizzards, and me a southerner! I thought I'd just die of frostbite that winter. Know something? I haven't been near a ski slope since. But," she added triumphantly, "it paid off! I was engaged by the spring thaw. The thing is," Rosemary scolded, "you have to show some enterprise, some ingenuity. You have to smoke them out in their native habitats, find their hiding places. The slopes. The ballparks. The gyms. Club Meds. Put your body and soul into the job. Fight! Like the poet said, 'Do not go gentle—' "

"I think Dylan Thomas was referring to death," Diane commented, "not spinsterhood."

"Same difference," Rosemary said. "The fact is, it's a sorry state of affairs when women like you can't find husbands. But that's only because you haven't organized it properly."

"Suppose we don't want to get married?" Bernie shrugged. "I sure don't—at least, not now."

"I don't believe a word of it," Rosemary retorted. "Of course you want to get married. Every normal woman does. It's just a question of—of—"

"Of?"

Then inspiration struck.

Rosemary paused, clapped her hands, widened her eyes. "My God!" she exclaimed. "I have just had the most fantastic idea. An absolute brainstorm. You girls are going to love it! You'll be thanking me on your honeymoons."

"We lay siege to the Downtown Athletic Club?" Fleur offered.

"Better! Beaucoup better! In fact, I can practically guarantee results. Think back," she said. "You were all so competitive in college, it was fierce! Remember one year you had a contest about getting to the top of the class?"

"Some contest!" Fleur laughed. "Diane left us all at the starting gate."

"But as a result, all three of you made dean's list, right? That's exactly what I mean. You have the competitive spirit going for you. So harness it, put it to work where it really matters. Well?" She looked around her with a satisfied air. "Don't you see?"

"See what?"

"We'll have a contest!"

"A contest?" Three voices shouted in unison.

"A contest." Rosemary beamed. "A race—to see which of you can get to the altar first."

"Get serious!" Bernie groaned.

"I'm perfectly serious, and it's a splendid idea. Just the kind of incentive you girls need. Let's see, it's September now. You'll have all of Christmas, the party season, New Year's Eve—that's good hunting—then spring and a young man's fancy. . . ." She made some mental calculations. "Okay. Let's shoot for final results by June."

"Nine months," Diane commented. "A proper gestation period."

But Rosemary was already absorbed in the minutiae of rules and procedures.

The Husband Hunt. With a little silver pen, she wrote the title on the back of her Bloomingdale's shopping list. Then she underscored the heading with a flourish. "There should be quotas," she urged. "Incentives. So many points for meeting prospects. So many points for follow-up calls."

"Just like Brownies," Fleur snickered. "Do you give merit badges at the end of the game?"

But Rosemary rattled on, unperturbed. Monthly reports were to be submitted by all contestants, she proposed, with a minimum of ten hours a week devoted to the search.

"I have never in my life punched a time clock," Bernie protested.

"I'm only making these rules for your good, darling," Rosemary replied. "And most important of all, at least one new man spoken to each day. That's a must."

"On or off the job?" Diane asked.

"Both. Think of every place you go as an arena, a battlefield. It might be useful to keep a record."

"Too many rules." Fleur shook her head.

"And you left out the most important one." Bernie could barely keep a straight face. "What's the law on poaching?"

"Poaching?"

"Poaching! Stealing! Whatever you want to call it. Suppose Fleur finds her Mr. Marvelous and Diane decides to lure him away?"

"Fat chance," Diane said.

"What I want to know is, would that be allowed?"

"Oh, absolutely," Rosemary ordained. "All's fair in love and husband hunting."

"Are you saying"—Fleur narrowed her eyes—"that anything goes?"

"Anything!" Rosemary nodded. "Everything! That's the first rule of the chase."

"The only rule," Bernie affirmed.

"Finders keepers—" Fleur said.

"Losers, weepers." Rosemary grinned.

"Fair enough. But what I want to know," Diane asked, "is what about prizes. After all, you can't have a contest without prizes."

"Prizes!" Rosemary flung up her arms. "Good Lord, woman! You talk about prizes! Why, you'll have won the biggest prize the world has to offer. The prize is a husband! What else?"

TWO

"**I**f you're heading toward the East Side," Fleur said, "I'll keep you company. I'm in no great hurry to get back to the office."

"Lucky you!" Diane gave her a quizzical look. The two women swung down Fiftieth Street into Rockefeller Plaza. The air had turned crisp. In the banks of flowerbeds that lined the promenade, a gardener was removing yesterday's gloxinia. Golden armies of chrysanthemums waited in the wings to take their place.

"Flowers dying," Fleur murmured. "Summer's end."

"That sounds very—valedictory. Is something wrong, Fleur? I had that feeling all through lunch."

"Psychic you," Fleur said. "I thought I put up a pretty good front back there in the restaurant. But actually"—they were closer than the others and Fleur could be open with Diane—"things are getting very hairy at the agency. There are changes looming. Austerity's in the air. Fact is, I could be out on my ass in another few months. You've heard what's going on at Saraband?"

"It's the talk of Wall Street," Diane replied.

"And Madison Avenue too. Got a moment for the details?"

Diane checked her watch. She was going to be late for the meeting, but she sensed Fleur's anxiety. Her friend was clearly bursting to confide. "Sure." Diane sat down on a low wall and folded her hands, the picture of lawyerly calm. "What are friends for?"

Fleur sat down beside Diane and began to talk. "Until a

17

year ago," she explained, "Saraband Enterprises was a privately held firm. Founded in the twenties by a Polish immigrant, Sara Bandinsky, the company grew, along with its advertising agency, Marsden-Baker, to become a giant in the beauty business. Skin creams, cosmetics, above all a successful line of fragrances made the name synonymous with *grand luxe* and prodigious profits.

"She was a tyrant, old Sara—a tantrum thrower, sadist, breaker of balls—but by God, that woman had an instinct for marketing that amounted to genius. She could take plain old shaving cream, christen it Wonda-Whip, price it at twenty bucks a fluid ounce, and foist the stuff off as a revolution in skin care. Magic, that's what she had, and I loved working for her. You know, when you're talking about the beauty business, the word 'product' is a misnomer. There is no product. Not really. Basically the stuff is all the same—the same emollients and chemicals and dyes, slightly reformulated. You want to know what the difference is between one lipstick and the other, between dimestore cold cream and those expensive cleansing gels?"

She went on, not waiting for an answer. "Hype. Packaging. That's all. We're not in the business of selling products. We're in the business of selling dreams. Hopes. Illusions. Use this perfume and men will kill for you. Buy our face cream and you'll look like Elizabeth Taylor, only thirty years younger. Rationally, we know that it's bullshit. Emotionally, oh! how we crave to believe! What suckers women are! Me too, I suppose. But there's nothing there, don't you see? Nothing real, nothing concrete. What I do is comparable to trying to sculpt the Venus de Milo out of smoke. I'll say this for Sara Bandinsky—with all her craziness, she had a profound grasp of women's fantasies.

"Then the old tycoon died, leaving the business to her sons, and, among the assets, the formula for a new perfume. What she couldn't bequeath to her children was her drive and dedication. The company was put up for sale.

"A few months ago, Saraband Enterprises was acquired by Consuma-Corp, a Pittsburgh-based conglomerate with divisions ranging from patent medicines to electric guitars. At Consuma-Corp, all talk of 'dreams' and 'illusion' fell upon deaf ears. Their only measure of worth was 'bottom line.'

"Let me tell you about my new clients," Fleur continued.

"They're zombies, number crunchers, just looking for an excuse to dump our agency. 'Show us the figures,' they keep saying. The marketing director is a total wimp with the IQ of a canteloupe. As for the ad manager, she came straight from Nasal Decongestants. Her claim to fame is that she's the first person to have demonstrated all eight sinus cavities on TV. Try to go deal with these people. Anyhow, they've told us straight out that if this new perfume flops we've had it."

"Is it a good fragrance?" Diane hesitated, not wanting to sound like one of the suckers. "Would I want to wear it?"

Fleur considered the question, then said, "It's your basic floral with an overtone of musk. In fact, it has a quite distinctive bouquet. Heavy. But as for good or bad—that's a subjective judgment. It'll be as good or bad as the marketing makes it. Thus far, the plan is to position it against Poison and Obsession, both of which have done enormously well. Strong. Sexy. All that jazz. But we're a long way from the launch pad. Hell, we haven't even got a name for it yet. I suggested Bitch in Heat, because that's essentially the promise"—she gave a brief laugh—"and you know what? Those jokers from Consuma-Corp took me literally. Jesus! I thought I was going to be canned then and there. You can believe I did some fast talking. But it was scary, Di. On the other hand, do I want to spend the rest of my life alternately groveling and throwing up?"

"It sounds to me like you're suffering from mid-life crisis," Diane remarked. "Isn't that a bit premature?"

"Not on Madison Avenue. Over thirty and you're considered geriatric. You simply cannot imagine how much pressure there is to be 'with it' all the time. After a while, the creative juices run dry, so if you're not at least a vice president by the time you're thirty-five, you're pretty much dead meat. My big fear is that one of these days I'll reach into my head for the new concept, the prize-winning commercial, and come up empty. Little old brilliant me—plum out of fresh ideas. But I ask you—how many new things can you say about some crappy shade of lipstick or yet another overpriced perfume? I don't know." She sighed. "Ten years of beating my brains out at the agency and for what? Shit! I don't live half as well as Rosemary, and all she's ever done is get married."

"Maybe you'd feel the pressure less if you managed better," Diane suggested.

"Like how?"

"Spend less on clothes, make a few prudent investments. Mutual funds, maybe, or I could suggest some tax-free municipals."

"Listen, Diane. The most prudent investment I can make is looking fabulous. What capital do I have? My face, my body—that's it. And they ain't gonna last forever. Sure, I spend a lot on clothes and at the hairdresser, but let me tell you, I expect to earn some very handsome dividends."

Diane sighed. It struck her that Fleur was her own best customer, subscribing to the very illusions she had been mocking a few minutes ago. "By dividends," she said, "I suppose you mean men."

"I mean *a* man. One is all it takes, Diane." There was sudden steel in Fleur's voice. "You know, when I came to New York after Smith, I thought wow! This place is the end of the world. Emerald City, I used to call it, where all your wishes came true. But Emerald City isn't a place, Diane. It's a man. The right man. I've done New York. I've done the career bit. I'm sick and tired of living by my wits, running the gauntlet every day. I want to get married, settle down, be cared for, be with somebody at the end of the day."

"Why, Fleur!" Diane was genuinely surprised. "I don't think you've been without a man two nights running."

"I'm not talking sex, Di. I'm talking wedding rings. Kids. The whole bit. That waiter today"—she smiled fondly—"what a cutie. A couple of years ago, I would have taken Rusty home to bed with me and spent a few pleasant hours exchanging nothing more substantial than bodily fluids. Not even last names. Christ, when I think of all the fabulous sex I've had over the years with guys I hardly knew! To say nothing of my numerous romantic interludes. If I ever write my autobiography, I'll call it 'A Thousand and One Night Stands.' *Et je ne regrette rien*. However, them days are gone forever. And so are them nights, regrettably. New joke in town. You know what they call someone who has AIDS and herpes and a dose of clap? An incurable romantic. Funny, huh?"

"I'm not laughing," said Diane.

"Neither am I. I'm absolutely through with casual sex. So you see, there's nothing left to do but get married. I want to be someone's 'lawful wedded.'" It was *a cri de coeur*. She turned and looked Diane square in the face. "I'm going to win the prize, get a husband. And I don't expect to take nine months to do it."

"Well," Diane said, "if you've made up your mind, then it's no contest. Poor bastard may as well throw in the sponge." For as long as Diane had known her, no male had successfully resisted Fleur. Her boast of a dozen proposals was probably true.

"So who's it going to be?" Diane ran down the list of Fleur's most recent victims. There was that Wall Street broker.

"Unh-unh!" Fleur shook her head. "Guys like him come six in a box."

The Lufthansa pilot.

"The sex was lousy. Erich was always coming in for a landing even before I got off the ground."

The model from last month's cover of *M*.

"We were three in a bed," Fleur replied. "Me, him, and his ego. I couldn't manage to service them both. Nope. The man I have in mind"—her dark eyes grew suddenly soft and luminous—"is someone very special. Strong, smart, decisive, prominent in business—a genuine grown-up. Everything you'd want in a husband."

"My my!" Diane was impressed. "He sounds terrific. Where'd you find him?"

"Around," Fleur said. "Practically under my feet. The problem is, he already is a husband. Someone else's. But one of these days that man is going to be mine. Only he doesn't know it yet."

Diane got up slowly, her face sad. "Don't do it, Fleur. Don't even think about it. It's emotional suicide. Besides, they never leave their wives. I should know. I went that route back in law school, and all I got out of it was a broken heart and an abortion. Remember?" She began walking, and Fleur fell in step beside her.

But Fleur shook her head. "I remember you mishandled it, start to finish. For a smart lady, Di, you can be awfully dumb, at least when it comes to men. You could have married Leo. All you had to do was play hardball."

"Like how? Put up a notice on the Yale bulletin board threatening suicide—or some cheap trick? The man had a wife and two young children. Anyway, there's no such thing as a shotgun divorce."

"The fact remains, you let him get away. Well, I don't share your scruples. As far as I'm concerned, it's open season. Besides which—" she stopped at the curb. Her eyes were shining, radiant with near-religious fervor. "I'm in love, Diane. Crazy, loony, helplessly, head-over-heels in love, just like in the storybooks." She hesitated a moment, then said, "No, not like in the storybooks because this is the real thing. And there's no way I'm going to let him go. I want your blessing, Diane. You're the best friend I have in the world, and I want you to stand by me. Just wish me well is all I ask."

Diane was nonplussed, reluctant to approve behavior she deemed morally wrong. And yet Fleur seemed so needy, so desperate. "Of course I wish you well, darling. I want you to be happy."

"I knew you would." Fleur planted an exuberant kiss on her cheek.

Across Fifth Avenue, the shop windows beckoned. "Come on." Fleur took Diane's elbow. "Let's pop into Saks for a few minutes and treat ourselves. Speaking of wardrobes, yours could use some jazzing up."

But Diane, already late for a meeting, begged off.

Funny, she thought as she hailed a cab. The contest was only one hour old and already it seemed to be over.

Once inside Saks, Fleur felt her spirits lift. She would buy something. Nothing major—God knew she couldn't afford it—but some charming trifle that would add a bit of zing to her wardrobe. She shut her eyes to conjure up the gray Missoni dress she'd bought last week. Terrific, but it needed a splash of color. Clunky jewelry, maybe. Or a zippy scarf.

Somehow, Fleur brooded, the more clothes you had, the more holes there were in your wardrobe. Each new outfit called for something special: the perfect shoes, the ideal belt. Accessorize, accessorize, accessorize. Wasn't that what *Vogue* was always preaching? Yes, the Missoni definitely required the right scarf. What the hell, she rationalized, you're only young once—if thirty-two could still be considered young. It certainly wasn't according to the TV spots, including her own. She hardly ever used a model over twenty-five. However, what was the point of spending eight hundred dollars on a designer dress and then not springing for a few bucks more to make it sing? For want of a nail . . .

Fleur headed for the scarf counter.

"I need something to liven up a very gray dress."

"Let me show you our new scarves from the Private Collection," the saleswoman said. "They just came in."

"Oh, God!" Fleur breathed as the counter filled with half a dozen brilliant silks. "Don't wrap them up, I'll eat them here. They are gorgeous!"

After some hesitation, she narrowed the choice down to two. Which would it be, the eau-de-Nil print, so restrained and elegant, or the dramatic fuchsia stripes? Maybe she'd splurge and get them both. But one look at the price disabused her of the notion. "A hundred dollars?" she gasped, "for a little scarf? I'll have to think about it for a moment."

The saleswoman smiled and went to serve another customer.

Fleur picked up the fuchsia scarf and folded it lovingly. The fabric was like a caress. Still, a hundred dollars for a square foot of silk! Outrageous. When she was a kid back in Waterville, that amount would have bought virtually a complete fall wardrobe at Dee-Dee Fashions on Front Street. A "best dress" surely ("None higher than $19.95"), a pair of slacks, a couple of Orlon sweaters (the kind that pilled after two washings) plus a winter coat. Moreover, Fleur would be expected to get three full winters out of the coat.

Chic hardly entered into it. For one thing, a hundred dollars probably represented the better part of a week's take-home pay for most people in those parts, money neither to be sneezed at nor squandered. For another, Waterville, like many another depressed New England mill town, was essentially immune to the dictates of fashion, New York being light-years away. Practicality and price were the criteria. Is it cheap? Is it warm? Will the gravy spots show? Can it be paid for on time? As for hemline fluctuations or chain-weighted jackets or (Fleur repressed a sigh) hand-rolled Italian scarves, who knew or cared about such subtleties when Fleur was a teenager. And even if one did get dressed up, there was no place to go except the local roller rink and Carvel's.

"Buy it a size larger," her mother was always urging when

she went shopping with Fleur. "You'll grow into it. Anyhow, you can always liven it up with lots of junk jewelry
from Woolworth's." So Fleur would buy a cheap dress and
a sleazy jacket a size larger only to have them fall apart in a
couple of months.

Dime store glitter was Belle Chamberlain's good-natured
answer to the drabness of life. That and her gaudy blond
hair and her four-inch spike heels and her Saturday night
blowouts at the Totem Pole Bar and Grille. "What the hell,"
she would say the morning after, while one or another
unshaven gent made his escape from the bedroom. "Everybody's entitled to a good time once a week."

And if Belle wasn't quite respectable, she was nonetheless
hardworking and cheerful, rarely complaining about the
difficulties of raising a daughter single-handedly on a wait-
ress's meager earnings.

Her mother asked too little of life, Fleur felt. She was
content to settle for shoddy goods and shiftless men. Even
now when her circumstances were a bit more comfortable,
Belle instinctively opted for the tawdry rather than the
beautiful. It was not just a question of taste, Fleur realized,
but of habit. Belle had felt miserably out of place in the
imposing precincts of Saks Fifth Avenue the one time Fleur
had taken her there.

"Come on, Ma," Fleur had insisted. "Let's get you something gorgeous. My treat." But Belle had balked at each
suggested item. "Highway robbery," she'd kept muttering.
Or "I could get this at K mart for a tenth the price." And
behind all her protests was the unspoken but profoundly
felt cavil: *We don't belong here, you and I.* Ultimately they
had wound up in Alexander's basement, with Belle rummaging happily among the bins.

But Fleur *did* belong. She had, through constant practice,
come to feel very much at home in the best stores and boutiques. She shopped with the authority of one to the manner
born. The salespeople never even suspected she was an
impostor, the poor-girl-made-good. There was a profound
pleasure to be derived not only in the wearing of beautiful
things, but in their acquisition as well. She loved the deferential attitude of the salespeople, their tacit assumption that
she was a woman of class and taste and property. It was a
delicious sensation, as gratifying as the creamy Italian silks
beneath her fingers.

Now, she turned her attention back to the matter at hand. Which would it be—the rich print or the fuchsia stripes. Yet in a far corner of her mind, she could hear mother's outraged shriek. "A hundred dollars for a little scarf! Are you crazy?"

Probably.

Fleur crumpled the eau-de-Nil and gently held it against her cheek, then studied herself in the mirror. The face that looked back was elegant, soignée, supremely Fifth Avenue. Sometimes even she found it hard to believe that this magnificent creature was her mother's daughter, Waterville's child. She shivered with a sense of what she had escaped.

No. Not crazy, she decided. What was crazy, after all, about desiring beauty and glamour, about choosing the best the world had to offer? The scarf was heaven. She could picture herself, the clutch of color at her throat, boarding the Concorde for Paris or lunching on a yacht off Newport. Eau-de-Nil. Even the name reeked of romance. The eau-de-Nil it would be.

But then again, the fuchsia was simply fabulous.

I must—I must— the little voice babbled like a subterranean brook. *I want—I want—*

Fleur dithered in an agony of choice. At the far end of the counter, the saleswoman was deep in conversation.

Neither then nor later could Fleur explain her impulse, but suddenly her bag was open just enough. In slipped the fuchsia scarf. In slipped the eau-de-Nil print. For an electrifying second, Fleur froze, unable to believe her own actions. She tensed, waiting for an alarm to ring. Already it was too late. There was no way she could put the scarves back unobserved.

Then, pulse pounding, eyes forward, she walked out of the store, turned a corner, and headed back to the office. Nobody followed. Nobody knew. Incredible!

At a corner of Fifty-second street, she stopped briefly to expel a huge sigh! *What a crazy thing to do, Fleur Chamberlain. Do that again and you're going to wind up in jail.* But—she felt a swift leap of the heart—it had been so dangerous. And so exciting! Almost like sex with a stranger. *What the hell*—she strode up Madison on an adrenaline high—*after all the money I've spent in Saks, they owe me a freebie.*

THREE

"**S**pareribs, beef with orange, fried rice"—Steve Godwin began unpacking the cardboard containers onto the white parson's table—"plus a double order of shrimp balls."

"I didn't know shrimps had balls," Bernie remarked.

"Very small ones. How was your day, sweetie?"

"*Fan*-tastic!" She opened the Coach satchel, which had grown in size since lunchtime, and pulled out a bottle of New York State champagne.

"I had lunch with my Smithies today at a place called the Café Karnak. An incredible, incredible experience!"

"Good chow, I gather?"

"I guess." She shrugged. "Food is food. You know me, Steve. I'm utterly incapable of forming a meaningful relationship with a restaurant. What was incredible was—well, I'll tell you when I've caught my breath. And how'd your day go, honey?"

"Medium rare." Steve had the laid-back accent of a native Californian. "We shot that hair spray commercial on Fire Island. Nothing but headaches. Supposed to be a guy and girl walking along the beach—mood stuff, you know, 'with the wind and the rain in your hair'—mist machines. And"—he laughed—"damned if the girl didn't get a hay fever attack every time we did a take. Jesus! The next time I shoot outdoors in ragweed season, I'm going to insist on allergy shots."

For the next couple of minutes they set the table in

happy complicity while the stereo belted out Genesis. Plastic dishes and paper napkins were the order of the day. Plus, for an uncharacteristic touch of elegance, the Tiffany champagne glasses that Steve had "liberated" from a food commercial shooting. Their movements were punctuated by smiles and small talk. They exuded the coziness of the long-established couple.

At forty, Steve Godwin had made his peace with life. Good nature resided in his clean blue eyes, the soft brown beard. The only remarkable aspect of his appearance was a slash of premature white in his hair, which he attributed to a wife who had stripped him clean in divorce court, divesting him simultaneously of bank account and children. The white streak, he claimed, was all Linda Godwin ever gave him—that and a permanent aversion to marriage.

He had met Bernie while on location in New York. The chemistry had been instant. That night they made love in her East Village loft. "No strings attached," she cautioned. "You betcha!" he agreed. A week later he sent west for his LPs and collection of old baseball cards. "Just for the time being," he insisted. "You know it!" she replied. Five years later they were still living together without a ripple.

"Our life-styles fit," she told everyone. Steve was amusing and affectionate. They had a wide circle of friends. And if his job in a production house had him on the road much of the time, there was no harm done. They appreciated each other all the more when he returned. Now, Bernie lowered the music. Steve reached for the champagne.

"So." He popped the cork and they sat down. "How about telling me what's the special occasion?"

Bernie raised her fists in triumph. "It looks like I'm going to be seeing air! Three weeks of yours truly on screen. Maybe even a regular spot on the show!"

Lunch that noon, though, had been a revelation, even more startling then the research team's statistics. "I thought Diane was going to have a heart attack," Bernie recounted to Steve. "And Fleur—wow! Even her makeup turned pale."

The moment the meal was over, Bernie had streaked back to her cubbyhole and started pounding out ideas on her typewriter. Three hours later she was beating on the executive producer's door.

"I have a proposal," she told Hy Feinstein.

"About what?"

"A proposal," she said, "about proposals. And it's perfect for our format."

She talked fast, competing with the buttons on Hy's phones that were always lighting up like a vintage Wurlitzer. Great idea, she bulleted. A real ratings raiser. Basic! Emotive! Wonder that *60 Minutes* or one of the big national magazine shows hadn't picked up on it already. Have to beat them to it.

"We're only a regional station," Hy reminded her.

"Well this should put us on the map. WHIZ—America's liveliest little station. Watch us grow!"

Briefly she reviewed the research study, then followed up with the gut reactions of her women friends. "And they're not unique," she claimed. "There isn't a female over twenty who won't be riveted."

Her proposal was to film a comprehensive tour of the marriage industry. "And it *is* an industry, Hy. We're talking megabucks."

"Everywhere you look," she continued, "people are trying to meet and mate, and paying handsomely for the privilege. There are singles bars, singles dances, singles cruises, and singles clubs for every conceivable subgroup, including vegetarians and people with herpes. There are computer dating services, videotape matchups—-even university courses on how to flirt, how to find. There are magazines," she reminded him, "of the highest quality that owe their financial health to the classified ads, all variations of Boy Meets Girl and vice versa.

'WSF requires TLC.'

'Jewish Juliet seeks Sensitive Romeo.'

'Nonsmoking blonde wants to set you on fire.'

And the object of all this feverish activity: Matrimony! It's number one on everybody's wish list. This town is Lonelyville, Hy, especially for working women. Busy days and empty nights. What I'm proposing is a complete guide for the single woman. And one of the single women in the story would be me!"

She envisioned the coverage stretched out over a three-week period, broken down into five-minute segments per day.

"I've got a budget roughed out, possible locations"—she tapped the sheaf of papers on his desk. "I've even got a title for the series. *How to Get Your MRS in NYC*. Cute, huh? Just the ticket for that *Heartbeat of New York* slot at the end of the show. Interviews with marriage brokers, social scientists, single men and women. Plus I could do a lot of the stuff with hidden mikes, cameras. Have the audience come with me when I make cold calls, follow up on blind dates. It's a natural, Hy, a grabber! Will Bernadette Hong land her man? Or is the Sensitive White Male Seeking Companionship really Jack the Ripper in disguise? Tune in tomorrow, same time, same station and find out."

"And how do you wrap it up?" Hy wanted to know.

"With a girl getting married," Bernie said. "How else?"

"You?" he asked.

"God forbid!" she grunted. "Well, Hy, what do you think?"

"So what did he think?" Steve put down a half-gnawed sparerib.

Bernie finished her champagne. "Barbara Walters, move over. Here comes Bernadette Hong." She giggled. "Actually, it wasn't that easy. We had to run it past the management, the budget guys—the whole schmeer. I pulled every trick in the book, including the fact that we are the only afternoon program in the tri-state area that doesn't have any ethnics on regular view. Even our weatherman is white bread. What I told them is that by giving me a regular shot, the station gets two brownie points for the price of one. A woman *and* an ethnic."

"I don't know if one Chinese grandparent qualifies you as a genuine ethnic."

"What's family for?" she came back. "Anyhow, you can't deny I qualify as a woman."

"The genuine article." He came over to where she sat and nuzzled her cheek. His touch was warm, urgent.

"The trouble with Chinese food," he said, "is it's a terrible aphrodisiac. Makes me want to go to bed with Chinese women."

He slid his hands under her sweater and began massaging her breasts. They were firm, compact, like the rest of her.

"Funny you should say that, Steve. 'Cause I've got this thing for Occidental men. Is it true you're built different?"

He laughed. "Come to bed and I'll show you. Let's leave the stuff on the table, just take the champagne."

As he loaded their glasses on a tray, he heaved a sigh. "Do me one favor, though, Bernie." A shadow passed over his face. "I think your idea is terrific. Really great. One thing is—don't take that shit too seriously."

She looked at him, astonished. "Seriously! My first real chance to get sustained TV exposure and you tell me not to take it seriously!"

"I meant the matrimonial part of it. Don't find yourself a husband en route."

"Is that all!" She swiveled and kissed him full on the lips. On the tray the glasses rattled. "You know me better than that, love. It's a story, nothing more. And I'm a professional. Besides, I've got everything I want right here and now. Bernie Hong—the Last of the Liberated Women."

An hour later she was lying in bed, "bed" being a king-size mattress on the bare wooden floor. At her side Steve was snoring gently. The only light in the room came from a barber pole.

"How can you live like that?" her mother would moan on her rare visits from upstate. "The place is a barn. No proper furniture, no decent china. You can call it the East Village, but to me it's the Lower East Side. I don't know what to tell them back in Binghamton." Poor Addie Hong in her suffocating gentility, scotch and sodas in hand, bearing the stretch marks of half a dozen pregnancies, worrying if this hat or that drapery was consistent with her husband's position at IBM. For if Ted Hong designed computer programs, Addie lived them. She was the perfect company wife, always blending into the woodwork and never quite grasping why her youngest daughter refused to follow her example.

Bernie sat up and rubbed her neck gingerly. She and Steve would have to cool the sex over the next few weeks. She could hardly show up sporting a bright red hicky at some lonely-hearts event, let alone on afternoon TV. When all this was over, they would take a long weekend somewhere. Hawaii, maybe, or at least Antigua.

She planted a soft kiss on his cheek, contentment flowing through her every pore. Thank God she didn't come home every night to an empty apartment, an empty bed, with no one there to share her daily measure of defeats and triumphs. Thank God for Steve. She was smart enough to know her good fortune.

Small wonder, really, that Diane and Fleur had given way to panic. Especially Diane. The man shortage was really tough on quiet types. But what idiots they were to think marriage would be their salvation! As if a few words mumbled down at City Hall could be a guarantee of anything except mutual bondage.

Bernie loved Steve. Steve loved her. And they didn't need a wedding ring to prove it. If anything, their relationship was richer, worthier because it was volitional on both their parts. Q.E.D.

When it came to wish lists, Bernie had her own, and it was at least a hundred items long. Meeting politicians, interviewing stars, getting on a first-name basis with the powers-that-be. Bigger office, bigger paycheck, bigger billing. Going live, going network. A slot on *60 Minutes*. Or *20/20*. Or anchor on the evening news. She wanted to appear on *Lifestyles of the Rich and Famous*—as an interviewee. To see her face on the cover of *Time*. It was a long list of wishes. And the starting point could be this series.

She was suddenly conscious of the irony. Here she was, a woman thoroughly committed to the single life, doing a survey on the marriage scene. In the dark bedroom, she began planning her show, her role. She would have to pass herself off as a genuine husband hunter, enlist the audience's sympathy en route. That might take some doing, but one of her skills as a journalist was the ability to fit into other people's skins. She'd need to "think lonely." She tried it now. Shutting her eyes, she envisioned herself as another type of woman: conservative, conventional, believing in tradition, and yearning for the emotional security of marriage. It was an unfamiliar role. She tried to picture herself married to Steve.

Interesting.

Of course it would never happen. But just suppose she did have those values, that she were that type of woman. She couldn't help wondering how Steve would react. "Marry me." "Or what?" "Or else!" ran the imaginary dialogue. She found it impossible to picture his response. Would Steve laugh it off? Or go along? Would he even hang in there if she brought pressure to bear? Or would he see her as another person entirely? As another Linda Godwin?

The thought was disquieting. Of course Steve loved her. *Her*, Bernadette Hong, with all her quirks and inconsistencies. ("I'm crazy about you." Those were the last words he had murmured before falling asleep.)

Moreover, these were the merest speculations, fodder for her show. She had no intention of asking for his hand in marriage! And yet . . . and yet the idea refused to be banished. What if she were to ask him, just for the sake of argument, as proof of his love? Would he head for the hills? She had the queasy feeling that his commitment to bachelorhood was greater than his commitment to her.

"Nonsense!" she said aloud. Beside her, Steve reorchestrated his snores. Nonsense it was. She would put that thought right out of her mind. Pronto.

Bernie sprang out of bed. In the kitchen were the remnants of dinner. She began putting away the half-empty cartons, nibbling a bit of beef, a strip of broccoli as she did. It was gelatinous but good. And say what you would about plastic plates, you didn't waste your time doing dishes. On the counter two fortune cookies nestled in a waxed paper bag, like Darby and Joan. She took one, crumbled it in her palm, and withdrew the paper sliver. "You will meet a handsome stranger," it read.

FOUR

In the living room the red light on the answering machine gleamed bright with promise. Diane went over to it and hit the Playback button. Invitations to the theater? To a dinner party? A call from someone new and attractive? But the sole message was a recorded reminder that her subscription to *Business Week* had expired. This news was followed by three wordless clicks. Wrong numbers, was her guess, or telemarketers moving in for the kill.

She switched on the lights, flooding the room with a thousand watts of brilliance. It was a handsome interior, sparse but elegant, with everything color-coordinated in tones of white, plum, and slate, from the Japanese graphics to the pale Berber rugs to the slim cluster of purple iris on weekly order from the Sixty-fifth Street florist. Sometimes, as tonight, Diane found the setting a bit austere, but everyone assured her it was a decorator's triumph, superbly suited to her New York high rise. And so it should be, considering the cost.

On the bar the onyx clock read ten-twenty. Another evening lost in the endless convolutions of *Simplexx Systems* v. *Harrigan Oil*, or, as she was wont to call it in her more discouraged moments, *Jarndyce* v. *Jarndyce*. The fight was long, bloody, and unrelenting—every inch of the legal terrain being disputed by two large and merciless teams of lawyers. Both firms subscribed to the litigation-is-war philosophy. "Take no prisoners" was the battle cry.

Diane's client, Simplexx, had scored the first round: Harrigan zapped them on the second. Simplexx had struck back with an appeal, at which point Harrigan filed for an injunction. Now both parties were gleefully gearing for the next burst of hostilities coming up soon in federal court. It was, as she had remarked earlier that day, a lawyer's paradise, a layman's hell, devouring most of her hours and energy.

She opened her briefcase, looked inside, then snapped it shut with a heave of disgust. Tonight she had no heart for further work. Bernie's news had taken the wind out of her. Never to marry. It was a life sentence. Worse. A death sentence.

"Byron," she had asked her closest colleague in the middle of a document review that very afternoon, "do you think that I am an unmarriageable woman?"

"What kind of question is that?"

"A frank one. I never seem to meet anybody suitable."

Byron was one of the few men with whom Diane could discuss affairs of the heart, or as it happened, the even more distressing lack of them.

Confidences had never come easy to her, least of all with men, and intimate matters were particularly off bounds. She was too proud, too self-contained to expose her vulnerability to imagined male derision. To this rule, Byron was the exception. For one thing, they had started at the firm at the same time. For another, their backgrounds (although he was from Virginia and she from Boston) were similar; they were both children of privilege. For a third, no sexual involvement was conceivable between them. Byron Elkington was gay.

As a first-year associate, he had made an effort at concealment, afraid a firm such as Slater Blaney would never extend partnership to a man of his inclination. But the strain proved too great. Rumors abounded of burly stevedores and mincing chorus boys.

He had turned up at work one morning with a face full of bruises and a broken nose. "Rough trade," he told a horrified Diane.

"You'll get killed one day," she said, "running around with lowlifes like that."

Byron was unrepentant. His brief encounter had been worth it, he claimed. "What's life without risk, huh?"

Shortly after, however, he met a young investment banker and the two settled down to a domestic routine.

The firm made its peace with Byron, although not with Byron and Jim as a couple. Their stipulation, tacit yet observed, was that appearances be met during office hours and at public functions. Byron obliged. With his aristocratic good looks and gentleman's wardrobe, he was a presentable man at a dinner party, and on those occasions when Diane needed an escort, she had no qualms about enlisting his aid. After Fleur, Byron was her closest friend.

Now he considered her problem. "Suitable? I couldn't say as to that. First you'll have to define your terms."

Diane frowned. What constituted "suitable"? He would, of course—this as-yet-undiscovered paragon—have to be smart. "You know me, I can't tolerate fools." And he would have to be successful. "I'll most likely make partner, Byron. He should at least be at my professional level." Dynamic. "Someone I can look up to—respect, admire."

"Is that all?" Byron arched an eyebrow.

"Now for the hard one." She gave an embarrassed giggle. "I want this terrific wonderful king of kings to be crazy in love with me! To be someone who can see past the diamond-hard surface of the brilliant litigator"—her tone became self-mocking, as though, God forbid, Byron should recognize how literally she took her own words—"discover the soft tender blossom beneath. How's that for impossible!"

"Not bad," Byron said. "In fact, I've got just the guy for you." He then named one of the attorneys on the Harrigan team.

She had nurtured a modest crush on Bill Shannon for months. When Bill was present, she went out of her way to dazzle him with pyrotechnics. "Look at me," she signaled. "How clever I am, how savvy."

She had last seen him at a lively deposition at his office. "You are one tough broad," he'd acknowledged with a smile. The admiration was professional, not sexual.

"Forget it," she told Byron. "I'm sorry I even mentioned the subject." But later that day she had asked her boss. "Do you think I'm tough, Frank? Be honest with me."

He studied her for a moment, taking in the high forehead, the intense blue eyes, the pale skin, and the imposing five-foot-nine frame. "Tough? You bet! You're the toughest damn lawyer on my team, Diane—bar none." Then he clapped her on the shoulder. "Keep up the good work!"

She had left for home, profoundly depressed.

But she wasn't tough—not in her personal life. At heart she wanted only what millions of other women already had: a husband to love, children to care for. Was that so much to ask?

No, she wasn't tough at all, Diane reflected as she sprawled out on the living room sofa. A tougher, less scrupulous woman would have exerted pressure on Leo Frankland back in law school, would have won him by means fair or foul.

True, married professors had no right to play havoc with the emotions of vulnerable students. Distinguished experts on legal ethics should know better than to climb into bed with women nearly young enough to be their daughters. That sort of behavior bred consequences. Yet Diane had done nothing to stop him, then had stood by helplessly and let the man she loved slip through her fingers without protest. Even now she thought of Leo with love and longing. He would always be "the one who got away," the haunter of her dreams.

Of course, she had been in awe of him back then, as indeed all the women students were. Physically and intellectually he towered above the herd—the arbiter to be consulted, the aphorist to be quoted, the final authority on matters great and small—and it was Diane's curse that she continued to measure other men against the length of his shadow.

She should, she now knew, have borne his child, even outside of marriage, even in the face of Leo's disapproval. She should have had the baby, and conventions be damned. She had lacked—what? Courage? The strength to buck the tide? The fear of her parents' disapproval? Yet had her nerve not failed, she would now have some part of Leo to cherish, some consolation for lost love.

Tonight for instance. Tonight she wouldn't be coming home to an empty apartment with spotless rooms. That child (for some reason she always presumed it would have been a boy), *their* child, would be seven now, full of fun and wit. Tonight she would have been greeted at the door by an explosion of life. There would be clutter around instead of sterility, and laughter instead of this heavy silence that crushed her with its weight, almost took the breath from her body. Not even the hum of traffic breached these walls. And on nights like this, she wanted to scream for loneliness. But she didn't. The Summerfields were not a screaming family.

For a while she lay there, wrapped in the quiet, but gradually her ears became attuned to a repetitive sound, barely perceptible yet invasive. Drip. Drip. Drip. She got up, checked the kitchen, then the bathroom. There it was. Drip. Drip. Drip. Slower than a heartbeat.

She flushed the toilet, and the water resettled only to recommence the pattern a minute later. No amount of jiggling would help. Drip. Drip. Drip.

Diane felt a flash of anger. Goddamn, this place was costing her twenty-eight-hundred dollars a month—a bloody fortune! Was it too much to expect that it included a well-behaved toilet? No way she was about to let that Chinese water torture continue untended until morning. By morning she would be certifiable. With energy born of frustration, she strode over to the intercom and buzzed the doorman to fetch the handyman.

"I don't care how late it is!"—her voice reverberated in the empty room—"I pay for twenty-four-hour service and I expect to get it. Send someone up right away."

"It might take some time. There are five hundred apartments in this building. He could be anywhere."

"I didn't ask for a statistical roundup. I asked for a handyman." There was a hysterical quaver in her voice. "Find him!"

She hung up the intercom, only then remembering some basic manners. "Thank you," she said to the fixture, instantly contrite for having yelled at the doorman. It wasn't his fault.

Minutes passed. The drip was growing unbearable. She turned on the stereo. Mozart responded full blast. *Ah, Mozart!* —Diane burrowed into the music—*I owe you my life!* Leaky toilets, lawsuits, even Bernie's grim prophecy—all were washed away by wave after glorious wave of melody. Diane drifted.

The doorbell rang. It was barely audible above the music. Diane, half-asleep, momentarily forgot having called for the handyman. "Who the hell ... !" She peered through the peephole. "What do you want?"

A man in a work shirt and jeans was standing in the hall. For a moment she mistook him for the waiter Fleur had teased at lunch. Same age. Same stocky build. What on earth was that fellow doing here? Her innate suspicion of all things in New York came to the fore.

"It's me," he said. "The night handyman." His artless blue eyes offered reassurance. So did the tool kit, the smile. No sex maniac or serial killer here, just a janitor doing his job.

"Yes, okay." Diane unlatched the door. "Come on in. I must say, you took your good time getting here."

Without further word, she led the way to the bathroom, pointed out the offending toilet, then left him to get on with it. Through the open door, she could hear him tinkering, flushing, clanking plumber's tools with gusto, whistling above the music. At a particular turn in the score, he began to sing in a hearty baritone. *"Voi che sapete."* Then followed a triumphant flush.

He emerged from the bathroom. "It's okay now, miss. I'm sorry about the delay." He had an accent of sorts, she noticed, but then so did most of the building staff.

The handyman stood for a moment in the center of the rug and looked around him with open curiosity. "What a nice apartment," he said. His voice was loud and blustery.

"Thank you very much." She nodded, sorry that she'd growled at him earlier. Why take her lousy mood out on the help? She considered tipping him, then decided against it. The man was only doing his job.

At closer range, he didn't look a bit like the waiter at the Café Karnak except for his stocky build. He was in his early twenties, fresh-faced, thick-necked, with broad Slavic cheekbones and wide, powerful hands. All told, he had the air of a healthy peasant.

She felt obliged to say something gracious, particularly as he remained planted expectantly in the middle of the room. But for all her articulateness in a court of law, Diane was hopeless at small talk with strangers. Working-class people, especially, made her feel ill at ease. She never knew what to talk about.

"I see that you're a Mozart fancier," she said, then flushed guiltily. There had been, she recognized, a note of surprise in her voice, bordering on disbelief. How insufferably patronizing that must have sounded. But the young man refused to take offense.

"What other possibilities are there in life?" he replied.

"Indeed!" His remark sent her reeling.

"Anyhow," he continued, "I grew up with Mozart, Haydn, and company. My father is with the Israeli Philharmonic."

"I didn't mean to embarrass you." She breathed a sigh of relief. So he wasn't working-class after all. "You're a student, I gather."

Yes, he told her. He had graduated from Hebrew University the year before and, always having wanted to see America, was now taking his master's at Columbia. The job at the Osgood Arms permitted him to live rent-free in a pleasant neighborhood and pursue his studies.

Of course. Diane nodded vigorously. How commendable, this nice young man working his way through college, just as Fleur had waitressed through Smith. And every bit as ambitious, no doubt.

"Please accept my apologies," she said.

"For what?" He furrowed his brow.

"For having mistaken you for a janitor." She blushed. And to think she'd almost tipped him.

"But I am a janitor. A carpenter—plasterer. How do you say it?" he rubbed his chin. "Ah! A jack-of-all-trades." Suddenly he looked like a peasant again.

"Well," she said, "I congratulate you on your command of idiom. Your English is excellent."

"So is my plumbing," he returned. "And if you need any more night work, just call and ask for Avram. Avram Gittelson."

She stared at him. Was that last crack a double entendre? If so, how crude. But before she could determine which way it was meant, his beeper summoned him to another apartment. And he was gone with a slam of the door.

Well, Diane thought wryly, at least she had met Rosemary's quota: one new man spoken to each day. Although hardly what one would call husband material.

She turned off the music. *The Marriage of Figaro*—of all things! There was simply no escaping the topic. But now, with the toilet drip fixed, the apartment seemed quieter than ever. Spooky. And the day's frustrations had left her with energy to burn.

Briefly she considered phoning Byron, who lived just a few blocks away, and inviting herself around for a drink. But it was getting late and Byron was, if not a married man, at least a domestic one. In all likelihood, he and Jim had already settled in for the evening.

Or she could call up Brent Wilson, and if he was available, they might spend a vigorous hour or two in bed. But she didn't like Brent, for all his Wall Street smarts and *Kama Sutra* skills. Sex with him was purely a convenience. He always called her "baby" when he came, most likely because he couldn't remember which one she was.

No, she didn't want Brent or any of that handful of occasional lovers who had walked through her life without leaving a trace. She wanted more than the mere mechanics of sex. She wanted warmth, love, permanence. She wanted to find another Leo, only available. She wanted—oh yes indeed!—to be first at Rosemary's finish line. Tomorrow she would start the hunt in earnest, she vowed.

With an air of resolve, Diane changed into her swimsuit, threw on a robe, and took the elevator to the rooftop pool. She swam forty laps without a break. A half hour later she returned, healthily exhausted and ready for bed.

The first thing she noticed was a damp smudge in the middle of her rug. The Israeli had left a footprint. It was a wonder he hadn't broken anything.

FIVE

———•———

It was nearly midnight when Alex Marshall, weary but keyed up from the long business day, arrived home. He let himself in with a minimum of noise. Yet again, he had missed Chris's bedtime. In the living room, his wife had dozed off in front of the TV set. Only Shelby, the springer spaniel, acknowledged his arrival. The dog gave a low growl.

"Sharrap!" Alex growled back, but the sound was sufficient for Rosemary to stir.

"Ah, you're home!" she murmured.

"To state the obvious." Alex brushed her cheek with his lips. "Long day. My ass is dragging."

"Did you have any dinner, honey?"

"I had a Mars bar on the train."

"A Mars bar!" She was fully awake now. "'That's no nourishment for a giant of industry. Come into the kitchen, I'll fix you something proper." She had a Southerner's feeling for good food and the ritual of communal meals. If she had any grievance about Alex, it was that he was rarely home in time for dinner.

Alex poured himself a scotch and followed her into the kitchen. The room, bright and cheery even at night, never failed to please him. It had the comfortable air of a French provincial farm, full of good things to look at and to eat. An example, *Connecticut Life* had written, of "the gracious use of modern appliances in a setting of antique cookwares and tiles." From the chef's oven, Rosemary withdrew left-

41

over cassoulet and set it atop the stove to reheat. The room grew fragrant with the herbs of Provence.

She set a place for one on the oaken table. "This is the third time this week you've been late," she said.

"I know."

"And it's only Wednesday!"

"I know."

"'One of these days you'll come home and your own son won't recognize you. 'Who's that stranger?' he'll ask."

"Now, Rosemary!"

"I don't know." She sighed and began heaping sausages on an earthenware plate. "We spent years trying to have a baby, and now that we have one, you're never here for his bedtime."

"Sorry," Alex said phlegmatically. "I'll make it up to you both this weekend."

"Promise?"

"Promise."

"After all, I don't want my one and only husband turning into a workaholic."

Alex grunted. There was no real rancor in this exchange; it had taken place almost nightly for years.

"There!" She put his plate down, then sat down herself and watched with satisfaction while he ate. "You look tired, honey," she sympathized.

"Bushed."

Alex munched for a while in silence. "What's this brown stuff?" He speared a crunchy morsel on his fork.

"That's *confit d'oie,* preserved goose. We had it in Toulouse last summer, remember, at Chez Louis? Anyhow, tell me about your day."

Alex put down his fork, the inner man fulfilled, and above the dark circles his green-gray eyes danced with excitement. He allowed himself a secret smile. "We were doing a run of press tonight, a stock prospectus, and I stuck around to see the job through."

As executive vice president at Leviathan, he had every reason to be satisfied. Ten years ago, when his classmates at Tuck Business School were scrambling for berths in investment banks and multinational corporations, Alex had seen the possibilities in the less glamorous world of financial printing. Leviathan was the third largest such firm in the country. It specialized in the printing of stock offerings, merger plans, company reports, and prospectuses. In addition to speed and accuracy, the firm promised its clients, mostly investment banks and law firms, an atmosphere of total secrecy. Not a word concerning proposed mergers or quarterly reports was ever to be leaked. Premature disclosure would be fatal. The typesetters themselves were often kept in ignorance of the material they were handling. To ensure confidentiality, documents were frequently set in code, with false names representing the actual companies. While the presses ran, associates from the participating firms stood guard to see that nothing went amiss.

But Alex Marshall hadn't spent those years in B school for nothing. He knew the corporate world, followed the market, kept tabs as to which firms represented which clients. On a couple of occasions, he had figured out what was in the wind, then bought the stock before it rose.

Legally, he felt he was on debatable ground. True, he wasn't a lawyer; he had taken no professional oath. Therefore, he couldn't technically be called an insider. But to be on the safe side, he had purchased the stocks in his wife's maiden name, figuring nobody would make the connection. His trading activity was unlikely to draw either the SEC's notice or Leviathan's. He wasn't a pig, he told himself, not compared to the real insiders on Wall Street. Those guys were making millions. Nonetheless, he liked to think he had done well for himself and his family, enough to add that extra gloss to their standard of living. Besides, a man would be a fool not to answer when opportunity knocked. It had knocked tonight.

"You know"—he scratched his chin thoughtfully—"it looks like AIDS is going to be a terrific investment opportunity."

"Oh?" Rosemary said. "Yes, it's awful. How about a piece of homemade pecan pie?"

"Yeah, sure."

"With a scoop of ice cream?"

Alex shook his head, preoccupied. "I could kick myself for not having cashed in on the condom market last summer. Guys were making fortunes. Okay, I missed out. But this little company—Jesus, it's a natural! Get this, Rosemary—"

She cut the pie and frowned. "And I think I'll put a little slice in Chris's lunch box for tomorrow. He'd love it."

"It's a blood bank," Alex went on, "only with a differ-

ence. You know how scared everyone is of picking up the
AIDS virus through transfusions, right? It's killing the whole
blood-donor business. Well, the idea these guys have—"

"Or maybe he'd be better off with an apple." She hesitated. "It would make less of a mess."

"What I was saying is, with this outfit, what you do is
you donate your own blood while you're healthy and they
file it away under your name. For your use only. You make
maybe three, four donations a year till you've built up a
substantial supply."

"In which case"—Rosemary polished a golden delicious
and slipped it in a brightly colored Care Bears lunch box—
"Chris can have his pie when he comes home from school—"

"That way," Alex continued, "say you need surgery, transfusions later on in life, you're guaranteed to get your own
blood back—"

"—with ice cream on it. Won't that be nice?"

Alex stared at her, frustrated. "Have you heard a single
word I've been saying?"

"I've heard, I've heard!" She wheeled around with a look
of barely concealed revulsion. She for one found the subject of AIDS utterly distasteful and wished to God everyone
would stop talking about it. "I just wonder, do you have to
talk about this sort of thing at the dinner table?"

"I'm the one who's eating," Alex reasoned. "I just thought
you'd be interested. The thing is, honey, the company's
going public, and I want to get in on it before the prospectus hits the street. Maybe take a flyer for ten thou or so. If
it sounds okay to you, I'll call my broker tomorrow."

"Whatever you think, Alex," she said, eager to drop the
whole topic. "You're the financial whiz."

He furrowed his brow. Was she being ironic? But that
wasn't Rosemary's style. Besides, he *was* the financial whiz.
As a teenager Alex had pledged to himself to make a
million dollars before he was forty. Not that a million was
all that much these days, but he could confidently expect to
achieve his goal with a few years to spare.

"And what did you do today, hon?" He got up from the
table and headed for the bedroom.

While they got ready for bed, Rosemary chattered on,
about lunch with the girls, some contest or other she was
involved with, how Chris was doing great in kindergarten.
Alex was only half-tuned in.

". . . these rush chairs I saw at Bloomie's. I was thinking how terrific they'd look on the sunporch."

Alex peeled off his shorts and tossed them in the general direction of the hamper.

"You want a rush chair, go buy it."

She paused. "Four chairs, Alex. We need four, if we're going to use it for a summer dining room. They're a bargain, honey, worth every penny. I saw them for sixty dollars more at Pierre Deux. Apiece."

Alex Marshall laughed. "Too bad Smith doesn't give degrees in Comparison Shopping. You'd have graduated top of your class. Yeah, buy the fucking chairs, whatever makes you happy." He yawned and fell into bed.

"Wake me up at six tomorrow, will you, love?"

"Six!" Rosemary snuggled up beside him. "How come so early?"

"Well," Alex began. He had a business breakfast at seven-thirty at the Carleton. The Delmo people were thinking of switching their account, of all things! American Litho had offered faster delivery dates. Christ, he didn't know what was wrong with his salespeople, letting American undercut them like that. . . .

He was just warming up, feeling a new surge of energy, when he noticed Rosemary was fast asleep. Wide-awake now, he began worrying in earnest. That American Litho business was going to be a bitch. He could use a little bodily comfort.

"Rosemary?" He placed a hand on her soft warm breast.

In her sleep she murmured and rolled away from him.

I bore her, Alex Marshall thought irritably.

Goddamn! Every day he gave his guts to the company just to pay for this elaborate ménage. The swimming pool. The expensive vacations. Rush chairs! He was busting his ass to provide her with rush chairs, but the moment he mentioned business, it bored her.

Too wound up to sleep, he got out of bed, flossed his teeth, then scrutinized himself in the mirror. He was getting thin on top, no doubt about it, just like his father who had been bald by the time he was forty, as Rosemary often remarked. The notion was too depressing to contemplate. He settled down in the den with some work.

SIX

"**W**ell?" Rosemary demanded at their next lunch at the Café Karnak. "Are we ready for a progress report?"

Diane looked sheepish. "I've been busy."

"Busy with all the wrong things, I warrant. And shirking all the right ones. Next time, darling, I expect a positive update. Names, places, the works. And you, Fleur?"

Fleur shifted in her seat. "I tried following up on that cute kid Rusty, remember him? But I hear he abandoned his promising career as a waiter for a part in a Broadway show." She gave a mock sigh. "Lost forever. Just when I was ready to pop the question."

"You're not taking this seriously," Rosemary chided. "I thought you had all these men on the string."

"There's a difference between having them on the string and getting them to tie the knot." Fleur sat up sharply. "What is this, the Spanish Inquisition?"

"I'm just trying to light a fire under you girls, that's all," Rosemary admonished. "You don't have to bite my head off."

Unexpectedly, Fleur smiled. "Sorry. The truth is, I'm working on a relationship that's got a lot of promise."

"Oh?" Rosemary's eyebrows arched. "Somebody new?"

"Reasonably new. I can't tell you the details, it's too early in the game. But believe me, Rosemary, I've been giving it my best shot. And if I pull it off, you'll be the first to know."

"Well, good for you," Rosemary said. "At least you're making the effort. Now I know I'm just den mother, but I've been following the field vicariously, thinking what I would do in your shoes, and do you know, *New York* magazine has page after page of classified ads with half of them sounding eligible? 'Handsome, serious, intelligent, rich,' plus looking for lasting relationships. Almost too good to be true."

"It is." Bernie laughed. She had spent a busy week following up on the personals and had met bachelors by the dozen.

"Actually," she reported, "I amend my statement. Most of the guys are nice enough, some of them are pretty interesting. It all depends on your expectations. My guess is I think you could find a husband in the personals, provided you're looking for one. Which of course I'm not. But I've come across all kinds through those ads, let me tell you."

The protocol was to meet in a public place for coffee or a drink and test the water before advancing to the "commitment" of dinner. Look for a man in a green sweater, she'd be told, or a denim jacket and a Vandyke beard. Bernie would arrive a few minutes late, case the subject from a distance, then decide whether or not to follow through. One guy pulled up in a sports car with balloons flying from it, tin cans clanking, and a sign that said Just Divorced. On the whole she preferred outdoor meeting places. "If he looks like he's loony-tunes, I just walk on past." But if the man appeared reputable, she would make contact. At the very least, she said, she heard their life stories, and there was usually something there that made good copy.

"And are they handsome, serious, intelligent, and rich?" Diane asked.

"Sometimes one, sometimes the other. The thing is, you have to know how to read the ads. They're written in code. For instance, if the ad says he's forty, read fifty. If he says he's in his fifties, try sixty-plus. And if he describes himself as 'mature,' that means he's been dead for ten years. Once you understand what the words really mean, you can more or less pick your customer."

She had worked out a glossary:

affectionate = horny
handsome = two eyes, a nose, and a mouth
artistic = thinks he may be gay and hopes you'll help

    him prove otherwise
rich = he'll spring for the coffee
intelligent = pompous
literate = too shy to make small talk
articulate = a nonstop chatterbox
levelheaded = accountant, dentist, etc.
sensitive = married before and still hurting
dynamic = short
down-to-earth = fat
great sense of humor = both short and fat

Rosemary frowned. "That doesn't sound like much of a field to choose from."

"I dramatize," Bernie said. "The point is, they're decent guys. Just lonely. And short," she added as an afterthought.

"Well, personally," Diane said, "I would rather die than advertise for a husband. Or even answer an ad like that. My God"—she shuddered—"it's so humiliating. Like standing on a street corner with your hand out."

"But you have to do something," Rosemary urged. "They're not going to come to you! How about the singles bars, discos? C'mon Diane, show some signs of life."

Diane made a face. "I can't."

"Of course you can," Bernie said. "Anybody can."

"I know myself, Bernie. I shrivel in those situations. I simply can't walk up to total strangers and start conversations. And no one seems to start conversations with me. I lack your gift of gab."

"Surely you're not shy," Rosemary clucked. "My Lord, you were the star of the debating team at Smith! Anyhow, I thought you lawyers do nothing but talk, talk, talk and argue, argue, argue—"

"She's dynamite in the courtroom," Fleur interjected. "I've seen her in action."

"It's not the same!" Diane said. "So will you stop ganging up on me. And it's not a question of being shy. It's a question of—of dignity! When I'm on the job, I'm dealing with facts, law, the realm of ideas. It's impersonal, an intellectual discipline. That's very different from putting myself up on the auction block, cornering some guy at a bar and forcing him to talk to me. Christ! I may as well carry a sandwich board: Lonely Woman Needs Mate."

"The men are lonely too," Rosemary began, but Bernie

intervened. "No no"—she raised her hand—"I understand. Diane's not the singles bar type. You're selective, Di, and so you should be. I always felt you were a class act."

"Thanks," Diane said doubtfully. "Put that way, I sound like a terrible snob. The thing is, meeting men under those circumstances—ads, singles bars, what have you—everybody comes off like marked-down merchandise. My feeling is, any man who's that desperate to meet women has got to be a loser, and I expect they'd feel the same about me. What am I, a charity case?"

"I know," Bernie said. "You're a Summerfield of Boston, and only the best is good enough. But you do want to meet men, don't you?"

"Nice men!"

"Good. Because this Saturday I'm going to something called the Professional Forum at the Park Plaza Hotel. It's a fancy word for—now don't get uptight, Diane—a single mingle. But the point is, this one costs forty bucks just to get in, plus you have to have a bona fide business card. The idea is you can meet single professional people, college graduates, without losing face. I hear they get a lot of doctors, investment bankers—"

"She'll go!" Fleur volunteered, and before Diane could lodge a further protest, her friend continued. "She'll not only go, she'll look absolutely gorgeous. Diane, I'll come by your apartment, ten o'clock Saturday morning. We'll go to Bergdorf's, Bendel's, the whole bit. I'll make an appointment for you with my hairdresser. Marco's fantastic with frizzy hair. Now don't give me any arguments. Just leave everything to me. I'm going to fit you out so fabulously, you'll break every heart in the room."

"But . . . but . . ."

But Fleur had the last word. "Ten o'clock, and bring your checkbook."

Coming home on the train that afternoon, it was all Rosemary could do to keep from bursting into smiles. It had been a glorious day, starting with lunch with the girls at the Karnak. But the high point of her day had come later, during Decorative Arts II at the museum. She had brought an earthenware milk jug into class, a curious piece shaped like an owl. It had been purchased at a country auction the month before. She had offered it for the lecturer's opinion. One look and he waxed ecstatic.

"Swansea," he said. "Early nineteenth century."

"Of course it was in with a whole bunch of junk," she said. "I only paid eighty dollars for the lot."

"Congratulations." Professor Gilmore fondled the owl with knowing fingers. "Yes, a splendid example of Swansea creamware, a genuine find. You have an eye, Mrs. Marshall, a connoisseur's eye!"

Yes indeed, she did have an eye, not perhaps as expert as her mother, who could distinguish sterling from silver plate at one hundred paces. But an eye, nonetheless, accustomed to seeking out the unusual, the charming. Combined with a nose for sniffing out bargains.

"Earthly goods," Alex called them. "Earthy" was more accurate. For Rosemary didn't chase after exquisite porcelains or Fabergé eggs. Instead, she concentrated on those everyday items, well made and beautifully cared for, that evoked the best of hearth and home. Marmite pots, antique cheese molds, pewter porringers, terra-cotta tiles from Tuscan villas. Simple, lovely, useful things that represented enduring values.

And they were enduring investments as well, she believed. Probably a lot more solid than those high-flying stocks Alex was always falling in love with. Why, the items she bought during their trip to Europe, she could have sold for five times what she paid. It was all very well for Alex to tease her about shopping, but no one could accuse Rosemary Marshall of being extravagant.

Certainly not like Fleur, who put every penny she earned on her back. To look at the woman, you'd think Fleur came from generations of careless wealth instead of some dinky mill town up in Maine. How they all used to shudder when Fleur's mother came to visit: pure brass and chewing gum, Belle Chamberlain was, with fingernails that looked like lethal weapons. Hardly the Seven Sisters type.

Rosemary couldn't resist contrasting Fleur's background with her own, or comparing Belle Chamberlain with Dolly Bainter. Her own mother, thank the Lord, looked and acted every inch the lady, with her neatly coiffed blue-gray hair (a little bluer, a little grayer in the three years since her husband's death), the well-cared-for hands, the gently buffed nails under a discreet neutral polish, the quiet voice, the innate good taste with which she handled every crisis from rose blight to coastal storms to sudden widowhood.

Breeding showed, Rosemary believed. It instilled basic values, with the result that she and her mother had remained close through the years, constantly visiting back and forth, while Fleur managed to keep her mother pretty much out of sight. Who could blame her! After all, Belle Chamberlain and Dolly Bainter hardly seemed to belong to the same world, let alone the same generation.

So much for mothers. As for fathers, Rosemary's had been a respected thoracic surgeon and treasurer of his country club. Whereas in Fleur's case—who knew if she even had a father!

Rosemary would say this for Fleur, though. She was a quick study, picking up clues on how to dress, how to talk, even how to eat, although no one had ever needed to teach her how to flirt. For that she was born.

In their college days, there were armies of girls who enjoyed busy social lives just on Fleur's rejects. "My outtakes," Fleur used to call her surplus men, handing them out left and right as casually as though they were chocolates in a box. "Rosemary, honey,"—she'd collar her on a Saturday morning—"how'd you like to go out with an Amherst senior tonight? You'd be doing me a favor. I'm double-booked. Besides, he's nice."

Not good enough for me but good enough for you, such largesse implied. Rosemary grimaced—and usually went. In fact, they *were* nice, the outtakes, but all they wanted to talk about was Fleur. Even after all these years, the memory stung.

Men, men, men. They used to hover around Fleur like bees at a honeypot, but now, apparently, she was finding them in short supply. For all her beautiful wardrobe, for all those long smoky lashes and that ravishing skin, Fleur was scared to death at the prospect of remaining single. It was enough to make you marvel, Rosemary thought.

If her claim of one dozen proposals were actually true, and Rosemary was highly skeptical, surely they all dated from her days in college. Fleur Chamberlain had grown into the kind of woman men slept with, not the kind they married. She'd been around too much and too long. She had squandered her capital; her credit was expiring fast. As for her chatter at lunch about having someone terrific on the hook, Rosemary put it down to bravado. You didn't need to be Ann Landers to recognize the sound of whistling in the dark.

And such a slob! She'd had the messiest drawers in college. There weren't too many men who'd put up with *that* on a day-to-day basis.

It was a pity, really, Rosemary thought. Imagine being thirty-three with nothing to show but a closet full of glitzy clothes and an ad portfolio! Once upon a time she had envied Fleur—the love affairs, the glamorous job, the travel. But no more. No way!

On occasion Rosemary couldn't help wondering what it was like to have gone to bed with all those men. Were they better than Alex? Worse? Or just different? Didn't it get boring after a while? How did you remember to call out the right name?

But now the realist in Rosemary pushed such speculation aside. Instead, she thought about the contest she had set up and wondered if it would have results. Not for Diane, she believed. She was too proud to scramble. Possibly Bernie would put the squeeze on Steve. As for Fleur, time alone would tell. But of course the contest, the real contest, had ended years ago. It had ended the day she married Alex.

Smith has been fine, she did not regret those years; but looking back from her present vantage point, Rosemary knew she had never belonged there. The intellectual competition was too intense. Having superachievers like Diane and Fleur for roommates had not enhanced her self-esteem. It was one thing, she discovered, being top of your high school class in Wilmington, North Carolina; quite another to make your mark at Smith. Sometimes Rosemary wondered if she had been admitted largely to achieve a geographic mix.

Well, she may not have been Phi Beta or magna cum laude, but, by God, she was clever enough to recognize her limitations and smart enough to know that marrying Alex was a genuine coup. A coup, mind you. Not a cop-out, as her classmates seemed to think. At the time, she had taken a lot of flak, as though she owed it to herself, to Smith, to the entire female sex that she go forth and carve out a career. But doing what? Rosemary hadn't a clue. She lacked Diane's steely intellect, Fleur's panache, Bernie's relentless drive.

But if at the time her friends had been critical of her decision, they weren't now. For along with her academic shortcomings, she also had strengths.

"You have an eye," Gilmore had said. A connoisseur's eye.

Alex was right. She should have majored, if not in shopping, then in something that would have fostered her abilities. Decorating, perhaps, or applied art, something of that nature. Hers was a case of talent not fully realized.

The train rolled through Larchmont with its neat houses, neat gardens, past the manicured autumn foliage of Rye. Pleasant towns, she thought, but not as nice as Westport. Pretty houses, but not as distinctive as her own.

You see, Rosemary Marshall had an eye. A gift.

Say what you will about the women's movement, and she considered herself a part of its flow, it tended not to laud those very real skills that went into the running of an establishment like hers. Just mothering Chris was a full-time occupation, to say nothing of all the efforts she made for Alex. The gracious ambiance, the dinner parties, the hospitality she provided for her husband's friends and clients—they required discipline. Organization.

"I'm more than a housewife and mother," she had wanted to tell the census taker. Was there such a category as "helpmeet"? Not that she had to justify herself, but that was a career too, she wanted to say. A legitimate one. In pursuit of that career as helpmeet, she had provided Alex with everything a reasonable man could ask for: a capable wife, a beautiful home, a wonderful son. And it had all taken work, work, work.

Especially getting pregnant. What a job that had been! It was nearly five years before Chris was conceived, and much of that period had been plain drudgery. The endless doctor's appointments, the fertility tests for both of them. The years of making love by the chart, by the calendar, by the dictates of the thermometer. That hadn't been much fun for Alex. Or her. It had taken the joy out of sex.

But of course having Chris was worth it. And even though she and Alex had never recaptured the ardent passion of their honeymoon days, well, to be honest, what could one expect after ten years?

"Kissing don't last, cooking do," the old adage went. Perhaps sex was an overrated commodity.

The train passed the state line into Connecticut. The houses grew prettier, larger.

"Westport next," the conductor called.

Rosemary took down her packages from the overhead rack and stepped out into the late afternoon sun. Still feeling good, she crossed the parking lot toward her car.

"Beautiful," Jacqueline Hermann called out. She was one of the mothers from kindergarten.

"Isn't it!" Rosemary beamed and unlocked the door. "Alex gave it to me for our anniversary."

Yes indeed. Rosemary Marshall had made ever so good a career choice. Much better than her old classmates had done.

She climbed into her brand new Porsche and drove home.

SEVEN

━━━━●━━━━

"**Y**ou look like gangbusters,"
Bernie said.

"I feel like Liberace."

"Will you stop being so self-conscious and enjoy?"

"I'll try."

With a doubtful air, Diane surveyed herself in the mirror
at the Park Plaza Ballroom. An oddly glamorous impostor
stared back.

She had spent the morning at Bergdorf's, buying what
Fleur called "killer clothes": a green sequined blouse, a
narrow black satin skirt, and long dangling earrings made
from peacock feathers.

"You're not," Fleur proclaimed, "going to a party lugging
that thing! Jesus, Diane, why do all your handbags look like
briefcases?" She selected a tiny emerald clutch with rhine-
stone closings.

"Now," she brooded, "height's the problem. We'll have to
go with strappy sandals. We don't want you coming across
like Mount Everest."

"I could always cut off my legs at the knees," Diane
offered.

"Don't be arch. You're going there to meet men, not to
trade wisecracks."

Fleur came over to Diane's house later to do her makeup.
"Industrial strength eye shadow, lots of liner"—Fleur hummed

as she worked—"and let's not be shy about the lip gloss."
Then she stood back to admire her handiwork.

"Not bad!" She nodded. "Not you, but not bad. Well, if I
do get canned from the agency, I can always hire out as a
personal shopper."

"I wish you'd come along and keep me company."

Fleur shook her head. "Nope. I've decided to stop dating
for the present. Maybe my special someone will get the
message . . . we'll see. But you go and have a wonderful
time. You look great, kid."

"Yeah, great," Bernie echoed the appraisal as they headed
into the ballroom. "Fleur did one helluva job. Too bad she's
not here. Who's this guy she's involved with, do you know?"

Diane frowned. "I think it's someone in her office, her
boss, maybe. Anyhow, someone important—and married."

"But it's Saturday night. He's probably out with his wife."

"Fleur says she wants to be faithful."

"It beats me why she should be faithful to some guy
who's playing around. However"—Bernie was perennially
nonjudgmental—"that's her business. Whereas ours is going
out—and getting men. Okay, Diane," she said as she headed
to where the crowd was thickest. "You're on your own."

There must have been three hundred people in the room,
mostly young, largely attractive. Any misgivings Diane had
about being overdressed quickly vanished when she saw the
competition. Such good-looking women! she marveled. So
well-turned out, so thoroughly attractive. And all—ye
gods!—in the market for men.

At the bar she gulped down a double scotch for courage,
then attacked the nearest prospect.

"Hi," she said, remembering to smile. "I'm Diane Summerfield. And you're—?"

His name was Arthur Blake, and he was in from Jersey,
where he had a lively practice in obstetrics.

He checked Diane's card. "I see you're a lawyer. My
problem is, whenever I go to a party, people are always
cornering me, telling me their symptoms, trying to get free
medical advice. I'd like your point of view as an attorney.
What can I do about it?"

Diane considered. "Send them a bill for services the next morning, at your usual hourly rate."

"What a good idea! But what would be my chances of collecting?"

"What's your home address, Arthur?"

He looked suddenly wary.

"Why do you ask?"

"So I'll know where to send my bill."

His eyes narrowed. "You don't give anything away, do you?"

His name was Win Braverman, and he had been divorced for thirteen months and eight days.

"We had a very vibrant marriage," he told her, and then began recounting its dissolution, play by play. The night she didn't come home till quarter to three. The time she left her diary in the john. What her therapist said. What his therapist said. The awful scene they had at Thanksgiving. The day she called him at the office.

After half an hour, Diane excused herself.

"It was nice talking to you, Miranda," he said.

His name was Colin Wasey III, and he was a broker with Shearson. He was interested in how she handled her investment portfolio. A single woman in her bracket should be able to put a good chunk away, but it took management, he said. What percentage did she keep in stocks? What percentage in CDs? Did she own or did she rent?

"Now I could recommend a really high-yield mutual fund," he told her, but the feeling wasn't mutual at all.

His name was Bart Connors, and he came to the Park Plaza quite often. He used to go to EST seminars two or three nights a week in quest of IT, but IT never arrived. Before that he had been active in HPM. "The Human Potential Movement, you know? It's an alternative way of exploring options. But it wasn't there for me, so I just keep looking."

"And what is it you're looking for, Bart?"

"I'm looking for a meaningful interpersonal relationship, you know, but one with a growth dynamic. And how about you, Diane? What are you looking for?" Earnest eyes beseeched her.

"I'm looking for the ladies' room. Excuse me."

*   *   *

His name was Marty Baker, and within ten seconds of meeting her he said, "I can see you're a nice person, Diane."

"No, Marty," she said. "I'm not."

"No fair hiding," Bernie found her in the powder room.

"I'm not hiding," Diane said. "I'm throwing up, metaphorically speaking. How about you?"

But Bernie was having fun, sopping up color, collecting foibles. She had a good-natured acceptance of quirky people and a reporter's curiosity about what made them tick. In the company of strangers she would smile, hum, nod, listen without a hint of disparagement, then file the experience away for future use. Even the deadliest bores, she claimed, were good for one juicy anecdote.

Diane envied her this ease, the casual way she drew people out. But Bernie was present that evening as an observer, she reminded herself, not a contender in the fray.

For Diane, however, the evening was over.

"You go back in there, Bernie. I'm heading home. There's an old Bela Lugosi on *The Late Show,* and from where I stand he's looking good."

"Coward!" Bernie laughed. "Preferring Castle Dracula to this!"

Coward she was, Diane reflected in the taxi home. A total coward of the cut-and-run variety. She lacked Bernie's detachment, and once in the cab, the strain of her effort began taking its toll. She was tired, disheartened, not just by the chatting up of unsuitable men, but rather by her skirmishes with the eminently suitable.

For despite her qualms, there *had* been lively and attractive men on the premises, precisely the kind she had come to meet. During the course of the evening, she had spoken to several of them. She had been—for her—quite persistent. "No one will bite you," Fleur had promised. "Stick with it." And so she had.

Without exception they were polite. Polite and restless. Whether through a darting eye or a cautious turn of phrase or a discreet drumming of the fingers, they made it patent— these eligible men—that they were entitled to something better, someone prettier than a tall gangly lawyer with a bush of red hair. At the first break in the conversation, they had made their escape to greener fields. Perhaps something in her demeanor had frightened them.

Had they smelled her loneliness the way dogs are said to recognize human fear? The thought made her sick. She wished she had never met them, never known they were there. At least, she might have spared herself this sense of rejection.

The hell with men! All she asked for now was a pot of tea and a mindless movie. Tomorrow was Sunday. She could sleep late, do the Double-Crostic in the *Times,* and stroll over to the Met later on. Sunday, bloody Sunday! On Monday, thank God, she would be back in the sheltering arms of Slater Blaney, where people liked and appreciated her. It was ironic, though, to think of one of New York's most litigious law firms as her refuge.

"Right here," she told the driver, "the Osgood Arms," and slipped him five dollars from the emerald clutch. It wasn't until she was at her door that she realized she had forgotten her keys.

"I've locked myself out," she told the man at the desk. "Can someone get the passkey?" The fellow phoned for the night man. Diane settled down on a couch in the lobby to wait.

It was another five minutes before he arrived wearing wrinkled khakis that looked as though they'd been slept in.

"Avram, isn't it?" she said. "Sorry, I hope I didn't wake you."

"That's okay, I was studying. You're 28R, aren't you?" he said as they walked to the elevator. "The leaky toilet."

Diane grimaced. What a way to go down in East Side history: Miss Leaky Toilet from 28R. But as they stood waiting for the elevator, Avram put his hands on his hips, caught her eye, and gave a smile of open admiration.

"You look very pretty, if you don't mind my saying."

"Why thank you!" His remark took her by surprise. Except for Bernie and the ever-loyal Fleur, no one that evening had offered anything close to a compliment. Oh, the power of sequins and peacock feathers to dazzle a poor student's eyes.

The elevator arrived. He waited for her to step in. "Did you have a nice time?"

His bluntness caught her off balance. "No! Not really." She felt an explanation was necessary. "Just a big dull gathering—hundreds of people milling around dressed to the nines—strangers."

He gave a quick sympathetic smile. "Beware of all enterprises that require new clothes."

Having Thoreau quoted to you in an elevator was not the sort of thing, she thought, calculated to lighten your spirits. Yet curiously it did. She looked at him with fresh eyes.

"What are you studying at Columbia, Avram? Literature?"

"Philosophy. I'm writing my thesis on Wittgenstein."

"Oh," she said. "I thought maybe your field was the New England Transcendentalists." There, that would let him know she had caught his reference to *Walden Pond*.

"No, Thoreau I read for fun. Also James. But Wittgenstein—ay, that's hard work."

He seemed eager to talk, and she wondered if he wasn't finding life in America difficult. "How's New York treating you, Avram? Are you enjoying it?"

He nodded. "But this a very fierce city you have here."

"It's not really my city," she answered. "I'm from Boston, along with all those Transcendentalists. Actually, New York isn't so bad once you know your way around."

"I'm sure that is so."

They got off at her floor. He let her into the apartment. For a moment, she felt sorry for him: young, broke, and so very far from home. Even lonelier than she, was her bet, and with far fewer resources. What a shock the inhospitable concrete of Manhattan must be compared to the healthy outdoor life of Israel.

Her mother used to throw monthly teas for the students at International House in Cambridge. They always arrived hungry, ate heartily, and left grateful. In the Summerfield family, such entertainments were considered a form of volunteer work.

On impulse, she said, "If you're free tomorrow afternoon, I'd be happy to show you around a bit. You might be interested in old New York."

His face lit up. "I'd like that very much, Miss—"

"Summerfield—Diane."

"Diane!" He pumped her hand with unselfconscious vigor. It was a clumsy yet appealing gesture. "That's a much prettier name than 28R."

"Thank you." She smiled. "Two o'clock in the lobby, unless it rains. Good-night." She went in. Through the closed door, she could hear him whistling on the way to the elevator.

Steven Godwin was sprawled out on the sofa watching "Great Moments in Basketball" when Bernie came home. "How'd it go?" Eyes glued to the set, he waved a bottle of Coors in her general direction. On-screen, Wilt Chamberlain was reaching for the impossible. They didn't make stars like that, anymore, he thought.

"Lot of fun," Bernie answered.

The evening had left her wired. Meeting people was her fix. New names and fresh insights provided her with an adrenaline high, and that night she'd enjoyed over a dozen encounters, some closer than others. They had been tough on the feet, but largely good on the ego. "I recognize you," one man had said. "You're that terrific gal from *Five on Ten*."

The terrific gal now waltzed over to Steve for a welcome-home kiss.

Head craned so as not to miss a second's action, he scrunched up his lips, brushed her cheek, then took a swig of Coors. "Go, baby, go!"

It was 101–97 and less than a minute to play. The Knicks were going to fight it right down to the wire—it was a classic!

"How about you, Steve? What'd you do all evening?"

"Had something to eat with Vinnie and the guys." He raised a hold-everything hand.

"Where'd you go?"

"I forget. Palm Too. Hey, honey—can you just wait till this play is over?"

"It's on tape, for God's sake. It's history. You can watch it any time."

She bent over, seized the remote control, and pushed Pause. Wilt Chamberlain froze in mid-basket.

"What d'you go and do that for?" Steve lifted puzzled eyes.

"I wanted you to know that I'm home."

"I know you're home. We talked, remember? Now can I just finish the game? Couple of secs. If you want a beer, there's a six-pack in the fridge."

With a touch of the Play button, Wilt sprang back to life.

She went to hang up her coat.

"Missed!" Steve was yelling at the set. "You mother! How could you miss a shot like that! Would you believe"—he turned to Bernie—"five seconds left to play and they blew it! Christ! It's enough to break your heart. Ah well, win some, lose some. So tell me, how's life among the Lonely Hearts?" that being Steve's nickname for her series.

"Interesting gathering, very productive too. I made a lot of notes." But even as she rattled on, the euphoria began dribbling away. She needed an audience to sustain the mood, and Steve wasn't tuned in. His heart and mind were still in Madison Square Garden.

"And did your pal Diane catch Mr. Wonderful?" He began fiddling with the channels. "I think there's an old Lugosi on tonight."

"Diane," Bernie said, "was cutting off their balls left and right. You know, if she had taken a solemn oath to virginity, she couldn't have done better. Every guy she meets is an obstacle course. She puts up these barricades—spikes, wisecracks, what have you—then expects someone to come along and discover her, just like in the storybooks. I love the woman dearly, but she's so fucking inflexible. Whereas I on the other hand"—she smothered a swift grin—"I was the belle of the ball."

"Uh-huh . . . good." He'd found the old Lugosi. Not Dracula after all, which he'd seen a hundred times, but some cheapo space thing.

"Aren't you jealous, Steve?"

"What's to be jealous? You were there on business." He patted the place next to him on the sofa, an invitation to sit and cuddle. The gesture was so casual, she found it insulting.

"You know, old pal, there's more to life than basketball and Bela Lugosi flicks."

"Like what, for instance?"

"Moonlight and roses," she snapped.

"What's that supposed to mean?"

"Nothing"

Steve shrugged. "Jesus, you're in a funny mood tonight." Then he let it ride. "This one's supposed to be a classic, by the way. *Harvard Lampoon* voted it one of the ten worst movies ever made. Right up there with *Attack of the Killer Tomatoes*."

Bernie sat down and clasped her hands behind her head. She turned thoughtful. The party had been enlightening, not just for the journalist in her, but for the woman as well. Total strangers had flattered her, confided in her, lavished attention on her. Several had asked when they might see her again. No one had taken her for granted.

"I'd like to know you better, maybe get involved," one man, a psychologist of sorts, had said. "But I have the feeling that you're more of an observer than a participant."

The remark vaguely haunted her. For years she had prided herself on journalistic detachment, but now she began to wonder if she hadn't grown *too* detached, *too* remote from the bustle and turbulence of life. Was she nothing but a bystander, a cool onlooker endowed with less than normal heart and soul? She hadn't set out to be. Whereas Steve— She observed him with a critical eye. He was engrossed in the movie, smiling, stroking his beard.

"Did you catch that credit, Bernie? Sets by Sham Unlimited!"

Another time she would have been howling along with him, but tonight the trash on the screen made her impatient. If there was any onlooker in this household, anyone in flight from the "real world," it was Steve. TV production people were all alike, she decided: obsessed with physical things, with appearances, with color and texture and line. They were concerned with novelty and visual wit, but hardly ever with feelings. For them, things *were* feelings.

Steve was of that ilk. Always bringing home some odd-ball prop from a shooting, like the red-and-white barber pole in their bedroom, the neon Eats sign liberated from an Alka-Seltzer commercial, the six-foot effigy of Mickey Mouse.

"Fun things," he called them, but whatever the term— kitsch, camp, trivia, tongue-in-cheek nostalgia—the point was you laughed at them. And all the while you laughed, you felt superior. Detached. Life was painless when viewed only through the camera's eye, and people like Steve preferred it that way. Always to be one remove from involvement. Ten removes from total immersion.

Any moment I can split was his dictum. To be honest, hers too. But Bernie felt herself capable of greater intensity, drama. Perhaps even of grand passion. Whereas Steve . . . for all his qualities, bless him, there was a part that couldn't be touched.

She watched the screen for a while with a rising sense of nausea. Some sleazy B movie from the fifties whose only virtue was how badly it was made. What was wrong with their lives that they pretended to like this shit? What was this cult of the ugly? The banal? God forbid an honest emotion should ever get in the way.

"Oh, gross!" Steve was laughing. "That is absolutely the pits."

Bernie jumped up and switched off the set.

"I'm sick and tired of camp," she said. "It's ugly. It's cheap. It's dumb. And it's boring."

"Hey" came the wounded response. "I was watching that."

"You, you, you," Bernie snapped.

Steve spread out his hands, a reasonable man at the mercy of an unfathomable woman. "If you wanted to watch something else, Bernie, all you had to do was tell me."

"It's not the goddamn television."

For the first time that night, he looked her full in the face. "You know, it'll be a good thing all around when you're done with this fucking husband-hunt story of yours. It's making you crazy."

"Maybe," she said. "Maybe not."

EIGHT

At dawn Diane awoke with a startled blink to find herself in bed with a six-foot teddy bear.

Unbelievable! Avram's broad fingers were resting lightly on her belly. His breath warmed the base of her neck. The room smelled of sleep and sex.

For a so-called smart woman, she had behaved absurdly, falling into bed with a stranger first time around. And an unsuitable stranger at that! As soon as he got up, she would put the situation to rights, nipping in the bud any foolish illusions he might have developed.

Yet lying next to him, so cozy, so intimate, she nearly choked with happiness. Avram was delicious. Lovable and delicious. Even as she planned her retreat, she nestled closer, enjoying the feel of his body, the scratchy bristles of his chest. Why spoil the dream just yet? It would end soon enough. For a long drowsy hour, she lay there quietly, trying to render yesterday's events into a semblance of order.

When she came down Sunday afternoon, he had been waiting in the lobby, a cheap Kodak slung around his neck. The sight of the camera reassured her. "Outing," it stated, not "date."

All morning long she had prayed for rain, for chicken pox, for some honorable excuse to cancel. A hundred times she had regretted having extended the invitation, worrying about the implications like a dog with a bone. She had been rash, unwise, intrusive, even patronizing. What impression could Avram have derived? Did he think she made a habit of picking up husky foreigners so much her junior?

Or—Diane would turn the matter over in her mind and attack it in reverse—was she the one being taken in?

Beware! the lawyer in her warned. *Proceed with utmost caution.* If she'd learned anything else in her years in practice, she had at least learned distrust. For if Avram had misread her intentions, chances were equally good that she had misread his. What appeared to her as his loneliness might well be sexual hunger. Depravity, even. What seemed to her friendly banter might mask the crassest sort of opportunism. It took no Wall Street lawyer to realize how profitable an intimate relationship with a wealthy woman could be. And coming as he did from another culture, who could say what his expectations were? He had a passkey to her apartment, it must be remembered. He could come and go as he chose.

Against these dark musings, she could only balance a cheerful smile and the fact that he liked Mozart. Had she been her own attorney, Diane would strongly have advised staying home. However, her word was her bond, and—the day being clear and brilliant—she could think of no plausible excuse.

She dressed for the event with scrupulous neutrality. There were to be no sequins and peacock feathers, no midnight glamour, simply a tweed jacket, old slacks, and walking shoes. That should dampen any ardor on his part.

But if her appearance disappointed, if he had expected some of the glitter of Saturday night, he disguised it wonderfully. The moment she stepped out of the elevator, Avram sprang to his feet and whipped across the lobby, hand outstretched.

"I was afraid you wouldn't come."

"Well, here I am," she said diffidently, "and it looks like a good day for sight-seeing." She had mapped a plan: The New York Historical Society, a tour of the Abigail Adams Smith House, winding up with tea at the Yale Club. She figured to be rid of him by six.

"That all sounds very interesting," he said, "except it's

much too nice to go to museums, don't you think? And if you're like me, I expect you spend the whole week indoors."

Instead, he proposed they take a Circle Line cruise around Manhattan. "Unless you've already done that," he amended.

Diane laughed, instantly relieved. It was the kind of sight-seeing jaunt every out-of-towner had at the top of his list: the provincials from the Midwest, Europeans on package tours. No New Yorker worthy of the name would ever admit to such an indulgence, any more than a true child of Gotham would dream of climbing the Statue of Liberty. Such day trips were for rubes.

"No, I haven't," she said, "and yes, I'd like to."

An hour later they were cruising up the Hudson while an erudite guide bared the city's secrets, most of which were new to them both. Diane wondered why she had never done this before.

During the course of the afternoon, they munched potato chips, drank coffee out of Styrofoam cups, and talked about college and grand opera and the novels of Henry James. But mostly they just "people watched." The boat was mobbed with tourists from all over—what Avram delightedly called a "mishmosh."

He derived enormous pleasure speculating about the lives of their fellow passengers. This one, he determined, was a Sorbonne professor of primitive anthropology on a field trip. The fellow with the black mustache was an Armenian maker of goat cheeses. That elderly couple was on their honeymoon. No! On second thought, they weren't married at all. They had run off on a whim, leaving their respective spouses behind.

"Run away from where?" Diane quizzed.

"Biloxi, Mississippi!" came the answer. The semanticist in him relished "exotic" American place-names. He had made a collection.

"And what about me?" She laughed. "What do you conclude?"

"About you," he said, "I will not speculate. I prefer to learn firsthand."

Some of his observations were funny, some astute, all were free of malice. "Go ahead—ask," Diane teased, "and find out if she really is an ex-show girl from Walla Walla."

"And spoil everything?" Avram laughed.

He asked her to take a photo of him against the skyline,

for people back home. He followed up by taking snapshots of Diane.

By the time the boat was rounding the Battery, her misgivings had vanished. Avram Gittelson was neither sex maniac nor con artist. He was, in all likelihood, neither more nor less than she had adjudged him at first sight: a friendly student trying to make ends meet. And a very bright one at that. In some ways he seemed older than his twenty-six years. In others, completely artless.

As the Wall Street skyline had come into view, Diane singled out one thrusting spike. "That tall white building," she said, pointing with pride, "is where my law firm is. One of New York's finest."

"Do you enjoy your job?" Avram asked.

"Yes indeed!" With relish Diane began describing the structure of the firm, her boss, her colleagues, and finally the all-devouring intricacies of *Simplexx* v. *Harrigan*.

Avram listened, intrigued. "It sounds," he said, "as if the key to the dispute is whether Simplexx had title to the patents before the merger."

"That's right!" Diane was delighted at how quickly he had grasped the essentials. "Of course our claim is, before, but it's a gray area. I had dug up a case from 1883 dealing with—now don't laugh—a company called Pneumatic Corsets that bears certain similarities. My hope is that this will serve as the precedent."

"Mmm . . . hmm." Avram chewed thoughtfully. "But between the two of us, it makes no difference, does it?"

"Make no difference!" Diane gasped. "We're talking about a billion-dollar judgment."

"What I meant," he said, "in the larger scale of things, what does it matter? One side is pretty much like the other, not so?"

"Well, it matters to me." Diane bristled. "My making partner might depend on it."

Making partner, she explained, was a seven-year process in her firm. It was what big-time lawyering was all about: the opportunity not merely to direct the fortunes of the rich and powerful, but to become one of their number. Partnership at Slater Blaney ensured a place in the top stratum of the American establishment. The rewards—social, financial, professional—were extravagant. Hence, the competition was rough, the chances of making it, slim. Yet already Diane had received informal assurances that she had a place on the inside track. With six backbreaking years behind her, she could expect to know the results by next summer.

"So you see, the outcome of the *Simplexx-Harrigan* case matters a very great deal to me on the personal level."

"Of course! Of course I can see that." He smiled, then stubbornly returned to his point. "Still, Diane, you have to admit that there is no right or wrong in this dispute, no moral principle involved. Tell me, do you ever wonder if it is worth so much of your time and effort? After all, you might just as well have been on the other side of the suit."

"Indeed I might," she affirmed. Avram was saying nothing she hadn't thought of before. Thought of and cast aside. Moral principles were irrelevant in such cases; moreover she was doing nothing unethical. Perhaps she had given him credit for too much acuity, too little awareness of American values.

"If I represented the opposition," she clarified, "you may be sure I'd work just as hard. Perhaps you don't quite fathom how our system of justice works." She then treated him to a five-minute discourse on the origins of Anglo-American jurisprudence.

"So you see," she concluded, "every attorney, no matter whom he represents, be it a mass murderer, a child molester, or a multinational corporation—although I don't necessarily mean to lump them together—every attorney, I repeat, is honor-bound to fight for his client regardless of the rights and wrongs. Otherwise, there would be justice for none."

"Oh, I understand," he murmured. "And I suppose that's as it should be." Yet she detected puzzlement in his eyes, a wonder that educated people should spend their time in such pursuits. It troubled Diane that he might think ill of her.

"I gather"—she came to her own defense—"you feel I should be working on behalf of civil rights causes or Amnesty International or some useful public service instead of a wealthy corporation—"

But Avram flung up his hands. "I never interfere with anybody's judgments," he said, "and please—" He gave his most appealing smile. "I'm sorry that I hurt your feelings."

"You didn't," she lied, then passed the ball into his court.

"And you?" she asked. "What are you going to do when you finish your thesis? Go on for a Ph.D.? I understand you can't get an academic job without one."

"More years yet? God forbid." He laughed. In fact, he hadn't the foggiest notion what he would do, but of one thing he was certain: He would not wind up a professional scholar. Grad school was full of them, driven young men and women piling up degrees ad infinitum, and for what? To shuttle from one university situation to another in search of grants, in hopes of tenure. He found the world of academia too suffocating.

"Perhaps I will tutor bar mitzvah boys. Or translate books from the Hebrew. My English is very good, no? Or," he mulled, "I could get a job as an interpreter. Interesting work, I am sure, but very much pressure. Sometimes I think of going home to work on a kibbutz for a while. But not yet. I like New York too much."

His attitude mystified Diane. To be so clever, to study so hard and yet have no specific goal was contrary to all her values.

"Or I could work for my cousin Lev."

His cousin, he told her, had emigrated to the States five years earlier, married an American girl, and built up a thriving radio-cab service in Chelsea. He liked to hire fellow Israelis, and Avram could always find employment there.

"Doing what?" Diane asked.

"Driver, dispatcher. What does it matter as long as it is honest work? Of course, everything would depend if I can get my green card."

"You mean"—she stared at him—"you are writing a thesis on Wittgensteinian semantics in order to drive a taxi-cab? What a waste!"

"No," he insisted. "Why a waste? I enjoy Columbia, and I am learning a good deal. I am even getting to like Wittgenstein a little. Besides, I had to go to university—"

"Had to?"

"To qualify for a student visa. Otherwise, I would not be able to stay here for any length of time."

"But what's the point?" Diane was nonplussed. She had assumed that his broader purpose in coming here had been to gain a professorship or write a book or become a consultant or enter medical school or find a job on the stock exchange or seek a post at the UN or explore any of the thousand avenues that the land of opportunity offered the upward-striving immigrant. Taxi driving was not among them. It was an occupation for illiterates, not intellectuals with advanced degrees.

She felt a strong protective urge. He was such a nice young man, with an accent on the "young." But so lost. It would be a real service to help him find direction.

She furrowed her brow. "There must be something you want to do, some walk of life for which you're fitted. It's just a matter of examining the possibilities. Let's think."

Like a conscientious student adviser, she began running down a list of "career options," searching for the particular color of Avram's parachute. There was business. The arts. The various professions. The prestigious world of academe.

Avram listened with an amiable grace, pleased and flattered by her exertions on his behalf. *You are being so nice,* his smile said, *so kind.* Yet he committed himself to nothing.

"How about the diplomatic corps?" she suggested.

But no, he'd served in the army and had enough of working for the government.

"I give up! Were you just watching my mouth move?" she asked. "Or were you actually listening?"

"Both," he laughed, adding that he still didn't know what was so awful about his driving a cab. It was useful, honest work.

"You're a marvel, Avram! You truly are! Given your attitude, I wonder why you even bothered coming to the United States. You could just as well drive a cab back home."

"True," he said. "But I wanted to travel, see something of the world. This is my first time away from Israel. In my lifetime so far, I have never seen snow."

"You will," she assured, and gave up the quest. It was pointless arguing; he was too immature. Doubtless in time Avram would adjust to the real world, find some calling worthy of his talents. He was young yet, and life had a way of beating people down. On the other hand, twenty-six was no longer such a kid. At his age she had been practicing law.

"Look," he said. "We're pulling into the harbor."

They hung over the rail for a moment, as the boat maneuvered into the slip. Behind them the sun was setting.

A sharp wind whistled up the river, wreaking havoc with Diane's hair. She fetched a comb from her handbag.

"I look like a wild woman," she said.

"Wait!"

Avram suddenly reached out and touched one wayward strand of hair. With a surprisingly tender gesture, he smoothed the hair away from her cheek. His thumb rested intimately against the skin of her neck. For a long silent moment, they held each other's gaze while the other passengers filed off.

"In the Sinai desert," he told her, "in a remote and beautiful spot, there is a bush that grows near an ancient monastery. No one knows how long it's been there, and some people say it is the Burning Bush of the Bible. Most of the year it looks like any other desert shrub, stark and thorny. But in the autumn, it turns a fiery brilliant red. The same color as your hair." Reluctantly, he let the shaft of hair slip through his fingers. In his eyes she read longing. For her? For the landscape of home? "The faithful," he said, "believe it to be a miracle." And she knew the longing was for her. Incredible! The man found her romantic. Even beautiful!

She turned from him, startled, her lips brushing his hand.

"I think . . ." she began, but the words fled.

In the gathering dusk, he loomed large and handsome, vibrantly alive. His eyes seemed to glint with captured rays of sunlight. She felt a swift lurch of sexual desire.

"Are you cold, Diane?"

She shook her head, then the guide tapped her on the shoulder.

"Sorry, miss. Everybody off."

Avram tucked her arm firmly in his and steered her on to the pier. "Let's eat," he said. "I am starved."

He chose a Hungarian restaurant where the food was plentiful and cheap, then scoured the menu for the heartiest dishes.

He ate. She nibbled. He chattered. She brooded. To go to bed with him or not to go to bed: that was the question.

Yes! Why not? She wanted to. What was the big deal? Two consenting adults, and no harm done. Truth to tell, she liked him better than most of the men she met on Wall Street.

No! Why get involved with a nobody on his way to nowhere? Why give him false hopes? Nothing serious could ever come of it.

Maybe. After all, there was no one else on her horizon at the moment and she was human . . .

From moment to moment she seesawed, wavered, changed her mind, then changed it back again. Suppose he wasn't interested. Suppose he didn't even ask—

"You're not eating!" Avram put down his fork.

She looked down at the heaping plate of goulash. "Heartburn," she said. "But you go ahead."

He ate his portion, then polished off hers while she emptied the bottle of Tokay.

They split the check. She waited for his next move.

"Do you like dancing, Diane?"

"I'm hopeless at discos," she said, uncertain where this was leading.

"You'll like this one."

There was an Israeli social club near Morningside Heights, he told her. He went there most Sundays. She could meet his friends.

The place was packed when they got there, dense with smoke, humming with noise and movement. Diane appeared to be the only non-Israeli.

On his own turf, however, Avram began visibly to expand. He knew a hundred people and felt she should too.

"Diane, I'd like you to meet. . . ." He propelled her through the crowd, stopping here and there. The air was thick with Hebrew gutturals. This one was a student, that one a real estate agent, a garment cutter, a psychologist, a diamond trader. "Don't be a stranger," one young woman welcomed her, and Diane decided the natives were friendly.

Everyone seemed to chatter at once, punctuating their words with gestures, half-shouting above the level of the music. Hands, arms, shoulders—all became extensions of the parts of speech. Fingers jabbed exclamation points and eyebrows curved into question marks in a manner that would have driven her mother to distraction, the elder Summerfields being of the belief that body language was a crime worse than arson.

But that was another time, another place. Diane was

happy to be here and now. The room temperature must have been in the nineties, and getting hotter, getting louder by the minute.

"Ah!" Avram gave a delighted shout. "The hora!"

A pleasurable buzz rippled through the crowd. They began linking hands.

Diane looked about her, then following the general example threw her jacket into a center pile on the floor. Avram took one hand, a small dark man with a Trotsky beard captured the other, and suddenly she was locked into a circle, a circle throbbing with life, bursting with energy.

She couldn't have fallen had she tried. The psyche of the crowd engulfed her, carried her along. Everyone was singing. She didn't know the words, but no matter. She sang anyhow and it was bliss. Avram's hand tightened on her own.

Oh the joy of letting go! The sweet divine sense of being part of a whole! The tingle of electricity flowing freely from body to body! She hadn't had that sensation since she was a small child at summer camp. While the music played, there were no outsiders. Everyone belonged.

The sweat began trickling between her breasts. Breathless, she looked at Avram. His brow was steaming with animal heat, his sandy lashes beaded with moisture. With luck the music would never end and they would dance themselves into exhaustion. Into oblivion. Into paradise.

Then it was over in a burst of laughter and applause.

Avram took out a large linen handkerchief, mopped his forehead, then patted hers. She raised her face to him awash with happiness, feeling—not thinking. Only one sequel was remotely possible.

"Subway home?" He asked in a voice urgent with sex.

"Taxi!" She grabbed his hand. "It's faster. My treat."

That was last night. In the gray of dawn it might all have been a fantasy were it not for Avram sleeping in her bed, big as life if not bigger. She wanted to hug him awake.

Their lovemaking had gone from fair to good to great, two people in the act of discovery. They'd both had less than three hours' sleep. Yet she felt refreshed, brimming with affection. She had to smother an urge to spoil him unconscionably.

"Avram," she said, kissing him. "You have an eight-thirty class. Get up and I'll make you a nice big breakfast."

He stirred, propped himself up on one elbow, and looked at her with naked admiration.

"Shalom," he murmured.

"Shalom." She smiled, pleased that she knew at least one word of Hebrew.

"How beautiful you look in the morning," he said.

"Oh, come on." Her pleasure dissolved in embarrassment. "What do you like for breakfast? How about some bacon and eggs or"— she paused—"is bacon against your religious beliefs?"

He laughed. "Only if it's not crisp. I will make coffee."

She started to head for the kitchen, but he gently pulled her back, then propped himself up on one arm to study her face.

"Yesterday," he said, "you asked me why I came to America, and now I know." Gently, he traced her lips with his finger. "I came to meet you."

NINE

———•———

"You know the basic difference between men and women?"

"I should say so," she said, regarding the naked figure on the bed with unmitigated pleasure. "In fact, I'd say we've just given a pretty good demonstration of it."

"Strictly physical. I meant psychological. The basic difference between men and women is that women have never developed a feel for sports. Take you, Fleur. Bet you've never played football—"

"Went to a game once, froze my ass off."

"Or basketball, hockey. You have no concept of what sports are all about, how gratifying they can be."

"I used to follow the Yankees."

"You're talking spectator. I'm talking participant, and that's where you women are out of it. The only time you fully use your body and mind in conjunction is for sex."

"You're not complaining, I trust." She sat down on the bed beside him and began massaging his shoulders in a rotary motion. He always liked that after lovemaking. Then maybe they could take a brief nap.

Nothing wrong with *his* body, she thought. Her fingertips explored the firm sinew of his arms, the tight cords of his neck, the powerful chest. A magnificent specimen.

He placed his hands behind his head and gave himself over to the pleasure of being stroked. "Yep. You won't really understand the masculine mind-set until you've had direct experience with sports. Contact sports especially.

The feel of muscle on muscle, flesh against flesh. Boxing, wrestling—"

"Yech!"

"Why yech? Boxing can be beautiful when it's done right. Wrestling too, if you know the rules and observe them. You know, Graeco-Roman wrestling is practically an art form. You see it depicted in classic sculpture all the time."

"What I see is a bunch of sweaty guys with Day-Glo jockstraps on TV."

"That's not wrestling, that's show biz and those jokers are just sides of beef. True wrestling is a matter of savvy, not size. What are you, Fleur? One-ten, one-twelve? What they call a flyweight. Not in bad shape, though. You could probably hold your own."

"I'd rather hold yours." She slid her hand downward and felt his body respond. Already? Again? The man was amazing. Well, she was willing if he was. However, even as she caressed him, he remained engrossed in his own line of thought.

"Okay, now picture this, Fleur. We're in ancient Greece. You are a young girl who's been captured, brought to Athens from some distant isle. In your own land you were a princess, but now you're about to be auctioned off as a slave. You're proud, but terrified too. Afraid of falling into the clutches of some disgusting old man, some pervert who will force you into unnatural acts. You stand there on a block in the slave market, naked, for every potential customer to fondle. The slave merchant is about to auction you off. You would rather die than submit to those beasts. Now, out of the crowd steps a powerful nobleman. He's young, handsome—"

"That's you, right?"

"—superbly virile. From the moment he sets eyes on you, he's thunderstruck. He's never seen such opulent breasts, full, almost pendulous—the nipples stiff and proud—"

"Opulent?" She frowned. "Does that mean fat?"

He cupped a hand beneath one breast and weighed it gently. Her nipples stiffened.

"Opulent breasts. A belly as smooth as precious Persian silk. Yes, in his eyes you are a magnificent creature. Voluptuous. He is immediately besotted. Naturally he would give everything he has to possess you, to have you at his feet.

The bidding starts, but he outbids all the competition. Money is no object. Sold! Your new owner takes you by the hand and leads you away. He desires you. And you, too. A part of you desires him. But he knows you are proud, virginal. And because he is a man of honor, he will let you fight for your purity. While the citizens of Athens look on, he challenges you to win your freedom in combat. A wrestling match."

"Between—?" Her heart was racing. Inner motors began to purr.

"Between—" He laughed, then sat up suddenly and locked his arms around her neck. "Between you and me, pet. God, that would be fantastic! If I win, I get to possess you outright. Do whatever I want with you. Should I lose, you can do what you want with me. Which could be nothing. In other words, winner takes all. Fair?"

Aroused as she was, she was also apprehensive. "But, darling, you outweigh me by about eighty pounds or so. Suppose you hurt me—"

"I promise not to hurt you, Fleur. Have I ever?"

"No . . . yes. Well, never deliberately. I mean, it's no contest. You'll have me pinned down on the floor in no time."

"Tell you what," he said thoughtfully. "If you're oiled and I'm not, you'll have a terrific advantage. You'll be very slippery, hard to hold. Okay"—he patted her on the rump—"go get your exercise mat and set it out in the living room, and I'll put on some music."

With long slow strokes he covered her with a fine layer of Vaseline. In the muted lamplight, her body gleamed like wet marble. To the sinuous rhythms of Ravel's *Bolero,* she struck a classic pose.

"Aphrodite!" He slid his hand lightly between her legs. "I sure don't have to grease you there! You're lubricated already."

His touch was instant orgasm with the promise of more to come.

"Now these are the rules," he whispered. There was to be no tackling, no tripping, no leg holds or rough stuff. Everything was to be done slowly, slowly, slowly, for the object was to inflict pleasure, not pain. To win, you were to force your opponent down and hold him helpless until three points of his body were pinned against the mat.

"For how long? Till the count of ten?"

He smiled. "Till the loser acknowledges the winner as master."

He faced her across the short distance of the mat, standing with legs apart, penis erect. "I'll demonstrate the basic movements as we go along. I'm sure you'll catch on. Ready?" he asked.

Fleur held her breath in an agony of desire. Then—

"Let the games begin."

For a mindless eternity they grappled with each other's flesh, delighting in unlikely juxtapositions: nipples against knees, mouths upon navels, noses against bellies, the shaft of his penis pushing against the nape of her neck. Then a swift, deft movement and all positions changed. It was a kaleidoscope of sensation.

"This one's called the Fireman's Carry." He slid a massive arm between her thighs and raised her off the ground, to be slung about his shoulder like a trophy. But her body was oiled, liquid, and in a quick supple movement, she slid through his grasp like quicksilver.

"Very well then." He dropped to his knees and locked his arms about her buttocks, pulling her down till his mouth was in her pubic hair, the weight of his body upon her. "The Double-Leg Pickup," he panted. She countered with her legs, spreading them wide. The soles of her feet formed a vise about his neck. Tight, tighter, she locked him in, even as he devoured her. Then suddenly, she broke free.

She stood up, winded, ears filled with the insistent beat of the music, the relentless crescendo. Perhaps he would call Time. Her head throbbed.

Then "The Cross-Body Ride!" he announced with a cry, he struck from behind, forcing her down by inches until her nipples brushed against the tight weave of the mat. With effort she raised herself onto all fours, her spine hard against his body. She could feel every hair on his chest, his belly. His cock nuzzled the crevice of her ass, playing up and down, riding her like a jockey at full trot. "Oh, God!" She began weeping with pleasure, holding the position fast until the palms of her hands were sore, her knees gave out.

And then there were no names, no words, nothing in the world but their two tangled bodies—back to back, front to back, top to bottom. Both were now bathed in sweat and

Vaseline; both more skilled, more adept than when they started. Wearier too. For one delirious moment, he slipped and she seized the advantage, wrestling him down on the mat. Two points! She had both his shoulders on the ground. All she needed was one leg. She straddled his chest, locked her hands, and began pushing hard against his thighs. Almost there. Another moment and victory would be hers.

Then with a mighty full-bodied heave, he flipped her over on her back. A moment later he had forced her hands above her head. All four points.

"Now—" he gasped.

She struggled, but he was so strong, overpowering, and as the music reached its climax, she found herself pinioned, incapable of any movement. He loomed above her, dripping sweat, his strong hands imprisoning her wrists, his knees in a scissors grip about her legs.

"Now," he panted. "Say it."

She lay there dazed, orgasmic, aching only for him to enter her, to drive himself so deep inside her that he would surface in her brain. To tear her in half. To fuck her until she was blind, deaf, and dumb. How else could this game end!

"Say it," he repeated.

"Master!" she cried.

"And you are?"

"Slave. I'm your slave."

He laughed softly, happily, and eased his grip. Then gently he kissed her and pulled her legs apart.

"That's better. And what would my slave like me to do?" The tip of his penis teased her swollen clit.

"Take me, Alex. . . . Fill me . . . fuck me. Please, I beg of you."

With a triumphant roar, Alex Marshall thrust his powerful shaft deep inside her, and in that moment she knew what heaven was.

Fifteen minutes later he was showered and dressed.

"You really have to?" Fleur asked.

"Can't miss the last train. I promised Rosemary I'd be home by midnight. You understand, don't you, darling?"

Fleur swallowed her pain. "I understand," she said thin-lipped.

He came over to the bed and kissed one brown swollen nipple.

"I'm sorry. If I could, I'd stay here forever." He kissed the other. "Just so."

"When will I see you again?"

"I'll call you tomorrow." Then he was gone.

For a few minutes more she lay amid the rumpled sheets, happy, tired, aching. Hungry too. They'd had nothing to eat all evening, except a handful of grapes. Briefly Fleur considered getting up and making herself a fluffy cheese omelet and toast, but wisdom prevailed. That was at least five hundred calories, and Alex liked her slim, despite that remark about "opulent" breasts.

She pulled on her robe and went into the tiny kitchen for a rice cracker and a yogurt. If she nibbled slowly, it would last longer, stifle the rumbles. It wasn't starvation, she consoled herself; each mouthful forgone was an investment in her future.

Only this morning she had seen her first gray hair, grabbed for the tweezers, and excised it at the roots. One swallow does not a summer make nor one gray hair a crone. Nonetheless it was a preview. A warning that time was running out. Balefully, she looked at her reflection in the toaster.

"You're a shit, Fleur Chamberlain," she admonished the image, then chewed on her biscuit. You win some, you lose some. And this was one she *had* to win.

Anyhow, it wasn't as if she'd set out to purloin Rosemary's husband in cold blood, she rationalized. She wasn't that much of a shit. If you had to blame anybody—and Fleur was largely indifferent to the assignment of blame—them blame it on the road.

Ah, the road—the road. Where anything goes.

Pittsburgh.

She had never borne the city any grudge until she started working with Walt McKerr. A small wraithlike man with a speech impediment, the new marketing director in charge of Saraband had raised nerdiness into an art form. Walt McWimp, Fleur dubbed him, and back at the agency the nickname took hold. "But don't ever let anyone at Saraband ever hear you say that," her copy chief warned, "or your ass is grass."

Once a month Fleur trooped to Pittsburgh with the latest

crop of ads, as Walt liked dealing directly with "cweative" people.

It was decision by committee, another way of saying the buck never stops anywhere. Certainly not with McWimp and his staff, known, none too affectionately, as the Wimpettes for their tendency to hum in unison in confirmation of Walt's every utterance.

Whatever his other qualifications (and Fleur hadn't a clue as to their nature), McWimp was hopeless as an adman, terrified of commiting himself to a decision that might prove erroneous, avoiding anything that might possibly be construed as a yes or no. Words failed him in every conceivable sense.

"What I m missing here," he would say, regarding the layouts spread before him on the table, "is something more— more—" A wimpish flutter of hands.

"More—" He searched his vocabulary for the correct waffle word. "More integwated."

"Mmmmmm . . ." hummed the Wimpettes.

"You mean, you want to see the gal with a black guy?"

"No, no! Fleur. You know what I mean. I mean more— more kinetic."

"It's a woman riding starkers on a big white stallion, Walt. I would call that pretty kinetic."

Then she would take him and the Wimpettes out for a very expensive lunch, after which it was back to his office for another round of shadow boxing.

"What I had in mind was something more—more stwuctured—"

"Mmmmm . . ." came the echo.

Four hours with McWimp was like four years with McWimp, and Fleur had just come from an eight-hour session that day.

The bar in the lobby never looked so welcoming. First a couple of margaritas to loosen up a jaw stiff from a day's worth of forced smiles, then maybe dinner in her room. She headed straight into the lounge.

That was when she saw him, a stolid emissary from the real world. He was hunched over on a barstool in a six-o'-clock slouch, popping macadamia nuts. She recognized the stance: another toiler in the vineyards at the end of a long lousy day with a client. He looked so solid, so prosaic. So familiar.

"Hey, Alex!" She went over and clapped him on the back.

"Hey, hey!" He blinked. For a moment she wondered if he placed her. Then he sat up, straightened his tie, and shifted his bulk to make room. "Have a pew. What brings you here, Fleur?"

"Bullshit business."

He laughed and signaled the bartender. "Me too. Buy you a drink?"

"Thanks. A margarita."

"Funny. I always figured you for the scotch-and-water type."

"Why, Alex!" she said. "I didn't know you had me figured at all."

The bartender appeared.

"The lady will have—" he began, but Fleur broke in, "a double scotch on the rocks."

"Make that two," Alex said.

They small-talked through one round. Alex ordered another.

On the second round, Fleur began to unwind. With gusto she told him about the unspeakable McWimp and the Wimpettes.

"Wimpettes?" he wanted to know. "What are they—his yes-men?"

"They don't have yes-men anymore, Alex," she chided. "They have yes-persons. Anyhow, this afternoon over lunch . . ."

She had taken her clients to Christopher's for something French and fancy and was leaning across the table to drive home a point.

"Then—crazy thing." She paused in her narrative and began giggling. "Like there I am, doing my dynamic adlady number when my goddamn contact lens pops out and goes into his ice water. McWimp doesn't touch alcohol, need I tell you, which doesn't make those fuckin' lunches any more fun. Anyhow, next thing I know—"

"Oh, Jesus." Alex doubled up with laughter. "Sonuvabitch drank down your lens."

"You know it!" And suddenly the two of them were howling like lunatics.

"You think you got troubles," Alex said, wiping his eyes, and proceeded to tell her his woes. "I only wish mine were so funny."

He had spent a frustrating day trying to salvage a major deal that inexplicably got unstuck. "Christ, I had them on the point of signing, when out of the blue, their purchasing agent waltzes in and starts fucking it up."

"Maybe the guy was looking for a kickback," Fleur suggested, brushing the palm of her hand. "It's been known to happen."

"You think?" Alex brooded. "Yeah. I thought so too, but I couldn't very well offer him payola with twenty other people present."

"A trip to the men's room would do it," she said. "My bet is, he'd take your cue, follow you out. And then you'd know."

"You're one smart lady, Fleur. Anybody ever tell you that?"

"Lots of people. Never the right ones."

"One smart lady," he repeated. He had cat's eyes, green-gray, flecked with dots of yellow. They gave an animal sexiness to his face. Strange she'd never noticed it before. Never given Alex a second thought. His being such good company was also a pleasant surprise.

Alex reached for a nut, then pushed the dish aside. It was empty anyway. "What say we have dinner, Fleur? Unless you've got something else on."

"Nope, nothing." She hesitated a fraction of a second. But surely Rosemary wouldn't mind. She would probably be grateful. "Dinner sounds good. Give me twenty minutes and I'll go upstairs and change into something a little more elegant."

"Why change?" he asked. "You look fantastic as is. Candy for the eyes."

His words went direct to her spinal cord. Was Alex coming on to her?

"Five minutes, then, and I'll fix my makeup."

She started for the ladies' room, then turned her head. He was watching her. So was every other man in the bar, nothing new. But Alex was also watching the other guys watching her, and on his face was a look of sneaky satisfaction. He was pleased, flattered to be in the company of a great-looking woman, to be the object of other men's envy.

Yes indeed, Alex Marshall was definitely coming on to her. Next question was, what now?

She spent an anguished ten minutes alone in the ladies'

room, doing and redoing her eyes, while she sorted out her
feelings. Alex Marshall of all people! She had never considered him as a lover—casual or otherwise. He was the husband of an old friend, for heaven's sake, as neutral as a
piece of furniture. Yet in a way, Rosemary herself had
provoked Fleur's speculations: always boasting what a great
guy Alex was. What a hotshot businessman. A good pro-
vider. A fabulous father. And—although Rosemary had never
put it quite in anatomical terms, her meaning had been
unambiguous—an absolute hero in the sack.

"I wish I could make a carbon copy of him," she was
wont to tell Fleur, "and give you a duplicate. Believe me, it
would solve all your problems."

Fucking condescending, that's what it was. But that was
Rosemary all over, always lording her married state over
her single friends. Always letting Fleur know, one way or
another, where she stood on the social scale.

Second-class citizen was how Rosemary made her feel,
right from the day she got married. Fleur, "good old Fleur,"
she would say in that patronizing manner. Good enough
for lunch with the girls. Good enough for going shopping
with at Saks. But not good enough for Rosemary to waste
her time with when her husband was around.

Couples counted. Singles sucked. That much was for
sure. In fact, about the only time Rosemary ever called
Fleur was when her husband was away from home. "Alex is
going out of town for a couple of days," she would say.
"Would you like to have dinner?"

Why, chances were she was ringing up Fleur this very
moment, seeing if she could fill in an empty evening.

"Alex is out of town—"

Well, so he was. And Fleur was out of town too.

There was something about the road that Fleur always
found stimulating. Aphrodisiac. Away from home, from the
conventional restraints, you could do anything and no one
was the wiser. The road was adventure, the place where you
could have sensational sex, anonymous sex. Even sex with
an old friend's husband.

Was Alex Marshall all that good in bed? For that matter,
who was Rosemary to judge? Fleur's bet was that she could
give him sexual pleasures that would make Rosemary look
like Bo Peep. And maybe Alex could show her a thing or
two in return.

"He's so wonderful." She could hear Rosemary's self-satisfied croon. Was he? There was one way to find out. From her handbag, she pulled out the ever-present perfume flacon and scented her neck, her ears, her nipples, her thighs, then returned to the bar in a cloud of fragrance.

He was waiting for her with hungry eyes.

"Mmm." He leaned toward her and inhaled. "You smell glorious. I ordered another round while I was waiting. Okay?"

"Fine." She climbed up on the stool and turned to face him.

"Here's to!" Alex lifted his drink and waited for Fleur to hoist hers. Instead, she placed a hand on his thigh. His flesh felt hot and muscular. Even through the smooth gaberdine she could sense the sexual tension, physical strength. His arousal triggered her own.

"Here's to us, Alex." She moved her hand till it came to rest on his throbbing genitals.

For a moment Alex sat there stunned, speechless, swelling beneath her touch, unable to believe his good fortune, yet, prudent man that he was, hesitant to make a false move.

"Well," he said, dry-mouthed. "Have you decided? What would you like to eat?"

"You," she murmured. "I would like to eat you."

Ten minutes later they were devouring each other in her room, like animals at the height of rutting season.

God! Alex Marshall was fantastic! And in ways that Rosemary had never imagined. He was a man, it struck Fleur, starved for passionate sex, a man with vast reserves of drive and sensuality. The things they did that night, themes and variations played, the intensity of sex taken to the edge of pain—all were clearly beyond the kind of lovemaking he found at home. But if he was greedy, and he was, he was also delirious with gratitude.

He flung his head back when Fleur took him in her mouth. "Oh, God! You are paradise!"

They spent the night in a wash of lovemaking, obsessed with the exploration of each other's bodies and tastes and desires. Toward dawn she fell into an exhausted slumber.

The wake-up call came at seven-thirty sharp. "I'm up, I'm up," Fleur growled, and rolled out of bed. Alex was already in the bathroom staring at himself in the mirror.

"Jesus!" He studied his reflection—the swollen lips, scratches, bite marks on his thigh. "What the hell will I tell Rosemary?"

It was the first time either of them had mentioned her name.

"Tell her," Fleur said, coming up behind him and laying her face against his shoulder, "that you were mugged in downtown Pittsburgh."

Alex laughed, reached back to cup her buttocks, and pulled her close. "And I plan to get mugged again as soon as possible."

That was four months ago. And the passage of time had intensified their passion. Yet since Pittsburgh, they had only managed two full nights together. Most of their meetings were like the one this evening, a couple of desperately passionate hours in her apartment, with an eye on the clock. Occasionally a matinee in a midtown hotel. But never enough, never enough. The sex was great, splendid, all that could be desired. But she wanted something beyond.

She wanted "afters." *Après sexe,* like *après ski.* Time to drowse in his arms after lovemaking. Or sit around drinking tea. Or watch *The Late Show* in bed with her head on his shoulder. At the end of their time together, she always felt deprived. Incomplete.

No, it wasn't enough what they had.

As this goddamn yogurt wasn't enough. Not filling enough. It wouldn't see her through the night.

She crawled back into bed and switched on the eleven o'clock news.

Alex would be pulling into the Westport station by now. She could picture it vividly. He was climbing into the little Audi he kept for a station car. The winding drive down Millpond Road, crunching over the piles of fallen leaves. Then the house, its fieldstone path gleaming white in the crisp November moonlight. Inside, all the lights were on, beaming a message of warmth and welcome. He opened the door, tossed his coat on the landing, then went into the kitchen.

His wife had made coffee, and now they sat down together, chatting and familiar at the end of a long busy day. The scene was so real she could taste it, smell it. The aroma of coffee mixed with the odor of woodsmoke. And she

could see the woman too. Alex's wife, moving smoothly
across the pretty tile floor, clearing away the coffee cups,
happy, smiling.

Only in her fantasy, the woman in the kitchen wasn't
Rosemary at all. It was *she*. Mrs. Fleur Marshall.

The train, in keeping with a venerable commuter tradition, was a half hour late. Alex slung his briefcase in the
overhead rack, then stretched out over three empty seats.
The Guilt Trip Special he called the late train, populated
largely by the overachievers and the screwers-around. He
used to be the one, now he was the other.

Adultery didn't come easy to Alex Marshall. He'd had the
occasional one-night stand on the road or at conventions
(what businessman had not?), but on balance, the game
seemed hardly worth the risk. He considered himself a
happily married man.

He yawned and checked his watch. Friday already. A
weekend of domesticity loomed in the foreground. He'd do
something with Rosemary and Chris, maybe take them to
the Essex Yacht Club for lunch. There was always some
kind of local dinner party on Saturday night. As a rule the
routine was pleasant enough, but since he'd met Fleur, life
had taken on a restless quality. He'd forgotten how exciting
sex could be. How gratifying it was to have a partner who
had no hang-ups, no qualms about the giving and getting of
pleasure. He always left there feeling like Superman.

Nor was it just the sex, Alex told himself. Fleur was
smart, quick, funny. Always ready for a laugh or a listen.
He could talk shop with Fleur, pour his professional angst
out, without her eyes glazing over.

And so beautiful it broke your heart! Just to look at her,
to smell her scent, to feel the bloom of her skin released a
streak of poetry in Alex that he never knew he possessed.
His wife always accused him of being a workaholic, and he
supposed he was, but that didn't mean a man had nothing
else inside him, that he was utterly devoid of aesthetic
sensibility. Fleur—the Flower—

He shut his eyes and remembered the brush of her hair
against his cheek. He woke to discover he'd slept past his
station.

"Shit!" Alex growled, then got out at Bridgeport and took
a very expensive taxi home. Halfway there, he remembered

he had left his briefcase on the train. Second time this month. "Double shit!"

It was all too much, too tiring. Something would have to give. Either the commuting or his affair with Fleur. Only not Fleur. Not yet.

When he got home the house was dark.

TEN

$\mathbf{B}$ernie, who never cried at weddings, cried.

The Rothstein-Weiss nuptials, scheduled to be the grand finale of her television series, had taken place that afternoon in a Brooklyn synagogue, and Bernie—the outsider, the cool, dispassionate observer of contemporary mores— had wept unashamedly.

The lucky couple (yes, they were lucky, Bernie realized, lucky in their love, their commitment) had met but three months earlier through the offices of a traditional Jewish marriage broker. Bernie had interviewed them twice already and decided they were perfect for the wrap-up. Sympathetic. Unpretentious. Typically New York.

Suzanne was a secretary in the garment industry. Not beautiful, but appealing in a homey way that viewers could identify with. Her new husband did something with computers.

"The first time I saw her," Alan Weiss had told Bernie in an earlier interview, "something clicked. We got engaged the next week."

"You've had very little opportunity to know each other," Bernie said. "What made you decide against waiting?"

"What's to wait for?" Suzanne had squeezed her fiancé's hand while the two exchanged rapturous looks. "Does life wait for us?"

Today at the wedding, Bernie sat with the guests instead

of the crew, fascinated by the lengthy ritual. It would have to be cut, the professional in her acknowledged, but the results would be terrific. The groom looked nervous, a nice touch. The bride was appropriately radiant. Hard to believe this was the same plain girl they had filmed a week before, eating lunch at her desk at Kid-Gro Fashions. Suzanne's mother, sniffling into a cambric hankie (Bernie prayed that the cameraman caught that), could be everyone's mother. Did Bernie fancy it, or was there a passing resemblance to Adelaide Hong?

Perhaps it was that likeness, perhaps some other chord had been struck, but halfway through the ceremony, Bernie found herself sliding from professional cool to subjective warmth, began imagining herself up there on the dais. Not that she understood a word of the service, but you didn't have to know Hebrew to read these people's faces. Something vital, something real was happening.

At one point, the groom smashed a glass on the floor. "What does that mean?" Bernie whispered to a neighbor.

"It goes back thousands of years, to the destruction of the Temple in the Bible, and it's to remind the new couple that their marriage is part of a long and holy tradition."

Bernie had a lump in her throat the size of a golf ball. "Tradition!" she sighed.

She spent the rest of the afternoon at the station screening the videotapes with her producer and a couple of people from Publicity.

"You don't think it's too Jewish?" Hy asked.

Bernie shook her head. "Universal. Those feelings are universal, believe me."

"Yeah," he muttered. "They sure are."

The tapes were sensational, the wedding a perfect "wrap." They would begin editing the next day and start airing the following week. The press releases were already in the works.

"You did good, kid," Hy said when she left that day. "Let's hope it gooses the ratings."

At home, Steve had laid on a bottle of Piper-Heidsieck. "Let's drink ourselves silly," he proposed, "in honor of the occasion."

"Which occasion did you have in mind?" Bernie asked.

"The end of the goddamn series, what else? Bye-bye

Lonely Hearts! Hello Steve. And not a moment too soon. What say we celebrate by your meeting me in Antigua weekend after next? I'm shooting a Schweppes commercial at Mill Reef."

Bernie sat quietly and sipped her champagne.

"What say," she murmured, "that we make it our honeymoon?"

Perhaps Steve didn't hear her. Perhaps he didn't believe his ears. She herself hardly believed her own. The words had slid out on a reflex. Did she intend them? She didn't know. But she did know what Steve's answer ought to be.

"I said," Bernie repeated, "that would be a great place to spend a honeymoon. Steve, I'd like us to get married."

He gave a nervous laugh. "You're kidding!"

Bernie's response was stony silence.

"You *are* kidding, aren't you?" Steve looked at her aghast. "This is your idea of a practical joke."

"Joke?" she burst out. "You think marrying me is a joke?"

A month's full of grievances began spewing out. He didn't really give a rat's ass about the inner workings of her mind, her private conflicts. "You don't even have the sensibility to be jealous!" she charged.

"Jealous?" Steve's look was one of genuine puzzlement. "What's to be jealous about? I trust you."

"And it doesn't bother you that I've been out on the town every single night in the last three weeks? That at least fifty different guys have made passes at me, asked for dates?"

"It doesn't bother me if it doesn't bother you," he replied evenly. "You're a big girl, Bernie, you can take care of yourself. You always have."

"There are times," she shot back, "when a woman wants someone else to take care of her for a change! Someone who gives a damn about her well-being, her safety. If you really loved me, Steve, you'd have insisted in being there to protect my interests. Protect yours too, for that matter."

"You didn't honestly expect me to play chaperon every night in the week," he replied. "What the hell, you had the camera crew lurking in the wings. Anyhow, I've got better things to do with my spare time than tagging along on your assignments—"

"What better things?" she yelled. "Hanging out with the guys? Watching 'Great Moments in Basketball'? And all the while you know I'm out meeting total strangers doing

God knows what? Well, let me tell you, another kind of man would have been concerned, dammit! Involved. But not my Mr. Cool! Oh, no! Not if it involves any effort. You're always telling me how much you love me and care for me, but they're just words, Steve, that's all. Because if you care about anything at all in this world—and sometimes I doubt it!—then it's that so-called freedom you're always ranting about. Freedom from what, Steve? From me? From responsibility? From real life?"

"How about"—he tried to defuse the situation with a tentative joke—"freedom from nagging?"

"That does it!" Bernie exploded. "You have never taken me seriously. Never ever! You think I have no feelings?" Her list of injustices began to build. "That I don't want what other women want? Husband? Children? What am I—a machine of some kind? An abnormal? Listen, buddy. I've met a slew of people this last month, people with a lot less to offer each other than you and I have. Okay, you call them lonely hearts, which I find goddamn snide. But at least they're going for it. They're sick and tired of playing it cool. They want to make commitments, get on with the business of life. The things that really matter, Steve, like buying a house, raising a family, kids—"

"Since when did you want children, Bernie? First I ever heard about it. Good God! You don't even want to take care of a cat!"

"Don't tell me what I want or don't want," she retorted, not too sure where she stood on motherhood. "The point is, life is passing me by because you're too frightened to take a chance. Every day ordinary men pledge themselves to ordinary women. It's a public statement, a proof of their love. They may not be hotshot TV producers, but at least they aren't scared shitless at the sight of a wedding ring."

"I already had a wedding ring—" he began.

"Yeah? Well, I haven't!" She paused to glare at him. "We share a laundry basket, that's all."

"I'll send my shirts out, if you like."

"Don't you dare smart-talk me," she exploded. "I've damn near had it. Five years together and the most you've ever put out is your half of the rent. A month at a time. That's your limit of involvement, the longest you can manage to look ahead. There's no tomorrow with you, Steve. With us as a couple! We live like gypsies, students, instead of grown-ups, for Chrissakes. And where is love in all this, I ask you? Where is loyalty? I'm a roommate, a sexual convenience, that's all."

Steve turned white. "I can't believe what I'm hearing. This fucking story has softened your brain. I knew it was trouble as soon as you told me about it. Jesus, Bernie, you're a journalist. An observer. You're not supposed to fall in love with the crap you write. You're only supposed to report it. Instead, you sound just like every other woman in the world. Marry me, marry me, same old song. I thought you were smarter than that, more independent. That's sure what you led me to believe. What'll it be next, Bernie? A frilly white apron and geraniums on the window sill?"

"Get out of the Middle Ages!" she snapped. "That's not the kind of marriage I'm talking about."

"Well, I'm not talking about any kind of marriage, sweetheart. Nada. Zilch. Watch my lips, Bernie. I've done that number. And as for family, get off my back! I've got two kids to support, remember? Eight hundred bucks going out every month, plus college fees coming up in another couple years. No way am I going to yoke myself yet again. Besides," he added bitterly, "we've always operated on the premise that either of us could walk away at any time. Those were the ground rules. You knew that for openers."

"Ground rules!" she screamed. "Openers! What is this—a fucking game? Well, I don't want to play it anymore. I want to be engaged—engaged with life, with the real world. And then I want to be married—till death do us part."

Her voice echoed through the depth of the loft. Steve waited until the reverberations died down.

"Talk that way," he said softly, "and we'll be parted a helluva lot sooner."

"If you loved me—" She caught her breath. The sound of her anger had frightened her but also steeled her resolve. "If you loved me, you'd want to prove it. You'd want to give something up for me."

"Like my freedom? No way. I love you, Bernie. Goddamn I love you. And I've been faithful to you all the time we've been together. But I don't equate love with sacrifice."

"And marrying me would be a sacrifice," she said coldly. "I see. And I see something else, Steve. You've been freeloading off me for the last five years, just taking up space. Well, this is my apartment, my furniture, my home, and I'm not going to share it with some man who panics at the thought of the simplest concessions. If marrying me is such a goddamn sacrifice, then I suggest you be out of here by the end of the month. Find some other free spirit to sponge off. I'm not going to waste any more time on you."

"Fine!" He was thin-lipped, quivering with rage. "Go get yourself a replacement. I'll be out of here by the weekend. Sooner if I can help it. Believe me, Bernie, living with you is no picnic these days. You've become so fuckin' emotional."

"Right!" she shot back. "Now out of my life. And take your goddamn barber pole with you!"

ELEVEN

———•———

"**W**ho is he?" Fleur demanded.

"Who is who?" Diane picked up a napkin, feigning ignorance.

"The man, sweetheart, Mr. Wonderful. No, don't bother to deny it. It's written all over you in Day-Glo letters six inches high. 'Here is Diane Summerfield, a woman being well and truly laid.' Listen, kid, you'd better tell me peaceably before the Grand Inquisitor comes, because you know Rosemary, she'll pry it out of you with hot tongs. So tell me, is he nice, is he sweet? I can see he's good in bed."

"What if I were to say there is nobody, Fleur?"

"What if I were to say you're a lousy liar?" She leaned across the table and patted Diane on the hand. "You can talk to me, Di. I'm not the enemy camp."

Diane hesitated. One part of her ached to announce to Fleur, to the world that she was crazy happy in love, but a sensible caution prevailed. And how could she (of all people) admit to Fleur (of all people) that she was engaged in a dead-end affair. For years now, Diane had been the voice of reason, pleading with Fleur not to throw herself away on unsuitable men. And sweet and sexy as Avram was, suitability was not among his assets.

Only a few hours earlier as she lay snuggled in his arms, she had pried a strange confession from him.

"Tell me," she asked, "that first night you came here to repair the plumbing, remember?"

"Of course I do, darling."

"Well, after you fixed the leak, you simply stood in the middle of the living room, dead still, and I had the oddest notion that you were waiting for something to happen. You looked so—expectant. Tell me, Av, did you know even then that we'd be lovers?"

"No," he nuzzled her, "how could I?"

"Then what were you waiting for?"

"If I tell the truth, you won't be angry?"

"I promise."

Avram reddened. "I was hoping for a tip, Diane. Sometimes, if I do a late-night job, the tenant tips me a few dollars. Not that I'd ask for it, but you know, I get virtually no salary. I can use the money."

She was shocked. Nothing could have illustrated more succinctly what she was constantly trying to forget: the disparity between them. She was the payer, he the paid. Except, ironically, she hadn't even tipped him that night.

She remembered the moment well: her doubts, her misplaced notion that his sensibilities would be "offended" if she handed him a few dollars. Since then, however, she had offered him a good deal more than mere cash. She had offered herself. The ultimate "tip."

The suspicion that she was making a fool of herself nagged incessantly. Was it credible, she asked herself, that Avram truly loved her? That alone among men, he should honestly care about her thoughts, her feelings? She was older, worldlier, and—it was not to be forgotten—had a good deal more money.

Even granting the sincerity of his affection, there was no doubt the affair was a great convenience for Avram. Perhaps he had slept with other tenants in the building. The Osgood Arms abounded in rich and available women, many of them as lonely as she. Avram did odd jobs for them after hours, a virile young man, always at their beck and call. There were other ways of "tipping" him besides money. How did she know she was the first?

"You were hoping for a tip," she mused, "and instead you got me. Tell me, am I the first woman in this building you've gone to bed with? I'm not condemning, Avram. I don't have proprietary rights."

Avram was grossly offended. "Even to ask such a thing,

you make me sound like"—he groped for words—"like a farm animal, a stud bull."

"God forbid!" she cried.

"I love you, Diane. I hope you love me. It's simple. Why do you find it hard to so accept?"

At heart, she believed him, but that only complicated the situation. The fact remained that theirs was a hole-in-the-corner romance, unsanctioned by her friends, her family. Ridiculous in the eyes of the world. The thought that her neighbors might have observed these goings-on was humiliating enough. And once or twice the manager had given her funny looks.

Should she have tipped Avram that night? Undoubtedly. But what a constriction that would have put on their affair! Poor dear Avram! She wanted so much to help him, but she couldn't bring herself to offer financial aid. For what should she pay him? As the reward for loving her? And what if he accepted? What hell!

"Yes." Diane turned away from Fleur, unwilling to meet her eyes. "There is a somebody, but nothing serious. More of a nobody, actually, than a somebody." Then despising herself for having betrayed Avram even at this remove, she waved for the waiter. "Why do we always eat at the Karnak? I'm sick of it. Anyhow, I could use a drink. How about a Bloody Mary."

"How about a Bloody Rosemary?" Fleur asked. "Because here she comes with Bernie. On time, would you believe!"

"The opera isn't over till the fat lady sings."

Diane and Fleur exchanged mystified glances at Bernie's cryptic announcement. She had spoken with an air of heavy significance.

"Granted, you've both had a three-month head start," she went on when Diane broke in with a comprehending gasp.

"You and Steve!" she said. "You're getting married! Congratulations."

"Steve who?" Bernie gave a homicidal scowl. "I don't know any party by that name. As for the rest of your statement, you're absolutely right. I am indeed going to get married. It's just a question of whom."

Fleur leaned back and folded her arms. Bernie looked ready to go the distance. There was fire in her eye, steel in

doubt, morally speaking, that she had been in the right. So why, she brooded, did she feel so utterly miserable?

What was required at this juncture, Bernie knew, was a graphic reminder of the merits of married life. And no one set a better example than Rosemary. Her friend was a font of practicality, of calm good sense, and of connubial bliss. She would console Bernie, fortify her in her resolve not to go crawling back to Steve.

By the time Bernie arrived at the station, she had reached an emotional pitch. She spotted Rosemary waiting on the platform with Chris in tow.

"Oh, wow!" Bernie broke into a trot. "Am I ever glad to see you! This last week has been holy hell!"

But Rosemary put her finger to her lips. "Little pitchers have big ears," she said with a cautionary glance at the child. "We'll talk later," she mouthed, then hoisted Chris up. "Now, lamb chop, give Auntie Bernie a great big kiss."

"Kiss, kiss!" He puckered and missed her face by inches, planting two sticky smears on the collar of Bernie's suede jacket.

"Sorry about that." Rosemary swiped at the stain. "It'll come off with a little benzine. We've just had pancakes, and we're a wee bit ooey-gooey, aren't we, sweetheart?"

"Ooey-gooey," Chris echoed with relish.

"And icky-sticky." Rosemary laughed.

"Fuzzy-wuzzy," he enthused.

They headed across the lot to Alex's Audi while Chris hummed a little ditty over and over. "Fuzzy Wuzzy was a bear. Fuzzy Wuzzy had no hair."

"You don't mind if Christopher sits in front, do you?" Rosemary asked. "He just loves pretending to drive his daddy's car."

"The backseat is fine." Bernie clambered in, dying to talk.

"And if it's all right, I thought we'd stop off at Safeway and do a quick shop."

"Sure thing," Bernie muttered, preoccupied.

"Cheerios!" Chris said. "Can we get Cheerios?"

"We'll see," Rosemary said.

"The problem is," Bernie said, "I'm wondering if I came on too tough with Steve—"

Rosemary craned her head and caught Bernie's eye. "Little pitchers," she reminded, while Chris rotated an imaginary steering wheel with the fervor of an Indy Five Hundred contender.

They rode a few blocks in relative silence, then Chris piped up. "Pictures don't have ears, Mommy. That's silly."

Rosemary giggled, but didn't amplify. "He doesn't miss a thing, that boy."

"Do they, Aunt Bernie?"

"Huh?" Her thoughts were elsewhere.

"Do little pictures have big ears? Mommy says so."

"Ummm . . . your mom didn't mean that kind of picture, Chris." Bernie tried to focus on the matter at hand. "In fact, it's not a picture at all, not the kind you hang on the wall. It's a pitcher—a jug—the sort of thing you keep water in. Of course they don't have ears really, either. Handles is more like it. Oh what the heck!" She gave up. "It's just one of those dumb things grown-ups say. Technically speaking, little pictures do not have big ears, Okay?"

Chris pondered this for a moment. "Do big pictures have little ears?" he wanted to know.

Rosemary burst out laughing. "Isn't that cute? Ah! Here we are at Safeway."

"Can I push the shopping cart, Mommy? Please can I push?"

"Only if you drive very, very carefully."

Once inside the supermarket, Chris commandeered a cart and pushed it manfully in the direction of the cereal aisle, with Rosemary and Bernie trailing in his wake.

"Cheerios!" He snatched a box off the shelf and triumphantly plunked it into the cart. "Yum! I want my Cheerios!"

"Do I hear a 'please'?" Rosemary said after the fact.

"Double please." Chris added a box of Honey Krispies for good measure. "Double means I can have two."

Sneaky, Bernie thought.

"Smart!" Rosemary grinned at Chris's fait accompli. "Just like his father. When he sets his mind on something, there's no stopping him. Such willpower! But you've got to admit he's adorable."

He was adorable, Bernie thought. Adorable and talkative and ubiquitous and charming and irritating and lively as a perpetual motion machine and hogging center stage every single moment, demanding nothing less than 110 percent of his mother's time and attention. Alex, smart fellow, was out playing golf, and there appeared to be no escape in sight from Chris's company.

As the day wore on, Bernie began to wonder if she would even have ten minutes alone with her hostess before it was time to go back to the city. Thus far, she hadn't got a word in edgewise.

"Doesn't he ever take a nap?" she whispered discreetly after lunch.

"We're too grown-up to take naps"—Rosemary winked at Chris in loving conspiracy—"now that we're great big kindergartners."

Bernie mustered up an agonized smile.

Toward three, mercifully, Rosemary packed her son in the car and drove him over to a neighbor's to play. Bernie watched him go with relief. God! Kids were hard work.

"Now." Rosemary settled down in the kitchen and began cleaning vegetables for dinner. "You can tell me all about it. You look rather peaked, I must say. Anyhow, there's coffee on the sideboard and some nice homemade pie, so relax and take your time. We're free till five."

Over half a dozen cups, Bernie provided all the details of her showdown with Steve, concluding with her ultimatum. "I told him to marry or move." But now, she confessed, she was having second thoughts. "What do you think, Rosemary?" Her eyes grew moist. "Maybe I overplayed my hand. Was I out of line, holding out for marriage?"

"Of course not!" Rosemary said vehemently. "You did the sensible thing. That little old wedding band is the only insurance we have in this world, and don't you forget it."

Bernie nodded. "You're right."

"It's your only emotional insurance, your only financial insurance. Your only guarantee that there'll be somebody to snuggle up to when you're old and gray."

"Too true!"

"Besides," Rosemary continued, driving the point home, "if a man really loves a woman, he ought to be willing to make that commitment, especially since neither of you is getting any younger. You weren't being the least bit unreasonable, Bernie, I assure you. Your behavior was not only absolutely proper but, if you don't mind my saying it, long overdue."

"Thank you." Bernie took a deep confirming breath. "You've told me what I've come to hear."

Rosemary softened her tone. "However, I myself have always been a subscriber to the bird-in-the-hand theory. And Steve is a very endearing person. I'm not saying you shouldn't hold fast to your principles. You should, you must! But don't you think there's a chance he'll come around?"

"None," she snuffled into the colander. "He's already made it impossible. For two whole weeks, I managed to kid myself that he'd see the light. I kept saying—he loves me, for Chrissakes, he won't let us break up over this. But since that night, nothing. Not even one lousy phone call. He just packed up his clothes and split. He'll never marry, I know it in my bones. He'd rather be hanged. And I for one will be goddamned if I'm going to make the first call, take him back on the same old terms. It's humiliating."

"It sure is," Rosemary clucked in sympathy. "After all, you have your pride. Marriage or nothing, Bernie. Stick to your guns."

"You bet your ass!" The more Bernie thought about it, the angrier she grew. "Okay, I accept the fact that he'll never propose and I won't go begging. Already I feel like a fool. I don't need that shit, Rosemary, not from him. If I want to get dumped on, I can go back home to Binghamton. They've got an ample supply of ego-downers ready and waiting. Why don't you do this? Why don't you do that? Why don't you get married and settle down? You know, I could make a million bucks and be on the cover of *Time* and my mother would shake her head and say, 'So why aren't you married like your sisters?' According to her, my sisters are the family success story—not me!"

Growing up in that brood had been a struggle of sorts, Bernie said. An endless clamor to be heard. "I wanted attention."

"Like Chris. I hope he didn't make a nuisance of himself."

"Of course not," Bernie said tactfully. "All children want attention. It's natural, I suppose. He's one lucky kid, having you all to himself. For me it was tougher, there was so much competition around. Believe me, Rosemary, when you're one of six and the runt of the litter, you learn to fight for your rights early. Otherwise, you get swallowed up whole. Funny thing, though, it's really no different when you're a full-fledged adult."

Take her job at the station, for example. If she hadn't been nagging, aggressive, persistent, the proverbial squeaky wheel, her series never would have seen airtime. She'd be condemned to six-by-six cubicles for the rest of her career, just another faceless name in the long scroll of credits at the end of the show. No one would know her. No one would care.

"You Don't Ask, You Don't Get is my motto. By the way," Bernie said, visibly expanding, "my new slot starts tomorrow, and already I'm the fair-haired child. There's been a surge of advertiser interest, we're hitting a younger, sharper audience. And frankly, it's thanks to me."

"But getting back to Steve—" Rosemary would not be diverted with shoptalk. She doubted the situation was as hopeless as Bernie claimed, and she knew they loved each other.

"There is no getting back to Steve," Bernie said. "That is truly yesterday's news. The man will not make a commitment—not now, not ever. You were right, Rosemary. Marriage is the only insurance you can have in a relationship, and I'm too pragmatic to waste any more time on a pipe dream. I've learned my lesson. Not like Fleur."

"What about Fleur?" Rosemary leaned forward in delicious expectation, just as Alex walked into the kitchen.

"Big pitchers . . ." Bernie whispered with a finger to her lips. "Tell you later."

That was yesterday. And now, wonder of wonders, here was Steve on the phone. Instantly Rosemary had visions of putting the former lovebirds back in their cage. A year from now they'd thank her for her trouble.

"You know, Steve," she gurgled, "Bernie was here for dinner— "

Dead silence at the other end. Then—

"I didn't call to talk about her, Rosemary. This is business. I've got a proposition for you."

His crew had been scheduled to shoot a commercial in the South of France, but with the recent terrorist scare the client was reluctant to go abroad. They needed a location, quick, something that could pass itself off for a Provençal kitchen. The Marshall house would be ideal.

"Two days next week," Steve explained. "One for pre-lighting, one for shooting, fifteen hundred dollars per day. An additional two thou if the shoot runs over. What do you say, Rosie? I need a fast answer."

Her first instinct was to ask Alex for permission, but what the hell—it was her kitchen, her home. And it would be enough money for a new fur coat, earned by her own superior taste.

Her house on TV! She felt a thrill of pride mixed with apprehension.

"What kind of product is it?" she wanted to know. Suppose it was Drano? Or even worse—Roach Motel!

"A line of frozen croissants from Gourmet de France. Terrific stuff. We'll send you a case."

Rosemary didn't have to think twice.

That night she pounced on Alex the moment he came through the door. "What do you think, honey. Did I do right?"

"Jesus," he said, laughing. "It's about time we got some money out of that kitchen after all the thousands I've sunk into it. Yeah—sure—fine. Unless you want to go back and see if you can jack them up in price. I'm sure Steve quoted you rock bottom for openers."

"Oh, no! I wouldn't want to take a chance on spoiling it. About the money, Alex—"

"All yours, sweetie. Treat yourself to something nice."

"Hot damn!" Nancy Goodrich held a blue-and-white flan mold up to the light. "Gorgeous. You sure have fantastic stuff here."

A stylist who specialized in food photography, she was tripping out on Rosemary's collection. "If I'd known you had kitchenware like this, I could have saved myself a lot of schlepping."

Nancy had arrived with crates full of china, flatware, crystal, even table linen rented from a dozen different boutiques. Nice things, but they couldn't hold a candle to Rosemary's own. Nancy said so herself. She had stayed behind an hour after the crew had gone to explore the contents of Rosemary's cupboards.

"Mmmm." She caressed an antique bain-marie as though it were a holy object. "Tell me, Mrs. Marshall—"

"Rosemary, please!"

"Rosemary, then. You have items I've seen nowhere else. Where did you find this piece, by the way?"

The bain-marie had come from an out-of-the-way shop in Litchfield County, and Rosemary's instinct was to share the information. Then she remembered Alex's first rule of business: Don't talk. Listen!

"I have my sources," she said cryptically.

"I see you do." Nancy gave her a long appraising look. "And you have a marvelous eye. How'd you like to free-lance for us?"

"Doing what?"

"Finding props, tracking down items for specific shoots. As you know, our firm specializes in food and home furnishings. We supply items for commercials, still photography, the occasional TV movie. The rule of thumb is, if it's cheap we buy, otherwise we rent. Mostly we rent. The important thing is that our props be distinctive. In other words you don't see a Campbell's Soup bowl in a Grape Nuts spot. So we're always on the lookout for what's fresh, unusual. That's where you'd come in. I'd tell you our requirements, you'd scout them out."

"You mean," she asked, incredulous, "that you're actually willing to pay me to go shopping for housewares? God! What bliss."

Nancy laughed. "That's one way of putting it. Plus we expect you to do some very shrewd haggling when necessary."

"Sounds fabulous. But I just don't know if I could take it on. You see, I've got a job already. I'm a wife and mother. I couldn't work a full nine-to-five."

She wouldn't have to, Nancy argued. That was the beauty of free-lance. She could set her own hours, plan her own itineraries. The arrangement was totally flexible; all that mattered was that she deliver the goods.

Right now, for example, Nancy was looking for an antique butter dish for a margarine shot. Something that implied the product was genuine dairy food.

Rosemary clapped her hands. "I know just the piece! It's English, white porcelain with the lid in the shape of a cow." And she knew where to lay her hands on it, too. Next week was no problem. They talked about terms.

"Are we in business then?" Nancy proffered her hand.

"My friend, you've made me an offer I can't refuse."

*   *   *

She would not buy that fur coat after all, she told Alex. Instead, she would invest it in building up stock.

"See, instead of renting the stuff and just passing the rental on, I would buy the piece, then have the stylist or the set decorator rent it from me. So I get A. the rental price and B. the goods, which can only increase in value, and C. depreciation for tax purposes. I already checked that with our accountant. Plus which I can rent the item again at some future date. What do you think, Alex? Does that make business sense?"

"Go for it, Rosie!" He looked at her with heightened respect. "It's a terrific idea. Especially the tax angle. And I think it's an excellent idea that you have money of your own for a change. Develop some outside interests." He nodded. "Yes, it would do you good to be a bit more independent."

"Rosemary Marshall," she said, giggling. "Career girl! Who would ever have thought it!"

Each Thursday, when the Nielsen ratings came out, a secretary from Sales would post them on the bulletin board. To those in the television industry, the ratings were report card, fever chart, CAT scan, lie detector, yardstick, and above all—dollars and cents. The figures regularly revealed how many viewers (or, worse, how few) had watched the show the preceding week, both in absolute numbers and share of sets tuned in. On the basis of these findings, advertisers and their agencies made their allocations; stations determined what they could charge for time.

For the past three weeks, Bernie had watched the Nielsens, hawk-eyed. On the Thursday following the end of her series, she marched into Feinstein's office.

"You've seen these, of course."

"Yes, very nice," Hy said warily, trying to strike a balance between congratulations and judicious restraint. It didn't pay, he knew from experience, to encourage notions of indispensability among the staff.

"Nice!" Bernie said. "They're fantastic! The salesmen are creaming themselves with these figures. And they don't tell the half of it. You should see the letters I've been getting from all over the tri-state area. Nothing short of sensational! For the first time since I joined this dinky station, we're actually competing with the national networks."

"Now, Bernie." Hy trod carefully. He knew she was looking for something far more substantial than plaudits. "Granted the series was excellent, but it wasn't the only reason for the rating surge. We've had a lot of good things happen the past few weeks. There was that big warehouse fire in Paramus. The triple murder in the Bronx. There was the Madonna interview—"

"Unh-unh." Bernie shook her head. "I don't buy it. You know and I know that what's turned people on—literally and figuratively—has been the lonely hearts stuff. So Hy . . . ?"

There was a long pregnant pause.

"So I'll buy you and your boyfriend dinner at Le Cirque."

"Fuck dinner," she said. "I want a regular slot on the show. I want to do the *Heartbeat of New York* segment, build up a following. Then I want to do some hard news, get a chance to anchor when the regulars are off—"

"You know I can't do that, Bernie. There are other people to be considered. Look, I'll try to get you on with more frequency, maybe once, twice a week, but as for a regular berth, I can't make that kind of commitment."

"Commitment!" Bernie looked at him unflinchingly. "Jesus, that seems to be the original dirty word. Once again with feeling. Hy, and I'm asking you nicely. Do I get a five-day slot, yes or no?"

"At the moment—no."

"Thank you." She turned and walked out. No purpose was served by arguing, in making threats she couldn't follow through. If she'd had another job offer, even a nibble, she might have indulged in some hardball with Hy. But the industry was tight at the moment; CBS and ABC were both laying off newsroom staffers by the gross. This was not the season for "or else."

Twice, she thought grimly to herself. That was twice in a month she had asked for a commitment and been turned down. First Steve, now Hy. It was rough on the ego.

Yet gut feelings told her Hy would do a lot to keep her—a lot more than he was willing to acknowledge. Should it come to either/or, she believed Hy would promote her, provided she didn't make him feel his back was to the wall.

At the station there was a large open space known as The Zoo, ringed by executive offices. There the bits and pieces of each day's programming were thrashed out. Stories were developed, continuity written while bookers tried to round up appropriate interviews. The noise level was horrendous, the gossip level even higher.

When Bernie wasn't on location or in her cubbyhole, she spent much of her time in The Zoo.

The following Monday, she was there as usual, another body in the *Five on Ten* team, working alongside Jamie McAllister. An hour before broadcast, she went into Makeup and returned to The Zoo camera-ready, wearing an elegant suit Jamie had never seen before.

"Hey, Jamie," she whispered. "I've got to leave early. Can you cover for me?"

"Sure," he said, then he took in her total appearance. "What gives with the makeup, Bernie? You're not on air today, are you?"

She bit her lips and seemed nervous.

"Look," she whispered. "Don't say a word about this, least of all"—she nodded in the direction of Feinstein's office—"to you-know-who."

She waited until she saw Hy open his office door and head toward The Zoo. Then she almost knocked him down in a mad rush to get out.

Hy was still standing there perplexed, when Jamie McAllister sidled up to him.

"Listen," Jamie confided, "you never heard it from me, but our little Bernie is out auditioning today."

"Oh yeah?" Hy probed. "She tell you that?"

"She leaves here with a face full of Pan-Cake, what does she have to tell me! She's testing for somebody this afternoon. My bet is NBC."

Jamie was wrong about NBC but right on the other matter. Bernie was indeed about to appear on camera in a test that was to yield twofold results. Of the myriad sources she had explored while developing the series, one in particular struck her fancy.

The People People was the name of the enterprise, a national organization that positioned itself as substantially more than a computerized dating service; rather, it was a place where a serious and successful person could meet his or her match. Selectivity was the key. Its members included corporate heads, theater people, international businessmen, Wall Streeters, lawyers, doctors, entrepreneurs—in short, those with more money than time. For them, the service was a valuable shortcut on the road to romance. The fees were stiff, two thousand dollars per year, which winnowed out the obvious failures. A "personal consultant" would analyze the client's needs, then, drawing upon the company's resources, provide recommendations tailored to fit.

Already Bernie had filled out a six-page form, detailing everything from her taste in music to her views on politics to those subtler areas of feelings and hopes.

"Are you looking for companionship?" the consultant asked.

"I am looking," Bernie said, "specifically for a husband."

"I see."

Among the services on offer was TPP's library of video-tapes. As a new member, the consultant explained, Bernie would make a three-minute cassette, a commercial of sorts, in which she spoke about herself and her expectations. At this stage no names were revealed, and the tapes were coded by number to prevent unwanted meetings.

Then the consultant would select a group of tapes for Bernie's consideration, men who might fulfill her stated needs. If she saw someone she thought she might like, that man in turn would screen Bernie's tape. Only if both sides professed interest would an actual introduction take place.

"So you'll meet only the men you choose to," said the consultant, "and you'll know that they also chose to meet you."

"Sounds terrific," Bernie said. "Lead me to the studio."

In front of the camera, she moistened her lips and gave her most professional smile, making sure her best angle was on view. And then—warm, delightful, cute as a button—Bernie charmed, charmed, charmed.

Even months later, looking over the tape, she could state with satisfaction that it was the finest performance of her career.

THIRTEEN

———•———

"Avram!" Diane called. "Come look out the window."

On the balcony, the first snow of the season was spiraling, whirling, whipped by the wind, settling briefly here and there into drifts and hollows, only to be lifted and sent dancing once more. The air was white, dense with flakes; the city beyond obscured. You could see nothing through this milky cloud—neither street nor sky. It was as though the two of them were cut off from the rest of mankind, surrounded by an infinite sea.

Enisled. Exactly so. She and Avram were enisled in every sense, existing remote from the familiar world.

At the start she had believed it would be a quick physical affair, burning itself out in a matter of weeks. Instead, their feelings for each other had broadened, deepened. Almost by accident, a pattern had sprung up, a kind of domestic routine.

Weekdays she would come home from the office to find Avram waiting. They would cook, eat, trade gossip, watch the news on TV. After dinner he usually worked on his thesis, filling yellow legal pads with yards of indecipherable scrawl, while she reviewed the contents of her briefcase. "How does this sound?" They would try ideas out on each other, then bat them around for mental exercise. She was getting the hang of Wittgensteinian semantics; he grew familiar with the *Simplexx* case. They shared a passion for argument, analysis.

Equally, friends, professors, and colleagues were discussed and dissected. "I'd like to meet this Byron fellow," Avram might say. Or "Your friend Fleur sounds very amusing."

"One of these days . . ." Diane would hedge, not sure if her reluctance stemmed from a desire to keep Avram to herself or the fear of subjecting him to general scrutiny.

They would finish the evening with a game of chess. Then a late-night snack and so to bed.

And through it all, they talked incessantly. About each other. About themselves.

"I don't like mystery," Avram said. He could be frank to the point of bluntness. For Diane, dwelling in a world where secrets were a stock-in-trade, self-disclosure did not come easily. Professionally, her role was that of receiver, not giver, of confidences. But little by little Avram chipped away at her reserve.

"Why did you do that?" he would often ask, and even more frequently, "How did you feel?" He was the first man, since Leo, who seemed to care about her emotional state. Nor would he be put off with easy answers.

"Why didn't you tell him he was behaving like a schmuck?" he asked when she complained about a man at Simplexx who told crude ethnic jokes.

"I can't do that," she said. "He's a client."

"But how did you feel about it?"

"I felt terrible. I wanted to haul off and sock him!"

Avram shook his head. "And you ask why I don't want to join a big corporation. You shouldn't have to tolerate that sort of thing."

"That's the real world, Avram."

"What's real about Wall Street? What's real about suppressing everything you feel?"

"Who do you think you are?" she asked uneasily. "My psychiatrist?"

Yet one of the rewards of Avram's company was the limitless freedom it afforded her. He was the one person to whom she could unburden herself, own up to fears and anxieties in the knowledge that her trust would not be betrayed. To whom could Avram betray it? He knew no one from her world.

She had often envied Catholics the relief and privacy of the confessional. To speak your heart, admit your faults, and be absolved—that was benediction indeed. In Avram, she had found a substitute. True, Diane had committed no crime except that of role playing, yet the deception haunted her. She had advertised herself as Diane the Strong, the Invincible. And the world had taken her at her word. The Iron Maiden, an adversary once had called her to her face.

"Do you think I'm a cold person?" she asked Avram after a particularly grueling day.

Avram gave the matter due consideration. "I think you have a cold analytic mind and a very warm heart. An interesting combination." Then typically, he asked, "Why, Diane? Do you think you're cold?"

Diane waffled. "Yes . . . no."

She didn't care to be viewed as a marshmallow, but it was preferable to the Iron Maiden role. "No, I'm not cold."

One night she told him about Leo, their affair, her abortion. To her own astonishment, she broke down and cried. "Crazy!" She sat up in bed, trying to stem the flood. "After all these years, I'm blubbering like an idiot."

She had expected a statement from him, some youthfully sage advice (*Leo wasn't worth it. That was years ago. You'll have other children. At the very least, don't cry.*). Instead, he put his arms around her and held her close for what seemed like infinity.

She finally pulled herself together. "Thank you."

"For what?"

On his own part, Avram had no dark secrets to reveal. He was one of three children, reared in a cultured but (by American standards) decidedly modest home. His mother taught kindergarten. His father, a Russian émigré and superb linguist, supplemented his musician's salary by translating poetry: Russian into Hebrew, Hebrew into English. His son had inherited these linguistic gifts.

Before entering university, Avram had served the mandatory three years in the army, much of the time stationed in the "territories," Arab villages that had fallen under Israeli domain after the Six-Day War.

"I hated it," he said. "I hated wearing a uniform, carrying weapons. Most of all, I hated being in that specific situation, neither at war nor at peace, neither at home nor abroad. You were always alert, suspicious, always with your Uzi submachine gun because violence could break out any time. The Arabs saw us as an occupying army, and in a way we were. Even the children looked on us with fear and loathing. But I was hardly more than a kid myself. I wasn't used to being anybody's enemy. It bothered me. I tried to make friends with some of the younger ones. They would hang around the caravansary where we'd go when off duty, begging cigarettes and Cokes. I learned a bit of Arabic, got to know some of them by name. For that I got a lecture from my sergeant. He saw them all as scum of the earth. Even worse—terrorists. But to me they were kids, that's all. Just kids, ten, eleven years old maybe."

The day after the invasion of Lebanon, a bomb exploded at the caravansary. Two soldiers from his barracks were killed. Within an hour, a suspect home in the Arab quarter was raided.

"We dragged people from their beds—women and children, forced them into the street. Arrested all the men. Then we began tearing that place apart—piece by piece, stone by stone. Smashing furniture, breaking crockery. One of the soldiers pissed on a copy of the Koran. It was dreadful . . . bloodlust. I don't know what else to call it. And all through this—this orgy of destruction, I could hear the women wailing. Arab women, they have this high, peculiar howl. It comes in waves and lodges in the brain, I tell you, like no other sound in the world. I hated myself for being there, for taking part. I'll never forget that sound." Toward dawn, they had planted demolition charges in the ground-floor rooms, then stumbled out into the street and waited for the house to blow. Behind the barrier, women and children were watching in horror. And there in that crowd, in the light of the explosion I could see Yusuf. He was one of my 'kids.' He shot me a look, Diane, of such pure hate as I hope never to see again. As for the women, I can hear them still."

"Was Yusuf's family involved?" she asked.

"I don't know," he said. "I don't think I want to know. A boy resembling him had been seen earlier, running from the caravansary. Perhaps I was naïve, perhaps it was a nest of terrorists. And who knows—such measures as we took may sometimes be necessary. But that night, I lost my innocence."

"About terrorists?" Diane asked.

"About myself. It made something very clear to me. There's that dark part in all of us, I suppose. But I do not

ever, ever"—he grew emphatic—"want to be in a position
where I'm called upon to act upon a judgment as to who is
good, who is bad. A position where you smother your basic
humanity and let your animal instincts run wild. I'm not a
policeman—I'm not a soldier—"

"Are you a pacifist?" she asked.

He sighed."I've given that a lot of thought and I can't say.
All I know is I refuse to think and behave like an animal.
Life's too short for that, Diane, too precious. All I ask is to
live in peace."

"I see," she said. And she did.

The six nights a week when Avram was on call, he kept
his beeper by his side. When his services were required, the
beeper signaled and he would phone the desk for instruc-
tions. Diane was certain the manager knew where Avram
was spending each night. Perhaps the entire staff was snickering behind her back. However, the formalities were strictly
observed. No one ever called her apartment directly.

And though the work itself was mundane, Avram found
the people intriguing. There was the Colombian coke dealer
in the penthouse. Who else could afford such a rent? Old
Mrs. Wetherby, 18S, living amidst a welter of canary drop-
pings, calling on Avram to retrieve delinquent birds. Then
there was 22J, the fashion model with the raucous love life.
Twice she had barricaded herself in the bedroom while
Avram ousted unwelcome guests in the small hours.

"A beautiful girl," he said, "and a big tipper."

"Yes . . . well," Diane muttered. "As long as I don't catch
you talking Wittgenstein with her."

"Never!" Avram laughed, then crawled back into bed.

Such were their work nights. Saturdays they shopped,
did household chores. Sundays they went out. Usually it
was to a movie or a concert in Manhattan (he had a comprehensive list of free music and lectures), followed by a cheap
Chinese meal or kabobs. Or coffee at his Israeli social club.

Diane longed to eat somewhere nice with him, a restaurant with tablecloths and a proper chef, but even going
dutch, such treats were well beyond his means. Avram took
for granted that he pay his own way. The question of
money perturbed her. She would have enjoyed taking him
to Barneys and buying him a few shirts and a couple of
decent suits. But even if Avram were to consent, she didn't

know if it was such a good idea. She had a recurring image of Gloria Swanson in *Sunset Boulevard* dolling up young William Holden with vicuna. Ghastly! And so they remained—enisled.

Now, he stepped barefoot out on the balcony, and bent over, consummately graceful, to scoop up a handful of snow. She watched with pleasure. He stood up, brushed the snowflakes from his hair, and caught her eye through the glass. He smiled and mouthed three short familiar words.

"Me too," she wanted to say, her heart welling with joy. "Yes, me too." Instead, she opened the door and called out, "Come on in, Avram. You'll catch cold."

The next morning at the office, Byron loped in and asked her if she could use a couple of tickets to the Met.

"*Turandot*," he said. "Gala premiere, great seats." He had been looking forward to it, but Jim hadn't been feeling well lately, and Byron felt he ought to stay home.

"So if you've got someone who'd enjoy it with you—"

"Oh, yes, Byron," she said, accepting the tickets. "Thanks."

Avram was delighted at the prospect. The seats were a gift, she assured him, and the best in the house. No remuneration was involved.

"You do have a suit, don't you?" she said. "It's a fairly dressy occasion."

"Why of course, Diane," he said. "I didn't grow up in the jungle."

Indeed he did have a suit. A suit of shiny blue serge, double-breasted, poorly cut, the kind that East European trade delegates wore to conventions. It was equally suitable for funerals. What ever happened, she wondered, to that great tradition of Jewish tailoring?

"Do I look all right?" He straightened his tie.

She swallowed. "You look very handsome, Avram." At least that much was true.

They arrived early, had a glass of champagne, admired the Chagall murals, then went to their seats.

"A box, no less." Diane grinned. "How very grand!"

But what Byron hadn't told her was that the box was shared. Worse yet, it was shared by Porter Reynolds III and his wife. Formidable son of a formidable father, Porter had made partner the year before. He was one of Slater Blaney's brightest stars. She knew his sister from boarding school. His uncle had recruited her for the firm.

"Well hello, Diane," Porter said, rising to greet her. "You remember Suzanne, don't you?"

Of course she did. Porter's wife was among the powers at Morgan Stanley. Resplendent in evening clothes, they both looked unspeakably elegant.

Diane introduced Avram without further ado. Hands were shaken, programs rattled, seats pulled out. Avram settled into one of the pretty gilt chairs, then crossed his legs revealing an expanse of hairy white flesh.

Over the calf, Diane cried inwardly. Why hadn't she told him to wear socks that went over the calf?

Porter's cool blue eyes didn't miss a thing.

Then mercifully, the lights were dimmed and the curtain went up. On stage, the drama of the icy princess began.

The next Monday she ran into Porter in the corridor.

"He was cute, your little date," he said with a twinkle. "Tell me, Diane, where did you find him?"

She turned scarlet. What could she say? That they had met when he came to fix her toilet?

"He lives in my building," she answered. It was an honest, if evasive reply. It would stand up in a court of law.

Minutes later she collared Byron in his office. "Why didn't you tell me you shared the box with Porter?"

Byron looked at her nonplussed. "What difference does it make?"

"I just didn't expect to see him there, that's all. Tell me, Byron, did he say anything to you about—about my date?"

Byron shook his head. She knew he was lying.

She jabbed her finger at his chest. "Come on, By! I know he said something, now talk!"

"What do you care what he thinks?" Byron shifted uneasily. "Your private life is your own business. Anyhow, it was nothing awful."

"Let me be the judge of that. Just tell me what he said."

"All he said was—well, you know how Porter likes to kid—" Suddenly Byron giggled. "What he said was 'Take me to his tailor.' "

Diane stomped out, wounded to the quick.

FOURTEEN

"Fleur is having an affair with a married man," Rosemary announced at breakfast one morning.

Alex choked on his coffee. His wife, however, intent on the microwaving of innocent croissants, rambled on, cheerfully oblivious.

"Isn't that awful, Alex? Ah! These are ready. How about some apricot jam? There!" She placed a hot croissant on his plate. "*Bon appetit, mon cher.*"

He sat for a moment, with the sense of living a nightmare. Instinct told him to dive for cover behind the *Times*; caution told him his trembling hands would give him away. Instead, he gulped down some juice and cleared his throat. What did Rosemary know? Was she playing cat and mouse? Hoping to shock him into confession? Not likely, he decided. She was the least conniving of women.

"Oh, yeah?" He feigned boredom. "Where'd you hear that?"

"Bernie told me." Rosemary sat down breathless, coffee cup in hand. "And Fleur's hinted as much herself. 'Somebody special,' she says whenever anyone asks. But no name, nobody's seen him. What else could it be but a married man? Bernie's sure it's a guy in her office. You know what I think?"

Alex was almost afraid to ask.

"I think," she went on, "that she's in trouble and it's my duty as her friend to save Fleur from herself. I can't stand

119

by idly while she throws herself away on some man who'll probably never leave his wife. That would be criminal."

No! Alex realized with an audible sigh of relief. Rosemary hadn't a notion, not a clue. He found a certain grotesque humor in the situation. And he was curious. How did Rosemary propose to "save" her?

"You're sighing," she commented. "I can see you feel the same way I do. The thing is, Alex, I'd like your help."

"You want me to talk to Fleur?" The absurdities were beginning to pile up. "Advise her like an uncle, maybe— play big brother?"

"Don't be silly," Rosemary snapped. "She wouldn't listen to you. What I want you to do, Alex, is find someone to fix her up with. You know, someone sensible, marriageable. When we were in college, she'd occasionally fix *me* up on a blind date. Well, it's my turn now," she announced with satisfaction. "Of course, the man doesn't have to realize he's being set up."

Alex watched her, fascinated. She was going about the task with such relish. Had she staked *him* out in this way?

"We'll invite them both out for a weekend." Rosemary unveiled her strategy. "Go for long walks, have an elegant dinner. Then let nature take its course. Think, Alex. Isn't there someone nice at the office, or one of your old classmates from Tuck? Divorced is okay, too. And a little older's all right. You know scads of people, hon. Find someone. After all Fleur's a very attractive woman, don't you agree?"

Alex grunted, speechless.

Rosemary mistook it for deliberation. "Well, Alex, who do you suggest?"

"I don't know anybody, Rosie. I'm not a marriage broker."

"Think!"

"I said I don't know anybody. Besides, I'm busy."

"Busy!" she said petulantly. "Why is it whenever I ask you to do a personal favor, something involving a little time and effort, you're too busy? Time for the office, but not for your family and friends! I should know better than to ask." She drank her coffee thoughtfully while Alex went for his coat.

"Bright idea!" she followed him out into the hall. "What about Lloyd Hageman?"

"Who's Lloyd Hageman?"

"You know," she said. "He lives in that big white house

over on Union. The periodontist. He and his wife broke up last summer."

"Guy must be fifty," Alex said.

"What does it matter? He's well off, he's pleasant. And Fleur's not in the first flower of youth, to make a pun. Besides, she's in no situation to be choosy."

He closed his briefcase, then headed for the door.

"Alex?" She pursued him. "What do you think about Lloyd?"

"What difference does it make what I think, Rosemary? You'll go ahead and do exactly as you please. As usual."

"Good," she said. "I'll call him today, see when he's available. Then I'll get in touch with Fleur. No problem. If she's running around with a married man, that means she has all her weekends free. She'll probably be grateful for the invitation, poor thing."

Alex made no reply. He would phone Fleur from the station, warn her what to expect, then insist that she make a tactful refusal. The situation was fraught with danger. And he wasn't certain Fleur could be trusted to behave.

"Kiss, kiss." Rosemary offered her cheek. They pecked each other. Alex got into his car.

But on the road to the station, Rosemary's plan began to take on a different cast. There was something exciting, erotic in the thought of having Fleur in his own house, in one of his own bedrooms.

In *having* Fleur—in every imaginable position—almost beneath his wife's nose, on those flowered sheets in the guest room. Like a goddamn pasha with a private harem. Or a scene right out of a racy French movie. They would have to be silent, very silent, but that might make the sex more exciting.

The mere thought of it gave him an erection. He sat in the car, aching with fantasy while one train after another went by. Then he stepped out with a whoop of laughter and went to the phone.

"A beard!" Fleur was aghast. "You want to fix me up on a blind date with a beard? A front man? Suppose I wind up liking the guy?"

"I'll take my chances," Alex said. "Only act surprised when Rosemary calls."

Fleur hung up the phone with mixed emotions. To enjoy

Rosemary's hospitality in these circumstances was unspeakably shabby. But, she mused, highly intriguing as well. It appealed to her competitive instincts.

Her last visit to Westport had taken place a year ago, well before her affair with Alex. It had been unmemorable, except for the food. This invitation was more opportune. At the least, it would offer her a closer look at the Marshall household, a clear picture of their married life. At best, it would give Alex a chance to compare the two women in his life. Compare and choose.

To give him his due, Alex never bad-mouthed his wife, at least not in terms that would give Fleur grounds for hope. Yet, she had the sense of a marriage grinding on essentially out of habit. There was money involved. A house. A child. A good deal of mutual convenience. Beyond that, she could only speculate.

Several times, she had tried to ascertain if Alex was still sleeping with Rosemary. The thought of his going from her apartment straight to the conjugal bed drove her crazy. The logic of the situation was irrelevant; she remained painfully jealous. Rosemary had almost everything Alex could give her: status, money, comfort, and ease. That she should have his sexual favors as well was intolerable.

"Are you faithful to me?" Fleur would ask.

"There's nobody else," he would assure her.

"There's Rosemary."

Faced with the direct question, Alex grew evasive. "I can't discuss this with you," he finally said in such a way that she decided to drop the subject for her own protection. Alex Marshall was not a man, she perceived, who would submit to emotional blackmail.

But one night, in a state of erotic exhaustion, he murmured that Rosemary "doesn't care much for this sort of thing." What kind of thing specifically? Fleur was dying to ask. A particular sexual act? Or did Rosemary eschew lovemaking in general? She suspected the latter, but Alex had sounded sad. She knew enough to keep her mouth shut.

She was at her desk an hour later, purportedly working, basically brooding, when Rosemary called. Years on Madison Avenue had made a seasoned liar of her; she had no trouble faking surprise.

"A really nice man," Rosemary gushed, "with a center-hall colonial, lovely garden. I told him all about you—"

"Not all, I hope," Fleur teased, but Rosemary bubbled on, ignoring the irony. "Well, naturally, I didn't say anything that would compromise you. After all, what are friends for?" In the hall, Fleur's art director was tapping his watch, glowering. Christ, she was late for a meeting.

"Yeah, I got it, Rosemary. Weekend of the twenty-fifth. I'll call and tell you what train to meet. Meanwhile, I've got to run."

"And look gorgeous," Rosemary said. "That's an order."

"I'll do my best."

Up in the conference room, the entire Saraband group had already assembled. The creative director was holding the floor.

"They want our warm bodies out in Pittsburgh a week from Friday," Scott Matthews said, looking as if he had swallowed a poison pill. "At which time they expect a complete presentation. Product names, copy lines, visual concepts, marketing plans. They've been doing their own research into perfume launches and have come up with several guidelines that we should all keep in mind. First of all, they want a one-word product name. A noun, ideally, like Opium, Obsession, Poison—"

"Shit!" someone murmured.

"Yes, that's a noun, although an adjective like 'Beautiful' will also be considered. Second," he went on grimly, "they want to position this—let's call it No Name for the time being—as an American fragrance. What with the 'new patri-otism' that's making the rounds, they don't want it coming off as French or Italian, nothing too elitist. They may ultimately decide to go downscale, K mart rather than Saks. They reserve that option. One way or another, our message will be, this product is born in the U.S.A."

"Springsteen!" Fleur suggested. "It fits all the requirements."

"Or Hoboken. Bottled at last! The unique odor of the New Jersey Turnpike. Now you're talkin' American."

"How about AIDS—so good, it's contagious," someone piped up.

"AIDS is African, not American, you jerk."

"Yeah? Try telling them that down in the Village."

"How about Sneakers! You couldn't get more downmarket than that!"

"And they've got a distinctive aroma too!"

"Okay." Scott waited for the babble to subside. "Now that you've all had your little giggle, back to business. For the record, I don't like working under this kind of restriction any more than you do, but those are the breaks of the game. And you must all remember that No Name is part of a hundred-million-dollar account. So keep the worst scenario in mind. Which brings me to point three. The advertising must be clean, in keeping with middle-America morality. Those orgy commercials for Obsession have brought in a lot of flack—"

"Brought in a lot of bucks too," said Ginny from Marketing.

"—so there is to be no depiction"—Scott permitted himself a smile—"of 'unabashed eroticism,' otherwise known as nooky."

An angry murmur rippled through the room.

"Gimme a break!" Art Gringold groaned. "Fucking sells perfume, always has, always will. Rule One: Wear this and you'll get laid."

"And No Name happens to be a very sexy scent," Fleur said. "My worry is, the stuff will wind up looking like a disinfectant. Lysol, for God's sake. 'Wear No Name and you won't catch anything—least of all a man.' What a downer!"

"The whole thing sucks! Okay?" Eddie Carducci stood up. He was Fleur's art director, wildly gifted in everything but self-expression, and still young enough to have ideals about advertising. "I mean we're the ones who are the experts. Okay? That's what they pay us for, our smarts, our savvy. Okay? We don't have to take this kind of crap from anyone. What are we, an ad agency or a whorehouse?"

"A whorehouse. Okay?" Scott smiled pleasantly. "Any more questions? Good. Then back to work. We'll have a creative review next Monday, take a look-see where we are, and everything's got to be on the Pittsburgh plane Thursday night. Including you all."

Consuma-Corp's headquarters was a stone fortress in the old business district of Pittsburgh. It had been modeled after a somber Sforza palace. All that was lacking (Fleur passed a note) was dungeons.

"I wouldn't bet on that," Eddie scribbled back.

God! she was bored. Bored. Bored. Bored.

For six solid hours they had been locked up in this vast,

overheated conference room furnished in Hollywood-heroic style with oaken seats that grew harder by the minute. Her ass was numb. And her mind wasn't doing so well either. The steam heating was enough to kill.

They were seven from Marsden-Baker pitted against two dozen people from Consuma-Corp. It was impossible not to think of the day as a battle, the client as the enemy. Through glazed eyes, Fleur surveyed their number.

There was McWimp with his underlings. Edna Royce of Nasal-Decongestant fame with her partisans. ("Edna and the Sinuses," Fleur muttered, and felt better.) Two product managers. One brand manager. One director of future planning—this title fascinated Fleur. Was it possible to plan for the past? And enthroned at the head of the table was the squat figure of Chairman Lewis J. Gibbs, liver-lipped, bald head shining as though epoxied, clenching a dank unlit cigar between his teeth. When one reached a certain level of wetness, he squashed it in an ashtray and took another. Fleur recognized the symptoms.

Oh the nightmare of dealing with people who'd just given up smoking! she grieved. Gibbs was brusque to the point of abuse.

Hours earlier the Creative Department had made its pitch. A list of over two hundred possible product names had been submitted, a favored six developed in detail.

Among Fleur's contributions was Fun.

"It meets all their criteria," she had said when presenting it to Scott the Monday before. "And it's a name you can have a lot of—well, a lot of fun with, as far as copy lines go. 'Ain't We Got Fun.' 'Put Some Fun in Your Life.' Go upscale, downscale. Get racy if you want to. Maybe show a gal dabbing some of the stuff on her thighs. 'The Best Place to Have Fun Is—' "

"Watch it, Fleur."

"Yeah, yeah. Anyhow, Eddie and I have been developing a visual of a laughing long-haired blonde, dancing on a meadow full of balloons. Very light, very airy. In feel, she'll be an update version of the gal in the Charlie ad, only even swingier—sunnier."

Once Scott gave the go-ahead to develop the concept, she and Eddie had worked around the clock. They had completed it on the plane coming in.

At a pre-meeting meeting that very morning, Scott had

decided to lead from strength. "Start with yours, Fleur. He sees the rest of the shit, maybe Fun'll look better," Scott grumbled.

"Well, thanks for your enthusiasm," she said tartly. "What the fuck can they expect on one week's notice?"

An hour later she made the presentation while Lewis J. Gibbs chomped his cigar to a pulp.

"Fun," she announced, then held up a red-and-white logo.

"Fun?" he read. "That's supposed to be a name for a perfume?"

"Yes, sir," Fleur said and went into a five-minute speech on the concept, the marketability of fun. How it was right on target with the new "lite" way of thinking, a life-style that was already changing American's habits in beverages, ice cream, even personal relationships.

It was spiel, pure malarkey, but she was good at it. Not good enough however for Lewis J. Gibbs, however, who listened with barely restrained impatience, shifting his cigar back and forth in his mouth. Lewis J. was not a "fun" person.

"Okay, toots," he said. "Show me the ad."

With a flourish, Eddie went to the easel and flipped back the protective sheet.

"It's a girl—" Fleur began to explain.

"I got eyes."

She shut up while he examined the visual. No one uttered a sound.

"How come the balloons don't break?" he said.

The visual wasn't to be taken literally, Fleur began, but Gibbs interrupted.

"Stoopid. A girl walks on balloons, the balloons are gonna break. That's stoopid. Okay, what else ya got to show me?"

And so it had gone, from that hour to this. Every creative idea they had presented was shot down, then trampled upon for good measure. Now the discussion had turned to marketing proposals. It was an area that Fleur knew little of and cared less about, a matter for technicians. She was bored, bored, bored.

The marketing people were pulling out their charts, arguing back and forth in that strange jargon incomprehensible to all but themselves. To Fleur this was always the worst part of these marathon meetings. You had done your number, yet you couldn't escape. You were expected to sit there, attentive, dutifully pretending to take notes on the profundities uttered.

By her side, Eddie was doodling on a scratch pad. Dogs, she noticed. Irish setters. Poodles. Great Danes. After a while he switched to cats. Occasionally, she would scribble him a note. Some were funny, some obscene—anything to break the pattern of boredom.

"Help," she lettered, "I am being held captive by Wimpettes on the thirteenth floor of Consuma-Corp."

She showed it to Eddie. He smiled. Then she crumpled it up and slipped it into her pocket. She wished to hell she could draw too, but even her stick figures managed to look like quadruple amputees.

Instead, she daydreamed about the forthcoming weekend. For the dozenth time, she mentally went through her wardrobe, finally decided on her flame-colored charmeuse with a voluminous skirt. Perfect for Saturday night. Alex had never seen it before (they went to so few public places!) and the color was sumptuous on her. By comparison, Rosemary was sure to look dowdy. What the hell, Rosemary *was* dowdy.

Fleur plotted the outfit—shoes, makeup, even stockings, but there was something missing. All the glitter in that dress was at the waistline. It would be lost over a dinner table. She needed—oh yes! she needed dazzling earrings. Long. Maybe even brushing the shoulder. Rhinestones were a thought, or else a tumble of silver.

If only this goddamn meeting were over, she'd scoot over to Kaufmann's before the store closed and pick something up. She tried to recall if jewelry was on the ground floor. In and out, that's all. It would only take a few minutes.

A heavyset woman began distributing thick mimeographed files down the length of the table.

"Hot in here!" Gibbs grumbled. A flunky leaped to open windows.

"Okay, now," Gibbs said. "Let's get down to business."

With sinking heart, Fleur looked at the file. Marketing Forecasts it was entitled. The fucking thing was eighty pages long. Charts. Graphs. Columns of tiny figures the size of fly specks.

She was going to die in this room! Die of ennui, of old age. Moreover, she would die single—an ancient, shriveled crone who had lost her one chance of happiness, forfeited the man of her dreams because she didn't have the right earrings for her flame-colored dress.

"Page one," someone announced. Thirty files flipped open simultaneously. Another hour went by of people talking numbers, the ennui broken only by an occasional trip to the coffee urn. Three o'clock became four o'clock and more than half the report still lay ahead. How late was Kaufmann's open anyhow?

A little before five, Fleur rose and went for coffee again, then stood by the window for a breath of air. Goddamn! She was going crazy in there. Another hour and she'd be foaming at the mouth. What was she doing there anyhow? She should be somewhere with Alex. Making love. Or sunning in Acapulco. Or both. She looked at the table. Thirty aching bottoms glued to torture-chamber chairs. Sixty bloodshot eyes trained on flyspecks.

God forbid she spend another hour there. She felt trapped, helpless like an insect in amber. Drastic measures were called for. Ideally, the sudden death of Lewis J. Gibbs. And no jury would ever find her guilty. She had nothing to lose but—? But what? The worst scenario, as Scott would say, would be that she got canned and Alex would come to her rescue. Not such a tragedy after all!

She fished the crumpled paper from her suit pocket, placed it on the ledge, then returned noiselessly to her seat.

Minutes later, a squad of Pittsburgh's finest burst into the conference room, guns drawn.

"Okay, what's going on here?" a burly officer barked. "Someone being held against their will?"

Fleur looked as astonished as everyone else.

For the next ten minutes, pandemonium reigned, and by the time the police were assured that it was a practical joke ("Some dumbo secretary, I suppose," Future Planning remarked. "If I find her, I'll have her ass"), the meeting had lost its impetus.

"Okay," Gibbs growled. "Let's call it a day."

In the elevator down, Fleur was jammed up against Scott. "You're skating pretty close, Fleur," he said. His eyes were knowing.

"Who—*moi*?" She smiled, then escaped into the street.

By six, she was examining the contents of Kaufmann's jewelry counter. The place was a find, another Bonwit's, with dozens of scrumptious things to choose from. She wavered between long silver swirls and a huge coral clip. "I don't know," she said, smiling at the salesgirl. The salesgirl smiled back.

"Decisions, decisions," Fleur said. "I'll have to think about it."

The saleswoman stifled a yawn and looked at her watch, which was all the time Fleur needed to slide the silver earrings into her purse. "Thank you," she murmured.

And thank you, Kaufmann's. She laughed once she was safely out on the street. Anyhow, what could happen? Worst scenario: Kaufmann's wouldn't allow her to shop there anymore. Big deal.

Because if all worked well, she would never have to set foot in Pittsburgh again. Never ever!

Westport, Connecticut, here I come.

FIFTEEN

He was educated. Successful. Clever. Urbane. And (if televised pictures didn't lie) handsome in the bargain.

Bernie's first reaction was "If he's so great, why isn't he married?" But he provided the most acceptable of reasons.

"That one!" She handed the cassette back to her consultant at The People People. "I want to meet that one."

"Splendid, because he's dying to meet you."

Yes, that one, she repeated a few days later when Roger Knowland appeared at her door.

Lean and muscular, with fine, even features and a head of blue-black hair, he was even handsomer in the flesh than on tape. He wore a beautifully cut suit, banker's gray, as evidence of serious intentions, and carried a bouquet of roses.

"You said in your videotape that you considered yourself an independent woman. I hope that doesn't mean you'll be offended by my bringing you flowers."

"Not at all," Bernie said, delighted. "It's nice to know that chivalry lives on. Would you like to come in for a drink?"

He smiled. He had wonderful teeth. "I thought you'd never ask."

Some men live by dreams. Some live by plans. Roger Ellis Knowland was one of the latter. Born thirty-five years earlier in Oklahoma City, he had grown up in comfortable circumstances. His father was an insurance executive, his mother sold real estate, and both parents had inculcated those values in their son that would ensure success in adult life. The "three P's," his mother called them: patience, precision, planning. To which she might have added pragmatism, for even as a child Roger manifested a talent for finding the shortest route between any two points. Theory didn't interest him. Results did. Given a head for mathematics, a taste for achievement, and a nose accustomed to the grindstone, he distinguished himself at MIT, graduating near the top of the class, then earned his master's at Carnegie Tech.

"Lucky for me the Vietnam War was over in time," he said. "That would've really thrown a monkey wrench in my plans."

After college he joined the firm of SI (Systems International) and was sent overseas as a technical consultant. "Two years in Brunei, setting up computerized drilling systems, one in Qatar, another in Nigeria, and the last three in Saudi Arabia." Within SI they were known as "shit locations" but, as Roger explained, as in the army or the Diplomatic Corps, if you expected advancement, you had to put in hard time. Moreover, it was a "learning experience."

He had a lot of respect for the Saudis, he said. They were shrewd businessmen. Fast learners. "But the downside of it was there was no social life there. Nothing going on culturewise either. Not that I'm big on poetry, that sort of thing. Still, I could have done with some singles bars, an occasional Broadway show. The nightlife was zilch. They have religious police, you know, patroling everybody's morals and the Saudis don't kid around. Just a bottle of booze could get you a jail sentence. And forget about a sex life!" Many of his colleagues had broken the rules with frequency, but he had preferred to play it cool. Why risk deportation or worse for a few hours of fun?

"Besides which," Bernie observed, "it's *their* country."

"I suppose. But more to the point, SI takes a very dim view when any of its people act up. It's the end of the line within the firm. What the hell!" He laughed. "The local ladies weren't that much of a temptation to begin with."

"Sounds like Boy Scout Camp," she marveled. "How did you manage to survive?"

He had played tennis, read a lot, then every six weeks

he'd gone to London for a week of R and R. "Wine, women, and a chance to see some new movies," he said with resigned good nature. "After which, back to Saudi and cold showers."

Now, however, those years of servitude were being rewarded with a fast-track job in the home office. No more road, no more flies and desert heat: henceforth, his career would be in New York. Until now, his personal life had been on hold; he was ready to make up for lost time. To marry. Raise a family. And rise within the firm.

He had picked his slot carefully "I wanted to be in a department where my boss wasn't too young, because I don't want to grow ancient waiting for promotion. But not too old either, because I don't want him retiring before I'm ready to step into his shoes. As it is, things look good. If all goes according to plan, I should make VP by 1990, senior VP by 1995, after which it's a hop, skip, and jump to the board." He paused and gave an apologetic shrug. "I imagine this sounds awfully calculating to a creative person like you, Bernie, that kind of long-range planning. It's very different in your business, I suppose. More volatile—"

"Unh-unh." She shook her head. "No apology necessary. When it comes to career building, I couldn't be more sympathetic." Strategic planning had just won her a regular niche on the show and an office of her own. She confided how she had fooled Hy Feinstein. "I held them up with a little toy gun, and they never even knew they were being robbed."

"Smart lady."

"Thanks. You know something funny? I started at WHIZ about the same time you joined your company. So we've both put in our seven years' hard labor."

"Like Jacob in the Bible," Roger said.

"Of course Jacob was sweating out a wife."

But then, she acknowledged, so was Roger.

He proved a most attractive companion, wonderfully presentable and with a taste for romantic settings. They had gone dancing at the Rainbow Room, taken carriage rides in Central Park, drunk champagne on the Staten Island Ferry, seen the dawn in with onion soup at the Brasserie.

"How'd you get to know New York so well?" she asked.

"I boned up on it when I was out in Saudi. You'd be surprised what you can learn from books."

He always arrived suitably dressed, with the evening's entertainment all thought out. His choice of restaurants was not to be faulted, his surprises meticulously timed. Yet despite the elements of calculated fun (Bernie recognized a romance-by-the-book when she saw one), Bernie enjoyed his company. Roger made her feel good about herself. Important. He sent flowers every time she broadcast live. He laughed at her jokes.

After Steve's breezy ways, she found it a relief to be treated as a personage. To be listened to with both ears. To be "rushed" like a deb at a ball.

It was a whirlwind courtship, Bernie told herself, right out of a movie. And if the scenes seemed to have been right out of a script, that was all right too, because within a matter of weeks, Bernie knew what the final fade would be. A two-shot. Bernie and Roger riding off into the sunset. Soft focus. Music up. Dissolve. End credits.

One day she took Roger to the studio, showing him off to her colleagues and vice versa. He made an excellent impression throughout.

"Wow!" said Bea Zimmerman. "Are there any more at home like him?"

"Go find your own," Bernie replied.

In every respect, Roger passed muster. Considerate, attentive, with the kind of deportment you could bring home to Mother, he was also possessed of a self-deprecating humor that kept him from the brink of pomposity. "You know me, Bernie," he'd say when she teased him about the conventionality of his views. "I'm all-American white bread."

Then without warning, everything came to a standstill, leaving Bernie profoundly puzzled.

From their first date on, Roger had charted a relentless forward course. Night One, a chaste brush of lips. Night Two, several pecks and a hug. On their third date, it was tongues. On the fourth, breast fondling.

Thus by calibrated stages, they had reached as serious a state of body exploration as could be conducted fully dressed. In numerous ways Bernie indicated her willingness to proceed, but Roger had inexplicably gone into Neutral. Neither an offer of sex nor of marriage seemed forthcoming.

What had gone wrong? Bernie was perplexed. Was he

concealing a deformity? Was he gay? Diseased? Or—the thought chilled her—was there somebody else?

They dated twice during the week and every Saturday night. When he didn't see her, he phoned. But that didn't really signify anything. There could be a Monday-Wednesday-Friday woman too. For although Roger had been *hors de combat* all those years in the Middle East, here in New York he was hot property.

On those occasions when marriage had been discussed— marriage in general, not marriage to each other—he had spelled out his criteria. His future wife had to be attractive, resourceful, independent, sociable, and committed to their relationship. Bernie felt she met those criteria; moreover, that he met hers. Yet the romance had reached an impasse. It was mortifying.

Only the week before, she had boasted of him at the Karnak. "A real catch"—her voice rang with triumph—"and he's crazy about me." Her friends had been avid for details.

"How soon can I meet him?" Rosemary trilled, and then had gone on to invite the loving couple to a weekend in Westport. "Fleur will be there, plus someone for her. Maybe you'll be able to announce your engagement."

But Bernie had demurred. She had no intention of letting Fleur inspect this piece of precious cargo before he was securely stowed. Another week or two, she figured.

Then, inexplicably, Roger had stopped his advance. Was it something she had said? Or done? If she had somehow offended him, he could either complain or cut and run. But he had done neither.

Then early that week, she divined a clue to his behavior. It had snowed that day, and coming out of her apartment building, Roger scooped up a handful of snow and lobbed it at her.

"Good shot!" she said.

"You're seeing me at my best," he said, giving her an odd smile. "In spring I'm a total wreck. Terrible hay fever. April, May, I'm a wipeout. But other than that, Bernie, you're looking at a healthy animal. Yep. I can assure you a clean bill of health."

Did she imagine it, or was there a message in this some-where? She thought about it the next day at work.

"A clean bill of health." The phrase was no accident. Roger did most things by design. Of course! she realized. He expected a clean bill of health from her.

Before royal marriages, she recalled, the bride would be inspected by a physician, then given a paper testifying to her virginal state. Well, virginity wasn't part of the social contract anymore, but a man might have other questions he wanted resolved. Especially in this era of AIDS and lesser diseases. If this was the sole impediment—

Then one night soon after that, they were dining at a smoky bistro on Spring Street. In the dark they couldn't see each other's eyes. It was a café designed for lovers' secrets.

"Roger?" she murmured when the brandy came.

"Yes, Bernie." He was running his fingers along her inner wrist. At the far end of the room, the pianist played a Cole Porter medley.

She leaned across the table and whispered something in his ear.

"You didn't have to do that."

"If you'd like, I'll show you the blood test. It's in my bag."

His answer was to slide his hand sensually up her arm. Then he bent over and kissed her open palm.

"You're a remarkable woman, Bernie."

"Thank you. You're pretty special yourself."

"One more question." He laughed softly. "Tell me, do you believe in sex before marriage?"

"Absolutely!"

"And after marriage too?"

Bernie gave a delighted squeal. "What the fuck are we sitting around here for, Rodge. Let's get the bill and go home."

Roger, who was good at everything—at math, at tennis, at work—was excellent in bed. He was skilled and thorough, with the endurance of a marathon man.

She caressed his firm buttocks. "God! You have a beautiful body."

"You too. Just great. Now roll over, sweetheart, and place your legs just so."

A half hour later, she lay winded in his arms.

"Don't tell me you boned up on *that* in Saudi Arabia." She sighed.

"Perfumed Garden." He gave her a playful punch in the ribs. "The illustrated edition, page eighty-six. What else could I do on those long desert nights?"

Around about dawn, they became officially engaged.

SIXTEEN

The Marshall house bore the distinction of being one of the few in the neighborhood without a name.

"That's Fourwinds," Rosemary informed Fleur on the winding drive back from the station, "and that big Gothic heap is called Kenilworth, which I think is kind of pretentious since the people who own it made their money in the rag trade."

Fleur devoured every detail, seeing the town as though for the first time, for Westport was now endowed with Alex's magic, the place she might soon be calling "home."

She didn't know if the houses they were passing qualified as "estates" except in the inflated parlance of real estate ads, but, for all the eclecticism of their styles, each conveyed an aura of wealth and stability. "Here to stay," their façades announced. Through bare trees, one glimpsed hints of summer pleasures: swimming pools now covered for winter, tennis courts, occasionally a stable. Private fantasies translated into the reality of glass and cedar and fieldstone.

Fleur looked at them with violent longing. She would have this white Greek revival with its Doric columns. No, the pretty Tudor with the greenhouse—As far as the eye could see, beauty reigned, poverty was vanquished. People here were happy, she could tell.

How different this seemed to her from Waterville where she had grown up. To her, the two towns might have stood at opposite ends of the world. Waterville was grim, industrial, populated by hardscrabble New Englanders and the despised French Canadian laborers (her father and a series of "stepfathers" among them) who had drifted in to work at the textile mills. In its day Waterville had boasted a few such spacious estates—the "houses on the hill"—but its day had passed. The factories moved south, the lovely houses had fallen into disrepair, the central city abandoned to decay. On the street where she had grown up, the houses were drab and utilitarian—narrow wooden structures divided into railroad flats, each with its screened-in "piazza" where laundry was hung out to dry, each with its weary linoleum in the halls.

Even as a child, Fleur had longed to escape. Her daydreams would transport her to wherever it was one might find music and laughter and pretty clothes. Life as it was in the romantic movies, in the television commercials—those same glossy commercials she herself now wrote. At first New York had fulfilled her expectations—the streets paved with sequins, so to speak. But lately the glamour had begun to pall. The city had grown menacing, even dangerous. The music had moved on.

Riding through the streets of Westport, she felt like a visitor from the third world, poor and piteous. Ten years of hard work had achieved nothing of permanent value: no home, no property. For all the cachet of an East Side address, she still lived in a railroad flat, smaller in fact than the one in Waterville, although considerably more expensive. This was progress?

Rosemary chattered on, a font of information about the houses, their owners, about fortunes both inherited and made. "That one, Springview, is a real showplace—with the most marvelous azaleas. Hence the name. If you had a country house, Fleur, what would you call it?"

"Mine."

"I beg your pardon."

"I said," Fleur repeated slowly, "I would call it Mine."

"I see." Rosemary giggled. "That's a name. Very witty. You should use your copy-writing savvy and think up a name for ours."

She stopped at an intersection, her capable hands in buttery leather driving gloves resting lightly on the wheel.

"You drive very well," Fleur observed.

"Thank you. Of course you can't survive here without a car. You drive, don't you, Fleur?"

"Nope. Never learned how."

"Really! Good Lord! I thought everyone drove, though I suppose there's not much point having a car if you live in Manhattan. I understand garages cost a fortune."

Rosemary turned down her street while Fleur pondered her remark. No, she had never owned a car, never had a license. That summed up the difference between Fleur and the gentlefolk of this world. It was the hole in her education, the gaping void that marked her as a born "have-not." She was a passenger, rather than a participant in life. Monday, she vowed, back in Manhattan, she'd arrange for driving lessons first thing. After all, you couldn't live out here without a car. . . . She had visions of meeting Alex each evening at the station.

"You're very broody," Rosemary remarked as they pulled into the drive.

Fleur felt a stab of guilt. "I'm sorry. How boorish of me. I promise not to be a grouch."

She stepped out of the car and looked up at the Marshall house with its half-timbering and red-tiled roof. A French farmhouse about forty miles from New York. That was fantasy too. Half a million dollars of real estate, Fleur marveled, so that Rosemary, like a latter-day Marie Antoinette, might masquerade as a storybook peasant.

Fleur smiled. "Call it Trianon," she said.

In the doorway, Alex was waiting.

They spent the afternoon being rustic, first a tramp through the woods (to Fleur's horror, those elegant suede boots that had cost a fortune at Ferragamo's were ill designed for this kind of use), then back to the house for what Rosemary called "defrosting": drinks and a roaring fire.

"The beard," as Fleur had designated Lloyd Hageman, proved to be a short, stocky fellow, polite and self-assured, although Fleur found it hard to work herself up into a romantic lather over someone who wore plaid pants and mined a living from gum disease. Far more interesting was the chance to observe Alex in his role as host and husband.

He knew his duties—the hanging up of coats, the mixing of drinks, the filling-in of conversational lacunae.

"Here we go!" he said, helping Fleur off with her sodden boots. "I'll put these in the sun-room to dry."

She snatched at the fleeting intimacy of his hand on her calf. "Not the proper shoe for a walk in the woods."

"Country mouse, city mouse," he said amiably, while Rosemary began trotting out hors d'oeuvres.

Fleur watched them closely, a tyro eager to pick up tips from seasoned pros. Whatever the reality of their private life, when it came to the care and feeding of guests, the Marshalls operated as a team. A tiny nod, the merest exchange of glances sufficed to determine who did precisely what and when. Years of marriage had produced a detailed division of labor, a seamless schedule of amenities. Fleur had come, half-hoping to see conflict, a household ringed with tension, a clash of temperaments, a domestic tantrum or two. Instead, she was watching the perfect functioning of a well-oiled machine.

Fleur began to grow depressed. How very much married Alex was! She could hardly trust her own memory. Was this domesticated creature the same wildman who had fucked her so well and so often? Today, his behavior was meticulous. She kept waiting for some clue, some mark of favor. Would she even have the chance to steal a kiss?

While Rosemary fussed in the kitchen, five-year-old Chris came into the living room, proud bearer of a tray of stuffed mushrooms. "Our unpaid help." Alex grinned. "Now what can I get you people to drink?"

"Do you think"—Fleur made a pointed reference to that night in Pittsburgh, willing him to make the same response— "I might have a margarita?"

But Alex smiled without blinking. "I imagine my skills are up to the challenge. Lloyd?" Then he went on to mix a drink for his wife, bourbon and water, no ice. There was no need to poll Rosemary.

"I'll bring it in to her." Fleur snatched Rosemary's glass and escaped to the kitchen. She should never have come. It was a strategic mistake. The comparisons she had sought to make in Alex's mind seemed to be weighing unexpectedly in Rosemary's favor. She discovered her hostess taking a tray of tiny quiches out of the oven.

"Have a piece of my zucchini bread. It's still warm." Rosemary put the steaming tarts on a cooling rack. "So, what do you think of Lloyd Hageman?"

Fleur, in a state of misery and awe, grunted a noncommittal answer. Rosemary's kitchen was an extraordinary place. The smells were marvelous—fresh herbs, melted cheese, shallots sautéing in a copper pan. Better than No Name perfume and probably far more potent with men. She wandered around the room, nibbling on a piece of bread, picking things up, then putting them down, often without a clue as to their function. Not only was Fleur Chamberlain incapable of running a car, she realized, but she couldn't even run a kitchen. Absentmindedly she cut another slice of warm bread. It was delicious.

The quest for Alex was lost, had probably been doomed from its inception. Diane was right. They never *do* leave their wives, let alone such exquisitely comfortable ménages.

What on earth had got into her—other than Alex Marshall's cock—to make her betray one of her oldest friends? For a guilt-ridden moment, she was tempted to blurt out everything, to lay her secrets bare and beg absolution. She was sorry, an inner voice cried. Sorry to be sleeping with Rosemary's husband. Sorry for herself as well.

I'm a shit, she wanted to blubber. *Please . . . forgive me.*

Instead, out of nervousness, she picked up a small wooden rectangle. On its front, a little angel was incised. "What's this, Rosemary, a Christmas decoration?"

"It's an antique butter mold," Rosemary said. "We got it in France last summer."

"Lovely." Her voice reeked of longing. "You have such beautiful things."

"I didn't know you were interested in all this domestic stuff."

"You get older, you get smarter." Fleur sighed.

"Well, you know"—Rosemary sat down at the counter with her drink—"you could do worse than Lloyd Hageman, although I don't think he'll be easy to land. By local standards he's a catch, there's such a dearth of men out here. Soon as anyone is divorced or widowered, they're practically deluged with invitations to this and that. Everyone's got an unmarried sister or daughter or—like me and you—an old school friend. The competition is fierce. You were lucky he could come on such short notice."

"*I* was lucky?" Did she imagine it, or was Rosemary's phrasing intentionally offensive? Fleur swallowed her rising

gorge. "In any case, I don't think your 'catch' is very interested in me."

"Then make him interested! Flirt a bit. Play up to him.
You used to be so good at it. I got him here just for you.
Honest to God," she said with a barely disguised satisfaction, "I never thought the day would come when I'd be
fixing *you* up with a Saturday night date. My, my, times
have changed."

Bitch!

Fleur gaped at her, thunderstruck. No doubt about it,
Rosemary was smirking. Luxuriating in this reversal of
roles, this long-awaited revenge. Revenge was the purpose
of this weekend, Fleur surmised. Revenge for all of Rosemary's dateless nights back in Smith, for all the young men
Fleur had so casually passed along. For an ancient and
largely imaginary loss of face.

Bitch!

And to think that Fleur had actually felt sorry for the
woman and nearly begged for forgiveness. One look at
Rosemary's face was enough to vanquish all thought of
remorse.

Yes, she would have Alex Marshall for her very own.
Tonight. Beneath his wife's nose. As for the first Mrs.
Marshall, Rosemary would have a lifetime to regret that
awful smirk.

Rosemary checked the wooden wall clock. "We'd better
be getting dressed. You want to look special for tonight."

"Thank you, Rosemary," Fleur murmured.

"For what? Introducing you to Lloyd?"

"For reminding me of my priorities."

They were to be eight at dinner, two local couples having
been invited to camouflage the fact that Lloyd was the
target for tonight.

Fleur had primped for an hour before descending in a
cloud of flame Charmeuse and No Name. The effect, to
judge even by Chris's reaction, was electrifying. There was
a moment of silence as she entered the living room, then—
"Yum!" The little boy buried his head in the layers of
silk. "You look yummy!" He wrapped his arms around
her legs, his eager nose practically nestling in her pudenda.
"And you smell so nice. Double yum!"

Rosemary gave an embarrassed titter while Alex made some psuedogallant remark about the privileges of childhood.

"Now say nighty-night to everyone," Rosemary said quickly, "then off to bed."

At dinner Fleur found herself seated between Lloyd and a neighbor named either William or Wilson or Willard. A few feet away Alex sat achingly out of reach. If only he would send her a sign, some private acknowledgment that of all those present, he and Fleur shared a special relationship. Instead, he acted the meticulous host, pouring wine, meting out his attention to all guests in equal part, smiling at everyone's bad jokes.

The food was brilliant, the conversation more mundane, focusing as it did upon local property values, country club gossip, and the relative merits of various prep schools. At last, those topics exhausted, the talk switched to the news of the day.

"I bow to no one in my admiration for the president," announced William/Willard/Wilson heatedly, "but this hostage business has gone too far. You can't negotiate with terrorists. I say we ought to stop pussyfooting around and nuke the lot of them. What do you think, Alex?"

Alex caught Fleur's eye.

"I think we should invade," he answered evenly.

"Invade Iran?" someone said.

"Invade. Cream them," he replied. "Full-scale assault. Go in there and make them holler uncle."

"A sneak attack?" Fleur's heart did a flip-flop.

"Down and dirty," he returned. "No horsing around. I say we hit them tonight with everything we've got."

"Tonight!" she echoed.

"Yep, while the world is sleeping, we penetrate their defenses. Catch 'em napping, vulnerable—and 'bombs away!' After all, are we men or are we mice?"

Yes! She shivered with delicious anticipation. There could be no mistaking that signal. The erotic possibilities were infinite. Even sitting across the table, she could feel his heat, his strength, his sexual drive. Yet his face revealed nothing.

She matched his blandness. "Is that prudent? Such a flagrant violation. I mean, that kind of thing could start World War Three."

"The hell with prudence," Alex responded. "Time to act.

Get in there and bang the bejesus out of them!" He returned to his key lime pie.

"Gosh, honey!" Rosemary exclaimed. "I didn't know you were such a hawk."

"Wow!" Fleur was equally breathless. "I'm impressed. But what I want to know, Alex, is—do we have the balls to do it?"

"Oh, we do," Alex wiped a smear of whipped cream from his lips. "We surely do. God bless America."

The party broke up around midnight with a good deal of neighborly pecking, though Lloyd Hageman neglected to ask for Fleur's phone number.

"Turn in, Fleur," Rosemary urged. "You must be exhausted, all this country air. Alex and I will just load the dishwasher and that's it. Everything else can wait till morning."

The guest bedroom was charming, decorated in a theme of fruit and flowers. From the floral trim of the wallpaper to the painted wooden fruit in a majolica bowl to the carved finials of the four-poster bed, the room was a garden of earthly delights.

Every detail that might add to its occupant's comfort had been anticipated. On the night table, Rosemary had put out the current *New York Times* best-sellers (both fiction and nonfiction), a clock radio, and a cluster of hothouse grapes. In the bathroom, thick thirsty towels were laid out in abundance, their tones in shades of shell pink to deep rose. The oaken cupboard offered a selection of shampoos, French hard-milled soaps, hand lotions, body lotions, deodorants, and talc. On the hook behind the door hung a terry cloth robe in the same deep rose as the shower curtain. And for the forgetful guest, a full range of toothbrushes.

Rosemary had talent, Fleur conceded. The room combined the amenities of a grand hotel with the stamp and taste of an individual. No plastic, no polyester—everything was authentic, pleasurable yet solid. Even the fruit, Fleur observed, picking a wooden apple from the pottery bowl. It felt good to the touch. Warm. Smooth. Luscious.

She rubbed it against her cheek, half-trembling. What a life she could have—safe, secure, surrounded by the fruits of the world . . .

There was a knock at the door, then Rosemary poked

her head in. "Checking to see if you're comfy. You have everything you need?"

"More than everything."

Rosemary came in to turn back the bed, ready to plunk down for a dorm-style discussion of life, love, and Lloyd Hageman, when Fleur foreclosed her with a yawn.

"Well, I guess you want some sleep," Rosemary said, "but be sure and shut your door. Shelby likes to roam around at night."

"Who?"

"You know, Shelby, our spaniel." Rosemary giggled. "You wouldn't want to wake up and find a great big hairy thing in bed with you, would you?"

"Sounds kind of kicky," Fleur said. "I hope his bite is worse than his bark. See you in the morning."

She washed, brushed her hair till the static crackled, then lay down naked on the bed. Five minutes later she was sound asleep.

"If you utter a sound, I will kill you."

Fleur awoke with a start, not only terrified but disoriented. It was dark, the room was strange. Where was she? Suddenly a powerful hand was clapped across her mouth, forcing her head down on the pillow. Oh God! She was the victim of a lunatic. Some rapist on the loose. Then she remembered where and who.

Alex! Thank God! The crazy conversation at dinner—and now he had come to make good. Almost instantly, her body changed from defensive to lubricious. She pressed her tongue against his palm. He tasted salty. In the pitch blackness, she heard body movement and wondered what he was up to.

"Now." His lips brushed her earlobe, his urgent whisper pierced her brain. "You know where you are?" She nodded, heart pounding. "Good," he said. "This is the situation. You are a member of the French underground who has been caught behind enemy lines. You possess important secrets, but you must not talk, no matter what they do to you. Your only defense is to pretend that you are mute, that you are incapable of speech. Make a sound, and you give the game away. They will come and torture you. Now close your eyes and lie still."

In a delirious quiver of apprehension, she lay there docilely while he blindfolded her and tied her wrists to the bedpost. "Does that hurt?" She shook her head no. The ties were loose, of some soft and pliant material. Her lingerie perhaps. Through the scented silk of the blindfold (yes, definitely lingerie), she could discern that a light had been turned on low.

"Now," the voice continued, "as you lie there wondering what will happen next, a handsome officer enters the room to conduct the interrogation. He is struck by your beauty, but he does not believe that you are mute. And he has ways of making you talk." Alex laughed softly as the familiar line took on new meaning. "Instead of hurting you, he will make love to you, try to make you cry and moan out of pleasure. But if you use your voice, you are lost. So . . . no matter what he does, no matter how exquisite his caresses, you must maintain complete silence. Once you so much as whimper, he will have achieved total mastery. You understand, *liebchen?* Good."

Pulse racing, she lay there and waited for the inevitable, her body braced and expectant, not knowing where his first touch would land. In the dark, each minute was an infinity. It would be a long night, an erotic one. Knowing Alex, there could be nothing so abrupt as outright rape.

She tried to sense where his vital parts were positioned in relation to her own. Her hands were useless, and in vain she waved her fingers. They fluttered in empty air. Lying there, she had no sense of space or time. For one panicky moment, it occurred to her that he might leave her there, naked and helpless, aroused almost beyond endurance, for as long as he chose.

Then like an electric charge, she felt a strong moist probe force its way between her toes. A tongue? No, not a tongue, for his tongue was elsewhere, the tip of his tongue was licking her navel. Fingers, then. Alex was working oiled fingers between each of her toes in turn with a slow, insistent rhythm, examining each crevice with a deliberate care. Sometimes he would skip one. It threw her off balance. Gradually his hands stretched to enfold her instep, her feet, the sensual rhythm remaining unbroken. Then upward to the hollows of her ankles, the swell of her calves . . .

She lay back in ecstatic suspense, anticipating the route those hands would take—over her thighs, into the tangles of her pubic hair. Then two strong fingers would slip between her labia and caress the secret places. Playfully. Purposefully. He would bring her one stroke short of orgasm, and only then would he enter her—virile, powerful—enter and fuck her roundly. She smothered a cry. Oh, but he knew what she liked. Already, she was liquid with excitement. She spread her legs to welcome him. His hands moved up her calves, rotated her thighs, slid upward to the delta of Venus. And then stopped.

Nothing! Not a caress, not a touch. She heard him move off, and contact was broken. *Oh, God! Alex*, she wanted to scream. *Don't do this to me. Don't leave me like this*. But if she made a sound, he would have won the game. She caught her breath and listened to her heartbeat.

He came back smelling of after-shave and sweat and one ·of those scented unguents in the bathroom. Tenderly he kissed her first on the mouth, then on the neck, his lips settling finally on her breast. Quietly he sucked her nipples, while a lubricated finger worked its way inside her ass. Teeth clenched, she moved with his rhythm. *Dear God, don't stop*, she willed. Every pore was ripe to receive him. Without warning, he pulled away.

Later (how much later?) she started in alarm. Something was brushing against her cheek, light and transient as a moth. His penis? His hand? Then it was gone. She could feel the heat of his body close, very close, but had no notion whether he was above her or below. It was maddening. She strained against the ties to get some sense of his position, but he dodged her flailing legs. Unfair, she wanted to cry. He had all the advantages: sight, strength, mobility. Ah there, there was the touch she had hungered for, the thumb stroking her clitoris, swollen and orgasmic, the fingertips smoothing the puckered walls of her vagina. She felt a pillow being pushed beneath her buttocks and arched her back waiting for the final assault. *Now*, everything within her cried. *Take me now*. She was coming—coming. She bit her lips to keep from shouting. He stopped. All was silence.

This night, Fleur knew, she was going to die. Die or else go mad. His game was to arouse her to the edge of ecstasy and then deny her. It was too cruel, too exciting. Time and again she lay there like a brute animal, while unnamed parts of Alex explored her at will—kissing, probing, sucking, massaging every orifice, every crevice and curve. Beneath this onslaught, her entire body had become an erogenous zone, capable of infinite pleasure, exquisite agony. Never once did he mount her. And never once did she cry out.

At some point, perhaps it was close to dawn, he untied her hands and kissed the soft skin of her wrists. She heard him leave the room, the sound of running water. He was washing up. She lay there, too weary even to think.

He came back and removed her blindfold.

"Enough of this foreplay," he said. "Let's fuck."

Sunday morning, they partook of a boozy brunch: a huge pitcher of mimosas and the previous night's leftovers rewarmed. "You don't mind quiche second time around?" Rosemary asked. "I have a thing about throwing out good food."

The meal over, Alex went outside to do some chores on the property, while Rosemary drove Fleur to the train.

"Thanks for a terrific weekend," Fleur said. "I thoroughly enjoyed myself."

"I'm so glad, sweetie, although I'm kind of disappointed you and Lloyd didn't hit it off. I thought he was so nice."

"Yes, well." Fleur smothered a yawn. "Win some, lose some."

"Was your room all right. You sleep well?"

"Like a babe."

"That's good. I was afraid we might've kept you awake."

"You mean with the dishwasher?"

"Not exactly." Rosemary giggled. "I meant Alex and me. He gets pretty ummm—romantic after parties, all that wine I suppose. And when he gets going—well! You can hear him a mile away."

Fleur's stomach turned. Was Rosemary lying? Being deliberately provocative? Was she crazy? Or had Alex actually come to her bed with Rosemary's juices still upon him? No! The very idea made her nauseous. He wouldn't! He couldn't! Alex adored her, for God's sake. He had some sense of decency!

Alex and Rosemary. Alex and Fleur.

Was such a thing physically possible? she asked herself. Knowing Alex, the answer was yes.

Was it morally possible? That was another question. She preferred to think not, but given the intensity of Alex's fantasy life, his passion for games and novelty, the answer was more equivocal.

Perhaps Alex had been aroused by the prospect of enjoying both wife and mistress in a single night, a single house. Perhaps he had actually planned it that way. Men were peculiar creatures. They had no sense of loyalty—even the best of them.

Behind the wheel, Rosemary hummed a tuneless air. The closed car was stifling. The quiche sat heavy and undigested. Fleur started to sweat.

Alex and Rosemary. Alex and Fleur. Alex and Rosemary and Fleur.

Rosemary turned a sharp corner. Fleur's stomach rebelled.

"Stop the car, please. I'm going to throw up."

Seconds later she was vomiting her guts out into the prized azalea bushes of the Springview estate.

"You all right?" Rosemary asked when she climbed into the car.

Fleur nodded and wiped her lips. "Sorry. Too many mimosas." She fumbled in her bag for a Life Saver. "What the hell! It's probably good for the azaleas. Like mulch."

Later that afternoon as Alex lay stretched out on the couch watching football, Rosemary came in with a peculiar expression. "I've been cleaning upstairs and—something funny."

Alex's antennae were instantly alert. Had Fleur left incriminating evidence? Worse yet, had *he*? With effort he remained motionless, ostensibly absorbed in the game. In his neck, a pulse began to throb.

Rosemary roosted on the arm of a chair, pondering.

"You know that bowl of fruit I have in the guest room? Well, why should you?" she answered her own question. "You're never in there. Anyway, I had some pieces of carved wooden fruit we bought in Pennsylvania last year. Two oranges, three apples, and a banana. I got them to go with the wallpaper. Not expensive either. The fruit, I mean. The wallpaper cost a fortune. I paid, five, maybe six bucks for them apiece. The banana was more, I remember. Anyhow one of them is missing."

"One what, Rosemary? You're not making sense."

"One of the fruits, Alex. A wooden apple. I think Fleur took it. Now why should she do a thing like that?"

"Oh, for Chrissakes." He rubbed his weary eyes, relieved it was nothing serious. "What do you do, take inventory every time a guest leaves? Why don't you count the silver while you're about it?"

"You're so cranky lately," she remarked.

Alex turned his attention back to the game.

"Well, you are," she maintained.

"You're imagining things, Rosie." And that was that.

SEVENTEEN

On Monday morning Diane sat in her office, door closed, phone calls on hold, hunched over a yellow legal pad.

She had drawn a line down the middle, dividing the sheet into columns. On the left she had written "Pros," on the right "Cons." The right-hand column was half-filled in her clear strong script. The left-hand was blank.

It was a technique she had learned from her father, along with how to balance a checkbook, ride a bike, reef in a sail.

Tom Summerfield possessed more skills and blessings than any one man was entitled to. Scion of one of Boston's oldest families, inheritor of both status and wealth, he had, upon leaving Harvard, set out to make another kind of name for himself, as an independent force in the financial community. He succeeded admirably. "Tough" was the verdict on State Street. "Firm but fair" was the description Tom preferred.

He married young ("beneath him," some said), his choice of a bride being the vivacious redheaded daughter of a Waltham physician. From the start, Frances Summerfield knew she had scored a marital coup, and ever mindful of her good fortune, immersed herself in the exact observation of what was and was not done in the upper reaches of Yankee society. Before long, Frances had learned to drop her r's, lengthen her a's, and generally acquire the tastes and prejudices of Boston. The minutiae of rank absorbed her.

"You're more royal than the king," her husband would occasionally twit her, to which she would answer, "Standards have to be maintained, darling. I'm doing it for the clan."

Notwithstanding, theirs was a happy marriage, the big Chestnut Hill house a happy home. And of Tom Summerfield's three wonderful children (two boys and a girl), Diane occupied a privileged place. She had inherited her mother's vivid coloring (though not her social skills), her father's sharp features and keen intellect. Tom adored her to distraction, although he scrupulously maintained that all his offspring held equal sway in his heart.

"Now, princess," he used to counsel, "whatever you want to do when you grow up, you can do it. Whatever you want to be, you can be. Don't be put off by the fiction that because you're a girl, you ought to settle for less. You're as much a personage as your brothers. So remember, only the best of the best is good enough."

At first she thought she wanted to be an investment banker like her father, then a diplomat like her uncle Drew, only later discovering the excitement of law. But one goal was constant from early childhood on: she wanted to marry and have a family of her own. Moreover she knew exactly what was required of a husband. He should be successful, dynamic, elegant, loving, secure, respected.

Tom Summerfield was a tough act to follow.

Diane pondered the lengthening right-hand list. "Cons."

> Difference in age
> Difference in religion
> Difference in background
> Difference in nationality
> Difference in income
> Difference in prospects

She could go on forever. Instead, she pushed the pad from her with an anguished sigh.

Avram's proposal of marriage had shaken her to the core. They had been lying in bed, yesterday morning, amid bagel crumbs and a ravaged copy of the Sunday *Times*, "schmooz-ing" (Avram's word for cozy small talk, surely one of his finest talents), content with the world and each other, when he had launched his thunderbolt.

"I'll be done with Columbia in a few more months," he declared. "I've already spoken with my cousin about a job, so by June I'll be in a position—not to support a wife, exactly, but at least, thank God, to support myself. And I expect you want to continue in your career. So now we can seriously think of getting married—maybe start planning a family."

"But—but—" She could do little more than splutter.

"The difference in age?" he'd finished her sentence. "I know it bothers you. You find it embarrassing. But really, what does it amount to? When I'm ninety, you'll be ninety-six. It's such a trivial matter when you consider all the things we have in common. Music and books, so many basic values. Anyhow, we belong to the same generation. More important, we love each other. We make each other happy. Why shouldn't it always be like that? Just the way it is right now?" He began stroking her cheek.

She pulled away. "Avram! This is hardly the time and place to discuss it."

"You mean because we're in bed?" He laughed. "Well, there are worse places for arriving at decisions, but I re-spect your qualms. I'm not asking for an instant answer, unless of course the answer is yes. Just promise me you'll think about it."

She promised, but in truth the very thought of his offer filled her with panic and guilt.

This dalliance, this crazy infatuation—and what else could it be?—had the makings of an all-out disaster. The fault was hers. She should never have permitted Avram to think they were engaged in anything more than a stopgap affair. An interlude—romantic and enjoyable—that would end once either or both of them found more suitable mates.

But coward that she was, she had encouraged him, led him on, winning his love and his trust, giving her own in return, yet all the while refusing to face the inevitable consequences of such behavior. Avram's offer of marriage was such a consequence.

She felt she had behaved dishonorably. Not only would Tom Summerfield have disapproved of Avram as a son-in-

law (that went without saying); he would also be censori-
ous of Diane. To toy with people's affections, to hold out
hope where there was none was thoughtless or cruel or
both.

At the least, she owed Avram the courtesy of considering
his proposal with the utmost seriousness.

She scanned the "Cons" with a critical eye.

Avram was right. Age was a secondary issue. So too were
the differences of faith and nationality. Neither of them was
observant or flag-waving and, other things being equal,
such obstacles might be overcome. The difference in class
was more troubling. On the one hand, Diane considered
herself a thorough-going egalitarian; on the other, it was
naïve to argue such distinctions did not exist. But even that
might be conquered if Avram were only willing to make
something of himself! If he would find some proper metier,
direct his talents to achieving an eminence of sorts.

He was a man without a résumé, which was understandable in one so young. But he was also a man without a
dream. How could Diane explain to others what she could
hardly explain to herself?

She had teased him once saying he was a "flower child,"
but he hadn't grasped the reference, and on examination it
was false. Avram lacked the idealism, the naïveté that had
characterized the sixties rebels. He had a sharp, sophisticated mind. Moreover, he liked his creature comforts. Yet
his bourgeois habits made the absence of ambition more
baffling. Had he been an aspiring writer, a composer strug-
gling for recognition, it wouldn't matter that he was poor.
At least he would have the status of the artist. She could,
for example, have introduced him (undertaker's suit and
all) to Porter that night at the opera as a young man of
promise, a future Bellow or Stravinsky. Then she herself
would be perceived as a patron of the arts. It was a socially
acceptable role, even in marriage, in a manner that a union
with a cabdriver was not.

He was not competitive. That was the heart of the matter.
Some days earlier they had gone jogging in Central Park,
twice around the reservoir having been the goal. It was a
crisp sunny morning. Halfway through the first lap, Avram
stopped. She halted too, thinking he was winded.

"What's that?" He pointed toward the trees.

"A blue jay," she panted. "It's a common bird in these parts. Come on Avram, we're supposed to be jogging."

But his eyes remained on the bird. "What a magnificent color. I've never seen one before."

Diane tugged at his sleeve. "Avram, you're breaking the rhythm."

"No rush." He fell in with her step. "After all, we're just running around in circles."

He stopped again a little farther on to start up a conversation with a dog walker who sported a political button.

"You go ahead," he said, and waved. "I'll catch up with you. If not, I'll meet you at home."

He arrived forty minutes after her, with fresh croissants and an unrepentant expression. "Interesting fellow," he said of the dog walker. "He believes that Eva Perón isn't really dead but is living undercover in Spain, operating a brothel. That's a new one."

"Terrific," Diane said. "You should have brought him home so we could all discuss the possibilities."

"You're angry that I talked with him," Avram said, "but he was amusing."

"I'm angry," she retorted, "that you waste your time on cranks. We were there to jog, remember? To accomplish something. Twice around the reservoir, we had said."

He viewed her thoughtfully. "I think we differ about the meaning of accomplishment. A matter of semantics. However, if you like we'll go jogging tomorrow, and I won't say a word."

She mulled this over. "You're a snob, Avram, in certain ways. I never realized that before. You seem to think your judgments are more valid, morally superior to—" She paused. She didn't want to say superior to her own. That would have put Avram on the spot. "Superior to those of the vast number of working people in this culture."

He refused to take offense. "Not at all. I think I have the same values as most other people anywhere. I hope to live in peace, have a family, friends, make a reasonable living, enjoy life without harming anybody. That hardly argues moral superiority. They're the most modest of goals. Your problem, Diane—"

"I wasn't aware I had a problem."

He scratched his chin. "Very well. Let me rephrase that. The problem of a great many people who live in this

building, for instance—what is the word for them, yuppies?—
is that they assume their condition is normal. But it's not.
They produce nothing that is either useful or beautiful—
unless money fits that definition. And they don't seem to
enjoy the money very much! What is normal, I ask you,
about working a hundred hours a week, of earning more
than you have time and inclination to spend? It's crazy!
The fellow in 28N, for instance. He's an investment analyst,
something like that. He tells me he's up every morning at
four to see what's happened on the London exchange. He
says this gives him a competitive advantage before he even
sets foot in his office. He rarely comes home before ten at
night, when the Hong Kong market closes, then the cycle
starts all over again. How can a man like that hope to
marry, raise children? Where does he even find time to
date? He's my age, Di, but he has the eyes of an old man.
What's the point of all this frenzy? What purpose is served?
It's another form of going around and around and around
in circles. Like a snake with its tail in its mouth."

She was silent for a long time, close to tears. He had
articulated some of her deepest anxieties. Held a mirror,
not to the precise image of her life, but to what her life
could easily become.

"Does this mean," she said hoping to end the discussion
on a less painful note, "that you don't want to go jogging
tomorrow?"

He came over and kissed her, delighted at the chance to
return to affectionate terms. "Of course I'll go if it will
make you happy. And I promise not to say a word to
anyone."

So much for the "Cons." Diane took up her pencil once
more and poised it over the "Pro" column. But what was
there to put down? What assets were there substantial
enough to offset the weighty list of negatives?

The touch of his hand on her hair. Words spoken in the
heat of passion, endearments murmured over late-night
coffee. Little insights, foolish jokes, small intimacies, shared
secrets, a private language meaningless to everyone but
each other. Avram's lively sense of the absurd, the pretentious.

A few weeks earlier, they had gone to see an off-Broadway
production of Andromache, updated to the Vietnam War.
Above their battle fatigues, the actors wore stark white

masks. "You cannot kill me for I am dead inside," Orestes shouted at one point. In the background a minichorus chanted "dead, dead, dead."

Avram, as always very live inside, began to laugh: first a titter, then a chuckle, then a full-throated roar. Diane caught the contagion. They were escorted from the theater by an angry manager and were still laughing when they hit the street. "I can't take you anywhere." Diane, wiped her streaming eyes, and for the next few days "dead inside" was the byword for everything pompous.

Yet in a way, she couldn't take him anywhere—other than their usual anonymous haunts. Off-Broadway was one thing, Wall Street another. She couldn't, for instance, take him to the annual Slater Blaney dinner dance at the Waldorf, or to a posh country weekend at the Marshalls, or to Boston next month for her parents' anniversary.

Not that Avram would disgrace himself. His manners were good, if informal; he had plenty of charm, and she would see to it that he was dressed for the occasion. No, Avram would survive the ordeal. She might not. What she feared was her own humiliation.

The differences in age, in wealth, in class were so glaring, one might conclude he was little better than a paid companion. Would people think she was so needy that she preyed on the young? Diane—who wouldn't set foot in a singles bar? "Well, well, well"—she could hear the tongues cluck. "How the mighty have fallen."

Yet sometimes she could envision herself and Avram married, living happily—if not in a hut, as the romantics would say, then in a comfortable apartment in Queens. With children, of course. Avram would be wonderful with children. The vision was warm, nourishing.

"*Il est doux, il est bon.*" The lyrics of a tender French song came to mind. He is sweet, he is good. And moreover—

And moreover, on the "Pro" side was the most compelling argument of all. She loved him.

Diane held the pencil against her lip and sighed, shy of actually writing the words as if the very act of notation would make it final. For a moment the dream seemed feasible . . .

Suddenly, there was an angry blast of the intercom, then Frank Merriam was hollering into her ear. "Where the fuck are you, Diane? We've been waiting in the conference room since ten." She glanced at the desk clock: 10:18. "Get your ass down here, pronto. You know, kid, you're hardly ever around when we need you these days. Shape up, okay?"

She spent a long day crowded with meetings concerning the latest development on the Simplexx case. Tuesday she and Byron went to Washington to file for another postponement. Stall, stall, stall was the present legal tactic; it seemed to apply equally well to her own dilemma. The trip was a welcome break from Avram and their problems, although Byron, usually such a pleasant companion, had been in a dour mood throughout.

"Anything wrong, By?" she asked on the ride back from the airport. "You seem troubled about something."

"No—nothing," he growled.

"You and Jim?" she probed, at which point Byron exploded. "Do I ask questions about your personal life?" he snapped. They drove the rest of the way in total silence.

At home, there was a message on her answering machine from Bernadette Hong. "Tomorrow, lunch at the Karnak, twelve-thirty sharp. I've got the scoop of the year."

EIGHTEEN

———•———

"In this corner"—Bernie Hong clasped her hands above her head in the manner of a victorious boxer—"the lightweight champion of the world." On her left hand a solitaire winked brightly. "Winner of this year's Rosemary Marshall Award for Fighting the Good Fight—" She could proceed no further without laughing.

"You did it!" Diane clapped her shoulder.

"You betcha!" came the answer. The reigning champ lowered her arms and submitted her engagement ring for close-range inspection and a suitable number of oohs and ahs. "Rodge and I picked it out yesterday at Tiffany's. Personally, diamonds don't mean a thing to me, outside of their symbolic value—"

"Some symbol!" "Some rock!" "Some people have all the luck!"

"—but my mother is over the moon. And Roger's parents are thrilled too. We called them last night in Omaha. They sound like lovely people. Now all three of you are going to be my bridesmaids, promise?"

There was a hum of happy assent. "Big June wedding?" Rosemary asked, but Bernie shook her head. "We're shooting for April. It's not as if we were kids. And speaking of shooting, my producer thinks maybe we should tie the knot live on TV. Hy sees it as a sort of postscript to that singles story I did last fall. Not that I'd go that route—ticky tacky. Besides which, that singles story's as dead as Calvin Coolidge. Every talk show in the country's raked it over by now,

and I'm ready to move on. *How to get your MRS in NYC.*"
She gave a curt dismissive laugh. "Seems like years ago. Go
figure it would work out the way it did."

"Go figure," Fleur murmured.

Diane, however, was intrigued by the brevity of Bernie's
attention and her assumption that everyone else was equally
bored with the topic. In Bernie's world yesterday's news
was like yesterday's fish, suitable only for disposal. Dead,
dead, dead, as Avram would say.

"Why do you say the story's over?" she asked. "Fleur and
I are just as single now as we were back then. Plus those
theoretical four out of five other women."

"Over for me, I mean." Bernie shrugged and shifted her
attention to more immediate concerns. They would have a
simple church ceremony followed by a champagne breakfast and a brief honeymoon in the Caribbean. Neither of
them could get away for more than a week. Roger and she
were in total accord as to the importance and vitality of
career. Naturally she would keep her maiden name. Separate but equal was the watchword. Already they had started
condo hunting in locations halfway between her TV station
and his office in White Plains. He agreed with Bernie's
mother that the East Village was too scruffy for family life.

"It hurts me to give up the loft," Bernie said. "I love that
old barn. But before I go, I plan to throw one helluva party.
Then it's into the arms of Riverdale respectability. However,
as the whole world keeps telling me, marriage is a compromise."

"You can say that again." Rosemary nodded. "You know,
you have me to thank for all this. If I hadn't suggested a
little friendly competition, you'd probably still be living
with Steve. Well, one down and two to go. Who's next?
You, Fleur? Diane? In every horse race there's win, place,
and show."

"We're not horses," Fleur protested.

"Thoroughbreds." Rosemary smiled.

Diane decided not to bring up her own situation. Compared to Roger Knowland's near-mythic status as a "catch,"
poor Avram was scarcely worthy of mention. Besides, today
was Bernie's day, the limelight all hers.

Yet Diane couldn't rid herself of the idea that Bernie
seemed more in love with the prospect of marriage than the
man himself. "Successful," Bernie kept saying of Roger.

"Suitable. Attractive. Ambitious." That was a far cry from an avowal of passionate love. If there was triumph in her tone, there was remarkably little rapture. This nuts-and-bolts approach troubled Diane.

"And what about Steve?" Diane asked gently. "Does he know you're engaged?"

Several times in recent months, Steve Godwin had phoned Diane, ostensibly as an old friend calling to chat, but clearly out of a need to keep informed of Bernie's progress. She had asked him around for drinks one evening, and he kept her up till three, talking wistfully about "the good old days." She'd felt sorry for the man.

But at the mention of Steve's name, Bernie's voice plunged to subfreezing, and she narrowed her eyes. "Steve had his chance. He could have married me. All he had to do was say the word. Well, maybe with the next woman in his life, he'll be capable of handling commitment. Anyhow, that's his problem—not mine."

The rest of the lunch passed in a flurry of delicious plans: buying furniture, choosing china and silver, the white sales now going on. "What would you like for a wedding present?" Diane asked.

"I'll have to check with Roger."

At one-thirty, Rosemary said her good-byes. "I hate to be the party pooper, but I've got oodles of work. We're shooting a spot for the New York State Tourist Board, and I have to find a spinning wheel somewhere."

"Business is good, I take it?" Fleur asked.

"Booming. I'm employing a neighbor and a part-time bookkeeper, and I'm still shorthanded. I'm thinking of having my mother come to help me. She's got sources you wouldn't believe. Alex says maybe I should incorporate—"

"You mean with him?" Fleur sat up.

"I guess. I don't understand these things"—Rosemary grinned—"simple country girl that I am. In any event, gotta dash."

She stood up and blew kisses at her lunch mates. "Same time next month? And let's see what you two can do for an encore."

That afternoon Fleur couldn't work.

Bernie engaged, just like that! One, two, three—and mission accomplished. Such efficiency left her numb. Not that she begrudged her old friend a fiancé, but Fleur had a paralyzing vision of her own quest losing momentum, of the prize slipping from her hand.

Despite Alex's bedroom fantasies (only yesterday he had Federal-Expressed her a set of sexy black lace lingerie to replace the damage done Saturday night), despite his declarations of love and passion, he had never once mentioned marriage.

Why should he? Fleur asked herself. Why should he choose between chocolate and vanilla when he could continue indefinitely enjoying both flavors? Alex was a two-scoop man. She had hoped the Westport weekend would spur him to action. Instead, it had reinforced the status quo.

Now time was running out. In a matter of months, possibly weeks, if she knew anything about men, the sexual heat would start to cool, the hungry eye to stray. If he wasn't secured by then, the battle was lost. Conceivably their affair might drag on for years with diminishing returns and increasing misery. Or, he might pick up and leave any day. Either way, control was in Alex's hands, along with the keys to her apartment.

It wasn't fair, Fleur brooded. Their entire relationship was riddled with inequities, unbalanced in every way. He could call her in the dead of night. She couldn't call back. They met at his convenience, rarely at hers. She had a vague sensation of being used, being passed from one Marshall to another. Just as Rosemary used to phone her to fill in the vacant evenings, now Alex was doing the same. Fleur felt powerless. How was it that she, a smart professional woman, had got herself into such a bind?

Intellectually, she knew the answer. Love had robbed her of leverage. Emotionally, she was unable to act. The prospect of life without Alex was more than she could bear. Without his love and protection, she was just another graying copywriter on her way to obsolescence. Another candidate for a lonely old age.

Briefly she toyed with the idea of an ultimatum—"Marry me or else!"—but the risks were too great. Alex was not a man to crumple under pressure. "I'm a pretty ballsy guy," he had said once, while describing a business coup, "and nobody shakes me down." Indeed it was this very ballsiness that made him so attractive, and she would be crazy to put his claim to the test. Yet if she did nothing, she would lose him: That much was clear.

All afternoon she puzzled over the problem. At quitting time she called in Ruthie Novak from the secretarial pool.

Ruthie owed her one. Hell, Ruthie owed her a couple of dozen. Fleur had given the girl the key to her apartment at least that many times for lunchtime quickies with the aptly named Bud Alcock in Accounts. And her a married woman! Fleur suppressed a grin. Yes indeed, Ruth Novak could be counted upon to keep a secret.

"Come on in and close the door," she said when Ruthie appeared. "I'd like you to do me a little favor."

"Sure, Fleur."

"Okay, I want you to make a phone call. Here." She scribbled out the number and a message. "Call tonight at ten P.M. sharp and don't wait for an answer. There's nothing to worry about. It's a practical joke. You understand?"

The two women exchanged swift glances.

"I understand," Ruthie said, smirking, "and good luck."

Diane returned to her office to find half a dozen "See me" messages from her boss. "Where the hell have you been?" Frank Merriam said when they finally connected.

"Sorry," she said equably. "A dear friend of mine just became engaged, and we were having lunch—"

"Well, okay this time," he growled. "But I've been meaning to speak to you lately. Your billable hours have dropped off woefully in recent months. I look for you at eight o'clock, your office is empty—"

"Eight A.M. or P.M.?"

"Both."

"Well, my office may be empty," she said, "but my briefcase isn't. I do my work, Frank. I just take more home with me these days. Why?" She stared him down. "Is there a falling off in quality?"

"Not in quality," he conceded, "but in—what shall I call it?—in commitment. Enthusiasm. Fire in the belly, if you will. You're beginning to veer off the partnership track, Diane, and that would be tragic. These next few months are crucial. The senior partners are weighing final considerations. As you well know, hours served are a major factor and while I don't begrudge my associates a private life—"

"Point taken." Diane nodded, and they got down to business.

She went back to her desk with a sense of relief. As things stood now, the pressure of work provided an excuse for fending off the pressure that Avram was exerting. She would shelve his proposal for another few months (at least until her partnership was secured), by which time their mutual ardor might have cooled and the whole question of marriage become moot or not a question at all. It seemed a prudent course. Experience had taught her to beware the premature decision. As Leo Frankland used to say back at Yale, fools rush in where lawyers fear to tread. Dear Leo! That man was a font of wisdom.

Rummaging through her desk, she came across the yellow pad with its list of Pros and Cons and placed it in the back of the bottom drawer. More urgent matters called.

She was working away, happy and absorbed, when Byron came in chalk white. "I've got a deposition with Bob Singer in half an hour. Could you take it for me? I don't feel up to it."

"Of course." She tried to suppress a startled quiver of anxiety. "What's the matter, Byron? You look as if you've seen a ghost."

He stood immobile, then fell to studying his feet. "Yes," he said finally. "Well put. You could say I've seen a ghost. What the hell, I can tell you. I have to tell somebody." He looked up at her with bloodshot eyes. "Jim has AIDS."

"Oh my God!" she cried out. "How awful!"

"I'm so fucking mad!" He began pounding her desk with his fist. "It's so fucking unfair. And there's no way to fight—not a goddamn thing I can do. We got the diagnosis last Friday, but I think we both knew before then. He's had one infection after another all winter long. Colds, sore throat. We kept lying to each other—" He began to weep.

There was nothing she could say, only one thing she could do. Diane stood up and held his trembling body tight. He felt frail and delicate in her arms.

He stopped shaking at last. "I'm sorry. I didn't mean to make an ass of myself."

She handed him a tissue. "If there's anything I can do—"

"Thanks, love." He blew his nose, straightened his tie, adjusted his jacket, made an effort to reclaim the usual unruffled Byron. "Send a message to Lourdes and tell them to hurry."

She scraped up a wan smile, hoping to mask a deeper worry. "And you, Byron? Will you be okay?"

"I've tested negative so far. Could be positive tomorrow. The likelihood is I'm all right. But will I be okay in all the ways that count?" He shook his head slowly, eyes misted. "I can't say, Diane. Jim and I have been together nearly five years. We love each other. We were a couple. What the hell—we still are."

But Diane's mind turned to the practical questions involved. "For safety's sake, Byron, wouldn't it be wiser if you made separate living arrangements?"

He stared at her. "You're advising me to cut and run? Is that what love means to you?"

"I was only suggesting prudence, Byron. You have to consider the risks involved."

"Fuck the risks," he spat out. "I want to make him happy while I still have that chance. Jim will die. Very soon. That's the given. And when he does, Diane, I'll still have to live with myself. If he were my wife, if he were my child, I'd behave the same way, and you would never dream of saying a thing. Or maybe you and I have different definitions of love. Sorry." He rubbed his eyes wearily. "I didn't mean to preach. Now if you'll excuse me, I'm going home."

She left for the deposition with a heavy heart. It struck her, and not for the first time, that the price of love could be unbearably high.

NINETEEN

———•———

The invitation was in the shape of a big red heart.

PARTY PARTY PARTY
FEBRUARY 14

Bernadette Hong and Roger Knowland invite
you to celebrate their engagement
Good food!
Good fun!
Good-bye to the single life!
P.S. Bring your own valentine or meet one.

"A hundred fifty people, would you say?" Rosemary pushed through the crush to Diane.

"More!" Diane shouted over the disco music. "Haven't seen this many live bodies in one place since the Macy's parade. Bernie must have asked everyone she's ever known since kindergarten."

The big room throbbed with motion, vibrated with music, was deafened with the babble of a chic bright crowd. There were slim-hipped models, record company execs, shining girls who popped letters on quiz shows, assistants to the mayor, off-Broadway playwrights, just published authors, SoHo artists, Village Voicers, real estate developers, rising rock stars, young women who did clever things with batik, young men who played hockey, played Hamlet, played the commodities market. Bernie had scoured not only her address book, but plundered the station's master Rolodex as well. The result was a crowd that would do justice to the Silver Palate food, the Sherry-Lehmann wines, and the formal entry of Roger Knowland to New York City.

"Isn't this exciting!" Rosemary waved across an asparagus patch of trendy heads. "There's Fleur—Yoo-hoo!—looking gorgeous. Isn't this terrific? Just everybody and his uncle is here. The literati—the glitterati—"

"The shitterati," Fleur added, coming up to them. "I was just swapping trade secrets with the Mayflower Madam, would you believe. Bernie's pulled out all stops for the occasion. Looks like a combination of outtakes from *The Tonight Show* and the Ten Most Wanted List."

"Well, I for one like a bit of glamour," Rosemary said. "Anyhow, Bernie's making this huge effort for Roger, which I think is perfectly splendid. You see, he doesn't know a soul in New York."

"Yeah? Well, I don't think Bernie knows half the souls here either. That is, presuming they have souls. Shows how far people will go for free booze."

"The point is, Fleur, they *came*!" Rosemary said. "After all, Bernie's something of a celebrity herself these days, now that she's a regular on the show. And Roger must be thrilled, meeting so many movers and shakers all at once. Have you met the groom, by the way?"

"One could hardly avoid him," Diane commented. "The man is positively ubiquitous."

Roger Knowland was in his element, moving here and there, charming and disarming, shaking hands, showing teeth, basking in the lively noisy milieu. He had a knack for voicing all the right sentiments, making all the right moves. He worked the crowd, Diane observed, like a politician, with the proper phrase, cunningly "personalized," for each contact. Diane was "that brilliant Wall Street lawyer," Fleur "the award-winning advertising writer," Rosemary "the best damn chef in Westport, Connecticut." To his credit, the man did his homework.

"Yes, Roger's very impressive," Diane agreed. "Quite a catch, I daresay. By the way, where's Alex? I haven't seen him in ages."

A shadow fell across Rosemary's face. "He's been so busy these days, the lamb, I practically have to make appointments to see him myself. He's knocking himself out on the job. Right now, he's home catching up on some sleep."

Fleur smothered a yawn and headed for the dance floor.

"Poor baby," Rosemary said, watching her walk away. "I guess she finally gave up on that guy she was involved with. I just hope he didn't louse her up too much. Well, maybe she'll meet someone nice tonight. How about you, Di? You shouldn't waste your time talking to an old married lady like me. Or did you come with a valentine?"

"I had a tentative date," Diane said, "but he couldn't make it."

Which was less than the truth. She had agonized for days before deciding not to bring Avram. "I don't think you'll enjoy it," she warned him. "Seriously. The place will be full of those snakes with their tails in their mouths."

"Would you prefer I didn't come?" he asked outright.

"I wouldn't go myself, love, if it were anyone but Bernie. You know how I loathe those big-production brawls."

Avram let her off the hook gracefully, claiming the pressure of his thesis, but she knew she had wounded his pride. In return she promised to come home early.

Rosemary had spotted a TV producer she was eager to pitch her services to, and excused herself. Alone, Diane made her way to the bar. As she wriggled through the crowd, scraps of conversation floated past her.

"But nobody goes to Mortimer's anymore!"

"I hear you're the guy to see about nose candy."

"Ross would rather be flayed alive than admit he went to CCNY."

"They cut a flap behind your ears and pull the skin back, just like peeling a banana."

"Make it quick, buddy. I've got a stretch limo waiting."

"To me personally, Donald Trump is a great human being."

"Who do I have to fuck to get my face in *Womens Wear Daily*?"

Yes, she began revising her judgments, it was well that Avram hadn't come. Not that he wasn't good enough for this thrusting crowd of yuppies and hustlers (the Mayflower Madam, for God's sake!); they weren't good enough for him.

She ordered a double scotch, then moved to the edge of the crowd. In its midst was Bernie, smiling, chatting, skimming the surface like a pebble over water. On the far side of the room, Roger followed suit. Diane waited to see if they would exchange glances, secret smiles. They talked, she observed, to everyone but each other. At one point their paths intersected. Diane craned her neck, curious. Would they touch? Hold hands? Would Roger whisper into his fiancée's ear? Bernie smiled and said something. It must have been funny, for the people around her laughed, but it was certainly nothing intimate.

With a shiver Diane turned away. She felt like an innocent bystander who had stumbled upon a terrible secret.

Fleur materialized at her side. "I'm splitting in a couple of minutes. I'm exhausted. You want to share a cab home?"

"Fleur?" Diane gazed out the cab window at the frozen park. "What did you make of Bernie's fiancé?"

"They seem right for each other."

"Really?" They were passing the pond. Too late for joggers. Diane turned to her friend. "I know it's none of my business, but I have—what would you call it?—bad vibes? Yes, I get bad vibes."

"Why? You think he's hiding some dark secret?"

"Secret!" Diane pounced on the word. "Yes. I think so, but what sort of secret?"

"Bigamist? Ax murderer? You tell me. You obviously have something in mind."

"No no! Nothing like that. But I had the weirdest feeling—"

"Yes?" Fleur was intrigued.

"—that there's nothing there!" she blurted out. "It's all done with blue smoke and mirrors. There's no feeling between them, no passion. It's as though they were allies rather than lovers. He doesn't love her, Fleur. That's the secret. He's using her to—oh, I don't know—provide him with entrée, people, vitality. Make up for what he lacks. I looked in those eyes, and they were empty. And you know something else? I don't think Bernie loves him either."

"So what else is new?" Fleur replied. "She made a considered decision. Bernie's no fool. My guess is, the two of them are using each other. As I said, they're an admirably suited couple. The perfect match. Look, Di, we are talking about two profoundly shallow people."

"What a terrible thing to say!"

"Okay, maybe 'shallow' isn't the word. Maybe 'scared' is. Bernie doesn't like to get intimate with anyone. The three of us are probably the closest friends she has, and even so she's always operating at arm's length. She weasels out your secrets, you never get a line on hers. Ever wonder why Bernie went into TV? Because it's quick. Casual. Slam, bam, thank you, ma'am. You skim the surface of the surface, ask a few dumb questions—'Tell me, do you sleep in the nude?' —smile, nod, thank your guest for a 'lovely interview' —and that's it. Over and done with." Fleur gave a smutty laugh. "You know, she's got a new series coming up next week, *Celebrity Refrigerators*. She goes into their kitchens, pokes around in their vegetable bins, their freezers. You see which star keeps champagne on ice, and which one has nothing but a few moldy sticks of celery and a bottle of Bud. The station's really hot on it. I suggested she do a follow-up called *Celebrity Garbage*—you go through their trash cans Monday morning. And of course *Celebrity Bathrooms*. That one she loved. The thing is, you're in and out in ten minutes, with no scars. You never get very deeply inside other people's skins. More important, they never get inside yours. Hello, good-bye, and tomorrow is a new cast of characters."

"But why, Fleur? What is she afraid of?"

"Feeling? Loving? Losing control?" Fleur paused. "Control, probably. My bet is she's terrified of surrendering the reins. And I can understand that. I'm not a shrink, but I'll tell you one thing: if Bernie wanted more, she would have got it. You think this guy is all that different from Steve? From any of the men in her life?"

"He's more self-serving."

"Agreed. And I like Steve better too, although there isn't an awful lot of depth there either. But that's your clue. Bernie likes lightweights. They don't threaten. They don't crowd. They don't make emotional demands. The main distinction between Roger and Steve is that Roger is willing to marry her, which at the moment Bernie thinks is the thing to do. Granted, it's not my concept of marriage, probably not yours. But it suits Bernie to a tee, so who am I to carp. Anyhow, she got what she wants, which makes her a helluva lot smarter than you and me, babe. She's in total control of the situation."

"And you're not, Fleur?"

"I wasn't" came the answer. "I was getting killed. But things are changing, coming to a head." She gave Diane a swift, affectionate hug. "I'm very close to being very, very happy. Oops! Here we are. Driver"—she rapped at the divider—"let me off at the next corner."

Diane rode the rest of the way in a quixotic mood.

What a marriage Bernie was contemplating! Such a compromise! Except if Fleur was correct, it was no compromise. It was a cold and reasoned choice.

Looked at in this light, marrying Avram didn't seem so outrageous. She would have to give it a good deal more thought.

"The Osgood Arms," she told the driver, "and step on it, please. I have someone waiting for me."

TWENTY

F orty years of marriage was not only an amazing achievement these days, it was also, according to *The World Almanac*, a ruby anniversary. Diane turned to Rosemary for advice. "I need help," she said. "I can't bring my parents actual jewels, but I'd like to get something appropriate. Ruby-colored if possible. Any ideas?"

"You leave it to Mama," Rosemary said.

The next day she called Diane from a Third Avenue antique shop, announcing she had found the perfect gift. Diane met her there, and Rosemary showed her a slim-necked decanter with circular stripes ranging from gold to deepest red. "It's amberina, and ideal for the occasion. It's from New England—just like your parents—and the color is a compound of real gold and rubies. Plus"—she lowered her voice—"this piece is a very good buy. I'm getting you the professional discount."

"My Lord, but you're knowledgeable," Diane said with respect while the salesgirl was wrapping her purchase.

Rosemary laughed. "I got tired of being written off as the class dodo."

Diane launched a protest, but Rosemary cut her off. "Those are bygones. Let's just say I'm a late bloomer. Anyhow, have a good time up in Boston, and let me know how your folks like the decanter."

"I will—and I wish you'd bill me for your time."

"I only charge clients, Di. I couldn't possibly take money from a friend. Remember me to your parents," she said,

171

then smiled as though the Summerfields' happiness were her own. "It's so nice to think of people staying married all that time. It warms the heart."

Diane left for the weekend with a sense of both pleasure and dread.

Pleasure, because going home was always a shot in the arm, a boost to the ego. Dread, because she had pledged herself to broaching the subject of Avram. As far as the Summerfields knew, he didn't exist, Diane having avoided even the vaguest reference to any romance. But now with Avram's proposal, she could no longer keep her family in the dark.

Not that she was asking her father's "permission"—she was too old for that. Indeed her age was one of the principal problems—but she had a keen respect for his judgment, his ability to read a situation quickly and accurately. Tom Summerfield was a no-nonsense man.

On Saturday night there was a large party at the huge Summerfield home in Chestnut Hill. Present were three generations of relatives, family friends, her mother's Back Bay circle, neighbors from their summer house in Maine, her father's business partners and tennis partners, and his classmates from Harvard. Though not a chic gathering in the New York sense, they were people Diane loved and respected. Real people, she told herself. Her people. The milieu she had known since birth: the well-born, the well-bred, the well-to-do.

And everyone was glad to see her, so interested in her life in New York. She floated through the rooms in a wash of affection.

"Well look at you!" she exclaimed, hugging her California sister-in-law, now hugely pregnant. "And look at *you*, Di." Sarah gave a mock envious sigh. "Just as skinny as ever."

She danced with boys she had known from the cradle: Rob Winthrop who broke her heart when she was thirteen; Jim Codman whom she took to her high school prom; Hank Sayre whose adolescence was marred by a near-fatal case of acne; Jay "the Animal" Brimmer who had more hands and tongues than an Indian deity.

How well they'd all turned out, these boys from the day

before yesterday. They were men now—serious, attractive, by and large successful—busy with talk of their wives, their jobs, their households, their children, their boats. Who would have thought that Hank Sayre would develop into a dashing journalist? Diane felt a quick sense of loss. What a crush he'd had on her when they were teenagers and how awfully she'd behaved. Perhaps she should have married young and stayed put. Except how could you foretell which ugly duckling would turn into a swan?

Her uncle Drew cut in. "How's my favorite niece?" he wanted to know and, predictably, "What's wrong with all the young men in New York that they let a lovely girl like you get away?"

The orchestra struck up the "Anniversary Waltz." Tom Summerfield pulled Frances onto the dance floor. "Still a handsome couple, eh?" Diane heard someone say, and unconsciously she nodded in assent.

Every now and then Diane tried to picture Avram in this gathering, dancing, making small talk. The vision didn't come easily. It was a homogeneous crowd, a classic WASP's nest. There were no black faces here, no Jewish names. With the exception of the British consul, no foreigners.

Not that people wouldn't have been pleasant to Avram; these were mannerly people, cordial and civilized, and he was not without charm. But would he feel the outsider? Be self-conscious, ill at ease? For all his frank good nature, Avram was sensitive to nuance. And what would the others make of *him*?

She had planned to speak her piece on Sunday, when her parents would have recovered from the party. Her sales pitch was how she thought of her speech. But no sooner had the last guest gone than her father, intuitive as ever, suggested they have a brandy in the den.

"We've hardly had a chance to talk," Tom Summerfield said, settling into his favorite leather chair. "And you're already off tomorrow. So, princess, how are they treating you at Slater Blaney?"

"Oh, Diane's doing fine," her mother interrupted. "Your father and his grapevine. He follows your progress like a hawk. Just the other day, he was speaking to Ralph Slater. More important, what the grapevine doesn't tell—what have you been doing with yourself? You know what I mean, darling. Socially. Have you—have you met anyone lately?"

Diane took a deep breath. She had asked for an opening, and here it was.

"Well, actually, yes I have!"

"Ah!" Frances said in triumph. "Didn't I tell you she was looking radiant, Tom? So, who is he?"

"His name is Avram—"

"Averell?" Frances furrowed her brow. "As in Averell Harriman?"

"Avram. His name is Avram Gittelson."

For a second there was utter silence, broken only by the sound of Frances Summerfield's ears being pinned back.

"Jewish, I gather."

"He's an Israeli," Diane said evenly, having foreseen this reaction, "and yes, he happens to be Jewish."

"Israeli too!" To judge by Frances's tone, insult had been added to injury. The man hadn't even the decency to be American. Diane began gearing herself for a sober defense, a call to tolerance, compassion, when her father preempted her appeal.

"Now, Frances—" He shot his wife a let-me-handle-this look, then continued in an amiable tone. "We don't want to prejudge Diane's young man. This is the twentieth century, my dear, and I personally have nothing but the highest respect for the Jewish people. Some of the finest gentlemen I know in business—" He went on to list notables at Goldman Sachs, Shearson Lehman, Salomon Brothers, awarding them his highest accolades. "A race of born bankers," he concluded. "Tough. Enterprising. Financially sound. And excellent family men, so I hear."

Diane listened to his assessment with sinking heart. Despite the reference to "family men," her father was veering woefully far afield. His assumption was that she was about to form an alliance with one of the lofty New York clans known as "our crowd," or at least a young man aspiring to those heights. Poor Avram in his ill-cut suit and short socks! She sniffed disaster in the air.

"Avram isn't interested in finance," she broke in, eager to limit the damage. "At the moment he's finishing his master's at Columbia. Not an MBA, I'm afraid." Why was she apologizing? Her task was to promote, pitch the goods. "Actually it's in philosophy. He's writing a brilliant thesis on Wittgenstein and I wouldn't be surprised if he gets a magna cum laude."

"Interesting." Tom frowned. "And of course if you like him, he must be a clever fellow. I'm not quite sure what one does with a master's degree in philosophy, though. Is he going on for a Ph.D.?"

Diane found herself in a peculiar situation. She had never lied to her parents and wasn't about to begin, but neither did she want to spell out the truth in graphic detail. She prayed the lawyer in her would rise to the challenge.

"He's a wonderful person." Diane turned advocate with a vengeance. For the next few minutes she employed all her eloquence on his behalf, espousing his merits, omitting irrelevancies (no purpose was served in saying that he was currently employed as a handyman), gilding lilies at every opportunity. Her summary was peppered with such words as *kind, decent, honest, forthright.*

Her father listened. Nodded. Smiled. *This isn't going to be so bad,* Diane thought. *He's probably relieved I've found a husband.*

Then the cross-examination began. What were Avram's goals? her father inquired. Who were his people? How had he supported himself thus far? Under the burden of Tom's shrewd but gentle questioning, an unwelcome picture began to emerge.

"If I understand you correctly, Diane"—he ignored the window dressing and zeroed in on the salient points—"this young man, this *very* young man, has no prospects in this country. No career of any sort. No driving ambition. I wonder, how can he afford a wife?"

"People don't 'afford' wives anymore, Dad," she said patiently. "I expect to pay my own way. I would no matter whom I married."

"Fifty-fifty, eh?" Tom asked, but the question answered itself. Eighty-twenty was a good deal more like it.

"Of course," she argued. "If he goes into business with his cousin, he can do quite well. Avram's a very hard worker."

That much was true. The taxi business might not be elegant, but it was certainly lucrative. Avram had taken her one evening to meet his cousin Zvi, who lived in a large, overfurnished apartment in Queens amidst the electronic fruits of his success. The talk, at least Zvi's portion of it, concerned itself mostly with business, money, and VCRs. Accent and taste in furniture aside, Zvi was hardly different from the Wall Street crowd. An Israeli version of a yuppie, she perceived.

"Avram could do very well indeed," she iterated. "It's a flourishing business."

"A livery service." Tom pulled his ear thoughtfully while her mother looked on, stricken. She was envisioning her son-in-law behind the wheel of a cab.

Tom's next line of questioning was devastating. "He has a green card, I hope."

Her heart sank. "No. Not yet."

"I see."

He fell silent, but she could read his mind. Her father believed, as others would too, that to Avram such a marriage must be a godsend. At a stroke, this penniless student would have won the right to remain in America. The precious green card. The promise of citizenship. How could Tom help but perceive Avram as a rank opportunist. And herself as a sentimental fool.

Yet her father was merely articulating her own worst fears.

"No, you don't see!" Diane flung herself into a passionate defense. "You don't see anything at all. Avram's not like that. He's the least venal, least grasping man I've ever known. Besides I love him and he loves me. He really does!—incredible as that may seem to you!"

"Why, of course he loves you, Diane!" Tom seemed astonished at her inference. "I don't doubt it for a moment. Indeed, what intelligent man wouldn't love you! You're a very superior woman, Diane. But we love you too, remember. And we're only thinking of your interest. Admit it, my dear, young Avram has got himself a catch."

"A catch? *Me*?" she blurted. "If I'm such a catch, how come no one's ever caught me before? Where are these terrific suitors lining up for my hand? Diane Summerfield: Catch-of-the day! It sounds like the blue-plate special in a seafood house."

"You set too low a value on yourself, Diane," her mother said. "I'm sure when you're ready you'll find some wonderful—"

"—wonderful man," Diane sang out in unison. She had heard it all before. "I'm ready, Mother, believe me! And

Avram is my wonderful man. All I ask is that when you meet him you keep an open mind. I'd like to bring him to Boston next weekend. He's eager to meet both of you."

"Splendid!" Tom patted his daughter's hand. "Although next weekend isn't terribly convenient. Next month would be better. Anyhow, there's no rush. And of course we look forward to meeting him. Doubtless he's everything you say—a charming young man. The only point I wish to make, Diane, forgive my candor, is that you are able to offer Avram much more than just love. Surely I don't have to spell out the particulars, and I'm glad those material benefits are yours to confer. But other than his affection, which I've no doubt is sincere, what can Avram give *you*? You're very much of a somebody, Diane. Top of your class at Smith, Law Review at Yale, and if my informants are correct, about to make partner in one of New York's finest law firms."

"And don't forget the *Social Register*," her mother piped in.

Tom smiled. "All that means nowadays," he said softly, "is that you're on yet another mailing list. However, your mother's point is well taken. On your side, you have a great deal to offer, including social position. You have a right to expect as much in return. But what is Avram bringing to this match? A man with so little future, so little ambition. Is he good enough for you, darling? Just ask yourself that. Is he good enough for our favorite girl?"

"Oh, Dad!" Diane didn't know whether to laugh or cry. "By your lights, who is good enough for me? The President of the United States? He's already married."

A deeply anguished Diane boarded the plane to New York. Her father was right. The match was impossible from every point of view. As a lawyer, she knew the only successful contracts, the only ones that endured, were those that provided mutual benefits. Equity. But there was no equity between her and Avram. Her father had made that much clear. If only . . .

If only Avram would do something prestigious, damnit. If only he would go out and make something of himself. As things stood now, she was ashamed of him. And ashamed of herself for being ashamed.

She remembered hearing a story that when Ingrid Bergman arrived in Hollywood, she was married to a dentist. The studio chiefs had recoiled in horror. Dentistry lacked glamour, panache. They sent him to medical school to be made into a doctor. Of course the story was contemptible. But understandable too. And Avram wasn't even a dentist!

Now if he were a medical man, their situation would be different. Religion or age would hardly matter. *I'd like you to meet my husband, Dr. Gittelson*. It had a nice ring to it. Or if not a doctor—

Diane set herself to some hard thinking.

By the time the plane landed at LaGuardia, inspiration had struck. She flew to a phone. "Avram! Wonderful idea! I'll meet you at my apartment in twenty minutes. All our problems are solved."

"You want to send me to law school!" Avram stared in disbelief.

"Why not? You'd make a fabulous lawyer," Diane gushed. "That smart Talmudic mind of yours is perfect for the bar. The wonder is, I never realized it before! And I'd help you of course, it would be kind of fun. With your grades, you should have no problem getting in. In fact, they look for diversity in background. Now it may be too late for Columbia"—she began scribbling notes—"but there's, let me see, NYU, which is excellent, St. John's out in Queens. Yeshiva has a good law school—"

Avram shook his head as if to dispel cobwebs. "Where on earth did you get the idea I want to be a lawyer? I don't! I never did—"

"Look," Diane's tone was reasonable. "I understand you wouldn't be happy in corporate law, but once you've passed the bar, there are a hundred fields you could enter. Industry, banking, immigration. You know, that's getting to be quite a nice specialty, immigration law, and you're so marvelous at languages—"

"I can't believe you're serious."

"If it's the tuition that bothers you, darling, don't worry about it. A lot of women put their husbands through graduate school. It's a way of investing jointly in their futures. Besides, once we're married, what does it matter whose money buys what?"

He stood up abruptly.

"I'm going out for a walk."

The suddenness of his departure stunned her. She had expected, if not immediate enrollment into law school, then certainly delight, joy—and yes!—gratitude that she was working so hard to make their marriage feasible. She had fought for him in Boston; the rest was up to him.

Ten minutes later he was back, puffing on a Gauloise, something he only did under stress. His expression was stern.

"Was this your father's idea, this law school nonsense?"

Diane was stung. "It's not nonsense. It was my idea, and frankly it's an excellent solution to our problem."

"What problem?" Avram said coolly. "I don't have a problem, Diane. You do. You think there's something gross about people working with their hands. Or providing a simple service. Yet for the last four months, I have heard you tell one story after another how fierce law school was, how hard they drive you at work, what thieves your clients are. I see you working twelve hours a day, coming home exhausted. Rat race, that is your term, not mine, and now you're telling me I should follow suit."

"It was a suggestion, that's all. A premise for discussion. Very well, if you dislike the law, choose some other career. Or else take your Ph.D."

"Why?" He mashed the cigarette out and lit another. "So you can call me 'Doctor'? Is that what this exercise is all about?"

"So you can make something of yourself, instead of frittering your life away. You could be somebody, Avram. At least you could try!"

He pulled himself up stiffly.

"I already *am* somebody. I am Avram Gittelson. It was my belief you loved me as I am. Apparently not, since you're determined to change me into someone else, someone I would probably hate. I'm deeply disappointed in you"—he held up an angry hand to forestall her protest—"deeply! I never thought you were such a snob, that you were a puppet dancing to everyone's tunes. I couldn't have fallen in love with you if I had. But one word from your father and you want to turn me into everything I despise. Well, I will not have it, do you hear?"

His outburst startled her. It was bad enough—she felt her

gorge rise—that she had to fight his battles in Boston; she shouldn't have to do battle with him as well. The strain of the weekend began to tell. The smell of defeat mingled with the pungent aroma of Gauloises. Both were equally alien.

Such resistance! Such anger! One might think she was his enemy, not his champion. And what was her crime? She had made him an extraordinarily generous offer—and had had her head bitten off in return.

She attempted to rein in her wrath. "I'm being perfectly reasonable, Avram, and you're being stubborn. It seems to me that if a man loves a woman, he should be willing to exert himself on her behalf. I'm not asking you to slay dragons or take on the labors of Hercules. I just want to see some show of ambition, some effort being made. If I'm worth having, surely I'm worth that. For God's sake, at least consider my proposition."

"I've considered," he replied. "And my answer is the same. You think you're the only one with grievances, Diane. I have mine too." Then to her chagrin, he began recounting a list of her offenses, most of which she was only too well aware. He had introduced her to his friends, his classmates, such family as he had in New York. Never once had she once reciprocated. Quite the opposite. She had specifically avoided bringing him into her circle in any way. Was he a criminal? A leper? She talked about her family, her pressures, her expectations. Did she presume that he had none of his own?

"Did you ever wonder how I'm going to explain you to *my* parents?" he retaliated. "You are not exactly what they had in mind."

"Explain *me*!" Diane was outraged. "You have to apologize for marrying into one of the finest families in Boston!"

"Explain that I am not only marrying a foreigner," he said, "and moving permanently to America, but marrying outside of my religion as well! That news will hardly make them happy."

"I never heard anything so arrogant!" She was breathless. She had come to him with gifts, kindnesses. How many women were there who would put a man through three expensive years of law school and ask nothing in return but his love!

"This has gone on long enough," she snapped.

"What has—you and me?" He looked thunderstruck.

"Yes—no!" She didn't expect the question to arise so nakedly. "Maybe." Their situation was absurd, hopeless. "I don't believe," she heard herself saying, "that we have any future together. You'll never be happy in my world, Avram. You won't feel comfortable. Certainly not as things stand now."

"Then come into mine!" At last—at last! He enfolded her in his arms and covered her face with kisses. "Forget your family, all your stupid prejudices. Let's get married tomorrow and to hell with the world. We could live for each other, Diane. There are worse fates."

But the moment had passed irrecoverably. In a flash of reality, she saw the truth. Avram, with his strong hard sense of self, would never change, never accommodate. To accept would be total surrender.

"I can't." She broke away and fought back the tears. "You were right. You are what you are. But I am what I am too, Avram. And nothing will alter that."

She held her breath, waiting against all logic for a reprieve—for one last plea, a statement of contrition.

Instead, Avram picked up his jacket and walked to the door. "I don't beg," he said, and then was gone.

The door shut. The apartment fell silent—that terrible silence he had dispelled for so long. But Diane didn't beg either.

She had trod on some part of Avram's self that was howling in pain. Had they married, she would do so again and again. Tom Summerfield was right. The match was impossible and love—"mere love"—was not enough. Avram was his own man. And for as long as he was, he could never be hers.

TWENTY-ONE

"Wallet—airline ticket—credit cards—" Rosemary ran down the list.

"Yep, I got everything, sweetheart." Alex grabbed his briefcase, snatched his overnight bag. "I'll call you from Chicago."

"—toothbrush—vitamins—"

A car honked in the driveway.

"Honey, anything I forgot I can pick up there. Gotta dash."

"Kiss, kiss."

"Yeah, I'll speak to you tonight."

"Good luck with your presentation," she shouted after him, but he was already in the taxi.

"Rush, rush, rush," Rosemary muttered to herself, then went into the kitchen to make fresh coffee.

Oh, Alex! You think you're so efficient! She shook her head. He had left his house keys on the breakfast table. Not that it mattered, he didn't need them on the road, and she would be home when he got back Wednesday night.

She brewed the coffee, then sat down, feeling troubled.

The truth was, she admitted to herself, Alex had been behaving oddly the last few weeks. The last few months, if she chose to inspect the matter more closely.

Then, too, there were those dreadful phone calls. There had been three in all, each from the same person, each with the same message word for word.

"It's ten o'clock," the woman would say in a nasal sing-song. "Do you know where your husband is?"

The first time, Rosemary assumed it was either a wrong number or a teenage prank. The caller had hung up before the words had a chance to register. Certainly she knew where her husband was. He was having dinner with clients from Skadden Arps.

A few nights later the episode was repeated. This time Rosemary got angry. "Who is this?" she had yelled into the phone, only to be answered with a click. Outrageous! Of course she knew where Alex was! He was working late at the office, they were printing some kind of merger plan that night. Rosemary Bainter Marshall was damned if she was going to lower her pride, humiliate herself by checking up on him in public. She trusted her husband.

The third time she checked up. Alex wasn't there.

"I called the office around ten," she said when he got home after midnight. "They said you'd left at seven."

"Of course I did," he answered without blinking.

"Well, where were you?"

"At a hockey game with Jim Rosen. I told you this morning."

"No, you didn't."

"Oh for Chrissakes, Rosie. You never listen. You're so all over the place these days with your goddamn business enterprise, you don't hear half of what I say. What do you want? You want to see the ticket stubs? Will that make you feel happier? They're in here somewhere—" He began fumbling through his pockets, plunking various objects down on the table. "Or maybe in my coat."

"Forget it."

"Nope!" Alex headed for the coat closet. "You don't trust me, I'm going to find you those tickets."

"I said forget it. Look, Alex, I'm sorry I mentioned it. Of course I trust you."

"Okay." He shut the closet door. "But next time I talk, listen."

That was last Tuesday. Since then Rosemary had been in an agony of suspense. Come ten o'clock, if Alex weren't home, she would wait in terror for the phone to ring.

In addition, there was the matter of the underwear.

She had always purchased his underwear, from the day they were married. Then around Christmastime, he'd come home with half a dozen sets of Italian briefs, in bright cheerful colors, as skimpily cut as bikinis.

Rosemary viewed his new acquisition with surprise. "You've got scads of Jockey shorts."

"Boring," he said. "A man gets tired of wearing the same boring white underwear year after year. Time for a change."

She picked up a skimpy garment, examined it, then put it back in his drawer. "Well, I don't know how these are going to hold up in the wash. They're practically G-strings. Honestly, Alex, what's wrong with good old Fruit of the Loom? Who sees them anyhow?"

"You do, honey."

Now she sat at the kitchen table, massaging his leather key case as if it would unlock these puzzlements. There were two bright shiny keys in the case, she noticed. They looked newly cut. For a split second, she succumbed to a wave of abject terror. Keys to what? To where? She studied the contents in greater detail. Alex's house keys were there, two or three well-worn keys most likely to the office, keys to the garage, to his locker at the Dartmouth Club. What else would he have keys for? "Talk, damn you!" she ordered, but the key case refused to render its secrets. She put it down with trembling fingers. Was she being blind? Willfully stupid? Or was she simply being a neurotic hysterical wife?

Rosemary hated confrontations, ugliness of any sort. She had been raised to look on the bright side of life. "People who expect the worst," her mother used to say, "invariably get it."

Rosemary concurred. She had no patience with what she called "the doom-and-gloomers," that mean breed of women who snooped through their husband's pockets, scoured their desk diaries, their receipts. Women who read adultery into every mild flirtation. *Seek and ye shall find,* Rosemary believed. Those woman were asking for trouble, and she was never surprised to hear their marriages had broken up.

Take her neighbor Dawn Hendryks, who now did Rosemary's books. A typical case. Dawn's union had foundered on the rocks of a mysterious item on a credit card bill.

"Why should Hank have charged a hotel room in Manhattan?" Dawn had agonized. Only one explanation fit the facts. Now Dawn, poor soul, was reduced to earning her own living. It would have been better had she never inquired.

But if, for the sake of argument—make that a giant "if"—Alex were up to something he would be wilier, more cautious than Hank Hendryks. Her Alex was one smart fella, Rosemary prided herself. An MBA, a top executive with a head for details. You wouldn't catch him in such a sloppy oversight. Besides, Alex's American Express bills went directly to his office.

But Alex wasn't up to anything. He was a good man. An excellent husband. And such a workaholic, he probably couldn't even spare the time for an affair. Anyhow, trust was the basis of marriage. She trusted him completely. Except perhaps when he was on the road.

That, she recognized, was a more ambiguous situation, a place where trouble was more likely to arise. Like everyone else, she had heard stories of misbehavior among business-men on the loose. Conventions, sales meetings, seminars: They were hotbeds of adultery. Alex himself had told her some fairly scabrous stories, though always about other women's husbands. Once or twice she had wondered if he too had enjoyed "one-night stands," but decided against it. Alex was a domesticated man. And he took good care of his health.

This morning, however, those doubts returned in force. Suppose today's Chicago trip was a smoke screen to hide a rendezvous. Suppose he hadn't gone to Chicago at all! If if weren't for those keys—

Despising herself for rank disloyalty, Rosemary picked up the phone and dialed the Palmer House.

"Hello," she said briskly. "I'm the travel secretary for Leviathan Press and I just wanted to confirm. Do you have a reservation for a Mr. Alex Marshall arriving at noon? You do? Good! And could you tell me, is that a single room or a double? A single!" She almost wept in relief. "Thank you very, very much. No—no message."

She hung up the phone feeling as though she had been reprieved from death. Or even worse—from betrayal! What a bitch she had been, even to suspect Alex of misbehavior. Thank God she hadn't left her name.

Suddenly her mood became festive. The good news, or more particularly the absence of bad news, seemed to call for a celebration, she told herself. She'd get a sitter, go into the city this afternoon. Do some shopping, have dinner with a friend.

Fleur! Of course. She'd call Fleur right now and see if she was available. Maybe they could eat at that Afghan restaurant on Second Avenue, catch an early show. Smiling, she reached for the phone.

"Fleur Chamberlain's office," the girl said.

"Is she there?"

"I'm sorry. Miss Chamberlain is in a meeting. She's tied up until one. Can I take a message?"

Rosemary's heart stopped. She knew that voice, the sing-song lilt, those Brooklyn nasal tones. For a moment she sat there, mouth open.

"Hello?" the voice on the other end repeated. "You still there?"

"Tied up till one," Rosemary gasped. "Could you tell me"—she drew a deep breath, shut her eyes, and prayed—"what time it is now?"

"It's ten o'clock," the answer came.

The voice—that voice! Could there be any doubt?

Rosemary hung up the phone. The room reeled. The walls receded, putting a distance between her and reality.

Fleur and Alex? Impossible! She could not bridge the gap between what her reason dictated and what her heart would accept.

Just a few weeks ago, Fleur had come to her home, slept on her sheets, patted her dog, played with her boy. She had sat at this very table, on that very chair, and eaten Rose-mary's bread.

Yes! Fleur and she had broken bread together, and in Rosemary's mind that imposed a near-sacred obligation. Hospitality was the holiest, most ancient of trusts; its be-trayal the most vicious of crimes. Yet even as Fleur sat there munching, she had hugged this dreadful secret to herself. Oh, how she must have gloated at Rosemary's ignorance while in the next room Alex had been mixing drinks.

Unspeakable! Beneath her feet, Rosemary felt the ground give way, affording her a glimpse into the abyss, as though the cheerful Italian tiles had concealed a Boschian hell. It was a vision of unfathomable depravity, of writhing bodies, sweating, copulating, commiting unnatural acts. And at the heart of this cesspool—Alex and Fleur.

She blinked. Briefly, the world snapped back to normal.

It was ten-thirteen on a crisp Monday morning, the sun was shining and Rosemary Marshall had been the victim of a hallucination or of a coincidence. Chances were, hundreds of New York secretaries spoke with nasal twangs. Thousands.

But in the recess of her mind, a tiny voice mocked, "Fool!" and nothing Rosemary did could silence it. This once, God help her, she had to know. Too much was at stake—her home, her happiness, to say nothing of Chris's welfare. She would never breathe easy, never be able to bear Alex's touch until that nightmare vision was exorcised.

She owed it to Alex to free him from the smear of doubt—and owed it to Fleur as well. The bedrock judgments of her life—the meaning of love, the value of friendship, the enduring virtues of home and hospitality—all would be jeopardized forever until that hellish image was dispelled.

For without trust, what was marriage? What was friendship?

On the table, Alex's keys glistened coldly.

Rosemary poured a jigger of bourbon into her coffee cup, then phoned her neighbor.

"Dawn," she said, startled that her voice sounded so casual. "Do me a favor and pick up Chris after school. I have an errand in the city."

An hour later she had squeezed her Porsche into a parking space across from Fleur's brownstone. It was nearly noon and the sidewalks were filling up with early lunchers, strollers, shoppers peering into the windows of expensive boutiques. A nanny walked by pushing a baby in an English pram. Normal people engaged in normal pursuits.

Rosemary felt like a criminal. Ladies didn't behave like this. Ladies did not break into people's apartments, any more than they went to the store with their hair in pink plastic rollers. Certain things were simply not done.

Suppose she were caught in the act? She envisioned the sharp glances of passersby, whistles blowing, police arriving, being yelled at, arrested, thrown into jail amid prostitutes and common thieves. And what if Fleur should come home? How could Rosemary explain her presence?

But Fleur was tied up for at least another hour, and she never lunched at home during the week.

That was the least of her worries, Rosemary decided. She was neither breaking nor entering. She was committing no crime. She was merely putting a key in a lock.

Assuming the key fit, which was doubtful.

In any case, she couldn't sit there forever. It was a sixty-minute parking zone. In her mind, matters large and small had become a jumble.

Don't fit—don't fit, she implored as she got out of the car and crossed the street. *Don't fit.* She approached the front door and took out the mystery keys. If neither of them fitted, she promised herself, if either offered the tiniest bit of resistance, she would not force it. God would have spoken. She paused for a moment in mute supplication.

The first key slid into the lock with the voluptuous ease of a man entering a woman.

Rosemary stepped into the carpeted hallway, propelled by some force beyond conscious thought. None of this was happening to her. It was delusion, a movie being played on a screen. She mounted the staircase to the top floor, wiped her feet on the mat and inserted the second key.

The place was a pigsty! How could anyone live like that—in this chaos, this mess! How could Alex stand it! But of course, he wouldn't. She knew her husband better than that. He had very high standards. Which proved that this trip was the product of an overheated imagination. She was inhabiting someone else's dream.

Out of habit, Rosemary picked a scarf off the floor, folded it, and placed it on a chair. It was a wisp of chiffon, as unsubstantial as all else in this room.

In a daze she glided across the living room into the tiny bedroom. Then she saw it.

"My apple!"

It sat on a table by the bedside, bold and bright red, a mocking reminder of trust betrayed. And that was real. Undeniable.

"Thief!" Rosemary grabbed for it, toppling the slender table. A bottle of perfume shattered on the parquet. The stench was distinctive, overwhelming.

"Thief!" She gripped the painted fruit with all her might until her knuckles whitened, her palm throbbed with pain. The pain was real. In dreams you feel no pain.

"Thief!" she screamed at the top of her lungs. "You stole my possessions. You stole my husband. You stole my happiness."

Thief! To have robbed her of everything that was most precious in life. To have cajoled, seduced, bewitched—with her sultry perfumes, her multitudinous salves and creams and lotions, her glossy pots of paint and powders and tiny sable brushes, her froths of lace and billowing silks and gleaming sequins. Her glamour. Her beauty. Her sexual wiles.

On the bed, in a dry cleaner's bag, lay one of the most beautiful garments Rosemary had ever seen, a delicate haze of sea-green organza, soft and fluid, the deep décolletage outlined with silver paillettes. With a sense of wonder, she picked up the dress and drew it out of the Polywrap bag. It was light as smoke.

"Thief!" With strong capable hands, Rosemary spread out the bodice and pulled with all her might. Kkkkrrrrrrk! The fabric ripped down the middle with a gratifying sound. Rosemary felt a rush of adrenaline, a sense of power and energy.

Crazy? Why shouldn't she be crazy! It was her right, her due. Thirty-three years of accumulated rage and frustration, of playing first the dutiful daughter, then the perfect wife! Thirty-three years of compliance, self-abnegation. Thirty-three years of fulfilling everybody's expectations and demands! And for what? For this?

All her life, she had behaved like a lady, only to be betrayed on every side. But Rosemary Marshall would be a lady no more.

"Thief! Whore! This should be you!" she savaged the dress with the force of a madwoman, the silver paillettes scattering everywhere. "This should be your body, you bitch! Your guts. Your blood!"

She flung open the door to the bedroom closet. Was there ever such an array of whore's fripperies? Ever such a theater for revenge?

The chiffons were easy, as were the laces and organdies and voiles. They yielded quickly to Rosemary's insistent fingers and rewarded her with rich delicious sounds. Cotton too. All you had to do was poke a little hole in it. A metal nail file would do. But other fabrics were more of a challenge. Silk crepe, for instance. Rosemary was surprised how resilient it could be. As for wool, that was virtually impossible.

She stopped to catch her breath and assess the situation. This would take organization, she realized, proper tools. She would require scissors for the wools and the knitwear, but Fleur must have a sewing box somewhere. Now—leather! That was going to be the big problem. Your ordinary scissors wouldn't make a dent. Leather was skin, after all, tough and seasoned. A good set of poultry shears would do the trick, but you could be damn sure you wouldn't find that particular item in Fleur's sorry excuse of a kitchen. Fleur cooking chicken? It was enough to make you laugh. Very well then—a good carving knife. Everybody had one of those! Aha. There it was. Perfect! That blue Fendi jacket Miss Fleur was so proud of—she wouldn't be proud of it anymore. It was like cutting into flesh.

And the clothes were only the start.

It was close to four when a grimy, disheveled Rosemary clutching a red wooden apple emerged from the building to find that the police had towed away her Porsche. She sat down on the curbstone and wept.

TWENTY-TWO

———•———

Fleur's first reaction on entering the apartment that night was an incredulous howl. Her second, after ascertaining that "that lunatic" hadn't savaged the phone wires, was to call Diane.

"Can you put me up tonight?" she pleaded.

"Why? What's happened?"

"Let's say the shit hit the fan."

A half hour later she was collapsed on Diane's couch, bolting down twelve-year-old scotch.

"Threads! Rubble!" she announced to a mystified Diane. "Every stitch I own. All I've got left are the clothes that I'm wearing. Thank God I'm wearing my Donna Karan."

"You have to report this to the police." Diane was horrified, though she had the impression that Fleur was relishing the drama. "They can dust for prints, make inquiries. For all you know it's some sex maniac—"

Fleur gave a hoot of laughter. "It was no sex maniac," she reported to a dumbstruck Diane. "It was Rosemary!"

"How can you say such a thing! And without proof!"

"Oh, I've got proof, Di. She took an apple, a wooden apple. A kind of trademark, you might say. It's too complicated to explain, but it was her, all right. I thought maybe you had it figured." Fleur poured herself another drink. "Alex and me, that is. We've been involved since last summer."

"Alex and you!" Diane could only echo. "No! I swear to God, it never crossed my mind!"

"Yeah. Well, it must have crossed Rosemary's sometime this very morning, because she visited my apartment like a biblical plague. The woman went bananas. Whole fucking place reduced to matchstick lengths! Dishes broken. Bathroom mirror smashed. Makeup, perfume dumped down the john. As for my wardrobe—ouch! The original chain-saw massacre! Shoes, stockings, the works. Underwear! Pretty kinky, wouldn't you say, slashing someone's panties? Plus curtains—pillows. Even the sheets—would you believe!"

"Especially the sheets, I should think!" Diane found her voice at last. "Fleur, how could you! I'm absolutely appalled. With all the men in the world, why Alex? My God, that's practically incest!"

"I love him!" Fleur stated, as if that were sufficient explanation. "And he loves me."

"Oh, love! I'm sick of the word." Diane burst into tears. "You think it's an excuse for every kind of behavior!"

"Jesus!" Fleur roared back. "You'd think you were the one who's got headaches!" She looked around her, puzzled. "Where's this guy of yours, by the way? I thought he was living here. Or did you boot him out tonight because of me?"

"No, no." Diane dabbed her eyes. "That's over, and I'd rather not talk about it. It hurts! I must say, Fleur, I don't see how you can handle this with such equanimity. I should think you'd be devastated—for Alex, for yourself. And what about Rosemary?"

"What about Rosemary?" Fleur retorted. "She's been needling me for years, with her Lady Bountiful act. Fleur the Pathetic. Fleur the Charity Case. The Dumb Canuck. Well, this time she overplayed her hand. Because if I know Alex— and I think I do—this is just the excuse he needs to get out. It was a lousy marriage, Diane, believe me. Otherwise, Alex wouldn't have strayed. Truth is, Rosemary did me a favor today. She shoved him right into my arms. Funny," she mused, "when this whole stupid husband-hunt thing started—and it wasn't my idea, remember?—Rosemary was the one who said anything goes. Her very words, so she really can't complain if I marry Alex. Which I intend to do as soon as possible."

"Well, I want to get married too," Diane shot back. "However, there are certain measures one doesn't—um—"

"Stoop to? Say it, Diane, You won't hurt my feelings. Sure,

you want to get married, but with you it's a luxury. Whereas with me—"

"It's a necessity? Why?" Diane started. "Are you pregnant?"

"Nope." Fleur pondered briefly. "At least I don't think so, though it's an interesting thought. What I meant was, no matter what you do, whether you marry or not, your life will be safe. You've got money, security, a big career ahead of you. And if you decide the professional hassle isn't worth it, you can crawl into the bosom of your family and still have status. What the hell, you're Diane Summerfield, Esquire. Whatever happens, you've got it made. Whereas I— Without a man, I'm nothing."

"Rubbish!" Diane said.

"Facts of life. Because if I fuck up now, I've had it. Chances are I won't even have a job, let alone a husband and a decent home when this is over. Yours truly, the Invisible Woman. Well, I'm tired of that shit. I want to be Mrs. Somebody, Diane. Have a place in the world. I want to be a member of the PTA and go to the hardware store and buy tomato plants and talk about real estate values and yell at the laundry because they didn't starch my husband's shirts and have people know me when I walk down the street. I'm tired of being anonymous, don't you understand? I want to put down roots. Without Alex, life's so fucking empty—and time's running out. You heard Bernie's statistics."

"I thought you didn't believe in statistics."

"I believe what I see—and what I see is that this could be my last chance to be happy. If I don't marry Alex, I'll just die—"

"I find that incredible," Diane broke in. "People don't die for love, Fleur. There's more to life. There has to be! Are you telling me that with all your smarts, all your looks, you can't do better than this—this sordid affair?" Yet despite her harangue, she felt sorry for Fleur. In a way, Rosemary was right. She *was* Fleur the Pathetic, eternally frightened and defensive behind the showy exterior, naked and vulnerable as a snail without a shell.

The phone rang. Fleur clutched Diane's hand. "Don't answer it. It's her."

"I have to. It could be—somebody else."

"Your guy? He can call back."

The fourth ring activated the answering machine.

Hello. This is Diane Summerfield. I'm sorry I'm unavailable to take your call.

Diane and Fleur exchanged expectant glances.

Please leave your name and number when you hear the beep.

"Diane, help!" Fleur froze as the grief-stricken voice sliced through the room. "It's me—Rosemary. Something dreadful's happened. I need a lawyer. A friend! I'll be up all night, so call me as soon as you get in, or else first thing tomorrow. Oh, God,"—she started snuffling—"I can't believe it. It's the end of the world."

There was a click, then silence.

"She shouldn't be alone at a time like this," Diane said. "I have to call her back. Excuse me." She went into the bedroom for privacy and emerged ten minutes later with red eyes.

"You didn't tell her I was here, did you?" Fleur gobbling peanuts out of nervous reflex.

Diane glared at her, then poured herself a drink.

"Well, Fleur," she said grimly, "you got your wish. You have successfully destroyed a long and happy marriage. How could you!" Her voice quivered with pain. "What real harm has Rosemary ever done you? She's a bit smarmy, but that's her way. She's always been a kind and faithful friend. She didn't deserve this. And Chris! Did you ever stop to think there was a child involved? No! All you cared about were your own selfish needs. It was a wicked thing to do. Wicked!"

Fleur nearly choked on the peanuts.

"Wicked!" she rolled her eyes. "What an old-fashioned word! I thought it went out with the chastity belt. But then you always were big on moral judgments. Very well, Diane, have it your way. It was wicked. And I'm a wicked, wicked woman. But what the fuck have I done that's so awful? I fell in love and followed my heart. Maybe where you come from that's a capital crime. But I'm not like you, Di—so cool, controlled, so infinitely superior to emotional storms. I've got needs, anxieties. Jesus, be human, for once in your life! Forget your goddamn principles—"

"I can't."

"Can't? Is it physically impossible? Don't you ever act purely out of passion—out of love?"

Fleur's question scored a direct hit.

"Wrong is wrong, Fleur, pure and simple. It's not a question of compromise. I know. I've gone down that road myself. But never again. What the hell. I've given up the two men I cared about most—"

"Two?" Fleur perked up. "Your Yale professor and who else?"

The cue was all Diane needed for the story of Avram to come tumbling out, unadorned and unedited. She had kept her own counsel too long. Fleur listened, entranced.

"My, my," she said as Diane wound down, "you're full of surprises. I figured you for one of those high-powered executive types in a thousand-dollar suit. What did this guy have that's so special?"

Diane wiped her eyes. "He gave me warmth."

"Don't knock it," Fleur advised. "Though I must say you always struck me as wondrously self-sufficient. The thing I don't understand is why you broke up. Okay, he's not husband material, but that's no reason to stop sleeping with him. At least till something better comes along."

"Because that would be using him," Diane explained. "Because I have standards, scruples. You'll say I'm being sententious. Possibly so. Nonetheless, one sometimes has to make sacrifices, forfeit personal pleasure for ethical reasons. It wouldn't be right, wouldn't be proper for me to give Avram false hopes. As it is, I feel responsible. I've caused a lot of grief. Besides," she was astonished to find herself on the defensive, "there is such a thing as dignity."

"Yeah! Well, you get into bed with your dignity on a cold winter night," Fleur retorted, "and find how much comfort it brings you. *You* snuggle up to it. Not *me*. I'm not the martyr type. I'd rather be cuddling up to Alex and scruples be damned. For the record, I didn't set out to screw Rosemary, and I'm sorry for her, but I have to look out for Number One. What did she say on the phone, by the way? Is she going to sue for divorce?"

"I can't discuss it, and moreover I have no intention of getting caught in the middle between you two. I love you both. All I can say is, it's lucky you weren't home when Rosemary arrived. She would have torn you limb from limb."

Fleur stretched, yawned, then gave Diane a good-natured grin. "Does this mean no Wednesday Club meeting this week?"

Diane made up a bed in the living room, then turned in, but sleep was impossible. Through the closed door she could hear Fleur talking on the phone. To Alex, she presumed. Warning him of what he might expect. Exchanging endearments, intimacies. She pulled the covers up over her ears, hoping to shut out those reminders of shared love. Fleur was right. Dignity was a very chilly bedfellow.

"Diane Summerfield informs me that you're the toughest, meanest, orneriest divorce lawyer in the entire Northeast," Rosemary said.

Arthur Grimes beamed. He knew a compliment when he heard one. Nonetheless, he felt beholden to do the politic thing. For a very expensive quarter hour, he spoke of reconciliation, counseling, divorce as "a last resort." "Are you certain you want to go ahead with the proceedings?"

Rosemary narrowed her lips. "Does a bear," she answered, "defecate in the forest?"

Two days earlier Alex had returned from Chicago, forewarned and bearing an uncomfortable burden of guilt, to find his household in an uproar, his son staying with neighbors and, even more alarming, his mother-in-law ensconced on the premises. Rosemary had sent for the heavy artillery.

"You have some nerve, Alex Marshall," Dolly Bainter said, standing in the doorway, arms akimbo, "even showing your face here after what you've done to my poor child."

"This is between Rosie and me." Alex could feel the sweat running down his collar. The last thing he wanted was an allied attack. The Bainters were a close-knit and powerful clan, especially when threatened. Alex's instinct was to turn tail and run.

However, this was his home, Rosemary his wife, and he knew exactly how to handle her. The best defense was an offense, experience had proved. With this in mind, Alex charged into the kitchen.

Rosemary was sitting at the table, polishing silver, steadfastly refusing to acknowledge his presence. She had aged ten years since Monday morning. The usually cheerful face was pale and ravaged, the blooming complexion now the color of chalk. Alex had never seen her look so unattractive. Briefly he wavered between pity and shame, but pity was a trap. He girded his loins. To show signs of weakness would be fatal. Rosemary would pounce. Given the slightest advantage, she would go for the jugular, insist he give up Fleur on the spot. He'd be in sackcloth and ashes for months.

"You did a foolish, crazy thing, you realize," he began in his authoritative head-of-the-household voice. Rosemary didn't reply. In the corner Shelby, the springer spaniel, growled ominously. "You're aware," Alex continued, "that Fleur can sue the bejesus out of us? Charge you with trespassing, theft, malicious mischief? We're talking thousands of dollars damage plus who knows about punitive, and I'm not insured for that shit. Hell, woman, you're lucky she's not bringing criminal charges."

"Fleur sue *me*!" Rosemary put down a serving spoon and folded her arms. "That's a hot one." Shelby snarled in assent.

Alex straddled a chair and studied his wife more cautiously. For the first time in his life, it occurred to him that Rosemary might be dangerous. She certainly was going to be hell to live with.

Briefly he shuffled two possibilities. One: beat a strategic retreat to New York till things blew over. Or two: deny, deny, deny. The Big Lie. It had worked for Hitler, for Al Capone, for the generals in Vietnam. It was the basis of many a business transaction and nearly all ad campaigns. It was worth a stab.

"I want to make this marriage work, Rosie. I love you and I have done everything in my power to make you happy. I have, God knows, provided till my back teeth ache. But this business with Fleur! You seem to have jumped to some kind of conclusion which is totally unwarranted. Totally! I don't know what you imagine is going on, but just because you bear her a grudge of sorts, that's no reason to act like a madwoman."

"It's *my* fault?" Rosemary's carefully maintained balance began to wobble. "I'm the guilty party? You carry on with my best friend—correction! my worst enemy—and you expect *me* to take the blame?"

Before he could answer, Dolly Bainter materialized in the doorway to provide tactical support. She was a formidable opponent.

"I think, Alex, it would be better if discussion were left for another time. Rosemary's very upset and needs a few days to think things over. I've packed a couple of bags for you—they're in the hall—and I've reserved a room at the Waldorf. You'll be more comfortable there for the present."

Alex hesitated a fraction of a second. The Big Lie wasn't washing—frankly he hadn't thought it would—and New York beckoned as did Fleur. Yet he was wary of abandoning the field quite so swiftly. He had a sense of being outmaneuvered on all sides.

Dolly marched him into the front hall, with Shelby holding up the rear. Three suitcases were lined up, waiting to go.

"I'll drive you to the station."

"About Chris—" Alex said.

"We'll arrange something, don't worry." His mother-in-law began hustling him out the door. "We have no intention of getting between you and little Chris."

Alex teetered between remorse and relief. "You'll make her see reason, won't you, Dolly?"

Dolly Bainter gave a heartfelt sigh, which Alex took as reassurance. It wasn't until he was halfway to New York that he began wondering: Who the hell did Dolly mean by "we?"

TWENTY-THREE

———— · ————

For days Rosemary careered about the house like a maddened animal, fueled only by a profound sense of rage. In shifts Bernie and Diane came out to Westport to hold her hand and witness her agony and offer such solace as was within their means. But Rosemary would neither be comforted nor appeased. Her wrath was something dreadful to behold.

"Don't tell me to be reasonable," she answered Diane's plea against precipitate legal action, "when I'm bleeding from every pore. I want to destroy that man, grind him into bits. I want to put him through the kind of hell that he and that whore put me through."

Diane winced. "But divorce is so—so final, Rosemary. And you've had so many good years together—"

"Have we?" In the light of Alex's crime, she had begun to reexamine every inch of their marriage, interpreting each episode afresh, realigning familiar facts like a Russian commissar presented with a switch in party doctrine. She had been given new eyes and what she saw repelled her.

"He was always so wrapped up in himself and his precious career that he hardly knew I existed. And manipulative? My God! I was there to run a catering service, take his flak. When did my feelings, my aspirations ever come first? I was a piece of furniture, a pair of hands, that's all. He wasn't even particularly good in bed."

Diane ducked the reference to the Marshalls' sex life; she never speculated on such matters. But in other respects, she felt Rosemary was being unfair, both to herself and Alex. "That's not true—I mean about your being furniture. Far be it from me to defend his behavior with Fleur, but he was a good husband in lots of ways. Generous, hardworking. Remember how he encouraged you when you decided to start a business?"

"You bet he did, and you know why? So I wouldn't be a financial drain when he cut out! He and Fleur probably cooked it up between them. 'Let's get Rosemary to pay for herself.' Now he'll go into court and claim that his wife is an independent woman. Try to squeeze me out. Well, just because I'm capable of earning a living, that doesn't mean he can get off the hook. I want to see him crawl!"

There was more in this vein, much of it wild, some of it disturbingly accurate, all of it venomous. Rosemary made no distinction between fact and supposition. She had declared Alex guilty on all counts. Diane was staggered.

"Now, Rosemary." She tried to calm her. "Suppose you'd never found out about Fleur? What then? You'd probably still be living with Alex peaceably as ever. After all, you felt good about him right up until last week—"

"You're telling me ignorance is bliss?" she screamed. "Balls!" The new Rosemary took a perverse pleasure in vulgarities. "Ignorance is ignorance. When I think about how dumb I was, what a sucker they played me for, it only makes me madder. That man was my life, Diane, my whole reason for being. I'll never forgive him for what he did. Him or that sneaky bitch you still call your friend. Never, Di. Not as long as there's breath in my body."

"You have every right to be angry," Diane cautioned, "but try to maintain some kind of self-control. Rage is so destructive, and the person you're hurting most is yourself. Yourself and Chris. Try to put it behind you. Let it rest."

"You sound like my mother" came the bitter retort. "She keeps telling me about how when my father died, she learned to cope with grief and loss. She says I'll get over it. But Alex didn't die, worse luck. I wish he had. Instead, he betrayed me. Lied—cheated. That's a helluva difference. And is he sorry? Why, right this very moment he and Fleur are probably—oh, Christ, I don't want to think about it! Laughing, having a good time, in bed together, snickering. I can't bear it! No, Diane. It may not be very Christian of me, but I can neither forgive nor forget. Because the moment I stop hating him, I'll fall apart."

There was nothing Diane could do. Clearly, Rosemary would have to grapple through this crisis with such tools as she possessed, that murderous rage among them.

The next day Diane met Bernie for a drink at the Algonquin.

"Rosemary scares me," she confided.

"You think she's suicidal?"

"She doesn't have the time," Diane said, rapping wood for insurance. "She's too busy hating Alex. That's all she lives for these days. I came away feeling as though I'd stepped into an acid bath. Granted she's in a state of shock, and I personally would like to wring Alex's neck. But the way she's going on, all this talk of vengeance, she'll make it impossible for him to come back."

"Maybe he doesn't want to. Maybe he'll marry Fleur."

Diane wrinkled her nose. "They're such an odd couple, Alex and Fleur. Can you really see them living together? Fleur's got this image of herself in a frilly little apron, baking deep-dish pies. I give that fantasy ten weeks. No, Bernie. I think their affair will run out of steam and Alex will head home. Which is where he belongs."

"Why should Rosemary want him back after this?"

"Why?" Diane cried. "Because of Chris, because they're a family with ten solid years of marriage behind them. He was a devoted husband for a long, long time. Okay, self-centered and terribly driven, but maybe this whole business will make him appreciate Rosemary more. What I'm afraid of is, she won't give him the chance."

Bernie contemplated her gin and tonic. "Rosemary scares me too," she muttered, "but not for your reasons. What scares me is how she let herself get so fucked over by a man. Her entire emotional stock was invested in that marriage. Past, present, future—the works. It was Alex this, Alex that. She lived her life through her husband. She gave and gave and held back nothing for herself. Crazy! Ever see Rosemary's personal stationery? It's on this beautiful cream stock from Tiffany, embossed letters, very pricey. 'Mrs. Alexander Marshall' is how it reads. Not even her own first name for Chrissakes. Well, this is her reward for all those years of perfect service and self-suppression. A good thing she's started this little company of hers, with or without

Alex's backing. Since I've known her, it's the first positive step she's ever taken."

"Oh come now," Diane said. "Marrying Alex was a positive step, having Chris—"

"By positive," Bernie clarified, "I mean independent. Let's face it, without a career of sorts, she'd be totally destroyed. All she'd have is Chris and a big empty house. There's a message in there somewhere, Diane. A terrible lesson for all of us."

"I suppose." Diane nodded and signaled for the bill.

She pondered Bernie's "message" on the walk home. It had something to do with identity, she presumed. With the risk inherent in living your husband's life. Bernie herself was in no danger of ever becoming "Mrs. Him." Self-abnegation was not her style.

Diane wasn't sure which approach was worse: Rosemary's total immersion in marriage or Bernie's cool-headed caution. On balance, neither passed muster.

Nonetheless, all this flurry of impending marriage and divorce had a profoundly disturbing effect on Diane. It underscored her loneliness. She missed Avram keenly. Half a dozen times a day she found herself reaching for the phone, eager to share some thought, some intimate bit of gossip.

How was your day, sweetie? Mine was hell.

Will you tape *L. A. Law* for me tonight?

Don't forget your deadline for that piece on Chomsky.

She had seen an item in the papers, heard a funny story, twisted her ankle leaving court—and all her instincts cried out to share these with him. She worried about him, too, oftener than she cared to admit. How was his thesis going? Had he ever bought himself a proper winter overcoat? Above all, did he miss her too? Some days she felt she would have given a fortune just to hear his voice, to have him drop in for coffee and to "schmooze."

Lately, she had come to feel like a monk in a peculiarly harsh and restrictive order, alternating bouts of hard work and vast silences. But unlike the dedicated Trappist, she lacked the compensation of true faith. He, at least, held dreams of heaven. Diane had only *Simplexx* v. *Harrigan* to console her.

Life without Avram! Theoretically it should be neither better nor worse than in those days before he came along. It was worse. His love had spoiled her, made solitude more painful. The least bit of tripe reduced her to tears when she was alone. A sentimental movie. A travel poster. The banal lyrics of some stupid pop song. "Reach out and touch someone," the TV commercial suggested, and Diane's eyes brimmed. Touch whom? She was suffering withdrawal symptoms.

Everyone else seemed to have someone to touch. All her friends enjoyed intense private lives, no matter how chaotic. There was Bernie, scurrying about with wedding plans. Fleur utterly absorbed in her affair. Byron, poor soul, and his beloved Jim. Even Rosemary, for all her misery, was not alone. When the agony subsided, as Diane had no doubt that it would, Rosemary would still have Chris at the end of the day. And she would have him for years to come.

Men leave, children don't. Children are forever. Could that have been Bernie's message?

If so, then Diane ought to marry Avram and have babies. Or not marry Avram and get pregnant anyhow. A lot of single women took that route these days. It struck her as sensible. Or maybe adopt a child. Or foster one. Or get a pet, like Ginnie Hadsell at the firm had done.

"You live with cats and you never want for companionship," Ginnie was always saying. "My babies wait at the door for me every night." She spoke of Flotsam and Jetsam as though they were human. Warm and furry they might be, even affectionate, but Diane had yet to meet a cat who could schmooze.

What the hell! She hadn't sunk to the level of seeking feline company. What an admission of defeat!

Perhaps Fleur was right and Diane had been drawing moral distinctions where none existed. Her affair with Avram had been cloudless until the question of marriage arose. If he was willing to turn back the clock, pretend the proposal had never taken place, then so was she. She would call him next week. Sooner. Invite him around for coffee or a drink. If they couldn't be man and wife—and they couldn't! —perhaps they could be lovers. And if they couldn't be lovers, they could surely be friends.

Alex's exile to New York, which he had viewed as a temporary measure, produced an unexpected side effect. For the first time since his wedding day, his leisure hours were accountable to no one: not to wife, not to child. Best of all, not to the learned-by-rote-and-never-forgotten commuter timetable. Those trains that regularly crawled between Grand Central and Westport could crawl without him for a while.

This revelation burst upon him his third full day in the city. The preceding night he had left the office at eight and taken Fleur to a leisurely dinner. Afterward they had gone dancing at Limelight and stayed out till one. Why not? He had no train to catch.

The next morning his mental alarm clock awakened him at twenty past six. Mind and body were instantly alert, geared to catching the seven-forty-nine to the city, before he realized, with a surge of delight, that he was already in the city. He rolled over and went back to sleep.

He arose again at eight-fifteen, shaved, and caught a cab to the office, making a note of the time. Forty-five minutes from bed to desk.

Alex pulled out his pocket calculator.

Including the drive to and from the Westport station, his daily commute came to a total of three hours and ten minutes. Multiplied by five, that was a total of fifteen hours and fifty minutes each week. Call it sixteen, what with delays on the rail and snowy roads in winter. And that was a conservative estimate.

Next he multiplied sixteen by fifty (Alex scrupulously allowed two weeks for the vacation that he rarely took), and he arrived at a total of eight hundred hours a year. Then he divided that by twenty-four, the hours in each day—

Alex sucked in his breath.

Unbelievable! Every year he was spending thirty-three and a third days doing nothing but getting to and from his job. A month plus! One month out of twelve irretrievably shot. Hours, days of accumulated boredom, watching familiar landscape grind by, when he might have been pitching new clients or sailing or sleeping late or screwing Fleur or playing squash or just plain having fun. The scale of such waste was staggering.

He had squandered a twelfth of his adult life on the Metropolitan Transit Authority. One fifth of his waking hours. For what? For the privilege of the occasional Sunday afternoon cookout. The thrill of changing screens and storm windows twice a year. It didn't make sense.

In another thirty years he could be pushing up daisies. By which time, he calculated, he would have lost another 3.65 years of his life.

Alex put the calculator away, feeling very much an ancient being, suddenly blessed with a second chance at youth.

Like many a suburbanite, Alex had a limited knowledge of the city. His New York was bounded by the World Trade Center to the south, the Plaza Hotel to the north, and within that grid, restricted to certain locales: a handful of midtown restaurants, the Dartmouth Club, and Brooks Brothers. The only times he ventured beyond these limits had been to see an occasional ball game and visit Fleur.

But the rest of New York—the "Big Apple," throbbing with adventure, pulsating with excitement, the center of dreams and dazzling fantasies—that New York he knew hardly better than he knew Chicago or any other city on his business itinerary.

And then Rosemary, of all people, handed him this extra month! He might never again have such a chance to kick up his heels. Discos, theaters, jazz joints, piano bars, Broadway, sports events: All these enticements were now within a stone's throw. And Fleur would be a glamorous guide. New York glitz was her forte.

That weekend he took a three-month furnished sublet in a smart co-op a few blocks away from Fleur. "What do you think?" He showed her around his new apartment with a proprietary air.

"Very charming." She was wounded that he had rented a place without consulting her, but she was reluctant to criticize. "Awfully expensive, though. Why don't you move in with me instead?"

"I've already signed the lease, sweetie."

"Then suppose I move in with you. I'd love us to live together, like a real couple. How about it?"

Alex thanked her but shook his head. "Too small, too crowded." And also, though he left the thought unspoken, too much grist for Rosemary's mill.

"Well, maybe if we found something together—"

"We'll see." He smiled and kissed her. Maybe later, maybe not. In the meantime freedom was unconscionably sweet.

*   *   *

Except for Alex's choice in living arrangements, Fleur was in seventh heaven. They slept together every night, his place or hers.

"If Rosemary thought we'd get bored with each other," she told Diane over the phone, "she couldn't have been wronger."

Overnight, life had become a whirlwind of heady entertainments, with Alex opting for the best shows, the hottest discos, the smartest restaurants, the noisiest bars. Morning would find him with his nose buried in *New York* Magazine or *The Village Voice*, figuring what to see, where to go after work.

"I feel like the proverbial hick in town spending the egg money," Alex said, learning the steps to the Bird late on a Friday night at the Palladium. "What's our next stop?"

"How about home to bed?"

He clapped her on the shoulder. "Night's young, baby."

Once he accompanied her on a shopping spree. The replenishment of her wardrobe was a major project, and Alex promised to help, in compensation for his wife's misbehavior. "My God," he said as he handed his American Express card to the saleswoman at Bonwit's, "this stuff costs a bundle." But beyond that he never complained. He was used to underwriting women. Moreover, he liked Fleur to look smashing at all times.

Now that the need for secrecy was gone, he delighted in showing her off. He often took her along on business dinners with the injunction that she "knock 'em dead." Accordingly, Fleur dressed to kill every night, although it got a bit tiresome. Still, she knew her job: to charm, to chat, to make Alex Marshall look like the most fortunate man in the world.

He introduced her as "my good friend, Fleur Chamberlain," and enjoyed that you-lucky-dog look that surfaced on his clients' faces. Above all he relished their discovery that this chic sexy female was not some bimbo provided by an escort service, but a businesswoman of judgment and clout.

"Fleur is a vice president at Marsden-Baker," he once boasted. Later she had reprimanded him. "I'm not, you know. Not yet. If fact I'm just about the only person there who isn't."

"That's okay. No one's going to check up. Anyhow, one of these days you will be."

On the one hand she found this job enhancement flattering—Alex clearly had a great respect for her accomplishments. On the other it scared her. For come the day when she had the privilege of being Mrs. Alex Marshall, she might very well have no job at all. The whole situation at Marsden-Baker could go *boom* at any moment, and she'd be out on the street, let alone not making VP.

Besides, Alex didn't need a vice president for a wife. He needed someone to run his household, look after his interests.

She wanted to raise the subject of marriage—never far from her mind—but held back. She assumed his emotions were still too raw from his last encounter with Rosemary and that he required time to adjust. By then Fleur would have made herself indispensable.

Poor Alex! He was like a kid let out of school, eating his fill of hot fudge sundaes. But a grown man couldn't subsist permanently on a diet of strenuous fun and wee hours. Sooner or later he'd feel the need to settle down, remarry. She hoped it was sooner.

Every Sunday he dutifully took the train to Westport and spent the afternoon with Chris. From what Fleur could deduce, Rosemary made herself scarce on those occasions, and Alex usually came back looking glum. Whether it was the visit that depressed him or the return to New York, Fleur couldn't say. She always made a point of being especially good in bed Sunday nights.

She had stopped by his apartment one day after work, when Alex handed her a registered letter.

"This beats everything!" he said, looking stunned.

The letter was from Arthur Grimes of Grimes, Roylott Shapiro. It stated that Rosemary intended to start divorce proceedings, and it included a request for the name of Alex's attorney.

"Oh, Christ," he groaned. "Lawyers! All they ever do is fuck things up and charge royally for the privilege. Maybe the sensible step would be for me just to phone Rosemary and see if we can't thrash things out between us."

"I wouldn't do that!" Fleur's heart skipped a beat. "You'd probably just aggravate the situation. From what I hear, she's really furious. Anyhow, the last thing you want is a shouting contest, Alex. If you like, I can find a good divorce attorney for you. My boss—"

"I don't need any referrals. I know dozens of lawyers. Bloody hell!" He gave the coffee table a swift vicious kick. "Why does Rosie have to make such an issue out of everything!"

He dropped the subject, and Fleur hesitated to bring it up again. But he did see a lawyer the following week. Fleur was delighted. She felt it was a step in the right direction. Lawyers did indeed fuck everything up, and once *Marshall* v. *Marshall* was in the hands of competent attorneys and positions began to harden, the marriage, Fleur believed, was as good as dead.

On the whole she felt charitable. Let Rosemary have the furniture, the knickknacks, the Porsche, custody of Chris. Even that fabulous house. Fleur begrudged her nothing. The woman had been hard done by and deserved ample compensation. Moreover, Alex had implied that he had plenty of other assets. He could always buy another house. In Westchester, perhaps. Or Bergen County. Westport wouldn't do, after all. It was preferable to put a few miles between Alex and his ex.

Anyhow, what were bricks and mortar compared to love? Within reason they could be happy anywhere.

As Rosemary herself had once said, in the long run there was but one prize worth having, one prize greater than all other earthly goods. And now that prize was Fleur's.

TWENTY-FOUR

———•———

Diane, so assertive in professional matters, suffered agonies of indecision before picking up the phone and dialing Avram.

He was angry with her, she posited. She would lose face. He had—God forbid!—found someone else. Alternately, he was unhappy. Repentant. He'd been ill and couldn't call. Flu, pneumonia—that wouldn't surprise her. What could you expect of a man who didn't even own a decent winter coat?

She didn't know which image was worse: Avram, sick and lonely, or Avram, hale and happy and otherwise engaged. It took no imaginative leap to picture him with a pretty girl on his arm. Prettier, younger than she. New York teemed with lovely women who would be delighted to take Avram at face value. A "buyer's market," as Bernie had once observed.

Given the geography of the building, they never met by chance. He took the service entrance on his rounds. She'd had no domestic crisis requiring his aid. Thus years could go by without their paths crossing, even though they lived but an elevator ride apart.

The night before leaving for Washington for a court appearance, Diane tossed a coin. The result was unequivocal. Accordingly, she poured herself a double scotch, downed half of it, then, swallowing her pride along with the Chivas Regal, phoned Avram.

"It's been ages since I've seen you," she said in a scrupulously neutral voice.

"One month and two days—"

"That long?" As if she didn't know. "Actually, I'm going out of town for a couple of days," she went on, "and was just wondering how you've been. Are you free to come around for a drink?"

"Half an hour," he said. Her heart bounded.

She would not be nervous, she pledged. Would play the evening by ear. Since she had taken the first step, the next would be up to him. One part of her was geared to learn bad news. A month was like a year in a young man's life. Another part expected instant rapture.

He arrived wearing his black suit as a sign of good intentions, but its very sobriety placed a formal distance between them. He had let his hair grow, she observed. He looked different, unfamiliar.

"Hello." Diane suppressed the urge to shake hands. "Won't you come in?"

He seated himself on the wing chair. Had he brought a hat, he would have placed it across his knees.

They had a brief, noncommittal exchange of "How are you?" and "Very well, thank you." Diane asked politely about his thesis ("Completed, thank you") and he in turn made the proper inquiries of her. It was all so polite. Punctilious. It was all—such sheer hell! The magic had fled, vanished totally, along with Avram's T-shirt and khakis. The atmosphere grew strained and oppressive.

"I'm flying to Washington tomorrow morning," she said. "Harrigan has filed a motion to postpone."

"Oh, yes?"

"If granted, then we counterfile."

"I'd be most interested in hearing the outcome."

"Should we lose, of course, we shall have to explore whether we have sufficient cause for a Supreme Court appeal."

"I see."

"But we expect a decision very soon."

They sat for a moment in uncomfortable silence, then Diane remembered her manners. "Oh, but I haven't offered you anything to drink. Can I get you something?"

"Coffee, please."

"No milk, two sugars, right?" Diane recalled.

He gave an unhappy nod.

"I'll put it on." She seized the excuse to leave the room.

There was a special blend Avram was fond of, a biting mix of chicory and coffee beans. She still had some stowed away in the overhead cupboard along with other rarely used items. Temporarily shelved, she mused, like the man himself. She climbed the step stool. The coffee was nowhere to be found.

Ridiculous. Things don't disappear. She was upset, nervous. It had to be there. It was inconceivable that she had thrown it out! That would be tantamount to admitting she had never expected to see Avram again. She would locate the damn coffee if it killed her.

With set lips, Diane began unloading each shelf, crowding forgotten groceries onto the narrow counter. God! How much food there was in this tiny kitchen. Cans of imported tomatoes and soup stocks, dozens of spices, three kinds of sugar, jars of relishes, chutneys, fancy sauces. As though this was really a proper household where a proper family sat down regularly for cooked meals. What a joke! From the day Avram left, she had done nothing more complicated than arrange take-out sushi on a dish. It was all a pretense, a sham.

My life may be empty, she surveyed the piled-up food miserably, *but my cupboard runneth over.* Why had everything gone awry? She had set so much stock in this reunion, held such high hopes. All the possibilities had been foreseen except this dreadful stiffness on both their parts.

Calling him had been a ghastly mistake. Nothing was as dead as yesterday's love affair. Dead, dead, dead, The thing to do was find the wretched coffee, brew it, then send him on his way. The sooner the better. With increasing frenzy, she continued emptying the shelves. A can of tuna fish struck her toe and clattered to the floor.

"Damn!" The pain brought tears to her eyes. Avram came running.

"What happened?" He looked about the kitchen in dismay.

"I can't find it." Diane was close to hysteria.

"Can't find what?"

"Your coffee." She started beating her fists against the counter. "I looked everywhere—I can't find it."

He grabbed her arm. "This is crazy! What are we—strangers?"

"I have to find it!" She burst into tears.

"Diane, sweetheart." Suddenly he was cradling her in his arms. "The hell with the coffee. I didn't come here for that. I came because I love you—I missed you—"

"Me too." A monthful of pent-up emotions began to burst their boundaries and overflow. "I missed you so terribly!"

"Sha—sha—" He rocked her gently as a child, and at his touch, the last vestige of her reserve crumbled and was gone.

"Sha—sha—" The words, meaningless, were balm, soothing away a hundred hurts, comforting, seductive. Nothing existed except this moment, this intimacy. She buried her head into the depths of the black worsted jacket, the coarse wool rough against her skin, his breath on her hair. Even as she clung to him, myriad emotions swept through her: joy, shame, love, relief, nostalgia. Above all, a piercing sense of panic at how close they had come to losing each other.

She fumbled with the buttons on his shirt, seeking reassurance from the warmth of his skin, the solid girth of his chest. If she could, she would have crawled inside him.

Without another word, they went into her bedroom and slowly, carefully, like solemn children, undressed each other with exquisite care.

"Look." He took her hand and led her to the full-length mirror. There they stood, naked, side by side in the muted lamplight. "How beautiful."

And so she was, bathed in his love, his image of her. And so was he. They were matched. Perfect. She smiled at the handsome man in the mirror. He smiled back, then turned in profile. She swung to face him.

"I love you, Avram." The words had ached to be spoken.

His answer was to draw her close until they stood mouth to mouth, breast to breast, thigh to thigh. He placed his fingertips on her cheeks lightly, the connoisseur of a rare precious object, then slid his hands across her shoulders, down her body in loving definition. And so they stood, sharing the same breath, the same heartbeat. Then he drew her closer still. Against her, she felt him grow hard and strong, felt the hunger born of so many lonely nights.

Her body grew ripe and welcoming. "Fill me, fill my life with your love."

He enveloped her buttocks with his powerful hands, then

with one great heave of his arms, lifted her off the ground
as though she were weightless. A nymph. Some exquisite
creature lighter than air. Her knees burrowed into the small
of his back, her arms encircled his neck. Eyes shut, flesh
melting, she could feel him enter her, possess her, merging
their bodies into a single liquid flow. And then there was
no longer Diane and Avram, rich and poor, native and
stranger. They were nothing more, nothing less, than a man
and a woman become one.

That night they refused to squander a moment on mere
sleep. Dawn still found them in bed, making love, being
close, "schmoozing." One night hardly sufficed to exchange
all the confidences left unshared the past month. Sometimes Diane couldn't get the words out fast enough. "Oh,
God"—she lay with her head nestled in his arm—"I completely forgot to tell you about what happened to . . . ."

To Fleur, to Byron, to her brother in Santa Barbara. And
there was so much to catch up on from him.

"You tired?" he asked.

Diane giggled. "I could keep on talking right up to plane
time, there's just so much to say."

The alarm clock sounded. Reluctantly, she made a move.
"I have some packing to do." She kissed his nose.

"Don't go to Washington, Diane."

"I have to." She signed. "You understand. Anyhow, I
expect to be back tomorrow or Wednesday at the latest and
then . . . ." Her voice trailed off. And then everything would
be as it had always been. They would be together. Happy.
Close.

"And then," he said, "we'll get married."

"Married!" Diane was startled. "I thought we agreed not
to discuss it at this point. It's way premature."

Avram frowned. "I don't understand you. How can we
not discuss it? What has this whole night been about if not
marriage? Of course we'll get married. In light of how we
feel about each other, my love, anything else is absurd."

"I thought—" Her heart turned over. "I hoped we could
go back to what we had before . . . well, before you proposed. It was easier all around. That's how I want us to be,
darling. The way we were."

Avram got out of bed and pulled open the drapes. A

watery morning sun drifted in. Arms folded, he studied her
with a puzzled air.

"I'll make us some coffee," he said.

"If you can find it."

"I'll find it."

She heard him puttering in the kitchen, putting to rights
last night's mess, then sniffed the tart aroma of the chicory
blend.

"Where was the coffee hiding?" she asked when he entered the room with two steaming cups on a tray, but
Avram would not be deflected.

"We can't be the way we were, Diane. That's impossible."

"Why?" She began to feel anxious. In another hour and a
half she had to leave for the airport. This was hardly the
time for a major upheaval. "Let's not make an issue of it
now, darling," she pleaded. "Let's just continue for a while
as we were. I thought that's what last night meant to
you—that we still loved each other, that we could be happy
in the same old way. Nothing has changed."

"Everything has changed."

"Because you proposed? Suppose you hadn't?"

"But I have." He sat down on the side of the bed and
sipped his coffee slowly. "It makes all the difference. Once
something's been spoken—" He paused. "When I was a
small boy, my sister Miriam loved to tease me. We were out
playing once, it was very hot and I remember her saying,
'Stand behind the tree and think of anything in the world
except vanilla ice cream.' Well, of course I couldn't think of
anything in the world *but* vanilla ice cream, and I don't
particularly care for vanilla. But it obsessed me. Why?
Because once a possibility has entered the realm of discussion, it must be dealt with. Once I started thinking of
you—of us as a married couple, there was a new element of
seriousness present. What we were is over, Diane. What
matters now is what we'll become. Nothing remains static.
You must know from your work that certain actions have
their own dynamic. Besides, it's time. We're ready for the
next step, the next level. I want to get married, put down
roots, start a family. School days are over, Diane, and it's
time for real life. When you called me yesterday, I presumed you too had come to some sort of decision. Instead,
you tell me that you want to turn back the clock. Well, I
can't. The matter has to be resolved."

Diane got up, put a robe on, then got her overnight bag out of the closet. Whatever happened, she had to be on that plane that morning. It was already close to eight.

"Don't avoid my eyes, Diane."

"Why do you have to do this?" She swiveled to face him, aware her tone had taken on an edge. "Why can't you let well enough alone? If anyone's turning back the clock, it's you. Right back to the same impasse as last time. You're pressuring me, trying to get my back to the wall, but I don't hear you making concessions. I'm perfectly willing to discuss possibilities, negotiate, but you'll have to do the same. Tell me, have you reconsidered what I asked of you that day?"

"About my becoming a lawyer? Absolutely not. It was not a reasonable request." He shook his head, impatient. "It's not as if I were a playboy, Diane. I expect to work—and work reasonably hard. At what I choose to do."

"Which is?"

"I'm not certain yet, but honest work, I promise, nothing that will disgrace you. I'm a reputable man."

"Oh, Avram," she sighed. "That's not the question. We're too far apart on too many issues to even consider marriage. However"—she had turned the matter over in her mind a dozen times this past week and arrived at what seemed a tolerable solution—"I have a proposal—well, perhaps 'proposition' would be a better word, that I would like to put before you. We will remain everything we are now—friends, lovers, confidants. And I will offer you something else."

Her father's suggestion that Avram saw her as his passport to America continued to vex her. Yes, he loved her. Yes, he might even hope to marry her. But what had lent urgency to his suit, she believed, was his status as an immigrant. Suppose that were solved? Suppose she could secure Avram's stay in America without resorting to the finality of marriage? For all she knew, he too might feel this was the ideal solution.

She tried to put the matter tactfully, but however phrased, the proposition was clear. Diane was willing to put up bond and act as Avram's sponsor. With her as guarantor (to say nothing of her uncle Drew's connections), he was sure to be granted a green card.

"Which means," she concluded, "that you can remain here indefinitely, without restrictions. It's the first step to citizenship, Avram. And it would give us plenty of time to sort matters out."

He had listened patiently as she said her piece, then mulled it over. Diane finished packing.

"So that's what you think I want, Diane."

"That's what I think," she said cautiously, "is a reasonable and workable solution."

"I see. In other words, it's what *you* want." He went over to her desk, picked up the leather-bound Hebrew-English dictionary he had given her for Christmas, riffled through it until he found the word he sought. She watched him, edgy, heart in mouth and eye on the clock. She hadn't even showered yet, and had a plane to catch. Whatever he was seeking could surely wait.

"Let's take a quick shower, Avram. We're both pretty grotty. Anyhow, you needn't give me your answer this minute. There's plenty of time. We'll discuss it when I come back."

Avram stared at her, unmoving, then glanced back into the book. "You want me to be—am I pronouncing it correctly?—you want me to be your gigolo."

"Oh, for Chrissakes, Avram. That is the most absurd thing I've ever heard! A gigolo indeed! Why, the term's right out of Victorian literature. I'm trying to help you, that's all."

"A gigolo," he repeated. "A paid companion. A man who pleases a woman, for a fee. I offer you marriage," he said bitterly. "And you—offer me this!"

"Please, darling. You're taking it out of context. I didn't mean to offend you. Anyhow, I'm in a hurry. I have to dress, I have a plane to catch. We'll discuss it later. Just think about it is all I ask."

"There is nothing to think about." She stared at him, stunned at the anger in his eyes. But he was moving about, collecting his belongings.

"Catch your plane, Diane. I won't hold you anymore." He threw on his clothes, slap dash, shirt buttons askew, then headed for the door as though the devil were on his heels. He turned for one final shot. "And you're the one who talks so much of dignity!"

A half hour later, a pale and shaken Diane was in a cab on the way to LaGuardia.

TWENTY-FIVE

$\cdot$

Federal Judge Herman J. Kunicki dreamed of being remembered in legal annals as the "Great Mediator." He was that rarity among jurists: a man who genuinely loathed contention. The old gentleman preferred to settle those disputes placed before him in the quiet and reflective peace of his study rather than in the adversarial arena of court. Ideally, he preferred not to settle disputes at all.

Given murky law and hard choices, Judge Kunicki was happiest when the litigants themselves relieved him of the necessity of publishing decisions. *Simplexx* v. *Harrigan,* for instance. The case should never have come to court, let alone dragged on for all these years. Whichever side prevailed, the loser would immediately lay ground for an appeal. And if there was anything Judge Kunicki hated more than making difficult decisions, it was having those decisions reversed.

He scanned the powerful array of legal talent crowded into his chambers. Some two dozen high-priced lawyers, each somberly clad, each with briefcase and brain at the ready, poised to move in for the kill. "Tell me," he said adjusting his glasses. "With all you fellas here, who's home minding the shop?" There was a polite if uncertain titter while the judge aligned the mountain of papers on his desk. He scowled, then drew a deep breath.

"As Edmund Burke so astutely noted in his speech on conciliation with the American colonies . . ."

Diane squirmed in her chair. The last thing she needed at
this point was a lecture on English jurisprudence. Why
didn't the old man deliver his opinion and be done with it?
This trip, she suspected, would be nothing more than an
egregious waste of time. She shouldn't be here. It was time
to resolve the situation with Avram, then get on with her
life. With or without him. Their last two meetings had
ended with such rancor, a far cry from Avram's dream of
living in peace. Was it a preview of what marriage had in
store for them? Or merely the normal ructions of two
proud people? Reluctantly, she forced herself back to matters at hand, for the judge's voice was turning stentorian.

" '. . . indeed, every human benefit and enjoyment, every
virtue and every prudent act—is founded on compromise.' "

" '. . . and barter,' " Diane murmured, while Byron slunk
deeper into his chair. If the judge insisted on quoting
Burke, let him do it properly. The phrase was "compromise
and barter." Not that it made any difference. The judge
was playing to a captive audience.

She gazed about her. There were a few new faces on the
opposing team from Howland & Matheson, but most of the
participants were familiar. Longtime colleagues and adversaries, veterans of the same unending war, who had spent
the last four years marching in lockstep. There was her
boss, Frank Merriam, tense as a Chihuahua, chewing on his
lip. Irene Katz, brow knit, furiously scribbling notes. Byron,
bored out of his skull. At the adjacent table, that nit-
picking Carrie Johnson. Hank "the Crank" Benedict. Bill
Shannon looking handsomer than ever. She had seen the
notice of his engagement in the *Times* the past Sunday. To
a neurosurgeon, Diane recalled. Well, the doc was one
lucky lady, Diane thought enviously. But—to judge by Bill's
glowing countenance—he considered himself lucky too.
Bill caught her glance and winked. She must remember to
congratulate him later.

"So I have decided"—Key words. Diane pricked up her
ears—"not to rule on this question of postponement at this
time." There was a collective groan of anticlimax. "Instead,"
the judge went on, "I commend the great Burke's wisdom
to you. You men and women represent some of the finest
legal minds in our society. I cannot but believe that should
you enlist your considerable skills in the art of conciliation, pour your energies into the noble task of achieving

compromise, you will arrive at a wiser, more equitable decision than this court can hand down. I expect you to strain to that end." He checked his watch. "It is now eleven forty-five, Monday morning. My clerk will show you to a deliberation room. It is my intention that both parties of lawyers stay there and negotiate in good faith from nine until six each working day, longer should they require, until a mutually satisfactory agreement can be reached. This court will reconvene on Friday at ten. At that time, I hope to hear that you have arrived at a meeting of the minds." He looked from one table to the other. "Gentlemen, ladies, I urge you to think of your respected opponents not as adversaries but as colleagues in the quest for justice."

He clapped his hands over his ears to block any protest, then strode out of the room.

"Outrageous!" someone howled. "Forced mediation!" "Is this legal?" Marcia Wainwright wanted to know. "What's the precedent?" "Goddamn," Byron groaned. "I feel like I'm under house arrest." "I've heard of juries being locked up," Bill Shannon said as Kunicki's clerk came to lead them away, "but never lawyers!"

Like naughty children, the two packs of warring attorneys were ushered into a spacious oak-paneled room on the floor above and left to their own devices. The first two hours were spent squabbling over rules of procedure, followed by a heated argument about seating arrangements. The only point of concord between the forces was irritation with Judge Kunicki. "We're litigators, damn it," Marcia pointed out. "Not pantywaists."

And so they were. "Hired guns" and proud of it—trained to maraud, attack, ambush. To go for the jugular, the soft spot, the Achilles' heel, the weak sister. Above all to contest each point to the death while granting nothing in return. Confrontation was their life's work; the smallest concession an admission of cowardice. Thus even sending out for lunch became a test of strength, a battle of wills. Pizzas or hamburgers—the lines were drawn. They wound up ordering separately from different establishments.

After lunch each team held strategy meetings at opposite ends of the long table.

"What do you make of Kunicki's tactics?" Frank Merriam polled his associates. "And keep your voices low. Bob?"

"He took his cue from the Bible," Bob Warfield ventured. "Solomon dividing up the baby. As I read it, the judge is incapable of making up his mind and wants us to do his job for him."

"If he's incompetent to rule, he should recuse himself."

"On what grounds—stupidity?"

"I don't believe indecision is his problem" Diane said thoughtfully. "Or stupidity. I suspect he's already decided the case and is afraid of being reversed on appeal."

"I agree with Diane," Frank whispered. "Kunicki's a wily son of a bitch. My bet is that he's ruled but is still looking for an out. In which case, it's all over but the shouting. Somebody's lost. Somebody's won."

"But who?" Tom Eng rubbed his chin. "Us? Them? That's the kicker. If we turn out to be the victors, then we'd be crazy to negotiate. Why give those bastards a hairpin? Winner take all."

"But if," Diane pointed out, "he's found against us already, then anything we can achieve through negotiation is pure bonus. What do you think, Frank? Do you believe we've already won on the merits?"

But her boss, one of the most farsighted men she'd ever met, simply shook his head, bewildered. "God only knows," he said. "It could go either way. I ask you, what's to choose between us and them?"

Tweedledum and Tweedledee, Diane remembered Avram once describing the contenders. But she was astonished that her own head of litigation felt the same.

"I'd hate to gamble," he was saying, "and turn out to be wrong."

"On the other hand, we might never know."

"On the third hand—what the fuck! Let's negotiate."

"Right. But we should keep this in mind," Diane cautioned. "If they perceive us as *willing* to negotiate, that means they see us as having conceded defeat. They'll just toughen their stance."

"Good point." Frank nodded. "Okay, we negotiate, but from a position of strength. Dominance. No concessions of any substance."

At the far end of the table, Diane saw a huddle of heads, then a show of hands, and suspected they too had reached the same conclusion.

*   *   *

For three and a half arduous days, two unyielding teams of people tried to make their opposite number holler uncle. Hours were spent working out the most trivial concessions, then demanding monstrous boons as quid pro quo. It was tough, hard, stressful work, And, given the intransigence of all concerned, doomed from the start.

Friday morning the two sets of weary lawyers trooped into Judge Kunicki's court.

"And have you reached a meeting of the minds?" he asked.

"I regret to say not, Your Honor."

The judge poured himself a Pepto-Bismol.

"Have you tried?"

"With the utmost sincerity."

Kunicki downed his concoction and made a face.

"You may expect my decision shortly. Court stands adjourned."

"What a goddamn waste of a week!" Diane said. She and Byron had repaired to the bar at the Hay-Adams for a drink before boarding the shuttle back to New York.

"Yeah!" Byron yawned. "Although that little session must have racked up another couple of hundred thousand dollars in fees for the firm. So it wasn't a total write-off. Thank you, Judge Kunicki. Christ, I'm bushed. Let's you and I get stinko."

Byron's week had been even more strenuous than her own. Each night after work, he had flown to New York to be with Jim, returning on the early bird special the next morning. Now he twined his legs around the barstool, staking out turf like a homesteader.

"We'll miss the noon plane," Diane said.

"Fuck it. We're not going to get any work done today." He ordered a round of doubles while they second-guessed the events of the week. The first scotch went down like velvet. "We'll take the one o'clock," Diane said, then ordered the same again.

"Did I tell you, Di?"—the two clinked glasses—"Jim and I have decided to get married. Yep, we're going to tie the knot. A small, select wedding. You're invited. We figured" —Byron's speech started to slur—"well, there isn't a lot of time left, another couple of months. May as well do it while we can. Marriage is commitment, way I see it. Exchanging vows, all that jazz. Bartender? Remember the thirsty in their hour of need."

Diane, half-drunk already, was curious about the legal implications of a homosexual wedding. That area of the law was pure mystery. "How'd you do that, Byron? You go down to the municipal building to—what is it, the registrar's office, and file for a license? I mean, is there some kind of gay rights issue at stake?"

"Unh-unh." Byron shook his head. "No license. Private ceremony. No standing in law. Symbolic gesture, that's all."

"I understand," she said, unexpectedly touched. "And I hope you'll both be very happy. Funny how everybody's getting married these days. My old friend Bernie. Bill Shannon. Pretty soon probably Fleur. And now you. I'll be the only old maid left in New York." She began feeling sorry for herself. "I could've got married too, you know. If I wanted to."

"Oh, yeah?" Byron looked at her with pink-eyed interest.

"Yep," Diane snuffled. "He was sweet. A darling man, but too—too immature. Not suitable in the long run. What we had was—we had a dalliance, Byron."

"Nothing wrong with dalliances, Di. I like dalliances. Jim and I started as a dalliance."

"But I loved him, you understand." She dabbed her eyes.

"Was this the kid you took to the opera?" he asked.

"That's right. The one Porter Reynolds made that take-me-to-his-tailor crack about." Diane bristled at the memory, then something in her friend's terminology struck her as odd. "What made you call him a kid, Byron? He's of legal age. Why? What else did Porter say about him? C'mon, By. You can tell me now that it's over."

"Well, actually," Byron said reluctantly, "Porter said he was a bit on the young side—"

"And?" Diane demanded.

"And he wondered if you were planning to adopt him."

"Terrific!" she growled. "You've really made my day."

They ordered another round, then downed their drinks silently, each absorbed in a private train of thought.

It was past five when they got back to Slater Blaney to find the office in a uproar, hordes of people dashing around, noise level approximating that of an SST.

"What the hell—" Diane, decidedly the worse for wear, wondered if she had come to the wrong place when someone thrust a glass of champagne in her hand. From Frank Merriam's office came wave after wave of laughter over music.

For some arcane reason, Frank was throwing a party.

"Hey!" He waved a flowing bottle of Moët in her direction. By God, the man was drunker than she was. "Here comes the last of the A-Team," he called, then stumbled out of his chair to greet them while Ralph Slater himself refilled her glass and Mark Vanderberg—the world's mustiest, crustiest gentleman—launched an out-of-tune chorus of "Hail! Hail! The Gang's All Here!"

Only then, through an alcoholic scrim, it hit her.

"We won!" she screamed, and threw her arms around Byron.

"You bet." Frank embraced them both. "Total annihilation."

Judge Kunicki had made public his decision at noon that day, even as Diane and Byron were in the bar getting bombed. Twenty-six pages of closely reasoned text finally coming down in Simplexx's favor. "And you know what proved crucial?" Frank was saying. "That goddamn precedent of yours—what was it? The Universal Corset Company!"

"Pneumatic." Diane joyously gulped down another glass. Partnership! She could smell it in the air, above the scent of grape and nicotine. "*Pneumatic Corset Company* v. *Williamsport Whalebone*. You're gonna quote, Frank, do it right."

Victory! Complete vindication. Four years of hard labor ending in clear-cut triumph. She picked up the phone and called her father.

The party continued over dinner at Le Cirque, then brandy at the Café Carlyle, then wee-hour dancing at Regine's.

"You know something?" She wobbled across the dance floor with Porter Reynolds, proud that she was still on her feet. *What a glorious night! What a wonderful firm!* She felt deliriously happy. These people treasured her, loved her. This was her world, these her friends, Slater Blaney her natural habitat. "Know somethin', Porter? This is the first time in my life I ever got totally drunk in two different cities, same day."

"Is this a precedent?" He laughed.

She came home about three—happy, sad, elated, bone-weary, and very, very drunk—and fell asleep atop her bed fully clothed.

Diane spent most of Saturday in bed with an ice pack on her forehead, praying for death. Late in the afternoon she got up, dressed, brewed tea, swallowed three Tylenols, and decided to go on living. It was not only the booze, she told herself, that had left her hung over. Nor the joy of professional victory. It was in large part the aftermath of her emotional binge with Avram. That relationship was done with now, she conceded, and just as well for both of them.

He had left his jacket in her bedroom, but she didn't feel up to phoning him. Instead, she folded the garment neatly, put it in a shopping bag, then brought it down to the desk.

"This belongs to Avram, the nightman," she told the concierge. "Would you see that he gets it?" And then, because the circumstances might appear suggestive, she added, "He was doing some chores for me."

The man fingered the package doubtfully, then slid it under the counter. "Avram doesn't work here anymore."

"What do you mean?" She stared in disbelief.

"He quit last Monday and moved out. No notice—just like that!" *These foreigners,* his shrug seemed to say. "Okay, miss, I'll hold it for him, just in case he comes around one of these days."

She hesitated. Avram must have left a forwarding address, but she decided not to inquire. To what purpose? Why subject either of them to another painful battle of wills. As Avram himself might have put it, their romance was dead, dead, dead.

Instead of going up again, she went for a walk in the gathering twilight. The fresh air revivified her, cleared her mind. Avram's leaving was all for the best, especially now when she about to make partner. She would order her life in different ways. Perhaps some day she would meet someone else, perhaps not. She would think it all through more clearly tomorrow. Spring was coming. The first crocuses were pushing through the island gardens of Park Avenue. A new season. A new start.

It was dark when she came home, footsore and sober. The red light showed on her answering machine. Saturday night, who would be calling? Someone from the office, she presumed. Or else Avram looking for his jacket. Most likely, Avram.

Teeth gritted, she geared herself to hearing his voice and pushed the Playback button.

"Hello, Diane," a rich baritone rolled out. She froze. She played the message a second time and a third, then fell back on the sofa in a state of incredulity.

There was a God after all!

TWENTY-SIX

Given the state of hostilities between Fleur and Rosemary, the Wednesday Club ceased to exist.

"I refuse," a grim-lipped Rosemary had announced early on, "to share a table with that woman. It's bad enough having to share the same planet. Frankly, I don't see how it's possible for any friend of mine to remain a friend of hers."

But Bernie clung to her neutral status, as did Diane, doing her best to be nonjudgmental while keeping in close touch with both combatants.

The week before her wedding, Bernie asked Fleur and Diane over for dinner. "I'm actually cooking," she said. "Thought I ought to get a little practice in before the main event. It'll be just us girls, by the way. Roger's going to an office affair."

Fleur accepted with alacrity. "Alex is out of town anyhow," she said.

And would have the decency to stay out of town, Bernie hoped, through Sunday. His presence at her wedding would be an embarrassment, a red flag to Rosemary. The original invitation had, naturally, gone out to Mr. and Mrs. Alex Marshall, and while Bernie could hardly disinvite him, she dreaded the prospect of having him turn up with Fleur instead of Rosemary. Given such provocation, fur—if not wedding cake—would surely fly. Why couldn't people behave sensibly? Bernie wondered. As it was, it had taken all her persuasive skills to handle Rosemary, who had threatened to boycott the affair.

"You have to come," Bernie had pleaded. "You're a bridesmaid."

"But I don't have to talk to her?"

"Absolutely not."

"Or sit with her at the reception?"

"You'll be at opposite ends of the room. The only time you'll come within ten feet of Fleur is during the ceremony, and then just to walk down the aisle. Diane will stand between you. If you have to communicate, you can do it through her. Now promise me, no scenes. After all, it is a wedding, a joyous occasion."

"Only for you would I do this," Rosemary said.

Tonight Bernie planned to wring the same guarantee of good behavior from Fleur. Not that Fleur had any reason to go one-on-one with Rosemary now that Alex was hers. Unless, perhaps, to avenge the loss of her wardrobe.

Bernie was taking the chicken out of the oven when Fleur arrived in a hurricane of No Name perfume and Blackglama mink.

She handed her hostess a bottle of champagne, then swirled like a model on a runway. "What do you think? My very first, very own fur coat. Alex gave it to me."

"Magnificent!" Bernie felt the silky skins and uttered the appropriate words of admiration, winding up on a cautionary note. "Do me a favor though, sweetie. Don't wear it to the wedding on Sunday."

"Why?" Fleur hung the coat up with reverent care. "You think that a certain crazy lady will take a razor blade to it? Okay, I'll leave it home. Don't worry, Bernie. I plan to keep a very low profile. Besides, Alex will be in California. He sends his regards and regrets, by the way, but he's tied up in meetings out there. Poor lamb! He puts in such long hours."

Bernie laughed. "You sound just like Rosemary. She was always complaining he was a workaholic."

"Oh, yeah?" Fleur scowled. She didn't like being coupled with her ancient adversary. "Well, at least I don't *look* like Rosemary. The bubbly, by the way, is for Diane. She won that big boring lawsuit of hers and is currently the darling of Wall Street. Ah!"—the doorbell buzzed—"speak of the devil."

Diane came in looking, they both agreed, marvelous. "Success agrees with you," Bernie said, to which she replied, "Let's eat."

For a woman who claimed to have been born without taste buds, Bernie had turned out an excellent dinner. Watercress soup, chicken with apricots, a salad of endive and radicchio with vinaigrette.

Fleur was all admiration. "Compliments to the chef. I never knew you cooked."

"I don't. I just follow Craig Claiborne's directions."

"In that case, compliments to the chef's cookbook," Fleur amended. "But give me the recipe for that chicken. Alex would absolutely love it. He has to watch his cholesterol, you know."

Diane, preoccupied, ate a third helping and tuned out.

After cheese and espresso, the three women inspected Bernie's wedding presents, then settled down on her ancient sofa. The piece, a comfortable eyesore, had been outlawed by Roger and destined for return to the Salvation Army where Bernie had picked it up years ago. Their marriage would begin with everything brand new.

"We've been shopping our hearts out," Bernie said. "Rugs, draperies, the works." They had put a binder on a condominium in Riverdale. "Three beds, two baths, view of the Hudson. The mortgage should be approved by the time we get back from our honeymoon. We move in on the first."

"You getting a fixed-rate mortgage or an adjustable?" Fleur wanted to know.

"Thirty-year adjustable," Bernie replied, "with ten percent down. Since when are you into all this shit?"

"Well, you know, Alex and I are hoping to buy—"

Diane raised an eyebrow, but said nothing.

"Buy what?" Bernie asked. "An apartment?"

"No way! A proper house in the suburbs. Not Westport, though. He's had it with Connecticut. I was thinking Short Hills."

Bernie gave a low whistle. "That's pretty expensive stuff. Have you considered . . ." The two of them began comparing commuter runs and property values while Diane sat quietly, there but not there, nodding as required, utterly absorbed in her own thoughts.

She couldn't think ahead to next Sunday. She couldn't

think beyond Saturday night. What to wear? The green sequined outfit Fleur had picked out for her? Or the black chiffon she had bought for her parents' anniversary? The green was sexier, the black more elegant. Which persona did she want to project? Lofty-minded aristocrat or glitzy Manhattanite? She came down on the side of glamour. A glamorous Diane would surprise him no end. In which case, the green. It would make her appear more sophisticated, more woman-of-the-world . . .

"Which one do you think, Di?"

"Oh, the green."

"Green? What green?" Fleur peered at her. "Are you here with us earth people? We were discussing the relative merits of conventional mortgages vis-à-vis so-called creative financing. Green doesn't constitute much of an answer. Honestly, since you came back from Washington you've been in a dreamworld. Wakey wakey!"

Diane looked from Fleur to Bernie, as though caught committing a felony.

"Sorry, I was thinking about something else."

"About what?" Bernie said.

"About whom?" Fleur corrected. "It is a whom, isn't it?"

Diane gave a cryptic grin. "Yes, definitely a whom, not a what. I've got a major date Saturday night."

"With?" Two voices rang in unison.

"With none other than Leo Frankland." The words spilled out in a rush. "You remember, Bernie. The man I was so crazy about at Yale. The love of my life! At least he was back then. At any rate, he's coming to New York for the weekend, we're going to dinner on Saturday—dinner and dancing. He said he wants to make up for lost time. And oh! in case I forgot to mention it, he's divorced!"

"Congratulations!" Fleur clapped her hands.

"For what? Being listed in the Manhattan directory?"

"For hanging in there! When you told me you broke up with your little Israeli, I had vibes, Diane. I knew in my bones that something really terrific would happen. Don't you believe in destiny? I do! Oh, this is so romantic," she crooned. "You two were meant for each other. What happened with his wife, do you know?"

Diane shook her head, suddenly anxious. So much was being invested in this reunion. Perhaps her expectations were too high, or her memory too deceptive. After all,

seven years had passed. She and Leo were older now, both
survivors of pain and heartbreak. "I don't know," she answered Fleur's question, "although I expect I'll hear the
details on Saturday. He sounded rather bitter. This is not a
mating ceremony, by the way. It's just dinner with an old
friend. Who knows? It might turn into nothing more than a
long boring evening."

"Unh-unh," Fleur said. "It's kismet. What are you going
to wear? Of course, you have to look fantastic. The point is
to clobber him, make him kick himself for having been
dumb enough to ever let you go."

Diane laughed. She had been thinking the same thing.
"I've decided on my green sequined top with long earrings
and a simple black skirt. How does that sound?"

Bernie approved while Fleur, who had total recall concerning all items of dress, closed her eyes to conjure up the
details. Okay," she finally drawled, "but take out the shoulder pads. That football player look is *fini*."

"No shoulder pads." Diane made a mental note.

"He's quite a bit older than you, isn't he?" Bernie asked.

"Seventeen years."

"Well, that's okay," she said thoughtfully. "At least you're
dealing with a known quantity. You don't have to hang
around and wait for him to make good."

"Hardly!" Diane exploded with laughter. "It so happens
that the man is a nationally known authority in the field of
constitutional law. You know"—she lowered her voice—
"when I was in Washington, the scuttlebutt was that he's
being considered for the next vacancy on the Supreme
Court."

"Wow!" Bernie's mouth formed a perfect O. "Imagine
being the wife of a Supreme Court justice. Now that's what
I call status! You could kick ass from here to L.A. Just
promise me one thing, though. You and your Leo must
absolutely not—repeat not—run off to Gretna Green or
wherever on Saturday night, thereby beating yours truly to
the altar. You turn up at my wedding this Sunday, mad
passion or no. In fact, why not bring Leo along? Give him
the right ideas."

"I'd rather not," Diane said. "I don't want it to appear
that I'm putting my eggs in that particular basket. Anyhow,
all this talk of marriage, let alone elopement, is wildly
premature. Good Lord! It's only a dinner date."

But Fleur steepled her fingers and put on her wise-woman expression, a look she had been cultivating in recent months. "It's going to happen, Di. You and Leo. I feel it. I have an instinct about these things. Funny, when this whole husband hunt started last September, it looked as if none of us was going to marry, and now it appears that we all three shall. So much for statistics. If you'd hold off, Bernie, we might have a triple wedding."

The thought was both absurd and attractive, yet sobering enough to plunge the three women into a heavy silence.

Bernie was the first to break it. "I ran into Steve on Fifty-seventh Street last week. First time I'd seen him in months. It was weird."

"Did he know you're getting married?" Fleur asked.

"He does now. I showed him my ring. I must say"—Bernie frowned—"he looked absolutely crushed when I told him. Almost made me feel sorry for the guy. Still, there comes a time when you have to put sentiment aside and make a clean break with the past and move on, don't you agree?"

"I sure do." Diane thought briefly of Avram.

"Me too," Fleur said. "I wish to hell Rosemary would view things that sensibly." Then on impulse she reached for Diane's long bony hand on her left, Bernie's small nail-bitten one on her right, enveloping them both in her own exquisitely manicured hands.

"This is a very special night, my darlings," she said in a small low voice. "A special moment. And because it is, because you're my oldest friends, there's something I want to share with you." She squeezed both hands gently and her eyes misted over. "I'm pregnant."

"Really!" Diane was stunned.

"Yes, really!" Fleur replied. "The doctors have very sophisticated tests now that can tell results within ten days of conception. I had the news this morning."

"Fantastic," Bernie murmured. "Wonders of science. Congrats."

"And how does Alex feel about it?" Diane felt both envious and inexplicably upset. Consenting adults, she kept telling herself. Alex and Fleur were consenting adults, although Rosemary had consented to none of this.

"I haven't told him yet," Fleur breathed. "I thought I'd wait till he comes back from the Coast. But he'll be happy, I know. Very, very happy."

*   *   *

But would he? Fleur couldn't be sure. Her head said yes, her central nervous system was more equivocal. She couldn't sleep that night, thanks to a combination of anxiety and caffeine.

Based on the evidence, the news that he was going to be a father should be all that was required to push Alex over the brink into matrimony. She knew of the struggle he and Rosemary had had before Chris was conceived, of their regrets that the boy was an only child. And now, with Christopher not in the orbit of his daily life, what could be more gratifying than the offer of a second family? It was good. It was right. It was necessary.

If, earlier in the evening, she had deceived her friends on the imminence of her marriage, she did not deceive herself. Alex was dragging his feet.

Despite the increasingly abrasive noises emanating from both sets of lawyers (Rosemary was asking for the moon, Alex had howled), despite his unabating enthusiasm for sexual sport (Fleur sometimes wondered if it wasn't too much of a good thing), despite all these positive signs, he remained as elusive as ever. Even his gift of the mink, for all its extravagance, relayed a mixed message. It could as well signify a sop as a commitment. A payment for services rendered. For all the optimism she'd felt when Alex first moved to New York, essentially nothing had changed. Alex remained in control of their affair. And Fleur remained nervous about pressuring him.

Her strategy had been to tempt him with luscious pictures of domesticity, sweet images of creature comforts. Given the opportunity, she would have waited on him hand and foot, but the opportunity rarely arose. Time and again she tried to lure him into spending a cozy evening at home, replete with the trappings of slippers-and-pipe. "I'll make dinner tonight," she'd say, "something simple and nourishing," which only made Alex laugh. "Sweetie, you can't cook worth a damn. Now why don't you put on some fancy duds and we'll go to Giambelli's."

Wearily, Fleur would force herself into those three-inch heels that he loved and, like a politician on a campaign trail, proceed to smile and chatter and flatter and flirt, all the while trying to turn a blind eye to the succession of rich and fattening dishes. Had Fleur eaten everything put before her those nights on the town, she would have wound up the size of the Goodyear blimp, and Alex would have hated that.

As for marriage, that constituted even less of a topic than home cooking. "There's plenty of time to discuss it," he would say whenever she brought the subject up, "after Rosemary is sorted out." In truth, he relished his new-found freedom far too much to cut it short.

But for Fleur, each day's delay was fraught with danger. While Alex dawdled and discoed and enjoyed the high-caloric fruits of Manhattan, she grew increasingly desperate. Another month and she'd most likely be out of a job. How would he feel about her once she lost the Madison Avenue pizzazz and status? Would he see her as a drain? A clinging vine? Was he already looking to greener pastures?

His trip to California filled her with dread. She knew, as well as anyone, the temptations of life on the road, the distractions an overworked-up businessman might choose for relaxation at day's end.

The night before, she had called his hotel at six, California time, then at seven, then every hour on the half hour. It was nearly midnight when she reached him.

"Hey," Alex had sounded surprised, "it must be three in the morning your time. What are you doing up so late?"

What were you doing out so late? she wanted to ask, but didn't dare. She knew the stock answer: dining with clients. She also knew—from experience—that the answer might well be a lie. Tonight, despite her misgivings, she decided not to call. God forbid he should think she was checking up on his whereabouts. Bernie's likening her to Rosemary earlier that evening had upset her. Fleur, at least, would not become a nagging wife. If, indeed, she became a wife at all.

Everybody was getting settled. In a few days Bernie would have married Roger. Diane would be reunited with her true love. Yet here was Fleur, nearly one year into her love affair and hardly better off than when she'd begun.

But a baby! Ah, yes, a baby would bring Alex to heel—and soon. For Fleur was near the end of the tether, and time was running out.

"Time's running out, Rosemary," Dolly Bainter said. "And I think you've let this feuding go on long enough."

"Now, Mother." Rosemary poured them both a nightcap,

then settled down to watch the late-night news. "Let's change channels."

She was feeling good that night. It had been a most satisfactory day.

In the morning she had picked up a magnificent Victorian high chair at a barn sale in Trumbull. One glance had been enough for her to spot its potential even under layers of pink enamel paint. On closer inspection, the chair looked even better. Such purity of line! Such workmanship! All hand-turned. A museum piece. It had been tagged at forty dollars. "I'll give you thirty," Rosemary had said, while her heart was pounding. She would have paid five times that sum. She got it at thirty-two dollars without giving away so much as a smile. But inside she was triumphant.

Stripped and refinished, the chair would be exquisite. That was good oak under there, superb craftsmanship. She could picture the piece in a baby food commercial or in a layout for *House & Garden*.

"I thought," her mother said when Rosemary came home lugging her trophy, "that you were going to limit yourself to small portable objects. Where are you going to store that thing?"

Rosemary thought for a moment, then said, "I can put it in Alex's study. There's lots of room in there."

"Now, Rosemary . . ." Mrs. Bainter responded routinely.

Then that afternoon, the two women had gone to watch Chris in the school's spring pageant. He was dressed up as a wood sprite and had four whole lines to deliver. The night before, he had been terribly nervous, even weepy, and Rosemary had suffered agonies on his behalf. But today, in his green smock and brown cap he stood his ground un- flinchingly, belting out each word in a strong high voice like a veteran sports announcer.

"I am the spirit of spring," he chirped, "flying o'er glen and dale." And this time it was Rosemary who turned weepy. He was darling.

"If only Alex were here," her mother whispered.

"Now, Mother!" Rosemary groaned.

"A boy needs his father." Dolly shook her head.

It was a conspiracy. A propaganda campaign. The whole world—except for the two divorce lawyers and Fleur Chamberlain—was ganging up on her in a massive effort to get the Marshalls back together again.

"Don't be crazy," her bookkeeper Dawn Hendryks kept urging. "Learn from my experience." "I have been married and I have been single," her cleaning woman intoned, "and believe me, married is better." The other mothers at school picked up the same litany, to be echoed by all her neighbors and friends. Even Diane who, after all, was Fleur's greatest intimate, continually warned Rosemary against premature action.

On every side people beseeched her to make up. But the most persistent of the peacemakers was her mother. Dolly Bainter saw Alex every Sunday when he came to visit Chris. Rosemary, who made herself scarce on those occasions, had a notion they were exchanging more than just how-de-dos.

"I trust," she said after one of Alex's visits, "that you and my dearly beloved aren't plotting behind my back."

"Now, Rosemary," the older woman said. "I've always been fond of him. He's my favorite son-in-law."

"He's your only son-in-law," Rosemary observed dryly.

"And I'd like to keep it that way. You've punished him enough, darling. Let bygones be bygones."

Rosemary's answer had been a laser-beam glare, but Dolly refused to be put off.

"Did you ever think," she probed, "Alex might be repentant?"

"Dodie Schwartz saw him dancing at Private Eyes at three in the morning last week. That doesn't sound awfully repentant."

Tonight as her mother started in her familiar plaint, Rosemary kept her eyes assiduously glued to the TV. "Now's the time, honey"—Dolly was droning on—"before the actual court date is set. What do you say, darling?"

On the screen, the daily roll call of culprits presented itself for inspection: Wall Street swindlers, Washington "fixers," city officials caught with their hands in the till. Clean white collars, dirty deeds—

"And I ask you, are you doing right by Chris?" Dolly continued. Rosemary motioned for her to be quiet till after the weather report, then remarked, "Bernie's got a great forecast for her wedding. Fair and warmer."

"Rosemary! I'm talking to you. What do you say?"

"About what?"

"About my speaking to Alex and seeing what can be arranged."

Rosemary gave her mother a long equivocal look. "It's a free country," she finally said. "If you want to see Alex, that's your business."

"You're being very wise," Dolly gave her a hug.

"Yes." Rosemary smiled. She zapped a button and the screen went black. "Yes, I'm very wise."

Dumb! Diane could have kicked herself. Why had she been so dumb? She ought to have kept her own counsel about her date with Leo, at least until the situation was clearer. Instead, she had oversold the incident, practically boasted that Leo would come to her a-courting. And with such advance billing, Fleur and Bernie would surely expect her to provide a play-by-play rundown of the night's events—what he had said, what she had said, whether they had kissed, had they wound up in bed?—a report complete in every detail.

Suppose, after all her hoopla, it turned out to be nothing more than a dinner for old times' sake? *Hello. Good-bye. Nice seeing you again.* What a sorry tale that would be to tell.

Yet she felt that Fleur, with her reliance on intuition, was probably right in ascribing it to destiny. Kismet, she had called it, with the understanding that one must bow to the inevitable. And even Diane who believed that fate was an excuse for passivity, the excuse of losers and cowards, was forced to reconsider her definition of it. That Leo's call had come at this time, following so swiftly on the heels of Avram's departure, could hardly be coincidence. It was written. Destined. She had a sense of invisible forces, mysterious powers at play.

Moreover, she was certain that Leo—alert, sensitive to the tiniest ripples and probable consequence of every action—would not have called her simply for old times' sake. This reunion, she had no doubt, was equally significant to him. She had heard it in the gravity of his voice, his careful wording. "I've always held you in a special regard," he'd said.

Diane and Leo. Then. Now. For all time. It was a dream that had sustained her for seven lean years. Yet she couldn't avoid a faint sense of anticlimax. She was thrilled at the prospect of seeing Leo. Thrilled, but not overwhelmed. Happy, but not delirious. Intrigued, but also wary.

She blamed this on Avram. That final scene had cast a pall over all her subsequent pleasures, although she was not quite sure who had rejected whom. But since that morning a certain zest had gone out of her life. Even the joy of victory in Washington, so sudden, so dazzling, had been less than anticipated. In its way, almost a letdown. Harrigan was not contending the decision. The litigation had apparently been laid to rest.

"I should be happier," she said to Byron, "now that we've won."

"Postcoital depression," he said.

She *should* be happier: about the case, about her impending partnership, and most particularly about Leo. Instead, she was fearful and painfully anxious. Because if her hopes weren't realized this time around, she believed that she would never marry. Her future had to be planned accordingly.

There was an ancient partner in Slater Blaney, Edward Stringfellow, whose manner of dress and speech harked back to the old days. Thin and dry as the parchment paper he had handled in his distant youth, this desiccated bachelor had been for many years the mainstay of the Trust Department. His waking hours were spent drawing up wills and administering estates, vicariously living through his clients and their children, suffering through their multiple divorces, their squabbles and squanderings, indulging himself at second hand with the caprices of the rich and profligate. He worked twelve hours a day, then went home each night to a small spotless apartment in Gramercy Park. "He lives for the law," Frank Merriam said of him, to which Diane had responded, "Why, he doesn't live at all."

God forbid she should wind up like that. It was a surrogate life, a living death. She vowed to take every step necessary to fill the empty hours. She would become active in the Bar Association, join a tennis club, perhaps even take up the cello. She would get a car. Get a boat. Get a cat. She refused to wither up and die.

Tonight, however, those palliatives offered meager consolation, for the news of Fleur's pregnancy had unleashed in Diane an old and violent longing. She wanted a baby. If not now, she asked herself, when? If not through marriage to Leo, she asked herself, then how?

She was almost thirty-three. The longer she put off childbearing, the less likely the prospect became. She had given the matter an enormous amount of thought in recent weeks, examining it from every angle, yet postponing a final decision. But Fleur's announcement had tipped the scales. It was unfair that Diane, of all women, should be robbed of the essential female birthright. She would be an excellent mother—devoted, tender, affectionate. She had so much to give, so much love waiting to be lavished. Why should she grow old and sour and dry and barren? Fate couldn't be trusted. Suppose it proved to be unkind?

In that case, she would make her fate. Yes! She would do it.

"I'll do it!" She sat up in bed and said the words aloud. Tentatively at first, then louder. The second time around, they sounded fine. Yes, she knew her mind this time. She would do as her nature cried out. Whatever else the future held in store, it would hold a baby. With or without a husband, with or without her parents' blessing, she was determined not to go to her grave childless. And if she couldn't conceive, she would adopt. There was no stigma anymore, no shame for women who chose to go it alone. Instead, the independent mother was accorded a healthy respect for her strength and courage, her ingenuity in finding an acceptable solution. And rightly so, for maternity was the most basic, the most powerful of women's instincts, the most natural of all roles. God willing, she would not be cheated out of it.

But her body was not a machine capable of reproduction on demand. Age was a factor. And if, at last, she was going to do what she really wanted, become pregnant, it should be soon while she still had youth and energy. Time was running out.

Only a few years left.

Only a few days left.
Bernie looked at the luminous dial of the bedside clock. Three in the morning. She straightened out the bedcovers for the umpteenth time. She wasn't used to being insomniac. But then she wasn't used to getting married. And time was running out. It was Thursday already. Less than a five-day weather forecast stood between her and the altar. The hours of freedom remaining before what Roger called "the feature event" had already shrunk to the countable. There was so much to do between now and then. Get her

hair cut. Call the phone company. Change the beneficiary on her life insurance policy.

Naturally Bernie intended to keep her maiden name, Roger and she both agreeing on the separate-but-equal doctrine as the basis of contemporary marriage. Separate credit cards. Separate bank accounts. But not, he drew the line laughingly, separate bedrooms.

They were going to have two children, one to be born the summer of next year, when the station would be showing mostly reruns, the second by the time she was thirty-six or when Roger was made vice president, whichever came first. Personally, Bernie was in no hurry. It was a hair-raising responsibility.

Fleur's equanimity about her own unblessed event had staggered Bernie. Suppose Alex didn't come through? Imagine being left with an unwanted child! Why, the woman had no idea of the hassle involved in raising children. She was a hopeless romantic, poor Fleur, still believing in the benevolence of fate and the tooth fairy.

Perhaps, like Bernie, you needed to have grown up in a large family to grasp the problems children entailed. Kids weren't toys. They weren't like any other kind of personal possession. You couldn't decide they were defective or boring or just a pain in the ass, then ship them back to the manufacturer for a refund. They didn't come with a warranty. You couldn't escape from them. Or farm them out. Or donate them to a thrift shop along with last year's clothes.

And once they were on the scene, they ran the show. They were so indisputably, utterly *permanent*. Which was kind of scary.

No matter what Roger said about shared responsibilities, children remained basically "women's work." Their bearing, their rearing, the whole schmeer. After all, he wasn't the one who'd be growing fat and unwieldy, the one who'd have to suffer morning sickness and labor pains. And that was just for openers.

"There are only two ways to travel," some wag had said. "First-class—and with children." Of course people *had* them— life wouldn't go on otherwise—but Bernie remembered reading a poll that said childless couples were happier. Was it true? It might make an interesting segment on the *Heartbeat of New York*. She'd mention it to Hy when she got back from her honeymoon. Antigua! Funny how she'd planned to go down there with Steve once, and now she'd be going with Roger. Maybe Fleur was right about this kismet shit.

She tossed for another half hour, then threw in the sponge. She could not fall asleep, and that was that. Further struggle was pointless. War nerves, she recognized the symptom. Like preshow jitters: The mind at full tilt, the body a bunch of nerve endings. It occasionally struck before an audition or a major interview, but, it had to be remembered, on the big day, everything went superbly. She was a pro, a veteran at handling stress. And no purpose was served by thrashing in the dark. Had anyone ever done a good show on how people cope with insomnia? What do you do when you can't sleep? Terrific idea. Get some funny answers. Some fairly obscene ones, too, was her bet. She'd mention it to Hy in the morning.

Bernie went into the living room and stretched out on that old ratty sofa that had seen her through so many good times and bad, then switched on the TV. Some dumb Lugosi movie that she couldn't recall having seen. Looked like trash. Looked like fun.

Five minutes later she was sound asleep.

TWENTY-SEVEN

————•————

Bernie's wedding day dawned bright and unseasonably warm for April. By midday the temperature had soared into the eighties.

"A record breaker," according to the weather forecaster from WHIZ, who was packed, along with a couple of hundred other privileged guests, into the hard oaken pews of St. Swithin's-on-the-Square. The church, one of the oldest in Greenwich Village, made up in atmosphere what it lacked in air-conditioning. That day, in particular, it bore a gay and festive look.

Bernie had chosen a color scheme of violet, moss-green, and white ("the Bonwit Teller national colors," Fleur observed), which was repeated in the clumps of lilac and carnations and hothouse tulips, echoed in the flowing purple gown of the organist, punctuated by the store of helium balloons neatly cached, in lieu of rice, by the outside door.

"Going to be a fun wedding," her boss remarked to his wife, who was fanning herself with a handkerchief. "Especially the reception at the Rainbow Room. Leave it to Bernie to do things in style."

"At least it'll be air-conditioned," she grumbled.

Upstairs, in a little room off the vestry reserved for the bridal party, the thermometer was close to a hundred, but not hot enough to melt the ice.

"Will somebody," Rosemary asked frostily, "please open the window? The stench of cheap perfume is overwhelming."

No question who the offender was, since there were only

two other women in the room, Bernie and her family having not as yet arrived.

"The only thing I smell"—Fleur addressed her comment to Diane—"is the aroma of sour grapes."

Diane resisted the impulse to take their two heads and knock them together. Although she understood why, it grieved her to see grown women behave as children. Weddings should be joyous occasions. She said nothing, however, merely wedged open the high heavy window, and let in a sliver of afternoon air. It smelled of soot and carbon monoxide. Her spirits sank. The next hour was going to a Grade-One Ordeal, not least of all for her.

Bernie had meant well, she supposed, in her attempt to reconcile the two feuding parties, but it was a resounding failure. Fleur and Rosemary refused to address each other, and Diane was condemned to the thankless task of being intermediary, translator, and lightning rod.

"Tell your friend." Fleur would say, "that she's sitting on my good linen jacket."

"Tell that woman," Rosemary replied, "to learn to hang up her clothes."

Even the simplest matters of protocol become complicated and unpleasant. Bernie had assured the two former friends that they would not be sharing a table at the reception, with the result that Diane was left in limbo. To sit with either one would be tantamount to taking sides. "You understand my problem," Bernie said. "I'll have to find a neutral table." The solution was to seat Diane with Roger's relatives.

"But I don't know them," she complained, to which Bernie answered that she was certain they were "lovely people."

"Your wedding," Diane said, "and I have to sit with total strangers?"

"I'm sorry, sweetie" came the answer, "but I know you understand. You're such a good soul, Diane."

The good soul sighed and acquiesced. Yet she had a feeling of being punished unfairly for the childish behavior of others.

Better, however, to sit among strangers than to spend another minute in this room, she decided. It was an arsenal, ready to explode. If the ceremony didn't start soon, she feared that the sniping would get out of hand. Given sufficient provocation, who could predict the consequences? Fleur might decide to announce that she was pregnant. Or Rosemary, never loath to turn the knife, might drop heavy hints that she and Alex were about to reconcile.

Shortly before noon the minister popped in to count heads.

"Are you ladies ready to go?" he asked.

"Ready and waiting," Diane volunteered.

"Good. We'll let you know as soon as the bride and her party arrive." The Reverend smiled. "Which should be any moment."

The sooner the better, Diane thought, for not only were tempers nearing the boiling point, but the bridesmaids' dresses had begun to wilt from the heat. They looked bedraggled.

From the organ loft came the strains of "Sleepers, Wake."

"Twelve o'clock," Fleur remarked. "I always said Bernie would be late for her own wedding."

"Tell your friend," Rosemary interjected, "that I was the one who said that. Because she was late for mine."

"Your friend's got it all wrong, Diane. What she said was, 'Bernie would be late for her own *funeral*,' to coin a tired cliché."

"Are these barbs going to continue all day?"

"What barbs, Di? I was addressing my comments to you."

There was a flurry of activity in the hall. Diane poked her head out the door. The groom had arrived with his parents and best man in tow. He looked happy, hot, and flustered.

"Bernie's not here yet?" Roger inquired, and when Diane shook her head no, he frowned. "Traffic's terrible. See you in a bit. We're right across the hall."

More minutes dragged by. The organist finished the Bach and began another selection. "That's familiar," Rosemary said, frowning. "What's it called, Diane?"

" 'Panis Angelicus' by César Franck."

"Oh God, yes." There was a sudden quaver in her voice. "I remember. They played it at my wedding. Such a lovely affair—all white and pink. We had these beautiful *boules-de-neige* roses everywhere, mountains of them. Nothing but roses, except for the bridal bouquet. That was a traditional orange blossom. I guess Bernie must have caught it after all. Remember, Diane, we were wondering . . . ?"

With a sense of alarm, Diane awaited a foray down

memory lane to that other wedding so many years ago, but this once Rosemary refrained. Such nostalgia had to be doubly painful on a day like this. Diane knew what she was thinking and even Fleur had the decency to fall silent.

They sat for a while sweating in silence while the music droned on. From the nave came the muffled babble of voices. The guests were growing restless. *Come on, Bernie*, Diane willed. *You're holding people up.*

The Franck was followed by some Mozart, then the Gounod "Ave Maria," then a reprise of "Sleepers, Wake." Then the "Panis Angelicus" again. Everything but the "Wedding March."

Diane glanced at her watch. "Ye gods. Twelve-fifteen."

"Maybe you should call," Fleur suggested. "Could be something's happened."

"What could have happened?" Rosemary said. "Her whole family's there. She's late, that's all."

But Diane was worried and went to check from the pay phone in the hall. She came back mopping her brow. "Roger's going bananas out there. He thinks maybe there was an accident. Anyhow, I called the loft. The line's busy—"

"Which means they haven't even left yet!" Fleur growled.

"Which means, Diane," Rosemary corrected, "is that someone left the phone off the hook. Not to worry, Di. She'll turn up any second now."

But Diane, who never credited herself with having a sixth sense, felt a tremor of apprehension. Something was wrong her innards told her. Like music out of tune. But then, this wedding had been out of tune from the start. With each second's delay, her certainty grew, became a dull low rage intermixed with relief. A picture had emerged with the force of revelation.

"Bernie's not coming!" she gasped.

Fleur was out of earshot, but Rosemary heard and was outraged. "Shame on you!" she said, whipping around. "What a rotten thing to say!"

"I'm sorry!" Diane gave a guilty flush. "I didn't mean to blurt it out like that. It's just—it's just—"

It's just that this marriage was an affront to every concept she held dear. It was a business deal. A merger between two self-serving corporations that went against her own cherished image of what love and marriage were all about. And Bernie herself, now that it was almost too late, had finally come to her senses, thank God. She had cut and run. Couldn't Rosemary see what was happening? Couldn't everyone?

But Rosemary was looking at her aghast. "I'm surprised at you!" She shook her head. "You sound as if you don't *want* her to get married. Are you jealous? Is that it? Honestly, Diane, I thought better of you than that. Besides which"—she gathered her breath—"it just so happens that you're wrong!"

For outside there was a screech of brakes, then a slamming of doors, then a bustle of footsteps and voices in the corridor. "There!" Rosemary cried in triumph. "There they are!"

"And about time," Fleur snapped. "Another minute in this hole of Calcutta with Her Highness and I'd be dead of evil eye."

Rosemary straightened her dress, Fleur fluffed her hair, and the three of them stepped into the hallway.

Roger and his party were already assembled, and the ushers were milling about, the minister adjusting his robes. Any second now he would give the cue and the strains of the "Wedding March" would pour forth. Over half an hour late.

But the new arrival, far from the expected vision in a white veil and bridal lace, proved to a husky black teenager. He wore a crash helmet, bicycle clips, and a shiny blue jacket emblazoned with a bolt of lightning and the words "Spee-Dee Messengers" on the front and back.

"What the hell," Fleur said.

The young man had two sealed envelopes and a clipboard.

"Mr. Roger Knowland." He waved the first communication. Roger snatched it. "And this one is for a Miss Diane Summerfield."

Diane recognized Bernie's writing. She grasped the envelope between sweaty fingers, reluctant to open it, mesmerized, as was everyone else in the corridor, by the effect of all this on the groom. Roger Knowland had torn his envelope open and withdrawn a single sheet. Silence fell as his eyes whipped down the dozen lines of text, then returned to peruse it again in detail. By the second reading, all color had drained from his face.

"Jilted!" the word burst from bloodless lips, followed by a howl of animal rage. "That bitch! I could kill her for this!" With a flailing gesture, he ripped off his bow tie and began gasping for air. "It's suffocating in here—suffocating!" Instantly his family formed a protective shield around him as though to ward off further assault, while the rest of the principals stood about helpless.

"This has never happened before," Reverend North kept repeating like a litany. "Never—not in my thirty years of ministry!"

"The letter!" Fleur practically snatched the envelope from Diane's hand. "What did she say? For God's sake, Di, aren't you going to read it?"

Gingerly, Diane drew out the letter. It was scrawled in a hasty hand on a campy bright pink notepaper with a "Happy Face" imprinted across the top. The first words of the text jumped off the page.

"Can't. Shan't. Won't."

But before she had a chance to absorb the contents, Roger Knowland was elbowing his way toward the exit. "Let me out of this hellhole," he yelled. The wedding group parted as the Red Sea before Moses. He had taken off his jacket and rolled up his sleeves, squared his shoulders—no longer a bridegroom, but an angry young man in a hurry. His eyes, Diane noticed, had gone from blazing to ice-cold. His voice was hard.

"That woman!" Roger glared at the bridesmaids as though they were criminals. Worse—vermin! What other judgment could befit Bernie's friends? "That shallow, lying, treacherous cunt!" he enunciated each word. "I wasted nearly four months of my life on her. Damned if I'm going to stick around and play the fool one second longer."

"But the guests!" Rosemary spluttered. "There are over two hundred people out there, Roger. They've been waiting for ages. What will you tell them?"

Roger's answer was his departing back.

"I'll tell them," Diane said wearily, then crumpled her letter into a ball. "Our friend, Bernie, has allotted me that enviable task."

A minute later, Diane, the perfect lady, was standing in the center aisle of St. Swithin's, informing a large, noisy, and incredulous crowd that the Knowland-Hong nuptials had been canceled. "By mutual consent," she embroidered, hoping the lie left a better taste in the mouth than Bernie's own brusque words ("Help! I'm running for my life"). She followed with a brief but gracious speech of apology and concluded with a touch of her own, something that had apparently slipped Bernie's mind in the confusion. "And the bride has asked me to be sure and remind you that the reception will take place as scheduled. So please, just think of it as a party in honor of old friends and have a pleasant time on their behalf. Thank you."

Then Diane fled like a Mafia chief before a pack of investigative reporters. She went home, washed, changed, lay down for an hour with an ice pack on her forehead, then headed over to Bernie's loft. The phone was still off the hook there, but she believed that the worst of the storm was over.

An explanation was owed her. A proper one. Bernie's "Can't, Shan't, Won't" hardly sufficed, And while she applauded Bernie's decision to follow the dictates of her heart, she wished it had been done in a less callous way. The responsibility of breaking the news to the assembled guests should never have been delegated, least of all to Diane, who wasn't even a member of the family. That was presumptuous, if not downright cowardly.

It struck Diane, and not for the first time, that she was perennially being enlisted by those around her to execute unpleasant chores—finding a divorce lawyer or running interference between warring parties or announcing a wedding wouldn't take place. In trouble? Feeling chicken? Call Diane. She's a good soul. A lawyer too. Besides, she has nothing better to do. That was the assumption, and she found it wounding. Even her friends seemed to think she had no overriding interests of her own, no other calls on her time. That she—like poor old Edward Stringfellow with his persnickety wills and trusts—existed only to serve and was expected to suppress her own emotions in the process. By the time she arrived at East Tenth Street, Diane was fighting mad.

She was met at the door by a devastated Addie Hong in fuzzy slippers and crumpled beige lace. Bernie's two sisters and a brother-in-law were grouped in the living room, hunched over coffee and reams of wrapping paper.

"We were just going through the wedding presents." Addie rubbed her red-rimmed eyes. "What'll I do with them?"

"Where's Bernie?" Diane asked grimly.

"Do I know? On a plane going somewhere," Addie wept. "Paris?—Rome? All I can tell you is that she took her passport and left in a taxi. That girl is crazy. The entire day has been a nightmare starting from the moment she got up. I kept telling her it was just nerves. Everybody's nervous on her wedding day, God knows. She kept saying that she wasn't 'everybody.' But the more I pleaded, the stubborner she got. She just kept stalling. She wouldn't even put on her wedding gown. Then she barricaded herself in the bedroom. At noon, just when she should have been coming down the aisle, my baby, my little bride, called the messenger service and took off. With her new suitcase and all! How could she do this to me?"

"To everybody," Diane snapped, but there was no reason to take out her resentment on poor Adelaide Hong who had just seen her life's wishes go up in smoke. Diane squeezed the older woman's hand.

"Come in, come in." Addie pulled her into the room. "I understand you were to make the announcement in the church. So good of you—so brave. Bernie always said that about you, that you were a good soul. Oh, God!" She began crying again. "I don't think I can ever show my face in public again—this has been so humiliating. And the presents! Tell me, Diane—what can I do with the presents?"

The living room was strewn with open boxes and tissue paper, the contents of innumerable packages spread out on the floor. The pile had grown even since Diane had seen it on Wednesday. Silver salt cellars, a Cuisinart, a cocktail shaker in the form of a space shuttle, crystal His and Hers snifters, myriad linens, curios, and eyesores—the hundred and one items, some beautiful, some hideous, that were to launch Bernie and Roger on their married life. Heaped together thus, the gifts resembled a discount merchandise mart, in which all the items had become scrambled.

"What am I going to do?" Mrs. Hong was wringing her hands. "They have to be returned right away. And I have no idea who sent what. The cards are all mixed up."

"Surely," Diane said, "they can wait till Bernie comes back. I assume she *is* coming back eventually."

But Mrs. Hong had got it into her head that the gifts had to be dealt with on the spot. It seemed the only way she felt she could atone for her daughter's disgrace. She turned her tear-stained face to Diane.

"Please, Diane, can you help?"

Diane sighed. "Yes, of course. Bernie has a list of who gave what. It's in her desk somewhere. I'll find it. With five adults, it shouldn't take too long." But it took until midnight before they finished sorting out the presents and writing a brief note to go with each one.

"I don't know how to thank you," Mrs. Hong said. "We couldn't have done it without you. You were simply wonderful." She looked at Diane with unaffected emotion. "Wasn't she, girls?" she asked her daughters, then didn't wait for a reply. "You're such a nice person. So sweet. It just astonishes me. I have to ask—"

"What?"Diane was bone weary, aching to leave.

"How come a lovely girl like you isn't married?"

Diane gave a tired smile. "Just lucky, I guess."

The instant the nonwedding was over, Fleur flew to a phone to call California. She could scarcely wait to relate the startling developments and hear Alex's opinion. He wasn't in his room, however. And, though Fleur never dreamed it, he wasn't even in California.

For at that very moment Fleur was placing her call, Alex Marshall was seated with his mother-in-law in a quiet East Side restaurant, discussing any number of possibilities.

TWENTY-EIGHT

$\mathbf{F}$leur phoned Diane at the office first thing Monday morning.

"In the excitement yesterday, I forgot to ask you. How was your date with Leo the Lion?"

"Interesting."

"Oh c'mon," Fleur wheedled. "After all that buildup, you'll have to do better than just plain 'interesting.' What I want to know is, does that ol' black magic still have you in its spell? And what happened with his marriage, by the way? Does he still see his wife?"

"It's definitely over," Diane said cautiously. "She caused him a great deal of pain."

"Aha!" Fleur seized on this piece of intelligence. "Which means that he's aching and vulnerable and in need of affection. Sounds promising. Did he mention the L word?"

"No comment."

"You lawyers!" Fleur read between the lines. "So when are you seeing him again?"

"A week from Friday. We're going away for the weekend, some country inn in Vermont. Eat. Drink. Take nature walks—"

"Separate rooms?"

"No comment."

"Honestly—blood from a stone! Still a weekend is good, a sign of public commitment. Much more hopeful than just dinner. What do you think?"

"Why do I think about what?"

"Do you think he'll mention the M word, too?"

"Well." Diane permitted herself a small chuckle. "As Bernie herself noted on another occasion, the opera isn't over till the fat lady sings."

Fleur considered the implications. "Interesting," she concluded.

"So it is. And what's new with you?"

"Alex is coming back from the Coast tomorrow," she gushed. "Oh God, Di, I'm so excited. Kind of nervous too. He's going to be bowled over when he hears the news about the baby. Papa Bear," she sighed, "and Mama Bear and all the little bears in a rose-covered cottage in the country. I can see it now. For you too! So get cracking, because it's back to square one. Go ahead, kid, beat me to the altar!"

"Souvenir of California." Alex smiled and handed Fleur the box. She looked at the label. "You have to be joking. Fifi of Hollywood? How stupendously camp!"

"Would you have preferred a T-shirt from Disneyland? Go ahead, honey"—he was watching her with his cat's eyes—"open it."

Fleur unwrapped the package and examined the contents with a doubtful air. There was a bra of lace and black satin, matching bikini panties, black net stockings, and a bright red garter belt studded with frothy rosettes.

"Did I get the size right?" he asked.

"Honestly, Alex"—she knitted her brow—"you're not very observant. Nobody wears garter belts anymore! Hardly even in skin flicks."

"I thought it would look cute on you. Be a sport, love. Try it on." He stretched out on the sofa and began leafing through a copy of *Fortune* while Fleur went into the bedroom to change.

Alex's "souvenir" proved to be a remarkable concoction, beyond the dictates of fashion. More like a schoolboy's dream of sexy underwear. The bra was appliquéd with two lacy black roses, each blossom covering a breast. In the middle of each rose was a reinforced hole the size of a silver dollar. She put it on. Her nipples protruded through the openings, showing red and round like the closed petals in the center of a flower. The panties picked up the floral theme with a twining vine, cut to reveal a "leaf" of pubic hair. Next came the garter belt and the fishnet stockings.

She put them on, then examined herself in the full-length mirror. The effect was devastating.

What on earth had been on Alex's mind? she wondered. Did he think these items reflected her taste in lingerie? Dior, she wanted to tell him, was quite sexy enough. Or something pin-tucked and romantic from Samantha Jones. But this! She stifled a shiver of distaste. This was both too much and too little.

However, she was pragmatist enough to recognize that this was a poor time to pick a fight. She needed to put Alex in a sweet, compliant mood, his good nature being crucial to the task at hand. They would have sex tonight. Happy, tender, lusty, enjoyable sex. Then as he basked in its after-glow, all masculine contentment and pride, she would snuggle in his arms and break the news.

Accordingly, Fleur put on her highest, spikiest heels (the outfit seemed to demand them), doused herself in No Name, and stepped into the living room, self-conscious as hell. "What do you think?" She struck the classic Betty Grable pose.

Alex put down his magazine. He had undressed and was sprawled on the couch. "Mmmm!" He said with admiration. "Yep, the high heels really make it. The final touch. Turn around, sweetie, and let me look at you. Fantastic!"

Fleur swiveled slowly, feeling like an idiot, then faced him, her hands on her hips.

"Yep! Looking good, but where do we go from here?" Alex shut his eyes briefly to conjure up the appropriate fantasy. "Right!" He beamed. "Get this one. It's Paris, the turn of the century. The Belle Epoque. In all of history there has never been an age of such license and lasciviousness. Such devotion to the pursuit of sensual pleasure." He gave a happy sigh, then hit his stride. "But for the handsome young nobleman, Count Alexandre de Marechal, the joys of sex have vanished. A connoisseur of the senses, a weary roué, he has known every thrill, every erotic variation Paris can offer. He has become jaded. Bored. No woman can arouse him, excite him anymore. No woman can bring him to orgasm. Just stay right where you are, darling," he interjected, for Fleur had begun to fidget. The three-inch heels weren't designed for holding a pose.

Alex fixed her with a glance, then continued. "Jaded, as I was saying. He despairs of ever feeling physical passion again. One night, however, in his quest for novelty, he visits a luxurious bordello"—Fleur's spine stiffened—"where the most beautiful women in Paris ply their trade. He has been there many times but never found satisfaction. To-night, however, in the red-velvet parlor, there is a new-comer, an arrival from the fleshpots of Istanbul—"

"No!" Fleur muttered, but Alex ignored her and went on, "—a courtesan who has traveled the world and acquired the most sophisticated sexual skills. She has been the mis-tress of kings and sultans, is adept in every art and perver-sion, a seductress who has never failed in her quest. Once she hears the young man's story, she sees it as a challenge. She will succeed where other women have failed, will arouse him, bring him to orgasm. Now how will she do this, Fleur? That's the problem. What can this woman do that others haven't? What techniques will she use? Will she excite him by having sex with a stranger? Another woman, perhaps."

If Alex's mythical nobleman was having difficulties in achieving an erection, he himself was not. His hand rested lightly on his thickening cock. Fleur felt sick but said nothing. She merely thanked God there was no second woman there to complete his fantasy. Anyhow, it was all talk, just Alex playing games.

"Or perhaps," he fantasized, "she will taunt him by mas-turbating herself into a frenzy. With a dildo, perhaps, or some more unusual device." His eyes scoured the room looking for a suitable object.

Fleur's apartment had changed since he first began com-ing there, had begun to fill up with homey trinkets. Alex surveyed them now. "Let me see—a bud vase. A wine bottle."

On the cocktail table was a bowl of ceramic fruit. Apples, grapes. . . . the items looked, for a moment, familiar. Rose-mary had something like them back in Westport. Only hers were wooden as he recalled. He reached over, took a bright yellow porcelain banana and placed it on his groin. It gleamed cool and hard against his flesh. "Why, the damn thing's as big as I am," he remarked. "Yes, this will do. Okay, the woman takes the precious fruit, fondles it as though it were a sacred object. Toys with it, slowly, volup-tuously, runs it up and down her body. It is smooth, sensual. Almost as desirable as the nobleman himself. Then kneeling on the floor before him—"

"Stop!" Fleur cried. "For God's sake, stop! This is not a brothel! I am not a whore!"

"Of course you're not a whore, darling." He sounded astonished. The banana rolled to the floor and landed on the carpet with a dull thud. "What are you getting so upset about, Fleur? It's only a game."

"It's a lousy game." The tears began streaming down her cheeks. "And I don't want to play. Why are you doing this to me?"

"Doing what? Have I ever forced you, hurt you, Fleur? I asked you that a million times. Have I ever physically hurt you?"

"You're hurting me now."

"Jesus God, I'm not even touching you. And that banana thing wouldn't hurt you if you're careful. I don't see what the big deal is. I was only making a few suggestions I thought might be fun. For both of us. You don't want to do it? Okay, I accept that. I'm not a pig, Fleur. I've never insisted you do anything you didn't want. Although frankly I don't see what you're so uptight about. You're the one who's always saying sex should be wild, that I should let myself go, indulge my fantasies. You've never said no to me before. Of course, I understand that's your privilege. We're consenting adults, after all."

"Well, I don't consent, Alex." She was crying steadily now, unable to stanch the flow. This was not the act of love she had envisioned. "I don't consent to be decked out like a prostitute. I don't consent to being humiliated, debased. Debauched. Yes—debauched! I want to be your wife, Alex, not your whore."

"Please, sweetheart"—he rolled his eyes in despair—"let's not start that again."

"We have to," she blubbered. "It's urgent. You've got to marry me, Alex, or—or I'll kill myself. For God sake, man, don't you understand? I'm expecting your baby!"

Before he could muster an answer, she had fled into the bedroom and slammed the door. He could hear her sobbing from where he sat.

Alex got up heavily, pulled on his pants, then went into the kitchen to make coffee. When it was brewed, he knocked at the door with a tray.

"Let me in, Fleur. We'll talk this through in a civilized manner."

"It's not locked."

She was sitting on the bed, pale and tear-stained. The hated lingerie was in the wastebasket. In its place, she had put on a floppy pink chenille bathrobe. Rosemary had almost an identical one.

"That," Alex said gamely, "is about the most unerotic garment I've ever seen. What do you keep it for—to scare off rapists?" He handed her a cup of strong black coffee. "Okay, Fleur, now pull yourself together and tell me, what is this business about your being pregnant? You told me you were on the pill."

She swallowed a jolt of coffee and looked him straight in the eye. "Accidents happen," she said.

"Do they now?" he said quietly, and she felt a quiver of panic, for he appeared to be involved in some mental arithmetic. "I don't quite see how that could be, Fleur," he said finally. "If memory serves, you had your period—let me see, about three weeks ago. It started on a Friday. We had tickets to Springsteen—"

"That was in February," she hastened to assure him. "Two months back. I'm talking about last month, Alex. You weren't here. You were in Chicago at the time, honey. That big technology show, remember? I can't tell you how surprised I was—it was first time in my life I ever missed my period. I didn't say anything at that point, I hated to worry you in case it was a false alarm. But"—she leaned forward and took his hand in hers—"it wasn't. They have these tests now, you know. They can tell almost as soon as you conceive—"

"If not before," Alex murmured.

"Please." She tried to squelch a growing hysteria. "Please listen to me, Alex. I only want what will make us both happy. And having a child will make us both happy. I promise you, I'll be a good wife, a wonderful mother." She started crying again. "We'll stop this—this gypsy kind of existence and settle down, buy a house, build a life together. I would devote myself to you, darling. Body and soul. I'll make you so comfortable, take such good care of you that you'll be the envy of everyone. We'd be a world unto ourselves, darling, tucked away from all intruders, happy, peaceful, and secure. And your baby—our baby—

could be the first of—of as many as you want. Imagine, Alex! A proper family, a real home. And I'll learn how to drive. About time, I bet you're thinking. I've already started lessons, you know. And I'll take cooking lesson too, which I think is a terrific idea. I'm actually a very handy person—" She rattled on this way, scarcely pausing for breath, drawing a picture of domestic paradise, while Alex, arms folded, heard her out without a murmur. An unwitting observer might have seen in his demeanor the seasoned and skeptical businessman listening to a salesman's pitch. His face revealed nothing.

"—so I thought," Fleur wound up, "that when your lease on that apartment is up, we should get a place of our own. In fact, why don't we start house hunting this weekend? How about the Short Hills area, darling? I understand they have a very nice country club. And it's not a bad commute. Alex?" She clasped her hands together to keep them from trembling. "What do you think?"

"Short Hills." He nodded thoughtfully. "We almost moved there when we were first married. Pretty town. You're right about the country club, by the way. I see you've done your research. Amazing!"

"What is?" She could hear her heart beat.

"You are. Absolutely amazing. I look at you, Fleur, and I see Rosemary. I listen to you talk, and it's like I never left home."

"Oh, my God, Alex," she burst out. "I'm not the least bit like Rosema——" but Alex cut her off in a no-nonsense voice. "Did I interrupt you while you were speaking your piece? No. You made me a proposition. I listened carefully. Now I'm making you an answer. One." He looked her straight in the eye. She was the first to flinch. "If I wanted to live in a center spread from *House & Garden*, I would still be in Westport. Two. I never asked you to get pregnant nor can you say I did. Three. You knew I was a married man from the beginning. Four. If you think back to that first time in Pittsburgh, you will recall that *you* were the one who made the overtures. And Five. We saw Springsteen in late March. My memory is absolute in that regard."

Fleur had turned the color of death. "Are you calling me a liar?" she shrieked. "I'm pregnant, damn you. It's true—I swear to God. I'll kill myself if you don't believe me, and don't think I won't. I'll slash my wrists, jump out a window.

Do something so awful you'll regret it till your dying day. Why not? What do I have to live for if not you and the baby? You have to marry me, Alex. You have to!"

"I don't *have* to do anything," he said evenly. "So don't pretend to hold a gun to my head. Or to your own, either. If you insist that you're pregnant, suit yourself. You can handle it however you want. You're of age. I never asked for this additional burden, and I have no intention of shouldering it, financially or any other way. I've got enough on my plate as is. Now about those death threats." He gave a cryptic smile. "Fleur, my love, you're the least suicidal woman I've ever known, and you can take that as a compliment. You're a survivor. But remember, so am I. So don't try to fuck me around. Because there's one thing I guarantee you." His voice took on a dangerous undercurrent. "I will not be blackmailed. Not now, not ever. And when I feel I'm being hustled, I can get really mean. Enough said? I had hoped we might end on a happier note."

He got up and put the coffee cups back on the tray, then began talking in a more sociable tone. "We've had great times together, a lot of laughs, a lot of joy, and I've cared for you very deeply. I still do. But you've changed, Fleur. You've become so clingy, so dependent the last couple of months. It's not fun anymore, at least not for me. The spark is gone. I figured we might stay together a while longer, remain good friends—occasional lovers. And I want you to know that however things work out, you'll always be dear to me. But that's life, sweetie. These things happen to the best-intentioned of people. I thought you realized that when I bought you the mink—that is was my way of saying sorry. And I am. I'd be the first to admit that it's not all your fault."

"Well, thank *you*, Mr. Marshall!" Fleur burst out, not knowing which was worse, his inner rage or this why-can't-we-be-civilized-and-share-the-blame-together crap. His moderation was worse, she decided. Far worse. It was devoid of emotion. If only he would become angry. Get violent even! Then they might still wind up in each other's arms. Bed was where you made up this kind of quarrel. Bed was the only way she could hold him.

Wretchedly she trailed after him into the kitchen. He placed the tray on the counter and rinsed the cups. She watched him, paralyzed. Alex Marshall: the good husband.

Housebroken in every particular. He placed the upturned cups on the drainboard, then went into the living room to fetch the rest of his clothes.

"And that's it?" She stared at him incredulously. "You're going to walk away? Just take a stroll out the door as if none of this ever happened?"

"That's certainly it for today." He sat on the sofa, lacing up his shoes, then straightening his tie. "Perhaps we might get together in another week or two." He was putting on his jacket, ready to go.

She came over to the sofa, bent down and picked the ceramic banana off the floor. As she did, her robe fell open, revealing those luscious breasts that Alex so adored.

She held the shaft of porcelain in her open palm, then placed it crosswise against her nipples. Clear yellow against deep dark crimson. Their eyes met, and in his, those wily green-gray cat's eyes, she could read a renewed flicker of desire.

"I offer you my life," she said, enunciating each word with measured clarity. "I offer you my heart, my trust, my love, and loyalty. And you tell me—to go and fuck a piece of fruit!"

The flicker of desire suddenly narrowed to a pinpoint of fear.

"Holy Hell!" Alex backed away in alarm, but not soon enough. The banana came sailing through the air with the force of a rocket. It missed his eye by the merest fraction of an inch, slashing a hard red line across his temple.

"You lunatic," he shouted. His hand whipped up to the wound. It came away bloody. "You fucking lunatic. You could've killed me."

"Like you've killed me, you balding bastard!" she screamed at full throttle.

She leaped at him. But her curses, her pounding fists were in vain. For Alex Marshall was already out the door and gone forever.

TWENTY-NINE

Every morning Bernie arose at dawn, put on a bathing suit, and stepped out on the beach before breakfast. There was nothing to be seen but sea and sky, nothing to be heard but the occasional burst of birdsong or the lowing of a distant cow. The scent of honeysuckle hung lightly in the air. New York was a lifetime away.

For an hour, she would swim with firm measured strokes, then breakfast on the terrace, after which she disappeared into her bungalow to sleep and read until the heat of the day had passed. Toward evening, cool and refreshed, she would walk along the shore in quest of shells, returning in time for a solitary dinner. By nine o'clock Bernie had retired for the night. Except for hotel staff, she spoke to no one. Had it been possible, she would have slept the week away.

"A coral paradise," her travel agent had described Antigua in those happier days when she and Roger had made the reservation. The Hawksbill Hotel in particular had been described as both elegant and secluded. "The perfect island hideaway," the agent had enthused, "ideal for a honeymoon couple."

And other fugitives, he might have added.

Given the recent turn of events, Bernie believed it was the last place on earth anyone would look for her. If anyone was looking for her at all—except possibly to gun her down.

"And Mr. Knowland?" the manager had asked when she checked in on Sunday.

"Unfortunately," Bernie replied, "he couldn't make it. I plan to be very quiet while I'm here. I trust you will respect my privacy."

Her fears were ill founded. Out of season, the resort was populated almost exclusively by Britons who tended to keep to themselves unless approached. There was no one, she noted with relief, from her own circle. Not even a television set disturbed the calm. The perfect location for serious thinking.

Bernadette Hong was not a reflective woman. The world was divided, she believed, into those who thought and those who did. She aligned herself with the latter.

From childhood on, she had been action-oriented, finding her heroes in those who shot first and asked questions after, if, indeed, they asked questions at all.

She admired Alexander the Great for cutting the Gordian knot, Henry Ford for saying history was bunk, and Napoleon Bonaparte because the little corporal—like herself— required only five hours' sleep a night. He was up and doing, enhancing his career, while the rest of the world snoozed away. When, in the tenth grade, she first encountered Hamlet, Bernie gave the prince poor notices. No hero, he.

"Hamlet had it coming," she observed in class.

"But don't you feel for him in his plight?" asked her English teacher.

"Why should I? Hamlet's a waffler."

To Bernie, he typified the least sympathetic sort of person. A man undone by thought, immobilized by contemplation. If only, upon discovery of his uncle's heinous crime, the prince had taken charge, obeyed his impulse, grabbed his sword, and exacted swift vengeance on Claudius, the ensuing tragedy might have been avoided. At a stroke, Hamlet would have spared both himself and others a great deal of torment. Instead of which he had dithered well into Act Five, paralyzed by doubts, crippled by introspection, compounding the mess as he went along. By the fall of the final curtain, the body count was horrendous; dozens of innocents would have been alive and kicking were it not for Hamlet's vacillation. Better late than never, she presumed

Shakespeare's message to be. Her own sentiment was better early than late.

Now, however, in the drama of her own life, it was Bernie who had waffled. Bernie, who was responsible for pain and suffering. Faced with difficult and complex choices, she had steadfastly refused, month in, month out, to come to grips with her deepest emotions and take the necessary steps. Like Hamlet, she had equivocated, waited until the last act. Like him, she had wreaked havoc.

She sat on the beach in Antigua, hugged her knees, and counted the victims strewn on the stage of her life.

Roger—wounded and angry. How could she have humiliated him so in public? The man had done her no harm, except, perhaps, by offering marriage. On balance, she would have liked to keep him as a friend.

Her mother—devastated. Indeed, *heartbroken* would not be too strong a word, for Bernie had robbed her of her fondest dream. "My daughter's marrying such a wonderful fellow," Addie Hong had boasted far and wide. And now she was left to pick up the pieces.

Two sets of relatives, two sets of colleagues and friends—all dismayed, saddened, disappointed. Diane, especially, weighed upon Bernie's conscience. Dear old Di. She was the most sensitive of souls. What hell it must have been for her to face the assembled guests as the bearer of such tidings. But of everyone Bernie knew, Diane alone struck her as having the requisite strength and courage. Besides, she was a lawyer—she could present Bernie's case in the kindest light. But what *was* that case?

How had it happened, Bernie sat on the beach and brooded, that such a situation had come to pass? How was it that she of all people, so committed to independence and the single life, should have let herself be lulled by a dewy-eyed picture of wedded bliss without once pausing to examine the consequences until the last minute?

It was the contest! That silly challenge of Rosemary's, with its irresistible appeal to her competitive instincts. Even now she could recall the intoxicating sense of drama, the barely restrained braggadocio that day at lunch when she had announced her engagement. For although Rosemary's husband hunt was a contrivance, it was by no means unique in the history of women. Such races (though not always so baldly stated) occurred all the time. They were the norm.

Granted, a woman might marry for any number of reasons, she believed, but the competitive challenge had to be
among them. It was the supreme form of one-upmanship,
the female equivalent of macho. What woman could resist
the chances to impress (and possibly depress) her peers
with the consummate trophy? *Look at me. I'm engaged.
Nyah . . . nyah . . . nyah! Aren't I clever? Attractive? Beloved?
More so than you, poor dear.*

That was part of the stimulus, Bernie admitted, the desire
to be first at the finish. The trouble was that when you won
that particular game, you lost. But Bernie had won.

Wife. Mother. Helpmeet. The traditional woman's roles.
To which Bernie added Prisoner. Ultimately, one had to
choose, she believed, between freedom and intimacy. In her
mind they were mutually exclusive. She viewed marriage as
a regimen of burdens and restraints. Above all, as the loss
of control. All her life she had struggled against emotional
entanglements, terrified of having her fate inextricably in-
terwoven with the welfare of another. She didn't want to
live inside another person's skin, didn't want anyone living
inside hers. It was too high a price to pay for love.

From the day she became engaged, she had been subject
to random bouts of panic, premonitions. "Bad vibes," as
Fleur might say. Each time they arose, she squelched them,
if necessary with the assurance that there was always divorce. But what did divorce signify, if not an admission of
failure? And Bernie hated to fail.

The week before the wedding date, she and Roger had
seen less of each other than usual. The nights had been
given over to office parties, a bachelor dinner, an evening
with "the girls"—almost a ritual farewell to the social lives
they had known when single.

"We'll be seeing plenty of each other in the future,"
Roger had said before excusing himself for some stag affair.

"Every night," she murmured.

"You betcha."

The exchange, though brief, had given her pause. Roger's
job didn't take him on the road, as Steve's had done. He
would perpetually be, if not quite "underfoot," then most
definitely *around* on a seven-day-a-week basis.

Moreover, the man had definite tastes and habits. Hair in
the sink bothered him, as did cracker crumbs in bed or feet
on the cocktail table. "It's my house," she had wanted to

say, "and I'll put my feet where I damn well please." But soon the house would be both of theirs.

Her failure to replace the cap on the toothpaste tube was a continuing source of friction. "What does it take to screw it back on," he argued. "Two seconds a day?"

It was a perfectly reasonable request, as were the others, and she of course had some quibbles of her own. Would he please refrain from cracking his knuckles when he was tired? It drove her up the wall. And his beloved Limburger cheese smelled up the fridge. Could he try to live without it for a while? Small items, but left unaddressed they contained the seeds of war.

Compromise, everyone kept telling her. Marriage depends upon the spirit of compromise, of give-and-take. But over the years Bernie had become accustomed to having her own way in minor matters. So, she observed, had Roger. Bachelorhood was poor training for the married state. And Roger was tougher and more willful than old laid-back Steve, who didn't care enough about most things to make an issue.

Last Friday she and Roger had gone to Citibank to complete their mortgage application. Everything had been in order. The loan had been approved, the closing scheduled for the day they returned from their honeymoon. The Citibank officer handed her a sheaf of papers.

"Thirty years," Bernie gulped. "A thirty-year mortgage! My God, I'll be an old lady when it's paid off."

The loan officer and Roger both had reassured her that the long mortgage was to their advantage. It imposed no obligation that would root them to the spot. "I would hope," Roger said with a wry smile, "that by the time we're in our sixties, we'll be living a whole lot better than in an apartment in Riverdale. By then I'll probably be retired."

His words shook her to the core. Bernie in her sixties. Bernie and Roger in their sixties—together. Retired. Nothing but each other to occupy the time. He would be home not only every night but every day, all day. So would she. Thirty years of lockstep. Of sharing meals and vacations and bed sheets with the same man. Whatever children they might have would be grown and flown by then. Bernie and Roger. Alone at last. Forever.

Would Roger be cracking his knuckles thirty years hence? Would he be nagging her about the toothpaste cap? Or would they have fallen so deep into the morass of marriage that they had nothing more to say, not even to argue about?

Thirty years from now they might be sitting on the same Brazilian leather sofa purchased at Maurice Villency the day they had gone to complete their mortgage application. ("It costs a fortune," Bernie had protested. "But it'll last a lifetime," the salesman reassured.) She would be gray-haired in thirty years, Roger would be bald, and they would be sitting on that sofa side by side, bored, silent, with grown children, passion spent, illusions shattered, chained together till death did them part.

Thirty years. It was a sentence. Convicted murderers got less.

Bernie got up, dusted the coral sand from her feet, and marched into the hotel office. "I'll be leaving this Sunday," she told the manager.

"You're booked for a second week," he reminded her. "Didn't you find the hotel to your satisfaction?"

"Lovely place," she said briskly. "Perfect for honeymooners. But unfortunately, you don't have TV."

THIRTY

————•————

Alex gone!

Fleur couldn't believe it. Wouldn't! But the shards of yellow porcelain sprinkled across the living room floor like confetti offered irrefutable evidence that she had loved and lost.

Men didn't dump Fleur Chamberlain. That had always been the rule. She disposed of them at her convenience, when the romance had faded, the sizzle had cooled. She was always the first to say good-bye. It was the prerogative of beauty.

But the old rules didn't prevail anymore, she realized. At least not with the one man to whom she had entrusted her future. She had loved him. He had left her. She had relied on him. He had let her down. She had joined the infinite ranks of abandoned women.

Alex gone! Surely this was the end of the world as she knew it, the end of her power, her glamour. What was there left to live for? Alex was gone! Very well then. The time had come to make good her threat. She would kill herself without further ado. Tonight. It was preferable to facing the dawn alone.

Tonight, she would make up her face, put scent behind her ears, slit her wrists with Alex's razor, then step into a warm soothing bath and let her life's blood drain away. They would find her body in the morning, slim and lovely, dark tresses undulating on the surface, like Ophelia in her watery bier. And like Ophelia, dead of heartbreak.

But first, she must leave a note. A final message, as eloquent as only she could make it with her writer's art and brilliance. Each word would be crafted to wound, to move, to gnaw at the conscience, to haunt her faithless lover to the end of his days.

Oh yes, she knew the capacity of words to cause grief. Alex had given her a brief stunning lesson this very day. He had run the gamut: satire, cynicism, cruelty, and contempt. Tomorrow, however, she would have gone beyond the reach of his words, and he would be suffering as she suffered now.

Fleur lay down on the sofa with a notepad and a Pentel, and began to compose a draft.

"Dear Alex," she began.

No! Wrong opening. That swine was the author of her misery, thus "dear" no longer. "Dear" was reserved for the people she loved or, alternatively, for total strangers. Alex fell into neither category.

"To Alex Marshall"—

No. Why address him at all? Why dignify him with a direct appeal? Let him learn of her death from others.

"She didn't mention any name. Just referred to 'some unspeakable toad.' " Now *that* had a ring to it. Better yet— "some unspeakable toad with weird sexual hang-ups." Best of all—"some *impotent* unspeakable toad . . ." Oh! wouldn't that infuriate him. Everyone would know who was meant.

She tore off the sheet and began another.

"Dear Diane," she wrote, then paused.

Diane was going to be very, very angry with her. Very hurt as well. Plus quite possibly annoyed that Fleur had never got around to making a will, which Diane had said was the duty of every adult.

Perhaps, then, this letter should serve dual functions. Not that she had anything of substance to bequeath—hardly a penny in the bank. "Her face was her fortune," the mourners might say of her. "Poor thing! She possessed nothing else of value."

Except, of course, for one magnificent Blackglama mink coat. Would it fit Di? she wondered. Perhaps the sleeves could be let out.

"Dear Diane,
Alex has left me and I want to die."

She put the pen down and stared out into the blackness

of the night. There was really nothing more to add. It was the definitive statement: short, direct, complete in every particular. The perfect piece of copy. Alex was gone—and nothing would fill the emptiness he left behind.

Dear God! Had Rosemary felt this misery, this utter despair, in the days that followed his leaving home, during those lovely nights when he lay in Fleur's arms? The thought was too painful to endure. For the first time in months, she felt a peculiar bond with Rosemary. They were both Alex's victims.

Oh, the capacity of men to break women's hearts! And the pathetic willingness of women to let them! It was the oldest story on earth.

She crumpled up the page and began another.

"Dear Diane,

I know it seems that you wind up with the shit end of everyone's lives, but you're the only one I can trust."

Fleur began weeping. It was too brutal, too true.

She started a dozen other letters, all unsatisfactory. Toward three in the morning, she gave up the effort and went to bed. Sleep was out of the question. So, too, was suicide. Alex was right about that. She was not the suicidal type. Moreover, the sight of blood made her sick.

Shrewd, coolheaded Alex. He had called the shots from the beginning. "You're a survivor," he'd said. She sure as hell hoped so, but that depended on the definition.

If survival was the simple business of breathing in and out, very well then, she was a survivor. But if there was more to it than that, if surviving meant thinking, feeling, working through, and coming out whole—then she would hedge her bets. Suicide *per se* was out of the question but there were other ways to self-destruct. Like getting involved with a married man.

If only—Fleur shut her eyes and crossed her fingers—if only she could push the clock forward, skip the next few months of pain and healing, and arrive at a time and place where life would once again be feasible: when the ache had dulled, the scar tissue would be hardly visible, and the promise of a new love lay ahead. Emotionally, she couldn't even picture another man at this juncture. From experience she knew it would be her only recourse. Of course she would be older a few months hence. Less attractive. More "used."

The hard truth was that she had gambled everything on a man who had tired of her and walked away. Spendthrift Fleur, squandering beauty and love and passion and intellect as though tomorrow would never come. Now tomorrow was already here.

Toward dawn she fell into a light, feverish sleep. When she awoke it was past ten. The office was out of the question. She couldn't work. And why bother? She'd be out of a job in another few weeks. And even had she felt capable of thinking straight, she would never let her colleagues see her like this.

A look in the mirror confirmed her worst fears. The skin was pasty pale with a yellowish tinge, the eyelids heavy and swollen. Some more gray hairs had sprouted overnight. Small wonder, considering the ordeal she'd been through. It struck her that she was growing gray at an exponential rate. Pretty soon it would be a job not for tweezers, but for Clairol.

In a bright light, Fleur believed, she could have passed for a woman of forty. God had a way of kicking you when you were down.

"You look ghastly," she told the image in the mirror.

To which the image replied, "I look the way I feel."

Fleur hobbled into the kitchen, made herself some coffee, and faced the immediate problem—how to make it through the day.

A movie, maybe. Some nice dumb Mel Brooks comedy, or the new Woody Allen. In the darkened theater no one would be able to see how lousy she looked. But a newspaper check revealed nothing of interest in the neighborhood: the usual action schlock, war movies, and a Schwarzenegger flick. In her present fragile mood, she couldn't cope with the sight of Arnold's rippling pectorals. Otherwise, there were only depressing foreign films. And even Woody Allen was getting serious these days.

She might, as a classic solace for being deserted, find some dimly lit bar and get stinking drunk. Except she didn't enjoy booze all that much. It made her morose.

There was only one cure guaranteed to lift her heart, to raise her spirits. The ultimate fix. The supreme narcotic.

"You really think this skirt is long enough to be decent?" Fleur asked the saleswoman in Designer Dresses.

"No question" came the answer. "Now how about this Oscar de la Renta? It's sexy, dramatic. You can wear it to an important meeting, then straight through a late night on the town. And it looks terrific on."

"Oh, scrumptious!" Fleur fondled the bounce of peacock blue silk crepe. "You don't think it's a—just a little youthful for me?"

The saleswoman stepped back, arms akimbo, and regarded Fleur with professional savvy.

"With *your* face?" She shook her head vigorously. "*Your* figure? Not at all. You were made for this dress, dear. Go ahead. Try it on."

It's even better on than off. Fleur swirled before the mirror and felt a comforting resurgence of self. *Better not look at the price tag, though.* She looked. Winced. Put it down. Picked it up.

What the hell! She would worry about paying for it at the end of the month. Fleur uttered her favorite words.

"I'll take it."

"Cash or charge?"

Fleur handed over her American Express card, aware that she was perilously close to the top of her credit line. Next she went to the beauty salon, had a facial and a cute young haircut, then went downstairs to Accessories.

The trouble with minis, Fleur thought, was they forced you to revise your entire look. The change of hairstyle was just for openers. Now she needed different shoes with a mini, punchier stockings, belts, jewelry that evoked a sense of fun. And that particular shade of blue was tough to match.

An hour later she stepped out on the street, feeling much better, though a good deal less than buoyant. At least she didn't look like a washerwoman. There was always *that* consolation.

A quite attractive man caught her eye and came toward her. Oh God! He was going to try to pick her up. Fleur Chamberlain did not pick up strangers on the street, needless to say. At least, not anymore. Still, a mild flirtation might give her ego a boost.

"Excuse me, miss," the young man said politely. She turned to him and smiled. He flashed a plastic card.

"Store security," he said. "Please come with me."

Fleur's heart stopped.

"There's been some terrible mistake." She tried to smile through her panic. *Flirt*, her instincts commanded. *Look helpless*. A few feminine wiles would extricate her from this nightmare. He was a man, wasn't he? Men always responded.

"No mistake, miss." He remained stonily polite. "We've been observing you on closed-circuit television. It's all on tape. One silk scarf, three pairs of panty hose, and a Swatch watch and earrings from the jewelry department."

In a state of shock, she was led back into the store, up the service elevator, and ushered into a grungy yellow office.

"Sit down, please."

She perched at the edge of a hard oak chair while he inspected the contents of her handbag. The purloined items were spread out on the desk before him.

"In my life," Fleur pleaded, "in all my born days, I've never done such a thing before." She looked at the various items. What could they amount to? A couple of hundred dollars at most. "I'll make restitution, I swear to God, out of my next paycheck. Have a heart! I'm a respectable woman, a copywriter, not a thief, please believe me! I was out of my mind temporarily. The thing is, I've just broken up with my boyfriend—"

"I'm sorry, miss." He was singularly unmoved. "You can tell that to the judge."

"The judge!" Fleur nearly fainted. "Surely, the store doesn't intend to prosecute! My God! I've spent a fortune here over the years."

"I'm afraid that's our policy."

Fleur averted her eyes and prayed that the floor would open up and swallow her. She should have died last night, should have killed herself after all.

"Can I make one call?" she asked in a frightened voice.

O'Ryan handed her the phone.

She dialed. Waited for the voice on the line.

"Diane," she wept, "I'm in terrible trouble. Come bail me out."

THIRTY-ONE

All day Alex had sat at his desk depressed, unable to concentrate on the job. It was a new and unpleasant experience.

"What happened to *you*?" his secretary asked when he had turned up that morning with a jumbo Band-Aid on his forehead.

"Accident," he mumbled, then went into his office and shut the door.

Accident, indeed. "Pussy-whipped" was a more accurate description. He touched a finger to the injured area. It hurt like hell. Lucky he hadn't lost an eye!

Women never ceased to amaze Alex Marshall. No matter what you did for them, no matter how hard you tried to please, to flatter, it was never enough. They simply wouldn't let you live.

This notion of Fleur's that they were going to get married, for instance. It was sheer delusion. He couldn't imagine where it sprang from. Never once in their entire affair had he mentioned the faintest possibility of marriage. Not a hint, not the merest suggestion. From the start, he had known it was a dynamite word, and Alex Marshall was a cautious man. Nonetheless, once she'd got the idea into her head, there was no dealing with her. She'd heard only what she wanted to hear. Like Rosemary, in a way.

Women! They were so fucking irrational!

The pity of it was, Alex told himself, he'd been genuinely fond of Fleur. A little bit in love. Or perhaps "infatuated"

was a better word. That was it—he swooped on the definition: infatuated. She was bright, funny. Fabulous in bed.
Pretty to look at, especially when she was all decked out.
Yes, he and Fleur had had some marvelous times together,
which made her homicidal attack the more perplexing.

Christ! that was a narrow escape, he thought, and he had
done absolutely zilch to provoke her. On the contrary, he
had behaved throughout their entire affair with honor and
equity. If anything, he had been generous to a fault. A
woman who walked off with a six-thousand-dollar mink
could hardly claim to be abused. Alex had given it freely, as
a token of his esteem and affection. But marry her? Good
Lord! the woman couldn't boil an egg.

Besides, as Fleur knew only too well, he already had a
wife and child. Whom he'd been neglecting woefully the
past few months.

Alex frowned at the thought of Rosemary. He hadn't seen
her since that night she booted him out of the house. He
hadn't even spoken to her, except through lawyers. Time
and again he wondered how she'd been getting on without
him. Badly, he supposed. People got used to each other
after a while, became a habit. And Rosemary was addicted
to routine.

"Has Rosemary been dating anyone?" he had asked his
mother-in-law the preceding Sunday.

"I should tell you yes, you naughty man"—Dolly had
rapped his knuckles—"and make you hideously jealous.
But actually, there are very few available gentlemen around,
at least as far as I can see. And I've been looking for the last
seven years."

Alex drummed his fingers impatiently. He had no interest in his mother-in-law's never-ending quest for a man
to replace the late Mr. Bainter. She was over sixty, for
Chrissakes. Don't women ever give up? Whereas Rosemary . . .

"Well," Alex said, "Rosemary's kind of attractive in her
way, and after all these years a woman gets used to having a
man around. Tell me," he persisted, "did she ever mention
a guy named Lloyd Hageman? He's a periodontist, lives a
few streets away. I believe he's considered the local catch."

Dolly shrugged. The name clearly meant nothing, and
the talk turned to other matters while Alex smothered a
sigh of relief.

*   *   *

Alex leaned back in his swivel chair, clasped his hands behind his head, and sighed again. This time out loud. He hoped that Rosemary was behaving sensibly. The thought of his wife, the mother of his son, being physically intimate with another man was distressing. In fact, downright unsavory. With a periodontist, yet. God only knew what kinds of cavities they filled. Alex had heard his neighbor was something of a stud.

However, he consoled himself, it was not a likely scenario. Sex had never been of great importance to Rosemary. That was Alex's chief complaint. Once they were married, she seemed to lose interest. For all her other wifely virtues (and they were considerable), she was passive in bed, unenterprising. He sometimes wondered if she even enjoyed it. If not, that would certainly argue against her screwing around in his absence.

Besides which, Alex trusted his wife. Implicitly. She was the least deceitful of women.

And much as he would miss the fun and games with Fleur, it was as well that their affair was over. Their games had been growing kinkier of late. Almost brutal. Fleur had appealed to some streak in Alex that disturbed him, a dark underside to his nature that he might never have known existed but for her. It was almost scary. A man could do himself—or somebody else—bodily harm once he gave free rein to those impulses. Excitement was one thing, danger another. The time had come to call a halt.

For if Alex prided himself on anything, it was on his firm, hard grasp of reality. Reality now dictated he get back into harness. His wife had suffered the past couple of months. His son had suffered. Worse yet, his work had suffered markedly.

Alex was weary. Those late nights in those Manhattan hot spots had taken their toll. There were days too numerous to recall when he had arrived at the office nursing a world-class hangover, his ass dragging on the ground. Clients noticed things like that. So did competitors. And colleagues.

You spend ten years busting your tail to get the corner office, Alex brooded, *and the moment you stop for breath, some subordinate is trying to ace you out.* Every year there was a whole new crop of MBAs—younger men, hungry men—eager to take up the slack, steal your best customers, nibbling at your heels like a school of piranhas. Or sharks who had scented blood. Who could blame them? He'd do the same in their situation. He had done it in the past.

Big fish, little fish. That was the way of the world, and if you wanted to survive you had to obey the basic rules. Alex had them down cold. If Moses had his ten commandments, Alex had his five: Never turn your back for a moment. Never take anyone on trust. Never let up. Never wind down. And, as it said in that deodorant commercial, never let them see you sweat.

Not every man responded to pressure as well as Alex did, and he supposed in a way, he had his homelife to thank for that.

Boring it might be, but that's what family life was about. Refuge. Relief. Because home was the one place where you could let your guard down. Breathe freely. Unbutton your collar and your lip. Where you could vent your frustration in total security. He never had to worry about Rosemary betraying his business secrets, speaking out of turn. Hell— she hardly ever listened when he talked.

The time had come, he guessed, to head back to Westport and make up with the old girl. Her lawyers had been making tough noises lately, but Alex discounted that as being the nature of the profession. Not that Rosemary didn't have good reason for being pissed off, but he knew his wife. Now that he'd broken with Fleur, Rosemary would be falling-down glad to have him back.

What the hell—he'd be kind of glad himself. This two-household life was a strain. To say nothing of being damn expensive! He was down to the last of his ready cash.

He devoted the rest of the afternoon to strategic considerations. Alex Marshall would not grovel, that much was clear. If Rosemary perceived him as crawling back on all fours, she would put him in the doghouse alongside Shelby, and properly so.

With the care of a businessman embarking on major negotiations, Alex plotted his tactics and refined his approach. He would appear moderately repentant, he determined, but by no means guilt-ridden. Affectionate, but controlled. Firm, but not unkind. Because if he was going to work out a viable deal, then Rosemary was going to have to make a few concessions. After all, marriage was a matter of give-and-take.

They would sit down, like the two sensible people they

were at heart, talk matters through, and see what steps they could take to improve their situation. Given good faith on both sides, he had no doubt that their union would survive for many years, if not even be better for having weathered the storm.

Shortly before quitting time, Alex picked up the phone. "Rosie," he announced. "I'm coming home."

"Women!" He stowed the last of his suitcases in the backseat of the cab, climbed in after it, then stifled a yawn. "Can't live with them, can't live without them. You married?"

"No, sir," the driver said.

"Smart." Alex nodded.

"The dispatcher said you wanted Grand Central Station."

Alex surveyed his surroundings. The taxi was clean and well maintained. In his present mood, he didn't feel up to the train, with the familiar commuter faces and voices. *Hey, Alex, where the hell have you been? Back in the fold, huh, buddy?*

"What'll you charge for driving me out to Westport? Figure about three hours round trip max."

They haggled for several minutes, then Alex gave in. A bloody fortune, but what the hell! It wasn't every night in the year a man reconciled with his wife. Maybe he could write it off somehow.

"Yeah, all right," Alex agreed.

"Plus tolls and tip."

Alex checked the name on the ID plate. Avram Gittelson. Jewish. To judge by the accent, Israeli.

"You guys drive a hard bargain," he said. "But that's okay. I respect that. I'm a businessman myself."

He gave directions. The car swung out on to the FDR Drive and headed north toward home. With a pang of nostalgia, Alex turned for a farewell glimpse of the Upper East Side. The skyline glittered in the twilight. Fun while it lasted. *Good-bye, Fleur, my pet. And hello Rosie, my wife.*

The driver was both swift and skillful, Alex noted with approval, weaving in and out of the lanes with the ease of a slalom artist negotiating an Alpine slope. Not like most of these maniacs you found behind a wheel these days, half of whom barely even understood English. This one was polite and well spoken for a change. Plus he had a great head of hair, lucky bastard! That last crack of Fleur's had really hurt. Balding indeed! Well, she was getting gray—so there!

He began to relax, feel a bit talkative, even philosophical. Cabbies were like shrinks, it struck him. Or wives. You could confide your life story, complete with all the gory details, and not have to worry. They couldn't sell you out if they wanted to. They wouldn't know where. It was a totally anonymous exchange. For the price of the cab fare you bought yourself a captive audience. It was a helluva lot cheaper than a session on the couch.

"You wouldn't believe what I've just been through" —he checked the name again—"umm—Avram."

"Yes, sir, I would. I'd believe anything."

"Woman threw a banana at me. Porcelain banana. Nearly took the top of my head off."

"Mmmm—hmmm." The driver seemed unimpressed. He must have heard a lot worse.

"I suppose you get all kinds, driving a radio cab," Alex ruminated. "Drunks and lowlifes—hookers."

"All kinds."

As always, Alex found himself intrigued by the seamier aspects of New York, especially now that he was leaving it behind. "I bet you could write a book of your experiences," he said.

"Some book!" Avram returned. "It would have to be censored."

"Oh yeah? Like what?"

Under Alex's prodding, the driver began to unwind. He seemed a friendly fellow, and as they cruised down the Thruway he regaled Alex with a cabbie's-eye view of life, love, and general misbehavior as it occurred in the backseat of his car. Some of the stories were funny, a few were scabrous. The grand finale was an anecdote concerning an elderly gentleman with a wooden leg and two teenage prostitutes.

"Really!" Alex found the details fascinating. "Both of them at once! And you could see all that?"

"In my rearview mirror. I almost went off the road."

"Hmmmph!" Alex marveled. "The things people do! Kinky! I gather you find it interesting work."

"Interesting" came the evasive answer, "but not necessarily enjoyable. I'd like to quit and start a little business of my own."

"What kind of business?" Alex's ears perked up. When Avram told him, he asked a few specific questions, then nodded. "Sounds like a viable proposition. Why don't you go ahead and do it?"

"No capital, no visa, no green card," Avram said. "Anyhow, I'm returning to Israel next month. This is a tough country you have here."

"You're telling me!" Alex chuckled. "So what do you think of our American girls?"

"As I said, this is a tough country."

"Oh, come on! A good-looking guy like you must be beating them off. You mean to tell me you've been here all this time and you haven't scored?"

"Scored!" It was Avram's turn to laugh. "You make it sound like a sport, a soccer game." He paused, and Alex wondered briefly if perhaps taxi drivers didn't also regard their fares in the same anonymous manner, as people to whom they could confide freely. Apparently this one did, for the young man went on.

"To tell you the truth, I fell in love with the most marvelous woman here."

Alex picked up a note of longing. It sounded as though the poor bastard had a terminal case. "Was she pretty?" he asked.

"To me she was. And a wonderful person. A lawyer, by the way. Sweet. Cultured. Affectionate. And smart? Ay! Is that woman smart! Just being in the same room with her was a joy." His voice trailed off. The joy was clearly over.

"Let me guess," Alex broke in, convinced of what was coming next. "She started putting the screws on you to get married, right? Jesus! They're all alike."

"Not at all!" Avram turned around briefly in surprise. "Quite the opposite. I was the one who wanted to marry, but apparently she felt I wasn't good enough for her. Who knows? She was probably correct."

"Not good enough? Typical female response. You know what that means, don't you? It's spelled M-O-N-E-Y. They're all the same—all looking for a meal ticket, you know, no matter what they say with this women's lib crap. Why should they work when we can bust our asses for them? Smart? You bet they are. Count yourself lucky. You ask me," Alex volunteered, "your girlfriend sounds like a Grade-A shrew. You're well out of it."

"Oh, no!" Avram shot back. "You misunderstand. She's not like that at all. In fact, she's a real mensch at heart—you know, a human being. But confused. Very ambitious, hardworking. Too involved in her career. Not that it matters any longer, but she really cared about success. I guess more than she cared about me. Success! I'm sick of the word."

"Don't knock it, buddy," Alex rejoined. "Without success in this world, a man is nothing. And as for your girlfriend, well, I wouldn't mourn over it. There are always plenty of replacements just waiting in the wings. Listen, my friend." They had reached the Westport exit. Another couple of minutes and he'd be home with his wife. It made him feel for this kid, bleeding over some hard-hearted bitch. "How old are you, twenty-five, twenty-six? I've probably got ten years on you, so you can benefit from my experience. You know what the secret of managing women is? Never let them get control. Take my wife, for instance. We've had a misunderstanding the last couple of months, and between you and me, I was partly to blame. But I won't let her catch me looking hangdog—no sir!—or she'll have me on the rack the rest of my life. I don't say you shouldn't be kind to them, be thoughtful. They're wonderful creatures, in their way. But once you give a woman a taste of power, you're dead meat. It's like booze to a drunk. They don't know how to handle it. They go bananas." He massaged his injured temple for emphasis. "Literally!"

"Oh, I don't know—" Avram said.

"No you don't, but I *do*. My philosophy with women is never apologize, never explain—the royal prerogative. For all their yattering about tenderness and sensitivity, you know what women really admire? Strength. Decisiveness. That's how come Clint Eastwood is one of this country's top box-office stars. Believe me, women respect you all the more for being firm. And that's what it's all about—control and respect. And I'll tell you something else—" He paused, then felt a sudden thrill. There it was. Home! The lights were on, the house looked inviting. He could see her shadow moving in the kitchen. She was probably whipping up something special. Rosemary had a nice sense of occasion. "Yep, I'll tell you something else," Alex concluded. "A valuable secret. For all their bitching, women really want it that way. God made them like that. It's part of their nature."

The taxi pulled up in the driveway to the comforting familiar sound of crunching gravel. Music to the ears. Alex smothered a smile while the cabbie unloaded the luggage onto the porch.

"Okay, now remember what I said, fella." He reached into his wallet, paid the fare, the tolls, and a ten-dollar tip. Then, feeling philanthropic, he added another twenty dollars for good measure.

"Thank *you*, sir!" The cabbie smiled, surprised.

"Ah what the hell." Alex was glad to be home. "It's only money."

THIRTY-TWO

———•———

"**H**ow could you be so dumb?"

Having snatched Fleur from the jaws of prosecution, having calmed her, comforted her, dried her tears, wiped her nose, brought her home, fed her, and black-coffeed her half to death, Diane now felt entitled to vent some right-eous indignation.

It had been a hellish afternoon. Fleur's panic-stricken call couldn't have come at a worse moment, with Diane being paged in the midst of a large meeting.

"You need a criminal lawyer," she had whispered into the phone.

"I want you."

Diane had excused herself briskly, claiming "personal crisis," and grabbed a cab uptown.

What followed was a roundabout of pleas, negotiations, and endless waiting. The store wouldn't budge. Neither would Diane, hanging on like a Boston terrier. She tackled everyone from the security staff to the managing director to the store's outside counsel, before a settlement was thrashed out. The store finally agreed to drop criminal charges. In return, Fleur had signed a form admitting theft. Henceforth her name would be entered on a file of known shoplifters (the "shit list," as she put it) and circulated to New York's leading retailers. It was the best, Diane assured her, of a very bad bargain.

Now Fleur was curled up in a corner of Diane's sofa with

a brandy snifter for support. Diane pursed her lips and repeated her question.

"I said, how could you be so dumb?"

"Which dumb do you mean? My affair with Alex or the shoplifting number?"

Diane shook her head, exasperated. "Both," she declared.

"It wasn't easy," Fleur said, "but if it's any consolation, I give you my word—it's history."

"What is—Alex or the shoplifting?"

"Both." Fleur managed an acerbic smile. "And for all I know they were related. Honest, Judge Summerfield, I never swiped anything in my entire life other than the occasional advertising idea. Not until I purloined my Mr. Wrong. Tell me, Judge, is there such a charge as Grand Theft Husband? You know, it's like Grand Theft Auto, only not quite as much fun, especially now that the joyride is over. Anyhow, I suppose one bit of larceny leads to another. So there I was this afternoon, caught in the act, practically a candidate for Devil's Island. Well, Riker's Island, at any rate. I mean, can you picture me—*moi*, Fleur Chamberlain—togged out in some tacky prison uniform? Not even genuine cotton is my bet. More likely those disgusting man-made fibers. I mean, I like understated clothes as well as the next person, but one can go too far in the quest for simplicity. I believe the *mode du jour* in the slammer is your basic potato sack in dishwater gray. One size fits all."

"You don't have to, you know," Diane said.

"Don't have to what?"

"Pretend to make light of it. It's not a joke."

"Listen, honey, if I don't laugh, I'll cry and never stop."

"Oh, Fleur—"

"Oh, yes!"

They sat for a moment in crackling silence, then Fleur polished off her brandy. When next she spoke, the mock-ironic tone was gone. "Today, sitting in that goddamn security office waiting for you to come, I felt I'd hit bottom. It was the absolute pits! I know, you're going to say that it could have been worse, I might have wound up a convicted felon. With a record! For this I worked my way through four years of Smith! For this I came to New York!"

"Forget it!"

"I can't. You saved my life, Di, metaphorically speaking, for which boundless thanks. I don't have the foggiest what your legal fees are, by the way. What do you big-time lawyers charge? Two hundred, three hundred dollars an hour? I'm afraid to guess what this little caper is going to cost me."

"Forget that too. I'm not going to bill you."

"Oh, yes, you are!" Fleur insisted. "I want you to. I want to pay my own way. It would put a lot of things in proper perspective. Not that I can write you a check at this moment, but one of these days—"

She paused. "You know, it's funny. Ironic, really. There I was in the worst predicament of my life, sweating blood, the proverbial damsel in distress! And who came to my aid? Not a knight in shining armor. Not Prince Charming galloping to rescue me from durance vile. No. Not a man at all. A woman! Ain't that something?" She swiped at an incipient tear, then continued.

"It wasn't supposed to be like that, Diane. It's not how it is in the fairy tales. And I believed them, Di, all my life. I believed that men were the answer to every conceivable problem. That were going to save us from drudgery, protect us from mice, carry our luggage, kiss away the hurts, meet the first-of-the-month bills, and then put us up on the nearest pedestal as a reward for our being so sweet and helpless and feminine. Men were where you turned when you found yourself in deep shit. My hero! But when I was sitting there in that ghastly room, it never occurred to me to call Alex for help. That so-called tower of strength, the man who was going to look after me the rest of my life! In my heart, I knew he'd make himself scarce when the chips were down. My hero indeed!" she sneered. "Chances are he's already back in Rosemary's loving arms, being hand-fed banana bread and homemade truffles."

"I wouldn't be too sure," Diane interjected.

"I would! Rosemary will give him a hard time for a good full ten minutes, then it'll be business as usual. My bet is at this very moment the two of them are probably clucking in unison about what a vicious, immoral person I am. The irony is, I wound up losing them both—friend and lover! Still, it's just as well. There were things I never told you about Alex and me that were fairly scary. He liked to play games, you see. Weird games. The kind that involved domination, forms of bondage. They were basically power plays, I realize, because he always had to win, to assert his masculinity. In his fantasy life, I was the slave, the whore. The eternal victim, don't you see? As for Alex, he was the master with the whip. We brought out the worst in each other, I'm sorry to say. It was sick. Why, there was one time in a Chicago hotel—"

"Please!" Diane held up an admonitory hand. "I don't want to hear the details."

"You're right," Fleur conceded. "They're not particularly appetizing. Besides it's all over. Everything. Completely kaput."

Diane hesitated. "Not everything surely."

"What do you mean?"

Diane drew a deep breath, before continuing. "I realize that at the moment things are looking very bleak for you, but don't take it out on the innocent. Please, Fleur, I beg of you. Remember there's another life at stake. And if there's any way in which I can help—financially, personally. . . ." Her voice drifted off. She felt close to tears. But Fleur was looking at her with genuine puzzlement.

"I don't know what you mean, Diane. You've helped me so much already. I don't plan to sponge off you the rest of my life."

"The baby!" Diane blurted out. "I know it must seem like a nightmare, all this happening and your being pregnant. But don't do anything rash, I implore you! If you feel the situation is too much for you to handle, have your baby just the same, Fleur. I'll be happy to take care of it for you, bring it up. Life's too precious to throw away."

"Oh my God!" Fleur turned ashen. "Don't you know? Jesus Christ, Diane." For the first time she couldn't face her old friend. "There is no baby! There never was! It was a hoax, a fantasy. The traditional way to pressure a man into marriage. Only he didn't buy it—not for a single minute."

"How could you!" Diane recoiled.

"I never meant to deceive you. I only told you and Bernie I was pregnant so I could rehearse it, try it on for size, so to speak, before I sprang it on Alex. I was growing desperate, don't you see? I needed that extra crunch. And of course as soon as we were married, I would really have tried to become pregnant, but by then it wouldn't have much mattered. I'd have been safe. Set for life. Please don't hate me, Di. I hate myself enough already."

"You make me feel like a sentimental fool," Diane said sharply, "letting me put my heart on the line like that."

"No, Di"—Fleur took her friend's hand and refused to surrender it—"I'm the fool. The original Miss Dumbnuts, wasting my days on illusions, waiting for my prince to come and carry me off. Slim shimmering Fleur, delicate as a wisp of smoke, being crushed in his great manly arms. Happy ever after. If I had to sum myself up in a single word, Di, you know what that word would be?"

Diane considered. *Beautiful? Needy? Clever? Lonely?* "*Romantic,*" she hit on it. "That's it, isn't it? You're the incurable romantic."

"Not incurable, I trust. Actually, 'romantic' wasn't the word I had in mind. The word was 'hungry.' "

"Hungry!" Diane exclaimed.

"That's right. Literally physically hungry. Ravenous. Famished. Starved. Whatever term you prefer to describe caloric deprivation. All my life I've been hungry. By that I don't mean that we were so impoverished there wasn't enough to eat. But I always felt that if I let myself go, I'd grow fat and disgusting and no one would ever marry me. From the day I saw my first dog-eared copy of *Vogue* at the La Belle Beauty Salon in downtown Waterville, I knew what was necessary. And I've been depriving myself of food ever since. I had to be perfect because I was going to marry perfect. And if I suffered, big deal! Because everything was temporary, makeshift, right up until my wedding day when real life would begin. Till then, I was simply marking time."

"I know the feeling," Diane murmured.

"So I was going to come to New York, make a little money, have a lot of fun, and then get serious and settle down. Which is not to say I didn't enjoy those years playing the glamour girl. But it palled after a while, and so did the job. Because it wasn't real—any of it! Ever have that feeling, Diane, that you're playacting, pretending that what you do really matters? And you know it's bullshit. Pure fakery. Maybe it's especially true of people in advertising or PR, where you deal with intangibles all the time. Dreams. Images. Two-dimensional stage sets. A view of life that measures no bigger than a twenty-two-inch screen. Who can take that seriously as a way of life?" she snorted. "It's only stopgap until the right man comes along."

"But what if he doesn't?"

"Oh, but he must! It is written. You see, I believed that in all the world there was one person whom fate had ordained for me. He would find me and marry me. And my life's work would be done. Everything else, from earning a living to staying slim, was prologue. And of course, I had to be ready when this king of kings appeared. You know, there's one thing I've always resented about you, Diane."

"And that is?"

"Your ability to metabolize food. Not me! If it weren't for diet pills, cottage cheese, and massive doses of Jane Fonda, I'd resemble your essential large planet. So I starved myself and prepared my body and panicked if I got a zit or some guy discovered unshaven hairs in my armpit or, God forbid, an ounce of flab on my thighs. Then along came Alex—and I thought I'd hit pay dirt."

"But what was so special about him?" Diane frowned. "I always thought Alex was—well, a bit pompous."

"I ran into him at a very vulnerable moment, and part of his attraction—you're going to laugh, Diane—was that he looked so substantial, so well fed. The prototypical solid bourgeois. Real beef. I can't tell you how appealing that was. I liked the fact that he was so mundane. It proved that he was good husband material. And if I could only hang in there long enough, I was sure he'd marry me and all my problems would be solved. Then I wouldn't have to starve myself anymore. I could grow plump and happy just like Rosemary. Not that she's so plump and happy these days! But until that wedding ring was on my finger, I couldn't relax my guard for a second. One false move, one forbidden helping of french fries or Häagen-Dazs, and my chances would be ruined. So here I am, still thin as a whippet and I've managed to fuck up my life nonetheless. All that suffering for nothing! No man, no money, and in another couple of weeks, no job."

Diane was grateful for a change of topic. "I thought that your agency was going to make a final pitch for the perfume account."

"Perfume!" Fleur gave a bitter laugh. "Talk about unreality! Anyhow, our pitch is a guaranteed loser, total shit. It couldn't be anything else, given our client's dumb guidelines. For your information, No Name is now christened Snow Drop, complete with a smiling image of a rosy-cheeked homecoming queen. Stuff looks so goddamn wholesome, you need a virgin's license in order to wear it. Sugar-sweet and twice as cloying. Fwankly, it makes me want to fwow up, as somebody once said of a Shirley Temple movie."

"Part of the new morality?" Diane asked. "Is that the reasoning?"

"Fuck the new morality! Women want to feel that they're sexy, attractive, and the irresistible objects of masculine desire. They always have. They always will. And they're going to compete with one another on exactly those terms just as long as there's one man left on earth. I'd stake my career on it. With that thought, my dear Diane, I leave you."

Fleur opened her bag, freshened her lipstick, and then gathered her packages. "It's a dress," she explained. "A smashing peacock blue mini. And mine, I'm happy to say, honestly come by. At least until my American Express bill falls due."

"But what happens now?" Diane wondered, asking Fleur out loud.

"Now I go home"—Fleur pecked her good-bye—"fall into the typewriter, and get down to work. Who knows, maybe there's a way to salvage the account. 'Cause if I can't come up with something better than fucking Snow Drop, then I deserve to be out of a job. No Name!" she snickered. "The stuff that dreams are made of. Well, it may be indefinable, elusive, and all in the head, but I suppose it's as real as anything else in this impossible world."

She walked down Lexington Avenue feeling almost buoyant. The worst had happened and she'd survived. She still had two tickets to *The Phantom of the Opera* next week. And there seemed to be no place to go but up.

Her thoughts zeroed in on No Name. Everybody at the agency had slipped the track, herself included. What the product needed was verve, passion, some concept that sang with excitement and glamour. If only there were a way she could use her experience with Alex—its intensity, its emotion—if only she could package those sensations and put them in an ad—

Oh, sure! She chided herself. *That's what the whole affair was all about, schmucko, to provide a little personal grist for your "creative" work. You're not Tolstoy, remember?*

Still, bills were bills, rent was rent, food was food. And

even the skinniest sexiest creature in the world had to eat. Even the schmuckiest copywriter. That was reality.

The air was sultry with a promise of long summer nights, pungent with the scents of car exhaust and pizza stands and dog shit. The quintessential perfume of New York. Fleur inhaled happily. For better or worse, her city.

She picked up the bulldog edition of the *Times,* then stopped at an all-night deli to buy a pastrami sandwich, a quart of butter almond ice cream, and some Cheezits. Then she walked the rest of the way home, totally preoccupied, eating the Cheezits out of the brown paper bag.

THIRTY-THREE

Alex slipped his key in the lock with a sense of benediction. To his surprise it refused to engage. "What the hell—" He jiggled it a few more times to no avail, then rang the doorbell in exasperation.

Dolly Bainter ushered him in, all smiles.

"About time!" He gave his mother-in-law a perfunctory peck. "Jesus, I was beginning to feel like a door-to-door salesman."

"Sorry," she apologized. "Rosemary had the locks changed last week. Something about burglaries in the neighborhood."

Alex deposited his luggage in the entrance hall, then stood back to survey his realm. The house was spotless as usual. The brassware gleamed, the floors shone. He could see his reflection in the mahogany table. From the kitchen, a wonderful aroma was wafting in.

"Do I smell Chicken Maryland?" Alex's eyes sparkled at the prospect. "Or have I died and gone to heaven?"

"Chicken Maryland it is." Dolly smiled. "Rosemary's been fussing since the moment you called. She's in the kitchen right now, waiting dinner. Chris is already asleep, so why don't I just do my disappearing act and leave you two to get on with it? Welcome home, Alex."

"Thanks, Dolly." He kissed her again, this time with warmth. "It's good to be back."

He remained motionless for a moment, psyching himself for the imminent encounter, then followed his nose into the kitchen.

Rosemary was bending over, taking something out of the oven and Alex's first impression was "Hey, you look terrific! Have you lost weight?"

She stood up, oven mitts full of pecan pie, and smiled. "I've lost a few pounds."

"You sure have." He nodded in appreciation. "You look downright svelte. I know what you're going to say." He began picking his words carefully. "You're going to tell me it's because of all this anxiety you've been going through—"

"Please, Alex," she broke in. "Let's leave the heavy stuff till later, shall we? It's nine o'clock already and I'm sure you must be starved. I know I am. So why don't you sit down and let me serve."

There was Chicken Maryland as only she could make it, crunchy on the outside, moist and tender on the inside, bathed in a delicate cream sauce. Corn fritters that were lighter than air, tiny fresh-picked peas sprinkled with mint, glazed baby carrots, popovers still warm from the oven drizzled with fragrant herb butter. Real home cooking. The kind, Alex thought as he dove in, that you couldn't get in New York for love or money. Well, certainly not money, he corrected himself. Because "love" was what this kind of meal was all about.

"How come you're not eating, honey?" he asked, pausing in mid-fork. His wife had hardly touched her plate. She seemed content to sit and watch him as he savored each mouthful.

"Oh you know me." She smiled and poured him a glass of vintage Gamay. "I nibble so much while I'm cooking that I never have any appetite left over. But you go ahead. Enjoy."

He had seconds on the chicken and the popovers, then finished the wine while she cut him a slab of pecan pie.

"How about a nice dollop of whipped cream on that, Alex?"

He opened his belt a notch and gave a mock groan. "What are you trying to do, Rosie, kill me with cholesterol?"

For some reason she found that funny. "I'll make coffee," she said. She rose and began measuring out fresh Colombian beans. He watched her back as she fed the beans into the electric grinder. The aroma was intoxicating.

"The greatest smell in the world," Alex said.

"Better than perfume?"

For a moment he was caught off balance, uncertain if that was intended as a round-about swipe at Fleur. He doubted it. Rosemary was not prone to verbal sparring. But even if it was meant maliciously, she was surely entitled to this small revenge.

His wife, he decided, was a remarkable woman. Thoroughly civilized. There had been no scenes, no shrieks, no wild recriminations. No porcelain bananas flying through the air. Rosemary knew how to behave like a lady, bless her. *Class always shows,* Alex thought. And Rosemary had it. Plus she was one helluva cook.

Next she took off her apron, poured them both coffee, then sat down across the table from him. He couldn't get over how attractive she looked. She had chosen a black silk-knit top and a long black woolen skirt for the occasion, an outfit he hadn't seen before. She never used to wear black, he recalled, having always been partial to ice-cream pastels and Scottish tweeds. This new style of hers was both elegant and faintly unsettling.

She was making a heroic effort to please, Alex concluded, trying to show him that in matters of panache she could compete on equal terms with Fleur. It was flattering. Touching, in fact, especially since the only jewelry she wore were things he had given her. The pearl choker he had bought for her thirtieth birthday—damn thing had cost a fortune! And of course her wedding ring. Now the pearls gleamed warmly against the smooth skin of her neck. Alex felt himself growing slightly horny.

However—he caught himself short—it didn't pay to be impulsive. To fall straight into bed would simply incorporate the *status quo ante.* That would come later. First, he would present Rosemary with his bill of particulars, those terms so carefully formulated earlier at the office. What was required here was a good old heart-to-heart talk.

Moreover he could see by her quiet face and her folded hands that she too felt a summing-up was due. She doubtless had her own expectations, and these would have to be negotiated. Tact was crucial throughout, as was a measure of caution, especially now when he was mellowed by good food and drink. Had she been endowed with a craftier nature, Alex might have suspected her of trying to soften him up.

"More coffee, Alex?"

He shook his head, then began speaking his piece.

"We both have a lot of work to do on this marriage, to make it as good as possible, and I'd like to start by being very, very open as to how I think you can help to make it better." That struck him as tastefully phrased, and since she uttered no word of protest, he moved on, emboldened.

They had, he reminded her, enjoyed ten reasonably happy years together, yet had their marriage been more rewarding, he would never have strayed. A man had certain needs, certain sexual needs—he watched her closely, she didn't flinch—that had to be catered to. If she felt this matter was too difficult to talk about, then she might want to see a therapist to help her overcome her inhibitions. He would pay for it. But in any event, major changes would have to be made. He was a normal, virile man.

Then there was the matter of commuting.

He appreciated how much this house meant to her, to both of them, for that matter, but the daily commute was killing him. It was literally shortening his life by one month per year, and she didn't want to be a young widow, did she? They would sell the house, and make a fortune in the bargain. Over the years the place had tripled in value. They would take the profit, then purchase something closer in. Perhaps a condominium in the city. And if there was enough money left over, maybe buy a little ski place in Vermont. Which brought him to the next topic.

"You never wanted to do fun things anymore," he complained. "Not since the day we got married. All I ever hear about is the goddamn house. My interests, my hobbies don't seem to count for anything with you. Take skiing, for instance. It's the perfect example."

Before they had got engaged, she used to ski all the time, he reminded her. They'd had great weekends back in college. Now nothing could drag her on to the slopes. It was too much trouble, too boring, she always complained. "Same thing with football games," he went on. "Or Clint Eastwood movies. You can't be bothered. Well, it's high time my preferences received consideration."

Alex paused. He hadn't mentioned the most important points.

You never listen when I talk, he wanted to say. *You never hear what I'm trying to tell you. My thoughts, my feelings, my problems, my anxieties—they all go in one ear and out the other. If they even go in that one ear, which I doubt.*

It was, in fact, the greatest grievance of his married life: this profound lack of communication, her complete disinterest in his emotional well-being. He wanted more than food for the body, no matter how beautifully prepared. He wanted food for the soul and heart. He begged to be perceived as a man of wit and sensibilities and imagination. Appreciated as something more than a breadwinner. Fleur had recognized some of those needs and catered to them. Why was Rosemary so consistently blind and deaf?

Hear me!—he wanted to say. *For God's sake, hear me! See me!*

But as he reached this point in his declamation, the words froze on his lips. For Rosemary was listening now. Following his every word with such avidity, such concentration that he found himself sweating.

Finally! he thought. Finally, after all these years he had caught her undivided attention. He wasn't too sure if he liked it.

He said nothing more except, "I rest my case. Now I would like to hear yours."

It was clear that his wife had changed during their separation. Grown in stature. His absence must have been a salutary lesson, for she had learned to sharpen her focus, to listen with both ears.

He leaned back in his chair and awaited her response. Rosemary would defend her position, of course. Argue this, deny that. She would make a few concessions here and there. Selling the house would be a sore point, although in this matter, he was determined to prevail. Beyond that, they could begin serious negotiations. After which they would go to bed and make love.

For a long moment, she sat quietly, her eyes fixed on his face. Beneath her gaze he grew edgy. Unwittingly, he touched his injured head. It still throbbed. She watched him with interest. Then she smiled.

Alex gave a sigh of relief. It was going to be all right. For the first time, he could admit to himself he'd been a trifle scared, even as he ate. For some reason, he kept thinking of the Last Supper. But she was smiling now.

He smiled back.

"It's good to be home, Rosie," he said. "Really good."

"What's the matter, Alex?" Rosemary murmured. "Your bimbo throw you out?"

He blinked. Her voice was so soft he could barely make out the words, and "bimbo" was a most unlikely term for her to use. Moreover, she was still smiling.

"I beg your pardon? I must have misheard."

"I said—" the smile faded. Her face was expressionless, her tone clear but devoid of intonation—"did your bimbo throw you out? Or did you dump her the same way you dumped me?"

"Rosie!" Alex was startled. "What kind of question is that?"

"A simple question that deserves a simple answer."

"Fair enough." He shifted in his chair. She was going to put him through the wringer after all. "Although I never dumped you, as you put it. You asked me to leave. Let's say we had a misunderstanding, that's all. As for Fleur, she and I have arrived at a mutual decision to call it off. It's over. I promise you that, Rosie. You needn't worry about my having anything more to do with her. It was a kind of craziness. An infatuation, that's all."

He reached across the table to take Rosemary's hand, but she recoiled with a visible shudder of revulsion. Then she folded her arms, once again inscrutable as a Buddha.

"I see," she said in a cool factual manner. "You got tired of screwing her and decided to come home and screw me. Very touching. Only this isn't your home anymore. As you maybe have noticed, I've had the locks changed."

Alex was dumbstruck. Invective he could have understood. Wrath. Tears. Hysteria. Even flying objects! They would have cleared the air like a thunderstorm. Then once her anger had run its course, he would calm her down and kiss her fears away, after which everything would proceed according to plan. But this? This coldness—this calculation! How did you cool down someone who was already made of ice? He looked at Rosemary with wary respect. She was turning into a formidable adversary.

Don't panic! his every instinct warned him. *Maintain control.*

"Surely"—he tried to suppress the tremor in his voice—"you don't mean that! You're dramatizing. Of course this is my home. Just as you are my wife.

"This is no longer your home," she said, "and in another

seventy-two days, according to my lawyer, I will no longer be your wife."

"I don't believe this!" Alex smacked his forehead, setting off another round of pain. "I come back in the spirit of sweet reason, conciliatory, ready to work things out—and you don't even want to fucking talk! Jesus, Rosemary, what do you want from me? I'm willing to negotiate, to compromise, so will you stop being so goddamn preemptive? It doesn't make sense. If you feel this way about me, that I'm such a faithless son of a bitch, then why the hell did you cook me dinner? Chicken Maryland, all my favorite dishes—" A sudden chill struck his heart. "What was on your mind, Rosemary? 'The condemned man ate a hearty meal?' Is that it?"

"Something like that." Now she *was* smiling. It was the smile of an executioner.

"Okay, you've had your little joke."

"No joke, Alex. It was serious business, right down to the pecan pie. I wanted you to remember how good it was here. How much you've had and how you've thrown it all away. I want you to think of that dinner, this kitchen, when you're eating TV dinners off a hot plate. Or does your girlfriend whip you up gourmet delights?" She snorted, the image of Fleur in an apron apparently being good for a laugh.

"Jesus," he exploded. No, she hadn't changed after all. She was deaf and dense as ever. "It's all over with Fleur. Can't you get that through your head? You haven't heard a thing I said, have you? Same old Rosemary. You never listen, you never see. Goddamnit, that's the story of our marriage—"

"You're right, Alex," she conceded. "One hundred percent right. All those years we were together, I never saw, never heard a thing. And you know why? Because I was afraid to! Afraid that if I looked too closely, I might discover you had feet of clay and the morals of a cockroach. If I listened too hard, I might hear what was going on behind your words—all the lies, the slime. So I didn't look or listen, because I loved you, I needed you. And I didn't want to know the truth. But I'm a big girl now, Alex. I've made something of myself since you've been gone. I've earned my independence, my self-respect, and I don't need you around anymore."

"Okay, forget need," Alex shot back. "You're Miss Superwoman. Fine with me. But what about love? Because those were your words. You said 'loved' and 'needed' just then. Doesn't love count for something still? We're a couple. We have a family. We've put in a lot of time together. Or have you found someone else? That's it, isn't it?" He had a vivid insight. "You've got something going on the side. You've lined up husband number two is my bet. Why it's as clear as day! Because I know you, Rosie—you're the cautious type. You don't jump ship without a life belt. Who is it, that periodontist fellow? Someone at the club?"

"Don't be absurd! You know that I've been a good, loyal, and faithful wife and I daresay you'll never find another woman so devoted as long as you live. So eat your heart out, Alex Marshall, because they broke the mold of loving wives when they made me.

"As for Fleur," she continued, "it's immaterial to me whether you see her or not. I don't believe she was your first such entertainment, I certainly don't believe she'll be the last. In any event, I have no doubt you'll find consolation elsewhere. But not in this house. Is that clear? And not in my bed. You disgust me. Now what I suggest is that you make a list of your personal belongings, books, et cetera, that sort of thing and let me know where to send them."

She got up and began loading the dishwasher.

Alex felt sick and feverish. The meal lay in his stomach like the *Titanic* on the ocean floor.

"Am I allowed to use the bathroom?" he asked acidly.

"Of course," she said. "You know the way."

"You have any Pepto-Bismol?"

"Try the upstairs john."

Feeling like a disoriented houseguest, he went up the steps for the first time in months. Down the carpeted hallway, through the bedroom (once theirs, now hers) into the bathroom (once theirs, now hers). Everything appeared simultaneously familiar and alien—rooms seen in a painting or a stage set. The effect was disconcerting.

He filled the marble basin with cold water and plunged his head in seeking relief. The water stung his eyes. He groped blindly on the counter for his comb in its usual location, alongside his father's silver-and-ivory brushes. His hand came up empty. No comb, no brushes. It was a sharp reminder that he didn't live there anymore. With a jolt, he realized what was wrong in these rooms. It was the absence of masculine paraphernalia. Of masculine scents. His. Anyone's.

Rosemary had assured him there was nobody else, yet he remained skeptical. She was the marrying kind, the type of woman who couldn't envisage herself without a man. If there was no one waiting in the wings, then why this mad rush to divorce?

The husband in him hated the idea of her sleeping with another man. The pragmatist in him saw the matter otherwise.

For if one thing was clear as a result of their conversation, it was that Rosemary was going to try to stick him in court. He knew how the situation would look before a judge. The errant husband. The innocent wife. As things stood, he was going to come across as a Grade-A super shit. Unless—*Sauce for the goose.*

Alex gritted his teeth. The time had come to play hardball.

Quietly he opened the medicine chest and riffled through the shelves, seeking signs of male habitation: shaving cream, condoms, any piece of physical evidence to indicate that Rosemary might have trod the primrose path herself. Nothing. He then made a swift inspection of the linen cupboards, the shower stall, the laundry hamper. On tiptoes, he went into the bedroom, explored the closets, lay down on the floor to look under the bed. Zilch. Not even a stray sock. He pulled back the bedspread, sniffed the sheets. Nothing of significance there either, except that she'd taken to eating crackers in bed.

By all appearances, the woman was a fucking vestal virgin. Yet it didn't sit right. He couldn't believe Rosemary had chosen this path unassisted. Because if Alex Marshall knew anything, he knew his wife. She was a born follower. Always was, always would be.

He went back into the bathroom, sat on the toilet seat, and pondered the situation.

The marriage was over, of that there could be no doubt. The notion would take some getting used to. Still, he consoled himself, the way Rosemary was behaving, it was probably just as well. She seemed to have developed a bitchy streak the past few months. Truly petty. The way she'd led him on during dinner was downright mean.

Okay, she'd had her cheap revenge. And he had had an excellent dinner. It was a fair exchange. And one thing she said was certainly true: he wouldn't lack for female companionship in the future. New York was full of eager women and he was still relatively young, reasonably attractive. And very well-heeled.

All that remained, he supposed, was tying up the loose ends, some of which could be left to lawyers. Except he didn't like dealing with lawyers. They complicated matters and charged a fortune for the privilege. Besides, that attorney of hers was a bloodsucker of the first order, out for every last penny.

Better, Alex decided, to deal with Rosemary directly. He could handle her. He'd be firm but fair, he told himself, with the emphasis on *firm*. Alex stood up, swallowed half the bottle of Pepto-Bismol in one gulp, then made his way downstairs.

"Right!" he declared. "Let's get down to business. I gather you want to keep the house."

"I do," Rosemary said. "It's the family home."

"Uh-huh." He nodded, making mental calculations.

"And the furnishings," she added.

"As you wish," Alex said. "Now, we have to work out the question of equity."

The current divorce law called for a fifty-fifty settlement of all property acquired since marriage. If Rosemary wanted the house outright, that was fine with him. First, they would have to call in an appraiser and get a hard figure on the value of the house and contents. Alex's guess was, based on current market prices, they were worth well upwards of half a million dollars. Right. That was her share. Then, to square accounts, he would take the dollar equivalency out of their joint financial holdings. Whatever was left over in the trading account would be divided in half.

"So essentially," he concluded, "it works out that you get the house and I get the stocks."

"What stocks?" she asked.

He was bewildered. "What do you mean, 'What stocks?' *Our* stocks. The R.J. Reynolds, Computa-Rama, that little blood bank I got into last fall." He enumerated the items in their portfolio with increasing gusto. They were talking very big bucks, edging up to a million. "And let's not forget the Bio-Chem," he wound up, "which just split two to one."

Rosemary heard him out patiently, then gave a sweet smile.

"Bio-Chem, Computa-Rama—" She shook her head. "Well, I don't know of any such firms. But as you used to say, I'm terribly naïve about that sort of thing. Tell me, these mysterious stocks—were they purchased in your name?"

For the first time in his life, Alex Marshall had a vision of hell. Naked, gaping hell. "My God, Rosemary! You know perfectly well whose name they're in. Your maiden name, for Chrissakes! Rosemary Bainter. Which doesn't make them yours, you understand!" He began hammering on the table. "By no means. They're part of our communal property just like the house, the cars. So don't try to get cute with me or I'll haul your ass into court."

"My, my, such language," she clucked. "Better be careful, Alex. A man your age could get a heart attack. Funny. You always told me you kept your cool when you were talking business! Another little lie, I reckon. Well, all I can say is, I've never heard of such stocks. As far as I'm concerned, they don't exist. But if they did exist, mind you, if such stocks actually were in my possession, then I'd have to ask myself: Where did they come from? How were they acquired? Via insider trading? Gracious me! I do believe that's against the law. Of course I'm not one of your great legal brains. I'm such a dumbo, I let my husband trade under my name. But dumb or not, I know my duty as a public-spirited citizen. If such stocks existed, Alex, I'd feel obliged to inform the SEC."

"You wouldn't!" he gasped. But one look at her told him that she would.

"Lord knows what they'd do. And even," she continued, "if you managed to stay out of jail, why, it could be the end of your career! Because I can't believe that a man who stooped so low, an executive who would betray his company's trust, trade on its secrets, would ever find a job again as long as he lives. Alex, baby, you've had it!"

The blood drained from Alex's face. "Rosemary! What are you trying to do to me?"

"Exactly what you did to me!" The sugar coating was off. The cream had curdled. In her eyes he read unremitting hate. Alex felt his hair stand on end. He couldn't believe what was happening. That his own wife—nice, kind, good-tempered, bread-baking Rosemary—would rip him off after their years together! It was too cruel, too incredible. He had trusted her—

"I trusted you!" he blurted out. "I've always trusted you implicitly. How can you do this to me?"

"*You* trusted *me*!" she shot back with heavy irony. "Coming from you, that's wonderful. As to how I can do this to you? Let me tell you—*with the greatest of pleasure*! The mechanics were easy. All I had to do was follow your example. You taught me how to cheat and lie and steal and betray, and play the innocent at the same time. I'm a slow learner, Alex, but when I learn, it sticks. You should be grateful all I'm taking is your money, that I'm letting you keep your job. Because if it weren't for Chris, I would have cheerfully killed you. Just as you killed me with your lies. Only I wouldn't have taken ten years to do it."

"I don't know you anymore." His mind reeled at the size of the impending catastrophe. Who was this woman? Why was she doing these terrible things to him? What had happened to the Rosemary he loved? "I look at you," he said in horror, "and I don't recognize you."

"Oh, you should, Alex. You truly should, because I'm your reflection. Your mirror image. So take a good last look, then get out of my house, and out of my life."

"Have you no heart?" he cried.

"I had one once, but you broke it."

He staggered to his feet, only wanting to be free of this nightmare, this emotional carnage. But where could he go? Not back to Fleur. That was impossible. How would he live? What would he live on?

He stared at her, half-pleading. "Am I to have nothing then?"

"This!" Rosemary pulled at her wedding ring. It refused to budge, unwilling to leave its familiar haunt of so many years. She attacked it with all the strength of her body, forcing it over the joint. The knuckle was left bruised.

"This is yours. It's a souvenir." She rolled it across the table, then touched her string of pearls. "But these I'll keep," she said. "They have value."

Dolly Bainter heard the door slam, then saw the taxi driving off. She flew downstairs in a frenzy.

"Where's Alex?"

"Gone." Rosemary was still sitting at the table, trembling uncontrollably while the tears streamed down her face. "And this time I made sure he'll never come back."

"Oh, darling!" Dolly began wringing her hands. "I had such high hopes. What happened? What did he say?"

"A lot of things, some of which even happened to be true. It was a very instructive evening. But everything he said came too late."

As Rosemary related the events of the last hour, Dolly recoiled in horror. "You robbed him, Rosie. You had no right. How could you do such a terrible thing!"

"You think it was easy?" Rosemary cried. "It was the toughest thing I've ever done in my life. But I needed to do it. I couldn't have lived with myself otherwise. I needed to prove myself. Funny," she sniffled, then dried her eyes. "Back at Smith, everyone used to think I was such a softy, such a sentimental wimp. Diane, Bernie—even Fleur." She gave a mordant laugh. "They should have seen me tonight. They would have been flabbergasted."

But Mrs. Bainter was shaking her head, distressed. "Pride," she murmured. "Foolish self-destructive pride."

"Pride," Rosemary returned, "but hardly self-destructive. I netted close to a million bucks tonight. Not bad for a few hours' work."

"Money doesn't buy happiness—" Dolly began to espouse the old homilies, but Rosemary broke in impatiently. "Please, Mother, spare me the eternal clichés about love and marriage and loyalty. I was raised on them. What's more, I lived by those values scrupulously for over thirty years. And a helluva lot of good they ever did me."

"You've become so hard, Rosemary." Unwittingly Dolly echoed Alex's words. "So very hard I wonder if I know you."

"Mother"—Rosemary turned on the dishwasher and headed upstairs—"I've become what life has made me. Nothing more."

The following morning Rosemary phoned Fleur. "You want Alex?" she snarled. "He's all yours."

In the background she could hear the clatter of the typewriter.

"Oh, Christ, Rosemary," came the answer. "Who the hell wants an Alex Marshall!"

THIRTY-FOUR

-------•-------

The years had dealt handsomely with Leo Frankland. The touch of gray at his temples, the web of fine lines at the corner of his eyes—signs that in a less-favored man might have suggested the mere passage of time—had conferred upon Leo a mantle of added distinction. His rolling baritone was as magnificent and peremptory as ever.

"I'm a weathered old bastard," he stated with quirky pride. "Some have even called me cantankerous. The wonder is that a young woman like you would waste a moment with such a craggy old bear. I'm fifty, you know."

"Fifty isn't old," Diane hastened to assure him.

"I make no secret of it," Leo went on. "I despise people who lie about their age. Age means nothing."

Their first date in New York had been marked with gallantries and flourishes. Leo knew how to do things in style.

They had dined at Lutèce where his name and commanding presence evoked instant recognition. "I have dinner here whenever I come to the city," he said. "It's pleasant. I think you'll enjoy sitting in the garden."

They were led to the best table and given exquisite service, niceties that were not lost upon Diane. From the sommelier to the busboy, the entire staff seemed eager to acknowledge the man of stature. And, by association the woman of stature as well.

"Tonight is a celebration," he announced as soon as they were seated. "After all we have seven lean years to make up for. So if you don't mind, I'll order for both of us, beginning with champagne cocktails."

"Of course!" Diane agreed, too engrossed in the fact that she was sitting three feet away from Leo, that he was actually there in the flesh, to think of anything as mundane as food.

"Splendid." He smiled. "Then let us start with the escargots."

And if, during the course of that meal, he had mentioned neither the "L" word or the "M" word, Diane had no doubt about the seriousness of his intent. Throughout, his candor was amazing. He unfolded the story of his marriage, as Diane listened spellbound.

"My wife," he said, "whom I don't believe you had the pleasure of meeting, contrived to share her favors with every male under the age of ninety in the greater New Haven area. Professors, delivery boys, law students, disc jockeys, even our piano tuner. Anne was what you might call an equal opportunity fornicator, discriminating neither by race, religion, nor ethnic origin. Her embrace was as broad as the Statue of Liberty's. Still, I daresay these democratic policies sat well with her. She's the mainstay of the ACLU."

Diane was dumbstruck. How had all this come about? she wondered. How did it happen that the wife of such a titan—and, if memory served, such a passionate lover—should resort to behaving like a bitch in heat? She ached to know, but dared not ask.

Her qualms, however, proved unnecessary, for Leo's confidences poured out in an unstoppable flood. For years, he told Diane, he had dwelt in happy ignorance, oblivious of his wife's infidelities. Ever the trusting husband, the devoted father, he had been supportive of her in every particular. It was Leo who had insisted that she keep on with her studies, Leo who encouraged her to use her gifts, which might otherwise have not been realized.

"If not for my encouragement," Leo said, "Anne would never have completed her doctorate, let alone have achieved the modest success she has subsequently enjoyed."

"Modest!" Diane exclaimed. Anne Frankland was a major

historian, a winner of the Pulitzer Prize. "Why, her book on Jeffersonian democracy was superb. Full of insights."

"Thank you." Leo gave a wry laugh. "And forgive me if I take that as a personal compliment. That book never would have been written if not for my contributions, my help in her research. And it certainly never would have been published except that the publisher happened to be an old friend of mine, you know. I prevailed upon him."

Diane let the matter drop. Whether Anne Frankland's fame more correctly belonged to her husband, she couldn't ascertain. What was undeniable was the depth of Leo's bitterness, hardly disguised behind his façade. And yet he was entitled to it. The man had been cruelly betrayed, not only by his wife, it turned out, but by his protégé as well. And that, Diane felt, was the consummate turn of the knife.

Every September, Leo singled out a third-year student (Diane herself had been one of these) to be taken under his wing and molded into a future leader of the bar. The honor, though informal and unofficial, was highly sought after. To these select few, Leo gave of himself unstintingly. He coached them, guided them, groomed them like thoroughbreds for the championship race that lay ahead.

Well before the bar exams, he managed to place his favorites in enviable positions. The jobs he found for them were launching pads to high achievement, gateways to the top echelons of the establishment. Had Leo's protégés formed an alumni association, it would include many of America's most brilliant legal lights. Diane, on the brink of making partner at Slater Blaney, took pride in being one of that elite group. The Frankland Mafia, as one federal judge had dubbed it.

Two years earlier Leo's choice had been Burt Shaferman.

"A brilliant lad," Leo confided, "with that quick grasp of theory, that surface cleverness so characteristic of the urban Jew. A born fighter too. Not, I now realize, as profound a thinker as I had thought him at first, but no denying Burt was a remarkable talent. He could have waltzed into any law firm he chose, here or in Washington. And you know what his choice was?" Leo gave a perplexed laugh. "He wanted to work for Ralph Nader in consumer law. I told him, 'Burt, it's a waste. You'll be burying yourself alive.' I had invested a great deal of myself in his future. I wasn't going to let him throw it away. So, Diane—" he paused in his narration, "I managed to come up with the proverbial offer he couldn't refuse. What, I ask you, is the greatest, most prestigious opportunity a novice lawyer can desire?"

Diane had no hesitation. "A Supreme Court clerkship."

Leo nodded.

"Lucky bastard!" Diane sighed.

"Indeed he was. And certainly the 'bastard' part of that turned out to be true. I pulled a great many strings to secure that post for Burt. It took months of lobbying. And, no sooner was my mission accomplished than I come home on a Monday afternoon to find this sterling lad in bed with my wife. Performing an interesting act, I may add, though hardly one of gratitude. Extraordinary, eh? Twenty-four years old," Leo marveled, "and coupling with a woman twice his age!"

I thought age means nothing. Diane was struck by the discrepancy of his words. But Leo, poor lamb, had suffered enough. It must have been a ghastly experience. Diane didn't know how to console him. "Perhaps," she ventured, "the time has come to put it all behind you."

He changed the subject and they settled down to round after round of that wonderful storytelling in which Leo excelled. For the next two hours, he delighted her with tales of who was doing what to whom, be they the moguls of academia or the movers and shakers on Capitol Hill. For her benefit he told the true story behind the Iranian arms deal, who the next director of the Fed would be, plus gave her a firsthand description of the Caroline Kennedy wedding. Diane listened, fascinated. It was gossip on an Olympian scale. Thus they lingered over coffee and brandy, emerging at a late hour into a fine springtime drizzle.

"Do you mind walking?" Diane asked. "I need some air."

"A little rain won't hurt me." He tucked her arm under his elbow. "I've survived greater hardships. Now tell me, how's life at Slater Blaney? Are you doing your old mentor credit?"

"I expect to be offered partnership next month."

"Splendid! Of course your future was never in doubt. My dear Diane. I thought of you often during those dark times with Anne. Often and with great affection." His mood lifted. "Do you remember that snowball fight we had outside the law library? My God, you were a deadeye with a missile."

She had forgotten how very intimate Leo could be. Now

he reminded her as they strolled up Third Avenue, reminiscing companionably until they reached her building. "Forgive me if I don't come up," he said, taking her hand. "I have a breakfast meeting with Pat Moynihan, after which it's straight back to Yale."

She forgave him. They arranged to spend a weekend in Vermont. "And then," he said, "we'll really talk."

The next few days Diane found herself woolgathering at odd moments when she was alone in her office. She would push aside her papers, absent herself from the present, and replay bits and snatches of her dinner conversation with Leo. Or more accurately, his with her, for she had said remarkably little. She had but to shut her eyes to conjure up his presence, his voice. Leo left echoes wherever he went.

"I thought of you often," he had said, "with great affection." Now his words resonated in the empty room. She had thought of him too. More than often. Constantly. Obsessively, even. He had been the object of her wishes, her regrets, her deepest fantasies.

Merely to sit across the table from him, to have him exclusively to herself for those few hours—that alone had been a consummation.

"You ruined my life," she had wanted to tell him in the nicest sort of way. "You spoiled me for every other man."

However, that would have been an outrageously forward statement, and technically untrue. She had, after all, loved Avram as well.

In an idle moment, she wondered what the two men would have made of each other in the unlikely circumstance of their meeting. Her first instinct was that Leo would have viewed the younger man as so negligible as to be beneath contempt. But Avram was not negligible. He was, indeed, very much his own stubborn person, and Leo was fiercely competitive. Avram would have been polite but skeptical, she decided. In any case, a good deal less than deferential. Leo would have arched his back and lashed out with withering scorn.

That aspect of Leo disturbed her. In many ways—appearance, vitality, intellect—he seemed little changed from the lover of her younger days. He still exerted the same strong sexual attraction. Had he come up that evening, they surely would have gone to bed.

But in the clearer light of day, she couldn't shake free of that bitterness that infused almost everything he said. She didn't know whether to feel sorry for him, a man simultaneously betrayed by his wife and protégé, or to be angry with him for continuing to nurse his hurt. The whole story puzzled her. Why had Leo never suspected his wife was a nymphomaniac? And why had Anne, once the secret was out, chronicled her escapades in explicit detail? Indeed, according to Leo, she had taken a perverse pleasure in the narration.

Even more bewildering was the behavior of the young protégé. To chance the wrath of such a powerful figure, to jeopardize a promising career for a dalliance with a middle-aged woman was sheer lunacy.

Contrary to Leo's recollection, Diane had once met Anne Frankland. The occasion had been a student-faculty tea, and Diane had a sharp memory of a tweedy heavyset woman with capable hands and a no-nonsense manner. She seemed a curious Jezebel for even the randiest of youths, let alone Leo's chosen third-year law student. It didn't make sense.

"You look like you're trying to solve the secrets of the universe," Byron said, poking his nose through the door.

"I'm trying to figure out why people behave the way they do."

"Oh that one!" Byron laughed. "The answer is simple. They behave the way they do for a reason."

"Thanks a lot!"

The next week and a half passed swiftly, without leaving a spare moment for private thought.

There was Fleur and her problems to be dealt with. The return of a chastened if unrepentant Bernie. And finally—to everyone's assorted horror and delight, the reopening of the *Simplexx* case, Harrigan having found grounds for appeal. Diane had the feeling of having been put through the wringer, professionally and emotionally.

By the time she boarded the plane to Rutland, she felt more confused than ever. Leo had called several times in the interval, and they'd enjoyed intimate late-night conversations. Yet concerning their future, too many questions remained unclarified and unanswered. She would go to Vermont with an open mind and the best of intentions. Beyond that, she would have to play it by ear.

THIRTY-FIVE

Her first day back on the job, Bernie walked into Hy Feinstein's office with jaw set and fists clenched to ward off possible attack. She was still hurting.

"Before you say anything," she said, "I'm warning you not to say anything!"

"About what?"

"About you-know-what and you-know-who and certain events that may or may not have occurred at a certain church on the Sunday before last. Is that clear?"

Hy's smile was as bland as a baby's. "There was no Sunday before last, okay? And beyond that, I don't know what you're talking about."

"Good," she said. "Now can we get down to business?"

She had an idea for a series on *Heartbeat of New York*. An idea so simple, so corny his first instinct would probably be to throw her ass out of his office and hire the first person off the street as a replacement.

"I mean, you won't believe how obvious. When I was down—well, no matter where I was holing up last week— where I was there was an extraordinary rock formation out in the water. I could see it from my hotel room, it dominated the beach. The thing was huge, in the shape of a bird's beak, say you had a mile-high bird. It changed with the light—looked different in the morning, in the evening sun, and it was really spooky in the moonlight. I couldn't take my eyes off it. But the funny thing was, the locals never even looked at it. Because it was there, don't you see? And always had been. They were blind to its beauty."

It was the same thing with New York, she explained. There were dozens of sights that tourists from all over the world flocked to see. Yet true New Yorkers wouldn't even bother to lift their eyes, being either too blasé or hopelessly oblivious. You put a couple of Manhattanites together and they immediately try to one-up each other, by claiming to know the authentic New York. The more obscure, the more recherché, the better. This one's discovered some little Italian restaurant known only to the Mafia. That one's onto a SoHo gallery so new even the owners are unaware of its existence. Typical insider shit.

But her bet was that the so-called New York sophisticate had probably never set foot in the Statue of Liberty or walked across the Brooklyn Bridge or gone for a carriage ride in Central Park. Those "goodies" were reserved for tourists. Your committed Gothamite wouldn't be caught dead at Radio City. Yet the cornball could be fun. Why, a friend of hers, a most elegant woman, had actually taken the Circle Line and enjoyed it.

"Take yourself, for instance, Hy. Have you ever been to the top of the Empire State Building?"

"Me? Not personally. But I saw *King Kong* when I was a kid."

"There you are," she gloated. "Case proven."

Her proposal was a series that would introduce New Yorkers to their own hometown. All the visual clichés, all the familiar tourist haunts would not just be trotted out but revealed with the freshness of a first-time visitor. Discover New York, the theme would be. Everyone else has.

Hy nodded thoughtfully.

"Should be a real cheapo to produce," he muttered. "After all, you don't need to scout for exotic locations. You just check out the best-selling postcards and pick your spots. Okay, work out the details and I'll consider it."

For the rest of the week she immersed herself in planning shots and writing scripts, with a mental bow to Roger Knowland. If not for him, with his fresh-from-Saudi eyes and gee-whiz guidebooks, she never would have been to any of these places. *So thank you, Roger, for providing me with a week's worth of bright ideas.* She almost considered sending him flowers by way of acknowledgement.

How was he getting on? she wondered. Had he fully recovered? Would he ever forgive her? Chances were, he was already working on fiancée number two. In any event, he was not the kind of man who would suffer for long. The blow had been to his pride, not his heart.

When Friday morning rolled around, Bernie looked at her calendar. The entire weekend came up blank. There were no parties scheduled, no theater outings, not even a date for drinks. But then, she was supposed to be off on her honeymoon, after which, in her married state, her social life would presumably have been taken care of forever. That, she concluded, was the best thing about marriage: never having to worry about Saturday nights.

She rang up a few friends, hoping to wangle an invitation, but everyone was busy, busy, busy. Fleur was working. Rosemary had a local dinner party. And Diane was going out of town. She thought of phoning Steve, but no doubt he was well provided for by now. In this town the unattached male didn't stay that way for long. Besides, she had her pride.

At times like this, though, she could almost confess to being a little bit lonely. Still, she could have married—there was that consolation. Oh well, you win some, you lose some. And on some, you just break even.

She spent the weekend in her loft watching television.

"Jesus!" Scott Matthews looked at the layouts. "This is what you drag me in on a Saturday morning for? What the hell has got into you? You've taken every single directive Saraband has given us, all their guidelines and research, and flushed them right down the toilet."

"Which is where they belong," Fleur replied.

"I can't show this stuff in Pittsburgh." He rubbed his eyes wearily. "May as well ask me to open my veins."

"I opened mine," she said, "working this out. Eddie and I have been busting our asses on this concept. I haven't slept for a week. Be honest, with me, Scott. I want your professional opinion. Are these good ads or not?"

"No, Fleur." Scott gave a heartfelt sigh. "They're not good ads. They're fucking great ads! Best things you've ever done."

"But—?"

"But"—he spread his hands in resignation—"what's the

point in doing great ads for dumbnut clients? You're giving
them caviar when they want hot dogs. You know these
guys. They're barely down from the trees. I mean, we are
dealing with primitive life forms here, limited capacities.
Especially Mr. Lewis J. Gibbs. Personally, I'm afraid even
the Snow Drop campaign might strain his intellect. And
here you are presenting him with something in French."

"The meaning's clear enough," she said, "but if the mental effort tires him, I'll give him a running translation."

"It's no go, Fleur." Scott put the layouts down reluctantly. "We're in deep enough shit already. What's the
matter, kid, you don't like eating regularly?"

"I love it!" she said. "And that's why we have to run with
this campaign. It's our only chance. Look—"

She began arguing passionately, without giving him a
chance to interrupt. Every agency between Boston and L.A.
would be slavishly following the path set by the client.
During the week of presentations Saraband would be bom-
barded with a nonstop barrage of sweetness and goo. By
Friday she guaranteed everyone there would be suffering
from an acute case of marshmallow poisoning. That Snow
Drop campaign of theirs, coming at the end, would deliver
the final diabetic blow. Instant death.

"Let's do what we think is right," she said. "We keep
boasting we're the best agency in America for this kind of
product. Then let's behave as though we are. I'm tired of
Marsden-Baker going in there on all fours and then getting
screwed doggie-style. What's the worst scenario, Scott? We
lose the account? For all we know, it may be lost already.
But even if that's the case, let's go down in style—not with
a whimper, but with a big fucking bang! Let's show them
that they're dealing with experts, not whores. Give them
our best shot. If we're lucky, they'll have the good sense to
recognize it. If not, at least we'll be able to live with
ourselves afterward. What the hell, Scott, we've nothing
more to lose—except, maybe, our self-respect by chicken-
ing out."

"I hear what you're saying." He studied the layouts for a
long silent minute. "Can you write me a rationale for this
campaign?" he finally asked. "Something nuts-and-boltsy
that they can sink their teeth into?"

"Oh can I ever!" She felt a surge of joy.

"Okay," he said, and grinned. "Let's run with it. But

everything's got to be ready by Thursday at five—media schedules, storyboards, the works. Which means a crash effort starting right this minute."

He went to the phone and began rounding up all the members of his group, reeling them in from warm beds and green golf courses.

"Get your asses back here," he said, "We've either got a winner or the greatest disaster since the *Titanic*. You!" he barked to Fleur. "What are you hanging around for? Get to work. I want to see this theme developed in inserts, car cards, mailers, point-of-sale material—"

"Will do!" She grabbed her layouts. "And one more request. When we get to Pittsburgh, can I make the pitch myself?"

"Women and children first." He laughed. "You're on!"

"You certainly were out till all hours last night," Dolly Bainter observed over breakfast Sunday morning.

"Was I?" Rosemary yawned. "How about some more hotcakes everybody? Mother? Chris, sweetie?"

"Very, very late," Dolly scolded.

"Really?" Rosemary reached for the maple syrup. "It was only a neighborhood dinner party."

"Well, I waited up till two, watching *The Late Show,* and I didn't hear you come in. What time was it, Rosie?"

"Now, now, Mother," Rosemary said. "I don't want you losing your beauty sleep."

She buttered a muffin, surveyed her family, and smiled. "It's a glorious day, darlings. We shouldn't be wasting it indoors. Let's go to Mystic. They have a wonderful aquarium there, Chris, with beautiful fish and shells and electric eels. Did you know, an eel can actually light up a lamp? Well, it can! Plus there's a whaling museum and marvelous old sailboats you can visit. You could pretend you're a pirate, Chris. Wouldn't that be fun? So what do you say we all pile into the car after breakfast and take off?"

"Oh yes!" Chris bobbed his head enthusiastically. "And can I sit in front, just like Daddy used to do?"

"If you like," Rosemary said. "After all, you're the man of the house now." She bent over and smooched his sticky cheeks.

"Kiss, kiss," she said.

Chris puckered. "Kiss, kiss, Mommy."

* * *

"Did you have a good weekend, darling?"

"One of the best, Leo." She gazed at him fondly. "Everything was perfect." *Including you,* she wanted to add.

From the moment she stepped off the plane to find him waiting in a rented Mercedes, it had been the stuff dreams were made of. The inn was exquisite, dating back to the eighteenth century and furnished with an abundance of antiques. He had booked separate rooms. Hers had a fireplace, a four-poster, and a bouquet of wildflowers. His, unseen, was on another floor.

Diane was first surprised, then grateful that he refrained from sexual overtures. It was not mere discretion, she came to understand, rather a question of sensibilities. Such behavior would have cheapened their weekend, reducing it to the level of a "fling." Instead, she had a sense of being auditioned for the most significant role of her life. Are you the same delightful creature I once fell in love with? was the question in his eyes. Can there be a future for us?

Of course Diane was no longer (at least she hoped not) the wide-eyed acolyte with a schoolgirl crush. She was a successful lawyer, a woman of the world. Therefore such scrutiny cut both ways. Leo, too, was being subjected to reevaluation. And he was passing the test with flying colors. He proved to be charming, learned, witty, affectionate. Everything she remembered and more.

They had stayed up late Friday night before a roaring fire, in a conversation touching upon everything from art to cybernetics to the next Wimbledon finals. On Saturday he had announced the day was reserved for fun and had planned a schedule of rural delights. There was a country auction to be attended, antique shops to be explored, a backcountry ramble in search of an ancient covered bridge, then an elegant dinner of lobster and game.

Sunday morning Leo had the hotelkeeper pack them a picnic basket and they set off to hike on one of the mountain trails. The weather was perfect, the walk invigorating, and the views superb. When lunch was over, he brushed the crumbs from his Irish sweater and poured the last of the Dom Perignon.

They were perched on a smooth, flat rock at the mountain's edge, sheltered from the afternoon sun by ancient pines. Below them the village, with its crisp white houses

and steepled church, lay as serene and idyllic as a Grandma
Moses painting.

"Here's to you, darling." They touched plastic glasses.

"Here's to you, Leo." She smiled.

They sat for a while in pregnant silence, then he shifted
his eyes to some remote spot on the horizon.

"I'm going to say something, Diane, that's not easy for
me after all these years. You might conceivably protest that
I have forfeited my rights, but I beg you—hear me out."

She tensed, cognizant of what was coming and feeling
painfully self-conscious. This was it! The grand finale. Even
the birds seemed to fall silent. She turned to study him, his
rugged profile strong and handsome against the sky. He
would propose. She would doubtless accept. There was
something dreamlike in the prospect.

"I made a mistake," he said softly. "I should have married
you seven years ago, instead of wasting my time in that
hopeless situation with Anne. And I can pinpoint not only
the day but the very moment when I should have asked
you."

To her bafflement, he alluded again to the snowball
episode on the library steps. "You do remember, don't
you?"

"Vaguely," she replied. Insofar as she could recall, it had
been a silly half hour of undergraduate-type antics, ending
with Leo falling into a snowbank. The significance eluded
her. Yet to him, the memory had remained vivid. Suddenly,
the image of Avram popped into her mind, and his first
encounter with falling snow. How delighted he had been,
standing there barefoot on the terrace!

Leo, however, was another matter. He had grown up in
Minneapolis. Snow, therefore, could hardly have been a
novelty.

"What was so special about that day?" she then asked.

"Promise you won't laugh when I tell you?"

The Franklands, Leo reminded her, were a distinguished
Midwestern family, studded with high achievements in the
arts and sciences. His father was a federal judge, his mother
a concert pianist. One uncle had been a consultant to FDR,
another the guiding genius at Bell Labs. And in this lofty
milieu, Leo had been considered as showing special promise. Almost from birth, he had been trained and tutored to
play a major role in the intellectual establishment. He grad-

uated from Harvard at eighteen, went to Oxford as a Rhodes scholar, and passed the bar at a mere twenty-one.

"But not until that day with you at Yale had I ever been in a snowball fight. Ridiculous isn't it! But given my childhood, I didn't have a clue about what it was to be a mischievous boy. To be carefree. Playful. Not that our relationship was frivolous, Diane. But it was, at least to me, influential. You gave me youth and joy and laughter and freedom. Yes, I should have asked you to marry me on the spot, while I was lying on the snowbank. For the first time in my life, I'd fallen not only on my duff but on my dignity, and I quite enjoyed it. Why didn't I propose, can you tell me?"

"Why?" She was both touched and surprised. "Because of your children! I always understood that, Leo, and respected you for it. You had your obligations as a father."

Yet it had struck her as odd—the one discordant note in his chatty, intimate weekend—that not once had he mentioned his progeny. The boy must be nearly twenty now, the girl fifteen. How would they feel about their father's remarrying?

"My children!" he echoed. "I can't tell you how I adored them when they were little. They were so charming, so responsive. There are few things more rewarding, Diane, than the unquestioning love of small children. They make you feel like God. You're right. Of course that's why I stuck it out. For their sakes."

"And what are they doing now?" She was glad of the respite. "Your son's in college, I suppose."

The temperature of Leo's voice plunged to near zero.

"In his wisdom, Alan decided to turn down Yale, preferring to attend Stanford."

"So far away!" she exclaimed.

"Quite!" Leo's lips grew thin as he bit off the words. "So far away. I believe he's a junior by now. As for the girl, she lives with my ex-wife in Virginia. Regrettably, she has turned into just another tiresome willful teenager with a taste for cheap music. I don't see them often, I'm sorry to say. We've grown apart. I'm afraid Anne has poisoned their minds about me."

"Surely not!"

Her heart went out to him in his agony. Poor Leo. Poor lonely Leo! His success and fame were as nothing to him compared to the loss of his children's love! What a heartless bitch Anne Frankland must have been. Only a man of Leo's moral sensibilities would have endured such a marriage for so long.

She swallowed down a lump. The matter was too painful to pursue.

He drew his gaze back from the mountains and swung to face her. "That was then. It's finished, and as you said the other night, the time has come to put it behind me. No more remembrances of things past, I promise. What matters is now, Diane"—he took her hands in his—"today, tomorrow. The years ahead. So you see, I'm going to make that request I should have made so very long ago. Diane, I treasured you then, I treasure you still. Will you do me the honor of becoming my wife?"

Her first instinct was to say yes out of quick sympathy. Yes for old times' sake. Yes because she had loved him for seven unbroken years and always knew it would one day come to this.

But Leo released her hand and put a finger to her lips. "I won't ask you for an immediate answer, Diane. In fact, I would refuse to accept it as unfair to both of us. I want your decision to be one of reason rather than impulse. And also, I hope, one based on love."

There were many matters to be considered, he pointed out. Practical issues to be resolved. She had a promising career, and he did not expect her to curtail it on his behalf. Quite the contrary. He was proud that she was about to make partner and hoped it would be a stepping-stone to even greater achievements.

They would buy a house that was mutually convenient in one of those pretty Connecticut towns, halfway between New Haven and New York. Children? Yes. Most definitely. That would be like starting life all over again. A second chance at youth.

There was one possibility he was not free to mention, a post that might require his presence in Washington, D.C. How would she feel about living there?

Diane sucked in her breath. So! The rumor was right. Leo had indeed been canvassed for the next Supreme Court vacancy. The notion sent chills down her spine. By High Court standards, he was still a young man. An even greater honor might lie ahead.

She shut her eyes briefly, trying to picture herself moving in that exalted circle: wife to the chief justice of the United States. Even her father would salaam. It was heady stuff, dazzling to the ego, but not to be considered too closely. One didn't marry a position. One married a man. Still—

"If you went to Washington," she said, dry-mouthed, "I'm sure I could join a law firm there."

"Good." He got up and brushed off his corduroy pants while she packed up the picnic hamper. "Then let's leave things as they are for the moment and enjoy what's left of the weekend. I know you'll think this through from every possible approach and make a wise decision. Perhaps you'll let me have your answer by the end of the month."

She promised to do so and they began their descent back to town. It was a long walk and time was growing short. There were suitcases to be packed, the rental car to be returned, planes to be caught. With luck, they would have time for a farewell drink.

"My boss says," she remarked lightly, "that lawyers ought not to get romantically involved with other lawyers. They'd argue too much. I was thinking of that couple on *L.A. Law.*"

"*L.A. Law?*"

"You know, the TV series."

Leo paused to stare at her. "You don't mean to say you watch that trash!"

"It's fun! Of course, I don't take it seriously."

"It's total rubbish," he stated. "Shame on you."

His vehemence surprised her. She felt called upon to defend not only the program but herself. "I'm not saying it's an accurate description of life in the giant law firms," she amplified. "Certainly hardly typical of Slater Blaney. For one thing, we're all far too overworked to have any energy left for interoffice hanky-panky. And nobody up there looks like Harry Hamlin, worse luck!" She smiled. He didn't smile back. "But yes," she persisted, "I very much enjoy the show, and the legal aspects appear to be well researched. Come on, Leo. Ease up. I bet you've never even seen the program."

"I don't have to see it to know that it's trash."

"That's absurd! How can you make such a statement? I happen to think it's pretty good."

"Well, you're wrong," he announced.

"Wrong! It's hardly a question of right or wrong, Leo. It's

a matter of opinion. At least, reserve judgment till you've seen it. It's on Thursday nights. If you like, I'll tape it for you."

"Don't bother, darling. I have no intention of wasting my time proving to myself what I already know. I know exactly the type of entertainment—mental popcorn for morons. Frankly, Diane, I don't understand why you're being so argumentative. I should imagine you spend quite enough time being contentious in the exercise of your profession and that you might prefer to accede to my judgment on trivial matters. Ah!" He took her elbow and guided her down the last steep steps of the path. "There's the inn."

"Does this mean"—she turned to face him with a quizzical air—"that if we get married, we'll have separate television sets?"

Leo laughed and checked his watch. "It's five o'clock," he said, "I believe we still have time for a drink at the bar."

THIRTY-SIX

"Welcome to *Heartbeat of New York*. This is Bernadette Hong speaking to you from the viewing platform of one of the most famous landmarks of our town—the Empire State Building. If you want to make a date with King Kong, try your local movie house. But if you'll settle for one of the greatest views—"

She clutched the mike a little closer and raised her voice. Christ, it was noisy up there, what with the wind shrieking past her ears and the buzz of a low-flying plane. A few feet away, her director was gesturing to her in some incomprehensible fashion.

"—of modern times, then take the elevator to the hundred and second floor. Back in 1931 this was considered the daddy of all skyscrapers, and though they come bigger nowadays—the World Trade Center, for instance—they don't come any better. Over the years—"

What the hell was the matter with Tony? With the crew! They weren't concentrating on their jobs. Instead, they were craning their heads skyward. With her peripheral vision, she could see the tourists laughing, pointing, jabbering away. Something was up.

"—nearly sixty million visitors have made the trip to the top, though rumor has it—"

Now Tony was down on his knees doing funny things with the equipment. Hell, he was motioning the cameraman away from her and redirecting him upward. Flying saucers?

Superman in full regalia? Or had the Russians launched a sneak invasion?

Bernie could see Tony gesticulating wildly while the camera panned up and began tracking something just beyond her sightline. The din of engines grew louder.

"—that not one of them was a native New Yorker. On a clear day like today—"

She could no longer resist. If it was the end of the world, she had to see it. It could be some kind of scoop. Her eyes followed the line of Tony's arm upward to the heavens. It was—*noooooo!* She couldn't believe it!

Flying a few hundred feet above them was a two-seater plane. In its wake, a colorful banner streamed across the sky. She'd seen this kind of gimmick umpteen times at Fire Island. It was one of those planes that were rented out to advertisers for commercial messages. The banners usually touted suntan lotion or the latest book for the beach. Only this one . . .

"Oh my God!" Bernie blurted out. Now the plane was directly overhead, circling the building.

And there it was—in big red letters!

STEVE GODWIN LOVES BERNIE HONG. MARRY ME!

Talk about commitment! Bernie reeled. Talk about public statements! Talk about going all the way! This very moment Steve's proposal was being broadcast live throughout the entire tri-state area. Hundreds of thousands of people were watching.

For the first time since she had entered broadcasting, Bernadette Hong was speechless.

"Keep talking!" Tony was yelling. "For Chrissakes, we're still on the air."

But she could only stand there, gaping and bug-eyed, while the plane flew off in the direction of Wall Street. Only then could she muster up the barest intelligible minimum.

"This is Bernadette Hong—returning you now to Station WHIZ." She gulped and shouted, "Hey, Steve! I love you too!"

Then she dropped the mike and bolted toward the elevator, knocking down a small Japanese family en route.

"You crazy idiot!" she said when they were settled happily in bed, having made up for those lost months of deprivation. "What made you do such a thing? And how'd you know that I wanted you back?"

"I didn't," he confessed. "I took a chance. But I missed you so much, babe, I would have done anything. Hell, I'm doing anything. I'm proposing, for Chrissakes. Did you ever think it would come to this?"

"Nope."

"Neither did I." He seemed stunned by his own actions. "Shows you how desperate I was getting, but life hasn't been the same since we split up. And then, when Diane told me your marriage was called off—well, all I could think of was, maybe you still cared about me. So I got your schedule through Hy Feinstein—and the rest you know."

"And you really want to marry me?" Bernie couldn't help but remain incredulous. "You've always hated the whole idea of 'commitment.' The last dirty word, you used to call it. What's changed?"

"I guess I have," he said. "I came to the conclusion that if a wedding ring is what it takes to get us back together, then okay, I'm willing. Go ahead, Bernie. Call up the preacher. I'm yours."

"The supreme sacrifice, eh?"

Steve gave an embarrassed shrug.

Bernie laughed, then stretched out her hand to his, happier than she had been in many months.

"Just think, Steve. According to statistics, I should have thrown in the sponge and settled for spinsterhood, yet I've had two legitimate proposals so far this year. Not bad for a middle-aged broad, huh? Yep"—she grinned—"I managed to beat the odds twice over. It's nice to know I could. But I'll tell you something else, hon. I don't want to get married. Not now, not ever. Not even to you. Thank you for loving me enough to do what I know must have taken a lot of guts. A regular St. George going one-on-one with the dragon. A real hero. But I discovered I'm not the marrying kind. Commitment scares me. Motherhood too, I guess. It looks great on paper, but when it comes to the crunch, I'm not one for putting down roots, taking out mortgages. Like the song says, 'Don't fence me in.' So what do you say we go back to what we had? Independence, affection, companionship. The freedom to split—and the freedom to stay together for the next hundred years if the fancy takes us. All without benefit of clergy. How does that grab you?"

He squeezed her hand and sighed with the audible relief of a man newly rescued from the gallows. "But I want it to go down on record that I was willing to marry you," he said. "That's the important thing."

"I won't forget," she said, smiling. "And I know what it cost you."

"You mean the plane rental?"

But she hadn't meant that at all.

Toward midnight they sent out for Szechwan food, then snuggled up on her ratty old sofa to watch the late movie on TV.

"Mmm—Bela Lugosi," Steve said gleefully. "Looks like a dog. You seen this one, lovey?"

Plan Nine from Outer Space! She put her feet up on the coffee table, the act that used to drive Roger mad. "Nope, I don't think so. Isn't it supposed to be one of the all-time worsts? Looks like fun."

The credits unrolled. She leaned her head on Steve's shoulder.

All told, life was grand.

THIRTY-SEVEN

— · —

Same Gothic gloom. Same bottom-busting chairs. Same cast of characters. There was McWimp and the Wimpettes. Edna and the Sinuses. The assholes from Accounting. The pricks from Planning. The swine from Sales. And at the head of the table, the unspeakable Lewis J. Gibbs sucking obscenely on an unlit cigar.

The only thing that had changed was the room temperature. The last time Fleur was there, it had been winter, and the steam heat had boiled them alive. Now, however, the weather being warm, the air-conditioning was on full blast.

Fleur shivered. The place was like a goddamn tomb. Her own probably. Because once she did her number, the temperature was likely to dip even further.

For the occasion she had donned that peacock blue mini, the accessorizing of which had caused her so much grief. No matter what the outcome, she consoled herself, at least she would make a well-dressed corpse. With or without matching earrings.

Scott Matthews was making the introductory flourishes. "We have, today, a most unusual presentation, which I think everyone will find of interest. It's daring, different. One might even say controversial. And it's the brainchild of the young woman who has requested the privilege of making that presentation in person. Fleur?"

Good old Scott. He had managed simultaneously to compliment her and distance himself from the campaign in case of disaster. Sneaky but smart. Fleur forced a smile and rose.

"Thank you, Scott, and before I show you the actual art-and-copy concepts we've developed, I'd like to share with you the basis of our thinking."

Share! That was a good weasel word. *Now starts the heavy hype.* Years of advertising had accustomed her to spewing our marketing clichés by the yard. It was a trick, mere verbiage. Yet these miniminds seemed to feed on this sort of claptrap. This time, however, a few truths would be judiciously strewn in among the usual lies.

"Ladies and gentlemen—" She looked at Lewis J. Gibbs slavering into his cigar. The 'gentlemen' was a misnomer right there. "As hardheaded businesspeople, we all know that the launching of any new product is a form of continuing warfare. First, we must fight to win name recognition. Then we must fight to achieve our share of the market. Lastly, we must fight for domination. The perfume industry particularly is an arena of intense competition. Brand differences are subtle. Subjective. Industry critics might even call them nonexistent. Yet real or imagined, the consumer's perception of those differences can make or break a product. Therefore, we can never stop seeking the competitive edge, the weapon, so to speak, that will distinguish our product, pull it ahead of the pack, and ultimately establish it as the clear champion in the field. As many have observed, it's a jungle out there, full of predators, and only the fittest survive.

"In fact, the struggle for perfume markets might be called the second fiercest contest in America today."

The McWimps looked up. Was there an insult intended?

"The second, I repeat. There's only one competition that's fiercer. Tougher. Where the stakes are the highest of all."

She paused. The next step made her nervous. There were old copywriters, the gag ran, and there were bold copywriters. But there were no old bold copywriters. And here she was, angling to be both.

A dozen feet away, Lewis J. Gibbs motioned impatiently, then mumbled something to one of his flunkies.

I've lost him. Fleur thought. *I've hardly opened my mouth and I've lost the little bastard already. Terrific.*

The flunky fumbled in his pocket, got out a lighter, and lit his boss's cigar. Another reached for an ashtray. Fleur watched in amazement as Gibbs disappeared momentarily behind a dense cloud of smoke. Then a wave of relief flooded through her. The sonuvabitch! He'd given up giving up smoking! He was no longer deprived and in pain. It was an omen, a sign from the heavens.

With a lift of heart, she barreled on. "As I say, there's only one competition that's brisker, tougher, more strenuously fought. One turf where more blood has been shed. And that, my friends, is the competition among women for available men. Perhaps you've read the latest figures, and if you haven't, be assured that your customers have. I'm referring especially to those sophisticated women—smart, savvy, upwardly mobile with a sizable chunk of discretionary income—who constitute the prime market for this perfume. Which is to say, virtually every working woman in America."

Briefly, she reviewed the findings of the Harvard-Yale study, stressing the storm of publicity, the feverish response of women across the board, above all the verified shortage of available males.

"We could deceive ourselves and pretend that life is a 1940 movie, with one nice fella automatically apportioned for each nice girl, and all a gal has to do is look cute, smile, and keep her fingers crossed and her legs together. We could deceive ourselves right into Chapter Eleven. Because today's woman is realistic, hardheaded, and aggressive. She's not going to sit around and leave things to chance."

Fleur went on to demolish the entire premise of the Saraband brief. Sweetness and light didn't sell movies. Or books. Or records. Or blue jeans. Let alone something as potent as perfume.

For the contemporary woman knew that if Prince Charming wasn't actually dead, he was certainly an endangered species. Her first job was to smoke him out; her second, to win him away from other women with the same idea. And in this pursuit for husbands and happiness, no holds were barred.

"Look at it this way," she argued. "Precisely the qualities we need to achieve success for our product in the marketplace—the American woman needs to achieve success on a more intimate level. Like us, she has to beat out some fierce rivals before she can secure her foothold and emerge victorious. Like us, she wants all the ammunition she can get. Introducing"—she nodded to her art director—"Fleurs du Mal."

With a flourish of a prestidigitator, Eddie unveiled an enormous blowup. The effect was stunning. Even at a distance the art dominated the room with its smoky blues and grays. In the foreground a naked man and woman lay on crumpled sheets, bodies entwined in sensual abandon. The woman's head was thrown back in ecstasy, her long mane trailing almost to the ground. She was as dark as Fleur. In the background, vast and surreal, loomed the visage of a second woman. One could see only the eyes, watching and jealous, and hint of pale hair.

"Fleurs du Mal," Fleur repeated. "The Perfume for the Wicked Woman. The name I've chosen, by the way, derives from Baudelaire. It means 'flowers of evil,' but one hardly needs to have studied French to get the message. And, of course, the caption underneath says it all: Why Fight Fair?"

"The woman on the bed," she explained, "has wrested the man away from her rival—" She stopped. Some instinct advised her to be quiet.

For Lewis J. Gibbs was absolutely riveted.

He stared and stared. And then, across that broad plain face spread a smile the width of the Atlantic. A smile of revelation. Whatever he was seeing in that ad, whatever message he had found, there was no question but that it spoke to him at the most visceral level. All eyes were fixed on his. All hearts were put on hold until he spoke.

"That guy in the picture." He waved his cigar in Fleur's direction. "He's banging both those bimbos. Right?"

Her jaw dropped. He had missed the intent completely. It was no such thing. It was a romantic dream of Alex, of victory over Rosemary. It was wish fulfillment, nothing less. Instead, Gibbs saw it in the crassest of masculine terms: a man fucking two women. Inadvertently she had pushed his fantasy button.

You've got it wrong, she wanted to protest. *You're way off base, Lewis J.* But was he? For suddenly it dawned on her, Gibbs had got it just right. He had seen what she had missed. For that was exactly the situation, exactly what Alex had done from the start. And she and Rosemary were both bloody fools.

"There are, of course, many interpretations," she started to say, then stopped. In any case, her voice would have been drowned out, for around the table—following the lead of Lewis J. Gibbs—a huge hum arose. The hum of thirty

Wimpettes competing with one another in their haste to voice approval.

"I like it," Gibbs stated. "What d'ya call it? Floors-da-male?"

Fleur gulped and nodded.

"And what does everyone else think?" He scanned the room, that shitty grin still on his face. "Speak up—speak up! Anybody got objections? I'm asking honest opinions here."

Mmmmmmmm. The hum rose to supersonic levels.

"Yeah, I think so too. Jeezus," he mused, and scratched his head in wonder. "Both those broads! Imagine that! Well, toots!" He looked at Fleur, then held up his hand for silence. "You did a terrific job here. Very exciting. Although, lemme tell you, young lady—and I don't mean this as criticism—you got some dirty mind! Well, it looks like you folks at Marsden-Baker have won yourself a nice piece of business—" Before he could say another word, Fleur had jumped up, scooted across the room, and planted a big red juicy lipsticky kiss atop his shiny bald dome.

"Mr. Gibbs," she said. "You're one very smart guy!"

Monday afternoon the call came from on high. Dutifully Fleur presented herself in Roy Marsden's lavish suite on the fortieth floor.

If an upholstery tycoon had died and gone to heaven, he might have wound up there, in the office of the president. The room reeked of big bucks, with its inch-deep velvet carpet and glove-soft leathers and yards of Scalamandré silks. Advertising might be all smoke and mirrors, but the money was most concrete.

Fleur settled into the buttery depths of a suede-covered armchair and awaited her reward. A vice presidency at least. With canonization as a distinct possibility.

"So, Fleur," the agency chief said as he poured generous shots of twenty-year-old malt whiskey into Baccarat glasses, "how does it feel to be our knight in shining armor? I can't tell you how pleased we all are with your performance in Pittsburgh. Dazzling! Frankly, Scott Matthews felt you were taking one helluva chance but"—he grinned—"it looks like you read Lew Gibbs just right. He was on the horn only an hour ago, singing your praises. You made a conquest out there."

"I'm surprised he remembered my name."

"He didn't, actually," Marsden remarked. "He referred to you as the tootsie with the short blue dress and filthy mind. He was greatly impressed on both counts."

Fleur muttered appropriate sentiments.

"So how'd you like to be a vice president, my dear?"

"I'd love it!" She beamed.

"And creative director on the Saraband account?"

"I'd love it."

"And move to Pittsburgh and open a new branch of Marsden-Baker?"

"I'd ... *Pittsburgh?*" she shrieked. "Am I hearing correctly? Did you say—"

"Pittsburgh," he repeated. "The Golden Triangle. The scenic confluence of the Ohio, Allegheny, and Monongahela rivers—"

"It's out of the question!"

"—recently named the most livable large city in America—"

"Impossible!"

"—with its world-famous orchestra and museums and sports—"

"No way!"

"—and where a woman earning a hundred and twenty-five thousand bucks a year could live like a queen!"

They exchanged quick pregnant glances.

"Plus relocation money?" she asked.

"Of course."

"And performance-based bonuses?"

"Naturally."

"And stock options?"

"Something might be worked out along those lines."

"May I have time to think it over?" she asked.

"Of course." He checked his watch. "You have five minutes."

He went back to his desk to read reports.

During the past year or so, Fleur Chamberlain had envisioned several different futures: As a New York career woman. A Short Hills housewife. And briefly, as a body on a tray at Bellevue, prematurely dead of love and grief.

Pittsburgh had figured in none of these scenarios.

Her first reaction was see it as a kind of exile, punishment for having been a wicked woman. Her second response was to deem it as absurd. People didn't emigrate to

Pittsburgh. It was a place-name utterly devoid of glamour. It had, as far as she knew, never even inspired a popular song. People left their hearts in San Francisco or took Manhattan or enjoyed moonlight in Vermont. But Pittsburgh?

Yet in the harsh clear light that poured into Roy Marsden's office, romance was dead and alternatives were few. What was there, after all, to keep her here?

Love? She had exhausted all the available men in her circle, and a number of the unavailable men as well. Home? Her apartment was an overpriced hole of Calcutta, only not quite so roomy. Shopping? She was on the shit list of every department store in New York. Friends? That would be the only net loss. But there were planes and phones and the overnight express. New York wasn't all that far away.

Briefly she was tempted to call Diane for advice, but she had only a couple minutes left. Besides, this was one problem no one else could solve. The realist inside Fleur started talking.

To turn down Roy Marsden's offer meant beginning at a new agency, having to prove herself all over again, which was a veritable nightmare. And his offer was spectacular. Vice president in charge of the Pittsburgh office. It had a ring to it. It had clout.

Fleur Chamberlain would control the destiny of a major account. She would do the kind of advertising she'd always craved, be a force to reckon with within the profession. The idea was appealing. For, as the late unbeloved Alex Marshall was fond of saying, in the business world, you either kick ass or lick it.

She'd get her own creative team together. She would take Eddie Carducci. And that smart Filipino woman from Promotion. Plus such local talent as Pittsburgh could provide, which was probably considerable what with Carnegie Tech and the other schools around. She'd find good people, fresh and sharp and ambitious. Loyal allies in the never-ending Battle Against the Wimpettes.

But she didn't intend to stop with Saraband Enterprises. They were just the tip of the Consuma-Corp iceberg. Once Fleurs du Mal was launched, she'd go after new business with a vengeance. The decongestant account, for instance. There had to be a better way of selling that shit than shoving sinus cavities down people's throats. She'd think about it on the plane.

Of course she'd buy herself a house first thing. Something substantial. Or maybe she'd buy one of those vast apartments in Oakland, then go ahead and furnish it to the hilt. There was no point waiting for Mr. Right—or Mr. Wrong—to come along. Maybe he would, maybe he wouldn't, but in the meantime there was only one person in the world she could count on. The newest vice president of Marsden-Baker.

She looked around Roy Marsden's opulent premises. Sniffed. And sniffed again. The perfume in the air wasn't Fleurs du Mal or expensive leather. It was the intoxicating smell of success.

Funny! For all the dreams she'd had, all the fantasies chased, she had never managed to picture herself in the corner office. But today she could. And did.

"So?" Roy Marsden glided across the room to where she sat.

"So"—she accorded him her most glorious smile—"let's talk about stock options. And of course I'll want a company car. . . ."

THIRTY-EIGHT

Thursday evening Diane settled down with a Tab and take-out pizza to watch the latest installment of *L.A. Law*. Yet even as she dimmed the lights, she felt a stab of guilt. Mental popcorn for morons, Leo called it. A waste of time.

Whether it was his disapproval or her own edgy mood or perhaps a less-than-glittering script—whatever the cause, she couldn't concentrate on that night's episode. The wisecracks seemed flatter, the plot permutations more contrived. All told, the magic had gone. In fact, she doubted she could ever watch it again without feeling either guilty or foolish.

Damn you, Leo, she thought. He had taken one of life's smallest, most harmless pleasures and squeezed the joy out of it. Not only had he belittled a television series, but he had also belittled her taste and judgment.

She switched off the set and fell to brooding. In the week and a half since her trip to Vermont, she had yet to come to grips with Leo's proposal. The spontaneous "yes" she had felt on the mountainside had dwindled to a troubled "maybe."

She had, in fact, gone to considerable lengths to delay the moment of truth, jogging every morning, working late every evening, spending the balance of her free time with Byron who lived close by.

"What do you think?" she had asked him one night. "Should I marry Leo Frankland?"

"Do you want legal advice or romantic advice?"

"Romantic, I suppose. I just can't decide."

"How about flipping a coin?"

His own "marriage" had taken place the previous Sunday, at a small bedside ceremony in St. Luke's Hospital. A dozen people had attended: Byron's mother from Virginia, Diane, and a few other close friends.

There had been, of course, no service of legal standing, rather a simple oath of love and fidelity that Byron had written. Then the guests had drunk champagne out of plastic flutes, said individual farewells to the dying man, and gone their separate ways. Diane had returned home and cried herself to sleep.

In the days that succeeded, she grew more troubled and depressed. Her obligation to give Leo an answer was weighing heavily on her. She kept taking her emotional temperature, hoping for a renewed surge of love and rapture. But the old black magic had faded to dishwater gray.

Tonight she found herself thinking that Byron's "wedding" would be the last one for quite a while. She would probably turn Leo down. And all because of a television program. One might say that was absurd. That women don't break off magnificent matches, deny their kismet, over the question of which channel to watch. But it was more than a program. It was a clue, a piece of the puzzle. And Diane would, at her risk, ignore it.

A short time ago Byron had quipped that people behave the way they do for a reason. She had dismissed his answer as specious, one of those too-glib replies with which clever people tackle the inexplicable. But now, as she lay on the couch before a darkened television set, the last piece of the puzzle fell in place.

Of course! She caught her breath. The dispute about the show was the last piece of evidence—the Q.E.D. in the problem that had been eating at her since that dinner at Lutèce.

Suddenly she saw with brilliant clarity the solution to all the enigmas. She knew why Leo's children wanted no part of him, why his wife had deserted him, above all, why his protégé had betrayed him in such a spectacular manner. There was indeed a reason for everything. These were acts of survival. Nothing less!

Because—it struck her with the force of revelation—Leo had to control everything and everyone around him. He

must be the father, the mentor, the stern giver of the law.
Leo knew what was best; therefore he could never be
wrong. And heaven help the misguided fool who struggled
to go another way.

She knew, too, why Leo imposed such high standards on
his students, his family. They had to achieve worldly hon-
ors, not for their own sake, she realized, not for their
personal happiness. But for his own! Their glory belonged
rightly to him.

Leo's protégé was a case in point. If, after all, Burt
Shaferman's preferences were all that mattered, then let
him join Ralph Nader and do useful and honorable work.
But that wasn't prestigious enough for Leo. Not glamour-
enhancing.

"I invested a great deal of myself in Burt's future," Leo
had said. Ergo that future was now Leo's property. As was
his wife's Pulitzer prize. As was every accomplishment of
those within his realm.

It was a wonder he didn't claim Diane's forthcoming
partnership for his own. Sooner or later he would. "I had a
word or two with Ralph Slater on your behalf," he would
surely boast. "I told him, 'Ralph, Diane is one of my
people—'" And in doing so, he would rob her of all triumph.

Leo's people. He owned them, shaped them, helped them
to succeed. Indeed, he forbade them to fail. In return he
expected blind fidelity and trust. He exacted their souls.

Of course Burt Shaferman had slept with Anne Frankland.
And vice versa. They had coupled not out of sex or mad
passion, but in a last-ditch battle to wrench free of Leo's
smothering control. They hadn't merely gone to bed with
each other. They had mutinied. Small wonder, then, that
Leo's rage was so profound. For by this act, the unlikely
lovers had challenged not merely the man, but his image of
himself as all-wise and all-powerful.

Even now the recollection of his wrath made her wince.
What if, one day, that rancor should be loosed upon her? As
surely it would if she resisted his control.

Diane—the voice would drip venom—*has, in her infinite
wisdom, decided to*—to what? To take up yoga? Espouse
Keynesian economics? Paint the kitchen yellow? Watch
L.A. Law? It would hardly matter whether the infraction
was large or small. What would matter would be that Leo's
will had been defied.

Marrying him, she realized, would be akin to joining the Communist party, an act requiring the suspension of all independent judgment, all personal tastes. One followed the party line without a murmur or else suffered exile and abuse. Either way, disaster was inevitable.

How she had misjudged Leo all these years! How naïve and trusting she had been. Yet if Leo was not the god she had hero-worshipped at Yale, then neither was he a deliberate villain. He was, rather, a man terrified by his own inadequacies, requiring constant praise and reassurance. What she had formerly seen before as unwavering strength, she now knew to be weakness. What had once appeared to be firmness of mind, she now recognized as rigidity. He would never change. How could he? He lacked the spirit of compromise. Even to admit that change was required threatened the entire structure of his self-delusion.

In one corner of her heart she loved him still. Perhaps she always would for old times' sake. Yet she knew a chapter of her life was finally closed, and with it came a sense of liberation. Never more would a godlike Leo stalk her dreams, dwarfing all other men, promising an unattainable ideal. Leo was as mortal and fallible as the next man, if not more so. And far less capable of unselfish love.

Thanks to Avram she had standards of comparison. *There* was a man who knew what love was. Poor dear vanished Avram! The memory of what was lost broke her heart.

Tomorrow, she would write Leo a letter, tactful but firm, offering some excuse that would spare his ego. Then she would shut the book on the past.

But if life without Leo was something she could cope with—had she not done without him for the past seven years?—life without the dream of Leo was another matter. She felt lost without her familiar fantasy. Ill-founded though it was, nothing else was at hand to take its place. She felt achingly lonely.

Toward midnight, she rang up Byron. "Are you up and are you decent?"

"Yes and no."

"If I came over, could you give me some coffee and a sympathetic ear and maybe a Bessie Smith record?"

"Things that bad?" Byron asked.

"I'll be there in two minutes."

*   *   *

"You really think I did the proper thing?" Diane sniffled
into a tissue. "It was like giving up my baby blanket, you
know. Come those long lonely nights, I don't know what
I'll fantasize about anymore. And if I'd married Leo, at least
I might have had children. I'd be miserable, wretched,
squelched, and in a chronic state of outrage, but I'd have
that consolation."

"So why don't you have a child anyway?"

"I thought about it, Byron. In fact, I thought—what the
hell, I'll do it! If not by Leo, then through artificial insemi-
nation or some such. There are a lot of single mothers
around these days. I considered it from every practical
angle, but in the last analysis I decided against it. It struck
me as a selfish act."

"Having kids is selfish?" Byron raised an eyebrow.

"Having them for *your* gratification, I mean, rather than
theirs. I grew up in a happy household, with two parents,
and I'd want to offer my children the same. At least for
starters. Life's tough enough as is, even in a conventional
family. Why should a child's life begin with a handicap?
Anyhow, I'm sentimental, Byron. I believe in marriage and
all that jazz."

"Cheer up, Di," Byron said, pouring her a brandy. "You'll
find someone. What's the old saying, about men being like
streetcars? You wait five minutes and another one comes
along."

"Oh for God's sake!" Diane shot him a jaundiced glance.
"I didn't expect that from you. A. You sound like my
mother. B. Streetcars have been extinct in this town since
1925 or thereabouts. And C."—she checked the clock—"In
five minutes I'll be thirty-three years old—"

"Congratulations!"

"—thereby reducing my statistical chance of catching
either a streetcar or a husband to nearly zilch." She managed a smile. "I should have married you, Byron—"

"Me!"

"Yes. Why not? You and I are ideally suited on all points
except sexual orientation. We're smart and compatible. We
like each other. Love each other, I dare say. We could stave
off loneliness together."

She looked at him with real affection. Curled up in an
English wing chair, wearing plum silk pajamas under a

foulard robe, Byron was as cool and elegant as an ad in *The New Yorker*. But he didn't fool her. There was warmth beneath those posh Sulka wrappings, love and humor in those deep brown eyes.

Byron Elkington of Hollow Farms, Virginia, and Diane Summerfield of Chestnut Hill: a merger. Briefly, the idea seemed feasible.

"You know, By, there are a lot of married people who care for each other far less than you and I do. We share the same interests, come from similar backgrounds. One might say we were made for each other. By and Di!"

Byron looked at her oddly, unsure whether or not she was teasing, and at the moment Diane herself wasn't certain.

"Diane, my dear," he said soberly, "if I were straight, I would have asked you to marry me long ago. Marrying you would be a singular honor and joy. However, I leave that privilege to someone more deserving than I. It's always puzzled me why there isn't a great army of wonderful men lined up demanding your hand. The more fools they. But all it takes is one. I don't want to sound fatuous, Di, but you'll meet a special guy one of these days, fall in love—"

"I fell in love." She began weeping again.

"With someone nicer than Leo."

"I wasn't referring to Leo." She lowered her eyes. "I fell in love with somebody terrific and I blew it. Remember that Israeli student I told you about when we were getting sloshed down at the Hay-Adams bar in Washington?"

"The dalliance?" Byron recalled the details.

"Only he wasn't a dalliance. I was crazy in love with him. And vice versa, I might add."

"Then why the hell didn't you marry him?"

"Because—" She wanted to say, "Because of what he was: poor, young, unambitious." But the sentence came out differently. "Because of what I am, Byron. Because I'm a snob, I suppose. It's hard for me to marry down, if that's the term. I've always had a certain picture of the man I'd marry. My entitlement, so to speak. Mature, successful, prestigious. It's what everyone expects of me. Hell, it's what I expect of myself. I can't bear the thought of being a laughingstock."

"Why a laughingstock?"

"You know perfectly well what people would say. Older woman/younger man. Successful lawyer/casual laborer. Boston blue blood/penniless immigrant. Do I have to say anything more?"

"I see," Byron murmured. "So you'd rather be a crying-stock."

"Is that meant to be funny?" She dabbed her eyes. "Or cruel?"

"Neither." The clock on the mantel chimed midnight. "Happy birthday, darling." He kissed her cheek. "And now I'd like you to tell me something. Be frank. When Jim and I had that ceremony Sunday night, did you find me a laughingstock?"

"Byron!" Diane was horrified. "How could you think such a thing. I was moved—touched."

"Touched! By two homosexuals going through a bit of mumbo jumbo? Why did you find it touching?"

"Because—" She considered the question fairly. "Because I care for you and Jim, and I want your happiness."

"Exactly! And that's what the people who care for you really want. What do you think, your father is going to disown you? My bet is he only wants to see you happy. He adores you. That's all any of us want for you, with the exception of the late unlamented Leo. Remember, it's your life, no one else's, and unless you believe in reincarnation and various other metaphysical crap, you may not get another chance. Yes, I *was* talking nonsense about men being like streetcars. The good ones are few and far between. I should know."

He took her hand. "Now I'm going to offer some hard lawyer's reasoning as grist for that deductive mind of yours. Try looking at it as an exercise in logic."

What was it, he asked, that frightened women so about "marrying down"? Men had been doing it for ages. It had always been the norm. Older men married younger women. Executives married secretaries. Doctors married nurses. A Rockefeller had married a Norwegian housemaid. Even Prince Charles had married a commoner, after which his brother followed suit.

Had anybody laughed? Quite the contrary. Those unions were seen as laudable: the triumph of love. Why then, shouldn't the same precept apply the other way around? Older woman/younger man. Boston heiress/penniless immigrant.

Because, Byron argued, women had been conditioned to

"marry up." It was a convention as old as the hills. That made sense in the days when women were totally dependent on their husbands. Marriage was the only means they had of bettering their condition.

"But now, Diane, it's a whole new ball game. Women can pay their way. They enjoy freedom, legal equity, professional standing. Therefore they're entitled to exactly the same perks that men have had for generations. They can marry—not for status or economic need—but solely for love.

"What do you want out of life, Di? You've always told me a husband and children. Well, if that's your highest priority, then go out and grab it. Or is your pride worth a lifetime's loneliness? Are you really willing to forfeit the things that matter most for some outmoded notion of propriety? Answer me truly. What is it you want?"

"I want," she replied in a measured cadence, "intimacy. I want someone to share my laughs and fears with. I want warmth. Bustle. Companionship. Love. I want children. I want—oh God yes! I want to marry Avram. If he'll have me! Oh, Byron!" She felt the tears start again. "I'm so scared. Everything you say is true. But what if it doesn't work out?"

"What if it doesn't?" Byron shrugged. "There's no guarantee."

Her jaw dropped. He wasn't supposed to confirm her anxieties. His job was to refute them, to assure her that love was immortal and her marriage would last forever. Instead, he was still playing the lawyer.

"Look," he argued. "Say the marriage fails. What's the worst that can happen? You'll have taken a chance on love. And had some very good times in the meanwhile. The end of love isn't the end of the world. People survive such losses, I should know. Let's say, then, that the worst that can happen is that you break up and you're miserable for a while. But now that that's out of the way, I ask you—what's the best that can happen if you marry Avram?"

"The best?" She frowned. Then she smiled. Then she raised her hands in the air, in a gesture of total joy. "Oh the best—is heaven on earth!"

Byron reached for the phone.

"Where does he live, your Avram?"

"Oh Lord," she cried. "I don't know."

"Where does he work?"

"At Tel-Aviv Taxi." And when Byron rolled his eyes, she laughed. "It's not in Israel. It's a radio-cab service based in Chelsea."

Byron was already burrowing into the yellow pages. A minute later, he was on the phone. "Do you have an Avram—" He paused.

"Gittelson," she breathed.

"Gittelson in your employ? You do? When's his next shift? He's on radio call now, you say? No. He's not in any trouble. Quite the opposite. He's been recommended as a superior driver, and I'd like to have him pick up a fare at 522 East Sixty-second Street. He should ask for—" Byron covered the mouthpiece. "Does he know my name?" Diane nodded yes. "Tell him to have the doorman ring 16J and the party will be right down. Destination?" He gave a wry laugh. "I'm not absolutely certain. Conceivably, it could be a fairly long haul."

Byron hung up the phone. "Here in five minutes. You want to freshen your face?"

She headed into the bathroom and popped out immediately.

"Suppose he doesn't want to see me? Which I could understand. I've given him a very hard time."

"You're a lawyer," Byron said. "Argue him down. In the nicest possible way. Now will you put on some lipstick so he doesn't die of shock? This is a romantic reunion, not a horror show."

She emerged a couple of minutes later, with a strange expression.

"Byron?" She giggled.

"What's so funny?"

"While I was washing up, I remembered something I hadn't thought of in ages. You know my friend Rosemary Marshall?"

"I've heard you speak of her."

"Well, I just remembered who caught the bouquet at her wedding."

The downstairs buzzer sounded.

She turned to Byron, eyes brimming with happiness.

"It was I!"

Byron watched as the elevator door closed. Good old Diane. Always the grammarian.

"Name the first one after me," he shouted.

THIRTY-NINE

———•———

The street was dark when she slid into the front seat of the taxi. For a moment all he could make out was a tall, angular woman in a T-shirt and jeans. His first reaction was that this was one of the loony ladies with which New York abounded. His second, that she might be armed and dangerous.

"Hello, Avram."

Then he shook his head in disbelief. "Am I being hijacked?" he asked hoarsely. "Or is this a practical joke?"

Diane was at a loss for words. Although logic dictated that he might not fall into her arms at first glance, she had expected some sign of spontaneous delight. Instead, he was instantly on guard. She suppressed an anxious quiver.

Good intentions aside, Byron's phone call had been impetuous. She ought, in fairness, to have given Avram advance notice concerning her change of heart instead of sneaking up on him like this. Except, considering the havoc she'd already raised, he might not have shown up.

"I'm glad to see you"—she mustered her courage—"and sorry if I've taken you by surprise, but this was the quickest way I knew to get in touch. I hope you're not angry."

"Why should I be angry?" He jerked on the ignition and revved the motor till it roared. "You're a fare. I'm a cabbie. The meter's running. Where do you want me to take you, Diane? The dispatcher didn't say."

"You *are* angry." She placed her hand his arm. Through the thin cotton sleeve of his shirt, she could feel his muscles tense.

"No, I'm not angry, Diane. Just surprised, puzzled, and confused. Now, why don't you sit in back, like a normal passenger, and I'll take you where you want to go."

"I'm happy next to you, Avram. And as you say, the meter's running. All right! I'd like you to drive to some attractive spot—a quiet place, maybe by the water—"

"And then?"

"Then we can schmooze."

"You're the boss." He pulled out into Park Avenue.

"No, Avram. I'm not."

They drove through deserted streets down to the tip of Manhattan. It was an area Diane knew well. By day, it swarmed with life. Wall Streeters and tourists elbowed for bench room. Vendors jostled for territory on the pavements. From the nearby high rises, mothers came to push strollers while commuters dashed for the Staten Island Ferry. Sometimes on sunny days Diane ate her lunch on the wharf, watched the parade, and threw the crumbs to the gulls.

But at one in the morning, Battery Park was like a private preserve, with Diane and Avram in sole possession.

Avram parked near the ferry slip, then came around and opened her door with unexpected formality.

She followed him to a bench, then scanned the horizon. "That's my office over there." She pointed in the direction of Chase Plaza. Some of the lights were still on. Eager associates hustling to make brownie points.

"I know," he said.

They took a bench a few feet from the rail and watched the water kiss the stones.

"Here we are, Diane." In the slanted rays of the streetlamp, he looked grim. "Let's schmooze."

She drew a deep breath. "First of all, I love you very much."

He sighed. "I love you too, Diane, although that doesn't seem to have been sufficient in the past."

"Second," she continued, "I want to apologize for having trampled on your feelings."

"Apologize?" He turned and regarded her with curiosity. "What for? You voiced your sentiments about me and my future, that's all. Why should you apologize for being honest?"

"Third"—she swallowed her last vestige of pride—"I want to marry you—if you'll have me. Consider this a formal proposal."

Her words stopped him cold. For a long, tense moment, he studied her with the wariness of a soldier entering a minefield, on the alert for traps and hidden dangers. When he spoke, his voice was charged.

"What brought this sudden change of attitude about, Diane? Is it because today's your birthday?"

"You remembered!"

"Of course I remembered." He completed his thought. "And now that you're a year older, you feel time is slipping by? You don't want to be lonely anymore. Who does? But other than the passage of time, nothing has changed. I'm still the same person you turned down. Twice! The same unsatisfactory Avram. I'll never be your corporate executive or captain of industry or—or your distinguished professor of law at Yale."

Diane winced.

"I didn't bring him up to hurt your feelings," Avram continued. "Merely to explain my own. When you told me about Leo Frankland, I realized that he was your ideal of what a man should be. What you had a right to expect in a husband. Clearly, there's no comparison between us. And since I'll never achieve his sort of eminence, how could our marriage possibly work? As I said, we're still the same people, you and I. There's still the same difference in age—"

"Age means nothing!" Diane blurted, unexpectedly echoing Leo Frankland. And in this one instance, Leo was right.

"—and expectations. I believe I have your love, but I want more than that. I want your approval. How can we be happy if you make me feel that what I am simply isn't good enough?"

"Oh you're good enough." Her voice became urgent. "You're better than good enough! You're terrific. And I'm not the same person, despite all appearances. At least not when it comes to judging worth. Believe me, Avram, I don't want you to change—not a hair, not a whit. You're the most wonderful man I've ever known, the best, the most loving. Avram!" She took his hands in hers. "I'm pleading, not just for my happiness, but for yours too, darling. We belong together, I know it now."

"Why? What's changed?"

"I have," she confessed. "Since I saw you last, so much has happened. I've undergone what you might call a revelation."

To his astonishment, she poured out the story of Leo's reappearance, his proposal, her decision.

"So I'm turning him down, Avram. I don't want bitterness and selfishness and secondhand love. *He* was the one who wasn't good enough. For me. For any woman with a mind of her own. I'm grateful he came back into my life. It let me shut one door and open another. The door that leads to you. Because now I know what's in my heart. I want you, Avram. I want your warmth, your humor, your zest for life. I want your love. And once I have it, I don't intend to throw it away ever again. You can drive cabs, you can sweep streets—I don't give a damn what you do, as long as you marry me."

"You really mean that?"

She paused to consider. "Always provided that it's legal."

He burst out laughing. "Darling Diane. Ever the moralist! Don't change too much. I love you the way you are."

For the first time that night, he embraced her with his smile, and Diane felt the weight of years sliding from her shoulders. In its place came a warm, loving masculine arm. She rubbed her cheek gratefully against his soft denim shirt.

"Actually," Avram confessed, "I hate driving a cab."

"You do?" She was surprised.

"You were right. It's not the job for me. It was, oh—I don't know, a romantic challenge. I wanted to feel that I was in touch with ordinary everyday people, getting to know the authentic America. Grass roots—isn't that the term?"

"Did you see the real America, at least?"

He laughed heartily. "Mostly drunks, workaholics, and call girls. At least on the night shift. The peculiar thing is, the fares look upon us cabdrivers as fonts of folk wisdom. A combination of idiot savant and psychiatrist, with a little bit of the entertainer thrown in. I developed a regular routine about Manhattan low-life and colorful characters. Glorified schmoozing, really, but it worked wonders when it came to getting tips. I had one story, totally absurd, about a peg-legged man and two women. It is amazing what people will swallow! Of course, in return, I had to listen while my passengers delivered their own peculiar theories on everything from the Reaganomics to religion. I had one fellow last month, a businessman, who gave me a ten-minute lecture on how to deal with women. Never apologize, never explain, he said. And never let them get control. He claims women like it that way."

Sounds like Leo, Diane thought.

"Heaven help his wife. However," Avram said equably, "I let him rant on without argument and he gave me a thirty-dollar tip."

"Then you've done quite well, driving cabs?"

"Not bad. Of course, the schmoozing helped."

"I'm sure it did. Did it ever occur to you, Avram, that you might be a born entrepreneur?"

"An entrepreneur! Such a fancy word. But the curious thing is, Di, I've had an idea for starting a little business in New York."

"Yes?" Diane was all over him for details, and when he was done, she gave a delighted whoop of laughter.

"That's wonderful! And it shouldn't take an awful lot of capital. In fact, I'd consider it a public service. Suppose I help you write a business plan, and we can check it out with my father—"

"Your father?"

"It's the kind of oddball proposition he loves. Oh, he's going to be crazy about you, I guarantee." She couldn't help bubbling. "My whole family will be, once they get to know you. We'll go to Boston this weekend, you'll meet the crew—okay? And what about your parents? How do you think they'll feel about your marrying a foreigner and staying in New York?"

"Whoa!" Avram hollered. "I haven't said I'm going to marry you yet. And you may not want to when you hear me out. We still have some things to discuss—"

"For instance?"

"For instance"—his voice became grave—"I don't want a wife who's married to an office. To me, that's bigamy. The situation is bad enough now, but what will happen when you make partner, Diane? I'll never see you. It'll be the hundred-hour week. Well, I want to come home in the evening and know you'll be there too. I want us to have time for each other, with each other."

She felt a catch in her throat. "I'll be there. I know I sometimes appear to be yet another one of these driven career women who lives only for the next step up the ladder. Success—titles—money. They're fun, but they were markers, basically. Ways for me to measure my worth in the absence of other rewards. I never meant them to be the whole of my existence. I'm not denying I love my work, Avram, but it's not the most important thing in life. At least not anymore. It served when there was nothing else to consume my time and energy, but all those years I was climbing, I was waiting. Waiting for you. Waiting for the right person to come home to. I won't be married to the job, I promise. We'll merely cohabit from nine to five."

"Can you cut back like that?" he asked. "Is that possible?"

"I think so. I can continue as a permanent associate, if not at Slater Blaney then at some less-pressured firm. Anyhow, the fast track isn't the only track in town."

"But you'll never make partner," he realized aloud.

She put her arms around his neck and they kissed.

"I've found my partner," she murmured, "for life."

They sat there talking, schmoozing, dreaming, setting dates, furnishing apartments yet unseen, planning for the summer ahead while the harbor came to life. They wrangled amiably about their wedding. Diane wanted a big one in Boston. Avram preferred something small and simple in New York.

"Is this a major dispute," he asked at one point, "or a healthy division of opinion?"

Diane laughed. "Oh God, how I've missed arguing with you."

They settled on a big wedding in New York.

A little before six, the sun rose and turned the harbor to gold. Hand in hand, they headed back to the car.

"One thing I want to assure myself of, Diane."

"Anything!"

"Is your giving up partnership a sacrifice?"

"Good Lord no!" she said fervently. "Not a sacrifice. I see it as a compromise essentially. Like your promising to give up those smelly Gauloises. As the great Edmund Burke once said"—with a quirky smile, she recalled the day of forced negotiations in Judge Kunicki's chamber—"'. . . every human benefit and enjoyment, every virtue and every prudent act—is founded on compromise.'"

"'. . . and barter.'" Avram added. "He said 'compromise and barter.' If you're going to quote Burke, quote him properly."

They kissed, then he opened the door of the cab for her. "I've just gone off duty." He grinned. "Let's go home."

FORTY

———— • ————

Rosemary stepped through the latticed door and sniffed dubiously. The first thing that caught her eye was the ceramic umbrella stand in the shape of an elephant. The art deco sconces were gone; instead the walls were hung with the hot bright silks of India. From the dining room came the strum of a sitar.

"What have you done with the Café Karnak?" she demanded of the maître d'. "It says Sikh Transit on the sign outside."

"The Karnak went out of business," he said. "We took over the lease. The only midtown restaurant featuring genuine nouvelle Punjabi cuisine."

Rosemary frowned. "Dear me. I was supposed to be meeting friends at the Karnak. Do you have a party here by the name of Diane Summerfield?"

"Let me see." He scanned his reservation list. "Already arrived. Would you be—Mrs. Marshall?"

"Ms. Marshall," she said. "Don't trouble yourself. I see them."

She smoothed down the skirt of her black linen suit, checked her makeup in the decorative wall mirror, and adjusted her earrings. *Accessorize, accessorize,* as Fleur was prone to say. *It's the secret of chic.* The image in the mirror stared back at her, smart and trim. Then she made her way through a maze of diners to Diane's table.

"Di, darling!" Rosemary greeted her with a kiss. "You look marvelous! Counting the days?"

Next, with a clank and clatter of costume jewelry, she turned and bent over Fleur. Instinctively Fleur crossed her arms to protect herself from possible attack. Having lost one wardrobe to Rosemary's fury, she was reluctant to risk another. The necklace Rosemary was wearing looked positively lethal—like the fangs of a wild animal.

But the onslaught never came. Instead, Rosemary brushed Fleur's cheek mildly with her lips. "Hello, Fleur. How are you?"

Fleur choked back a sigh of relief. "Excellent, thank you, Rosemary. And you?"

"Splendid."

"You've lost some weight," Fleur observed.

"You've gained a little."

"You're looking very elegant, I must say."

"You too."

"Marvelous accessories. I particularly like the effect of that African necklace against classic linen. Are those real teeth, by the way? It's an interesting contrast. And what's that wonderful scent you're wearing?"

"It's called Bijan. And yours is?

"Fleurs du Mal."

"Well!" Diane beamed and uncrossed her fingers. "Now that you two fashion plates have got the formalities out of the way, what do you say we order drinks?"

"Shouldn't we wait for Bernie?" Fleur asked.

Rosemary shook her head. "Absolutely not. You know Bernie. That woman would be late—"

"For her own wedding," they sang out in unison.

Then Rosemary giggled and the ice was broken.

Getting the two combatants to sit down peacefully had been an enterprise requiring Diane's utmost tact and tenacity.

If Fleur was doubtful ("She'll probably come after me with a machete and who could blame her?"), Rosemary was adamant ("How can you ask me to sit down across a table from the woman who ruined my life?").

"Now, now," Diane soothed. "Your life has hardly been ruined. You seem to have come through with flying colors. Anyhow, what's done is done. I happen to know," she said earnestly, "that Fleur's genuinely repentant."

"She is?"

"Stays up nights brooding about it. She desperately wants

to make things up and be friends again. Fleur's always been very fond of you, Rosemary. Even a trifle envious, I suspect, but that's only because she admires you so much. I know you can't forget, but do try to forgive. Besides, she's moving to Pittsburgh, so you may not get too many more chances to see her. How about a last gala meeting of the Wednesday Club before we go our different ways? Be a lamb. If not for her, then for old times' sake."

"I was a lamb for thirty-two years," Rosemary said crisply. "The sacrificial kind. And as far as Fleur wanting to make things up, why should I cooperate simply to ease her conscience? Old times' sake indeed! I'm through with being sentimental."

"Then do it for me," Diane pleaded. "I'm getting married next month and you're both my bridesmaids. I don't want a repeat of the scene at Bernie's almost-wedding. I expect this to be the happiest day of my life, and it won't be if you and she are still feuding. I can't bear to think that two of the people I'm fondest of in this world should be at loggerheads. We've known one another too long, meant too much to one another, to write off our oldest friends. Please . . ."

Rosemary shot her a skeptical look. "Usual time, usual place?"

Diane nodded vigorously while Rosemary pondered.

"I'll come just this once," she said finally, "and I'll behave like a lady. But I want you to understand I'm doing this for your sake, not hers."

"You *are* a lamb," Diane assured her, but Rosemary was lost in thought.

"Were you serious about Fleur envying me?"

Diane gave a noncommittal mumble.

"And she sincerely wants to make it up? I'll be damned."

"Are you telling me"—Fleur too was disbelieving—"that Rosemary wants to be friends again?"

"She's always admired you," Diane hedged. "Even envied you a bit. And she's promised to be there on Wednesday. Now that's a sign of good faith. So come on, Fleur, how about it?"

Fleur sighed. "Only for you. But you have to promise to frisk her for weapons at the door."

Diane now looked around her. "I miss the old Karnak. We had some terrific lunches here. I hope the drinks are as good."

"*Plus ça change—*" Fleur signaled for the waiter.

"Cute!" Rosemary remarked, as a well-built young man approached, dashing in a white turban and red cummerbund.

He smiled. "Hello, I'm Eric and I'm your waiter for the day."

Fleur scrutinized him with a practiced eye. "Didn't your name used to be Rusty? Or was that in an earlier incarnation?"

"That's right." He nodded. "I changed it for luck."

"I tried to change mine"—Fleur made a wry face—"but it didn't work. Say, I thought you'd given up waiting tables to achieve fame and fortune on Broadway? What happened?"

He shrugged. "Ever hear of a play called *Murder in the Manse?*"

"Nope."

"Neither did anyone else, I'm afraid. Now, can I get you ladies something to drink?"

"I'm in the mood," Rosemary decided, "for a Beefeater martini on the rocks, twist of lemon."

"Make that two." Diane nodded.

"Make that three and make the third one a double. Plus, bring us a great big platter of those delicious Indian breads," Fleur said. "Plus some chutneys. I plan to overdose on calories today, it being in the nature of an occasion. So" —she turned to Diane—"how's the bride-to-be? And how's Avram coming in his new business?"

"It's looking very promising," Diane said.

"One hell of an idea, Di. Yours or his?"

"Definitely his. He told me about it the night I proposed."

Early one morning Avram had gone to the Bureau of Motor Vehicles in Manhattan to get his driver's license. By the time he arrived, the waiting room was packed, the lines still growing. He took a place, pulled out a book, and began to read. A couple of minutes later, a man in a pin-striped suit got in line behind him and by ten o'clock was climbing the walls.

"Oh, Christ!" he groaned. "We could be here all day. I'm a broker, a busy guy. You know what this goddamn scene is gonna cost me? Probably seven, eight hundred bucks in commissions."

The man was in agony, according to Avram, the proto-typical yuppie for whom lost time was lost profits.

"Is your office nearby?" Avram asked. "If you like, I'll

keep your place and give you a ring when your turn is next. Does twenty dollars an hour sound reasonable?"

Avram not only earned over a hundred dollars that day; he also got an excellent tip on an over-the-counter stock. Both parties were delighted with the bargain.

"It struck me, Diane," he told her as they sat in Battery Park and discussed their future, "that New York has thousands of people—executives, doctors, lawyers—who are just too busy to wait in line for licenses or passports or tickets for a hit Broadway show. On the other hand, there are plenty of New Yorkers with time on their hands, people who'd be glad to pick up some extra money. College students, teenage kids, retirees, housewives. What's needed here is a middleman, someone who could put the two groups together, the yuppies and the—ummm—"

"Gofers!" she said.

"Gophers?" He furrowed his brow. "Isn't that a breed of small furry animal?"

"Different kind. It's a slang term. Gofers are people who go on errands for other people. But how would you organize something like this? And how would you promote it?"

The plan would take capital, he explained. He'd need an office. A central phone setup, including a beeper service. He'd want to advertise in the business papers, *New York* magazine, *Manhattan, inc.*, the yellow pages. Maybe do some mailings to the big downtown firms. As for staff, Avram knew exactly where to recruit the personnel, starting with the bulletin board at Columbia. He had a million ideas.

"Anyhow"—Diane hoisted her martini—"he raised seed money from a venture capital firm and I drew up the incorporation papers last week. Go-Fers Limited. Don't you love the name? My father's crazy about the whole idea. Thinks Avram should test-market it here, then expand into other cities. Go national eventually, a sort of McDonald's for casual help. But Avram says no."

"Why not?" Fleur asked. "He got something against big bucks?"

"He refuses to become a workaholic. Which is fine with me, because I don't want to be married to one."

"Very wise," Rosemary said. "And I'm speaking from ten years' experience."

The table fell silent while the three women exchanged meaningful glances. Diane sensed they were sailing into dangerous waters as Alex Marshall's unseen presence made itself felt. Rosemary sighed.

"Do you see him at all?" Fleur asked softly.

"Who? The ex-Mr. Marshall?" came the grim answer. "I saw him in court last week, when I got my decree nisi. I believe he's currently living in a small apartment in Chelsea, eating Franco-American spaghetti out of a can. And that, my dears, is that."

Fleur nibbled at a papadom and collected her thoughts. Reluctant as she was to reopen old wounds, she was also consumed by curiosity. Curiosity prevailed.

"Well," she said hesitantly, "I've often wondered how you managed to stick it out with him all those years. I mean, the man had such a lurid fantasy life."

"Fantasy life?" Rosemary nearly dropped her glass. "Alex Marshall had a *fantasy life?* You've got to be kidding! Are we talking about the same guy? Alex has about as much imagination as—as"—she groped for images—"as the Dow Jones averages. As a matter of fact, they were kind of related. Whenever the Dow went up, so did Alex. But fantasy! Good God! I have no intention of going into physiological details, Fleur, except to say he was the original slam-bam man."

Fleur mulled this over. "I don't mean to be critical, Rosemary, but—where do you have grounds for comparison? After all, you were the virgin bride."

"More or less . . ."

"And the faithful wife." She stopped short, for Rosemary was wearing a cat-who-swallowed-the-cream smile. "Or *were* you? Rosemary! Is there something you haven't told us? We're your friends—your confidantes!"

Rosemary's newfound cool temporarily gave way. Her face grew flushed. "Well, yes, I've been seeing someone off and on—"

Diane stared in disbelief; Fleur gave a hoot of triumph. "I knew it! I knew it! Didn't I say she was looking fantastic, Diane? What else could it be but a man!"

"It's not like that at all." Rosemary had turned a deep crimson. "And if I'm looking nice these days, it's because 've, um, come into a good deal of money lately. Plus of course, I have to dress well for business."

"You're ducking the issue," Fleur drove on. "We want to know. Who? When? Where? How? Give, honey! We demand details."

Rosemary drew a deep breath. "If as much as a word of this gets back to Alex—" She was interrupted by a chorus of "We swears." "Although I don't suppose it matters now that I've got my divorce. You see, I didn't want to give him ammunition to use in court. Even my mother doesn't know. Actually, I've been having a bit of a fling with—you met him, Fleur—a neighbor of mine, Lloyd Hageman."

"The periodontist?" Fleur squealed. "Little guy with the toothbrush mustache? Why, I should think he'd only come up to here on you!"

"Little David was small but—"

"Oh my!" Fleur said, miffed that she had missed what was clearly a major erotic opportunity. "And he's that good in the sack?"

Rosemary cleared her throat. "Let me just say that during the few nights I've spent with Lloyd, I've had more pleasure in a greater variety of ways than I did in ten years of marriage with Alex!"

"Wow!" said Fleur.

"So!" said Diane. "Do you think it will develop into something permanent? He's eligible, I gather."

"Not only eligible," Rosemary wailed, "he's Mr. Eligible. By all reports, the one and only such in Westport, Connecticut. Which means the man is being pursued and pampered by every unmarried woman in town. He can pick and choose like a sultan, and from what I gather, does just that. Would you believe, he had a little cold last week and received twenty-two bowls of homemade chicken soup! Mine among them. Why should Lloyd get married? He's having the time of his life."

"Oh dear," Diane groaned. "But how do you feel about sharing him?"

Rosemary shrugged. "I relax and enjoy it. Half a loaf's better than none. Of course I hope it'll work out. Or at least that I'll meet someone else, but I'm not counting on it. The pickings are slim."

"Isn't it awful," Fleur sympathized. "There are just no decent men out there for us."

"You're telling me!" Rosemary finished her drink, then waved. "Hey, hey, there's Bernie!"

"Sorry I'm late," Bernie gasped, "but I had a bitch of a time finding this joint. What are you drinking? Some exotic Indian shit? Martinis—oh my God. I haven't had a dry martini in a zillion years. Waiter? Another round pronto. She pulled up a extra chair and plumped her packages down on it. The familiar battered Coach bag, her Sony tape recorder, briefcase, clipboard . . .

"Listen," she said when she was settled in. "You won't believe how I spent the morning. Fabulous story. Real dynamite. Something that could affect all your lives. I was with members of this Harvard-Yale research team. Why, did you know—"

"I don't want to hear it!" Fleur shouted her down.

"Not a word!" Rosemary howled.

"But—but—" Bernie spluttered.

"Keep your research to yourself," Diane said.

"Amen!"

"Ditto!"

"Gosh!" Bernie was puzzled. "I know you'd be interested. The research proves—"

"Nooooo . . . !" came the concerted howl.

"Have it your way." Bernie shrugged. It beat her why everyone was up in arms. It was an interesting story. About the effect of cholesterol on rhesus monkeys. However . . .

Rusty-turned-Eric arrived with a tray of drinks.

"Here's to." Bernie raised her glass.

"Here's to us."

"Jesus!" the maître d' scrunched over his coffee at a table near the kitchen. "Those four women have been at it since noon. Pretty soon the dinner crowd'll be here. What's going on, some kind of class reunion? Sounds like a bunch of bloody banshees!"

Eric smiled and rested his hand on the maître d's thigh. "Women," he said. "Who can understand them?"

The afternoon had degenerated (or improved, depending on one's point of view) to a nonstop feast of nostalgia, washed down with martinis, intermixed with gales of laughter.

"Remember that Amherst mixer where you popped out of your bra?"

"I've been trying to forget it for fifteen years."

"Ever date a guy named Hank Miller?"

"Hank of the thousand hands? I'll say. I still got the black-and-blue marks."

"He married Betsy What's-her-name."

"Betsy who wore granny glasses?"

"No, the one with the terminal dandruff."

"Same person."

"Unh-unh. There were two different Betsys. Hey, Eric, babe. Another round of martinis."

By five they had gone past the anecdote stage to the point where the mere mention of a name or a place or a punch line sufficed. Supply a half dozen words and fifteen years of communal memories took over.

"The Blue Note Café."

"The Brown-Williams game."

"The sweetheart of Sigmund Freud."

"Northland Deli's mystery meat."

"Is this Anthropology One?"

"My green coat with the beaver collar."

"Sue-who-joined-the-Peace-Corps."

"That night in Fort Lauderdale."

"That weekend at Bromley."

"Blizzard of seventy-seven."

"*Mein führer*, I can talk!"

"Mary Hersey's calico cat."

"Diane caught the bouquet. I remember."

I remember, I remember, I remember . . .

Shortly before six Fleur blew her nose and checked her watch.

"Listen, you guys, I've got a plane to catch. Got a date with a real estate broker in the morning. It's been—what can I say, the afternoon of my life. I love you all—you're my closest, my dearest, and it grieves me to say good-bye. But before I dissolve into a sentimental rag, I want to tell you that I plan to get to New York at least once a month. On the company. And you can bet your asses I'll try and make it on a Wednesday."

"Terrific!" Bernie nodded.

"Long live the Wednesday Club!"

"Betcha!"

"Next month? Same time, same place?"

"But by then," Diane said, "the Sikh Transit may be gone."

"No matter." Rosemary looked at her friends with brimming eyes. "Restaurants come and go . . ."

And men come and go. And years come and go. And houses and jobs and fashions and troubles and dreams all come and go.

And friendship endures.

"Waiter!" Diane signaled. "One for the road."

ABOUT THE AUTHOR

———————•———————

F REDA BRIGHT began her career as a concert pianist after studying at the Paris Conservatory. She was an advertising executive for many years in New York and London before writing her first novel, OPTIONS. Ms. Bright is also the author of FUTURES, DECISIONS, and INFIDELITIES. She has one daughter and lives in Montclair, New Jersey, with her calico cat.

OFFICIAL RULES

NO PURCHASE NECESSARY.

To enter identify this month's Bantam Book titles by placing a circle around each word forming each title. There are three titles shown on previous page to be found in this month's puzzle. Mail your entry to: Grand Slam Sweepstakes, P.O. Box 18, New York, N.Y. 10046.

This is a monthly sweepstakes starting February 1, 1988 and ending January 31, 1989. During this sweepstakes period, one automobile winner will be selected each month from all entries that have correctly solved the puzzle. To participate in a particular month's drawing, your entry must be received by the last day of that month. The Grand Slam prize drawing will be held on February 14, 1989 from all entries received during all twelve months of the sweepstakes.

To obtain a free entry blank/puzzle/rules, send a self-addressed stamped envelope to: Winning Titles, P.O. Box 650, Sayreville, N.J. 08872. Residents of Vermont and Washington need not include return postage.

PRIZES: Each month for twelve months a Chevrolet automobile will be awarded with an approximate retail value of $12,000 each.

The Grand Slam Prize Winner will receive 2 Chevrolet automobiles plus $10,000 cash (ARV $34,000).

Winners will be selected under the supervision of Marden-Kane, Inc., an independent judging organization. By entering this sweepstakes each entrant accepts and agrees to be bound by these rules and the decisions of the judges which shall be final and binding. Winners may be required to sign an affidavit of eligibility and release which must be returned within 14 days of receipt. All prizes will be awarded. No substitution or transfer of prizes permitted. Winners will be notified by mail. Odds of winning depend on the total number of eligible entries received.

Sweepstakes open to residents of the U.S. and Canada except employees of Bantam Books, its affiliates, subsidiaries, advertising agencies and Marden-Kane, Inc. Void in the Province of Quebec and wherever else prohibited or restricted by law. Not responsible for lost or misdirected mail or printing errors. Taxes and licensing fees are the sole responsibility of the winners. All cars are standard equipped. Canadian winners will be required to answer a skill testing question.

For a list of winners, send a self-addressed, stamped envelope to: Bantam Winners, P.O. Box 711, Sayreville, N.J. 08872.

THE LATEST BOOKS IN THE BANTAM BESTSELLING TRADITION

Experience all the passion and adventure life has to offer in these bestselling novels by and about women.

Bantam offers you these exciting titles:

Titles by Jean Auel:

☐ 25042 CLAN OF THE CAVE BEAR $4.95
☐ 25053 THE VALLEY OF HORSES $4.95
☐ 26096 MAMMOTH HUNTERS $4.95

Titles by Cynthia Freeman:

☐ 26161 DAYS OF WINTER $4.50
☐ 26090 COME POUR THE WINE $4.50
☐ 25433 FAIRYTALES $4.50
☐ 26092 NO TIME FOR TEARS $4.50
☐ 24790 PORTRAITS $4.50
☐ 27743 WORLD FULL OF STRANGERS $4.95

Titles by Barbara Taylor Bradford:

☐ 26534 A WOMAN OF SUBSTANCE $4.50
☐ 25621 HOLD THE DREAM $4.95
☐ 26253 VOICE OF THE HEART $4.95
☐ 26541 ACT OF WILL $4.95

Titles by Judith Krantz:

☐ 25917 MISTRAL'S DAUGHTER $4.95
☐ 25609 PRINCESS DAISY $4.95
☐ 26407 I'LL TAKE MANHATTAN $4.95

Bantam Books, Dept. FBS2, 414 East Golf Road, Des Plaines, IL 60016

Please send me the books I have checked above. I am enclosing $_____ (please add $2.00 to cover postage and handling). Send check or money order—no cash or C.O.D.s please.

Mr/Ms _____

Address _____

City/State _____ Zip _____

Please allow four to six weeks for delivery. This offer expires 3/89. Prices and availability subject to change without notice.